MY LADY OF THE NORTH

In the light of the fire I viewed her now for the first time.   Page 62.
— *My Lady of the North.*

My Lady of the North

The Love Story of a Gray Jacket

By RANDALL PARRISH

Author of
"WHEN WILDERNESS WAS KING"

A. L. BURT COMPANY, Publishers
⚘ ⚘ ⚘   NEW YORK   ⚘ ⚘ ⚘

———————

Published October 15, 1904

Third Edition, October 25, 1904

Fourth Edition, December 15, 1904

Fifth Edition, December 24, 1904

Sixth Edition, February 25, 1905

Seventh Edition, April 5, 1905

Eighth Edition, May 3, 1905

Ninth Edition, November 15, 1905

Contents

Contents

My Lady of the North

The Love Story of a
Gray-Jacket

CHAPTER I

A DESPATCH FOR LONGSTREET

IT was a bare, plain interior, — the low table at
which he sat an unplaned board, his seat a box,
made softer by a folded blanket. His only companions were two aides, standing silent beside the closed
entrance, anxious to anticipate his slightest need.

He will abide in my memory forever as I saw him then,
— although we were destined to meet often afterwards,
— that old gray hero, whose masterly strategy held at bay
for so long those mighty forces hurled on our constantly
thinning lines of defence. To me the history of war
has never contained his equal, and while I live I shall
love and revere him as I can love and revere no other
man.

"General Lee," said one of the aides, as I passed
the single sentry and drew aside the flap to step within,
"this is Captain Wayne."

He deliberately pushed aside the mass of papers which
had been engaging him, and for an embarrassing moment
fixed upon me a glance that seemed to read me through

9

and through. Then, with simple dignity, far more impressive than I can picture it in words, he arose slowly and extended his hand.

"Captain Wayne," he said gravely, yet retaining his grasp, and with his eyes full upon mine, "you are a much younger man than I expected to see, yet I have selected you upon the special recommendation of your brigade commander for services of the utmost importance. I certainly do not hold your youth to be against your success, but I feel unwilling to order you to the performance of this duty, which, besides being beyond the regular requirements of the service, involves unusual risks."

"Without inquiring its nature," I said hastily, "I freely offer myself a volunteer for any service which may be required either by the army or yourself."

The kindly face brightened instantly, almost into a smile, and a new look of confidence swept into the keen gray eyes.

"I felt, even as I spoke," he said, with a dignified courtesy I have never marked in any one else, "that I must be doing wrong to question the willingness of an officer of your regiment, Captain Wayne, to make personal sacrifice. From our first day of battle until now the South has never once called upon them in vain. You are from the ranks, I believe?"

"I was a corporal at Manassas."

"Ah! then you have won your grade by hard service. You take with you one man?"

"Sergeant Craig of my troop, sir, a good soldier, who knows the country well."

He lowered his eyes to the numerous papers littering the table, and then, leaning over, traced lightly with a colored pencil a line across an outspread map.

A Despatch for Longstreet

"You speak of his knowing the country well; are you aware, then, of your destination?"

"I merely inferred from what Colonel Carter said that it was your desire to re-establish communication with General Longstreet."

"That is true; but do you know where Longstreet is?"

"Only that we of the line suppose him to be somewhere west of the mountains, sir. It is camp gossip that his present base of supplies is at Minersville."

"Your conjecture is partly correct, although I have more reason to believe that the head of his column has reached Bear Fork, or will by to-morrow morning. Kindly step this way, Captain Wayne, and make note of the blue lines I have traced across this map. Here, you will observe, is Minersville, directly beyond the high ridge. You will notice that the Federal lines extend north and south directly between us, with their heavier bodies of infantry along the Wharton pike, and so disposed as to shut off all communication between us and our left wing. Now, the message I must get into Longstreet's hands is imperative; indeed, I will say to you, the very safety of this army depends upon its reaching him before his advance passes Bear Fork. There remains, therefore, no time for any long detour; the messenger who bears it must take his life in his hands and ride straight westward through the very lines of the enemy."

He spoke these words rapidly, earnestly; then suddenly he lifted his eyes to mine, and said firmly: "I am perfectly frank with you. Are you the man?"

I felt the hot blood leap into my face, but I met his stern gaze without flinching.

"If I live, General Lee, I shall meet his advance at Bear Fork by daybreak."

My Lady of the North

"God guide you; I believe you will."

His words seemed uttered unconsciously. He turned slightly, and glanced toward the door. "Major Holmes, will you kindly hand me the draft of that despatch?"

He took the paper from the outstretched hand of the aide, read it over slowly and with great care, wrote a word of explanation upon the margin, and then extended it to me.

"Commit that, word by word, to your memory; we must run no possible risk of its ever falling into the enemy's hands."

I can see it now, that coarse yellow paper, — the clear, upright penmanship, the words here and there misused and corrected, the sentence scratched out, the heavy underlining of a command, and his own strangely delicate signature at the bottom.

"*Headquarters, Army Northern Virginia,*
"*In the field, near Custer House,*
"*Sept. 23, 2 P.M.*

"*Lieut.-Gen'l Longstreet,*
   "*Commanding Left Wing.*
   "*Sir: You will advance your entire force by the Connelton and Sheffield pikes, so as to reach Castle Rock with your full infantry command by daybreak, September 26th. Let this supersede all other orders. I propose to attack in force in the neighborhood of Sailor's Ford, and shall expect you to advance promptly at the first sound of our artillery. It is absolutely essential that we form prompt connection of forces, and to accomplish this result will require a quick, persistent attack upon your part. You are hereby ordered to throw your troops forward without reserve, permitting them to be halted by no obstacle, until*

A Despatch for Longstreet

they come into actual touch with my columns. The success or failure of my plans will depend utterly upon your strict observance of these orders.

"R. E. LEE,

"*Gen'l Commanding.*"

I handed back the paper, and lifted my hand in salute.

"You have memorized it?"

"Word for word, sir."

"Repeat it to me."

He held the paper before him as I did so, and at the close lifted his eyes again to my face.

"Very good," he said quietly. "Now let there be no mistake; repeat it over to your companion as you proceed until he also has memorized it, and one of you must live long enough to reach Longstreet. I advise you to take the Langley road,— it is the most protected,— and not try to pass beyond the old Coulter plantation until after dark, or you will run the risk of being observed by the enemy's pickets. Beyond this I must leave all to your own discretion."

He paused, and I still lingered, thinking he might have something more to add.

"Are you one of the Waynes of Charlottesville?" he asked gravely.

"Colonel Richard Wayne was my father, sir."

"Ah, indeed! I remember him well"; and his face lit up with a most tender smile. "We were together in Mexico. A Virginia gentleman of the old school. He is dead, I believe?"

"He was killed, sir, the first year of the war."

"I remember; it was at Antietam. And your mother? If my memory is not at fault she was a Pierpont?"

13

"She is now in Richmond, sir, and the old plantation is but a ruin."

"War is indeed sad," he said slowly; "and I often feel that our Southern women are compelled to bear the brunt of it. What heroines they have proven! History records no equal to the daily sacrifices I have witnessed in the past three years. God grant it may be soon ended."

Then, as if suddenly moved by the impulse of the moment, he again extended his hand.

"Well, lad," he said kindly, the same grave smile lighting his face, "our country needs us. We must not waste time here in conversation. I am very glad to have been permitted to meet the son of my old friend, and trust you will remember me to your mother. But now good-bye, Captain, and may He in whose hand we all are guide and guard you. I know that a Wayne of Virginia will always do his duty."

Bareheaded and with proudly swelling heart I backed out of the tent as I might have left the throne-room of an emperor, but as I grasped the reins and swung up into saddle, I became conscious that he had followed me. Craig flung up his hand in quick, soldierly salute, and then, with a single rapid stride, the General stood at his horse's head.

"Sergeant," he said, — and I was struck by the incisive military tone of his voice, so different from the gentleness shown within, — "I am informed that you are intimately acquainted with the roads to the westward."

"Every bridle-path, sir, either by night or day."

"Then possibly you can inform me whether the Big Hickory is fordable at Deer Gap."

"Not for infantry at high water, sir; but there is another ford two miles north where it is never over waist deep."

" That would be at Brixton's Mill?"

" No, sir; the other way."

Lee smiled, and rested his hand almost caressingly on the trooper's knee.

" You are a valuable man for us to risk on such a ride," he said kindly. " But I desire you to understand, Sergeant, how deeply I value the service you are about to render, and that I shall never permit it to be forgotten or go unrewarded. And now, good-night, Sergeant; good-night, Captain Wayne."

As we turned into the main road, riding slowly, I glanced backward. The General was yet standing there in front of his tent, gazing after us, the rays of the westering sun gleaming on his gray hair.

CHAPTER II

THE NIGHT RIDE

BY five o'clock we were safe at Colchester, and while our horses rested and refreshed themselves on some confiscated grain, the two of us lay lazily back on a grassy knoll, well within the shadow of a ruined wall, and watched the round, red sun drop slowly down behind those western hills we had to climb.

We scarcely spoke regarding the work we knew was ahead, except to discuss briefly the better route to be selected for our hard night's ride. We were both old campaigners, inured by years of discipline to danger and obedience. This special duty, however arduous and desperate it might prove to be, was silently accepted as part of the service we owed the State. Reckless and hardened as I know Craig to have been, I have no doubt he reflected upon Lee and his kindly words and was touched and softened by their memory, as he lay there stretched at full length on the grass, his pipe glowing cheerily between his lips. But if so, his thoughts remained unuttered, nor did I feel inclined to dwell upon the theme; and so, in the strength of a simple comradeship which could remain silent, we waited patiently for the night to close us in.

As early as we deemed it safe to venture, we were again in saddle, riding now straight to the westward, along the smooth-beaten pike, until we caught sight of the black shadow of Colton Church in our front; then

16

The Night Ride

we swerved to the left, and still moving rapidly but with considerate care for the horses, headed directly across the more broken country toward the foot-hills.

It proved to be a hard, toilsome climb up those long, steep slopes rising before us; for we were extremely careful now to keep well away from every known route of travel, and our horses, although selected from among the best mounts of the cavalry brigade, had already been thoroughly winded by their smart trot up the valley. The short grass under foot, crisp from the hot sun of the long afternoon, caused many a slip of the poorly shod hoofs, while the darkness had grown so close and dense about us that we could barely creep through it, with only faith and a doubtful memory as guides. Every road, we well knew, would be patrolled by Federal pickets; only the broken country between could yield us the faintest prospect of success. But at best it must largely be guesswork, — Providence, luck, what you will, — and the slightest swing of the pendulum could easily frustrate our best laid plans.

An hour of this work passed. Whether or not we were yet within the enemy's lines was largely conjecture, for no human eye could pierce the enveloping gloom, and no sound, either of warning or encouragement, reached us as we strained our ears. The Sergeant rode slightly in advance as we toiled up the higher terrace, for our sole dependence as to direction and distance was upon his memory, and even that could scarcely serve for much on such a night as this. I traced his passage upward as best I might, and pressed close after him, guided not so much by sight as by sound, — the occasional rolling of a loosened stone, the rustling of leaves as he touched a bush in passage, the faint clinking of his sabre, and the heavy

2   17

My Lady of the North

breathing of his horse, — until at last his long, slender figure rose sufficiently above the dark hill surface to be faintly silhouetted in deeper shadow against the dim reflection of the upper sky. Almost coincidently with this my horse ranged up beside his, where he had drawn rein in evident perplexity.

"What is it, Dan?" I questioned cautiously; for all I could feel reasonably assured of just then was that behind any rock or tree in our front there might be crouching a Federal picket.

"It's nothin', Cap," he answered quietly, turning his face toward me as he spoke. "I'm just tryin' ter 'member some landmark yereabout ter guide from. Blamed if ever I see such a dark night; it's like bein' inside a pocket, sir, an' I reckon as how it must be nigh onter ten year since I run loose in this yere country as a kid. Thet thar cut-off we took a while back has sort o' confused me, that's a fac', and I don't just know whar I am; but I reckon as how the main ridge road we're a huntin' after oughter run somewhar out yonder." He pointed forward into the night.

"I supposed from the map it would be found farther back and considerably to the right of us," I ventured doubtfully.

"Never saw no map, Cap," he returned, with the easy familiarity of a scout on service. "But if I recollect clear, it sure used ter run mighty close ter the east edge. I reckon it ain't changed none to speak of, an' so it'll have ter be somewhere just along thar."

He spoke with such an air of certainty that I felt any controversy useless.

"Very well; hand me your rein, and see what you can discover out there on foot. Sitting here isn't apt to mend

18

The Night Ride

matters, and we surely cannot afford to cripple our horses among those rocks."

The Sergeant, a gaunt, tireless mountaineer, slipped silently from his saddle, swung his light cavalry carbine from his back to the hollow of his arm, and in another moment was lost to sight in the darkness. A snake could not have slipped away more stealthily. I heard a stone rattle under his foot, a half-suppressed oath, and then the night had completely swallowed him.

How utterly alone I seemed; how intensely, painfully still everything was! The silence felt almost like a weight, so greatly it oppressed me. Even the accustomed voices of nature were hushed, as if war, with its unspeakable cruelty, had cast a spell over all things animate and inanimate. It was weird, uncanny. With every nerve strained I leaned forward across the pommel of my saddle, listening for the slightest sound out in that black void. My head burned and throbbed as with fever, and I felt that strange, unnatural stillness as though it had been a physical thing; surely others besides us were upon this hilltop! For I knew well — my every soldier instinct told me—that somewhere out in that impenetrable mystery were blazing the camp-fires of an enemy. Vigilant eyes were peering everywhere in search for such as we. How far away they might lurk I could not even conjecture, — perhaps merely around some near projecting wall of rock, — and we might even now be within the range of their ready rifles. I could hear the quickened throbbing of my heart, and my hand fell heavily on a pistol butt in nervous expectancy.

The soft night wind, heavy with pine odors, began suddenly to play amid the leaves of a low tree beside me, and the pleasant rustling mingled like strains of music with the slow breathing of the horses, but no other sound broke a silence that had become a positive pain. Man at his best is largely a creature of impulse, and I confess to a feeling almost of terror as I sat there in utter loneliness. I glanced behind, hoping that there at least I might discover some object on which my gaze might settle, something that would relieve the intense nerve-strain of the black nothingness. I swept with staring eyes the half circle where I knew must lie the deep wide valley far beneath, but no welcome gleam of light greeted me. Far out yonder, as I well knew, was the cheery glow where our ragged, tired comrades rested around their night fires, but the bend of the land between shut it all off as completely as if I were already in another world, a denizen of those cold and silent stars so far away.

I recall it now as one of the loneliest moments of my life, one of those almost unaccountable conditions of mind and body when it seemed to me that the thin, sinewy fingers of an inexorable fate were closing down with a pressure which no strength of man might resist. I was worn with fatigue in the saddle, but did not dream of sleep; my mind, in a firm endeavor to cast aside the uncanny influences of the hour, recalled in swift panorama those three years of civil strife which had run their course since I, a slender, white-faced lad, had stolen forth into the moonlight from the portals of the old home, to ride away into the northward where the throbbing drums called me. In those days I understood but little of the cause for which I was so eager to fight and suffer. Possibly I cared even less; yet I had ever since blindly followed the faded, tattered flag of my native State with the same passionate devotion that possessed thousands of others, and with no clearer thought than to remain beside it to the bitter end.

What strange, exciting years those had been; how filled with adventure! Like pictures painted on a screen there flashed across my memory in vivid colors the camps and marches, the long night vigils, the swift sweep of the charging squadrons, the deadly shock of battle, the scouting across unknown country, the hours of pain while the soft moon smiled down upon a stricken field, the weary weeks in the low-roofed hospital at Richmond. It seemed hardly possible that I could be that same slender, untried lad who stole forth with quaking heart, fearful of the very shadows of the oaks about the old home. What centuries of experience lay between! The same boy, yet moulded now into a man; into the leader of a troop of fighting men, hardened to steel by service, trusted by one whom the South most revered and loved, — a veteran soldier in the ranks of the hardest fighting legions our world has ever known. Yet such had been the magic touch of war. So deeply had my every thought become merged in these musings that Craig, slipping silently as a ghost from out the engulfing darkness, laid hand upon my bridle-rein before I became aware of his approach.

"I got 'er all right now, Cap," he announced quietly, peering up into my face. "We uns are not more nor a hundred yards ter the right of the road, but I reckon you 'll find ther way a bit rough."

He led both horses forward, moving slowly and with that silent caution so characteristic of his class. With scarcely the scraping of a hoof on the flinty rocks we came forth in safety upon the defined, hard-beaten track.

"The south is over yonder ter the left," he whispered,

as he swung up into saddle, "an' the trend of the road is mighty nigh due west."

"But in which direction does their main camp lie, Sergeant?"

He shook his head gravely.

"Durn it; thet's just what I can't quite figure out, sir — whether we uns be to ther north or south of ther white church. Then, somehow or other, it seems like to me as if this yere road lay a bit too close ter the edge of ther plateau ter ever be the main pike what the Feds marched over. I reckon from ther direction it runs that maybe it might be a branch like, or a wood-road leadin' inter the other. If thet's the way it is, then them fellers we uns is tryin' ter dodge ought ter be down yonder ter the left somewhar."

I gazed vaguely out into the black vacancy to which he pointed.

"Well, if we should chance to run up against one of their picket posts we shall be soon enlightened," I returned, urging my horse carefully forward. "But we shall have to take the chances, for it would not prove healthy for either of us to be caught here by daylight."

I heard Craig chuckle grimly to himself, as if he found humor in the thought, but without other attempt to give utterance to his feelings he ranged up close to my side.

Not daring to venture on any gait faster than a walk along this unknown and ill-defined mountain trail, we slowly and cautiously worked our way forward for more than an hour, meeting with no human obstacle to our progress, yet feeling that each step forward was surrounded by imminent peril. That we were now well within the guarded lines of the enemy we were both assured, although where or how we had succeeded in

The Night Ride

penetrating the cordon of picket posts unobserved we could only conjecture. The darkness about us seemed intensified by the high, overhanging bank of rock at our left; on the other side, and but dimly revealed against the sky-line, I could perceive Craig's gaunt figure as he leaned far over the high pommel of his cavalry saddle, his short carbine well advanced, his trained eyes seeking vainly to pierce the mystery in our front.

CHAPTER III

AN UNWELCOME GUEST

THIS was the sort of work I had long ago learned to love; it warmed the blood, this constant certainty of imminent peril, this intense probability that any moment might bring a flash of flame into our very faces. Each step we took was now a stern, grim play with Fate, where the stakes were life and death. I felt my pulses throb as I rode steadily forward, fairly thrusting the darkness aside, my teeth hard set, my left hand heavy on a revolver butt.

How, in such a situation, the nerves tingle and the heart bounds to each strange sight and sound! Halt! — what was that? Pooh! no more than the deeper shadow of a sharply projecting rock, around which we pick careful way, our horses crowding against each other in the narrow space. And that? Nothing but the faint moan of the night wind amid the dead limbs of a tree. Ah! mark that sudden flash of light! The hand that closes iron-like upon the loosened rein opens again, for it was merely a star silently falling from out the black depths of the sky. Then both of us halt at once, and peer anxiously forward. The figure standing directly in the centre of our path, can it be a sentry at last? A cautious step forward, a low laugh from the Sergeant, and we circle the gaunt, blackened stump, as silent ourselves as the night about us, but with fiercely beating, expectant hearts.

An Unwelcome Guest

But hark! Surely that was no common sound, born of that drear loneliness! No cavalryman can mistake the jingle of accoutrements or the dull thud of horses' hoofs. The road here must have curved sharply, for they were already so close upon us that, almost simultaneously with the sound, we could distinguish the deeper shadow of a small, compact body of horsemen directly in our front. To left of us there rose, sheer and black, the precipitous rock; to right we might not even guess what yawning void. It was either wit or sword-play now.

I know not how it may be with others in such emergencies, but with me it always happens that the sense of fear departs with the presence of actual danger. Before the gruesome fancies of imagination I may quake and burn like any maiden alone upon a city street at night, until each separate nerve becomes a very demon of mental agony; but when the real and known once fairly confronts me, and there is work to do, I grow instantly cool to think, resolute to act, and find a rare joy in it. It was so now, and, revolver in hand but hidden beneath my holster flap, I leaned over and touched Craig's arm.

"Keep quiet," I whispered sternly. "Let them challenge first, and no firing except on my order."

Almost with the words there came the sharp hail:

"Halt! Who comes there?"

I drew the cape of my riding-jacket closer, so as better to muffle the sound of my voice.

"Friends, of course; who would you expect to meet on this road?"

Fortune seemed with me in the chance answer, for he who had hailed exclaimed:

"Oh! is that you, Brennan?"

There was no time now for hesitancy; here was my

25

cue, and I must plunge ahead, accepting the chances. I ventured it.

"No; Brennan could n't come. I am here in his place."

"Indeed! Who are you?"

"Major Wilkie."

There was a moment's painful pause, in which I could hear my heart throb.

"Wilkie," repeated the voice, doubtfully. "There is no officer of that name in the Forty-third."

"Well, there chances to be such an officer on the staff," I retorted, permitting a trace of anger to appear in my tone, "and I am the man."

"What the devil is the difference, Hale, just what his name is?" boomed a deeper voice back in the group. "We are not getting up a directory of the Sixth Corps. Of course he's the man Brennan sent, and that is all we 've got to look after."

"Oh, all right, certainly, Major," returned the first speaker, hastily. "But the night is so cussed black I supposed we must be at least a mile this side of where we were to meet. However, we have the lady here for you all right, and she is anxious enough to get on."

The lady! Heavens! What odd turn of fortune's wheel was this? The lady! I heard Craig's smothered chuckle, but before I had sufficiently regained control over my own feelings to venture upon a suitable reply, the entire party had drawn forward, the leader pressing so close to my side that I felt safer with my face well shaded.

"Where is your escort, Major?" he asked, and the gruffness of his tone put me instantly on defence.

"Just behind us," I returned, with affected careless-ness, and determined now to play out the game, lady or no lady. I was extremely sorry for her, but the cause outweighed her comfort. "The Sergeant and I rode out ahead when we heard you coming. Where is the lady?"

He glanced around at the group huddled behind him.

"Third on the left."

"All right, then. Nothing else, I believe"; for I was eager to get away. "Sergeant, just ride in there and lead out her horse. We will have to be moving, gentlemen, for it is a rough road and a dark night."

"Beastly," assented the other, heartily.

I fairly held my breath as Craig rode forward. If one of them should chance to strike a match to light a pipe, or any false movement of Craig's should excite suspicion! If he should even speak, his soft Southern drawl would mean instant betrayal. And how coolly he went at it; with a sharp touch of the spur, causing his jaded horse to exhibit such sudden restlessness as to keep the escort well to one side, while he ranged close up to our unwelcome guest, and laying firm hand upon her horse's bit, led forth to where I waited. It was quickly, nobly done, and I could have hugged the fellow.

"Well, good luck to you, Major, and a pleasant ride. Remember me to Brennan. Deuced queer, though, why he failed to show up on such an occasion as this."

"He was unfortunate enough to be sent out in the other direction with despatches — good-night, gentlemen."

It was sweet music to me to listen to their hoof-beats dying rapidly away behind us as we turned back down the dark road, the Sergeant still riding with his one hand grasping the stranger's rein. I endeavored to scan her figure in the blackness, but found the effort useless, as little more than a shadow was visible. Yet it was impressed upon me that she sat straight and firm in the saddle, so I concluded she must be young. Rapidly I reviewed our predicament, and sought for some avenue of escape. If we were only certain as to where we were, we might plan with better prospect of success. The woman? Doubtless she would know, and possibly I might venture to question her without awakening suspicion. Surely the experiment was well worth trying.

"Madam," I began, seeking to feel my way with caution into her confidence, "I fear you must be quite wearied by your long ride."

She turned slightly at sound of my voice.

"Not at all, sir; I am merely eager to push on. Besides, my ride has not been a long one, as we merely came from General Sigel's headquarters."

The voice was pleasantly modulated and refined.

"Ah, yes, certainly," I stammered, fearful lest I had made a grave mistake. "But really I had supposed General Sigel was at Coultersville."

"He advanced to Bear Creek yesterday," she returned quietly. "So you see we had covered scarcely more than three miles when we met. How much farther is it to where Major Brennan is stationed?"

I fear I was guilty of hesitancy, but it was only for a moment.

"I am unable to tell exactly, for, as it chances, I have never yet been in the camp, but I should judge that two hours' riding will cover the distance."

"Why," in a tone of sudden surprise, "Captain Hale certainly told me it was all of twenty miles!"

"From Bear Creek?" I questioned eagerly, for it was my turn to feel startled now. "The map barely makes it ten."

"It is but ten, and scarcely that, by the direct White

28

An Unwelcome Guest

Briar road, or, at least, so I heard some of the younger officers say; but it seems the Rebel pickets are posted so close to the White Briar that my friends decided it would be unsafe to proceed that way."

This was news indeed, — news so unexpected and startling that I forgot all caution.

"Then what road do they call this?"

She laughed at my evident ignorance, as well as the eagerness of my tone.

"Really, you are a most peculiar guide," she exclaimed gayly. "You almost convince me that you are lost. Fortunately, sir, out of my vast knowledge of this mysterious region, I am able to enlighten you to some extent. We are now riding due southward along the Allentown pike."

Craig leaned forward so as to look across her horse's neck to where I rode on the opposite side.

"May I speak a word, sir?" he asked cautiously.

"Certainly, Sergeant; do you make anything out of all this?"

"Yes, sir," he answered eagerly. "I know now exactly how we missed it, and where we are. The cut-off to the White Briar I spoke to you about this afternoon cannot be more than a hundred yards below here."

"Ride ahead carefully then, and see if you can locate it. Be cautious; there may be a picket stationed there. We will halt where we are until you return."

He swung forward his carbine where it would be handy for instant service and trotted ahead into the darkness. The woman's horse, being comparatively fresh and restless, danced a little in an effort to follow, but I restrained him with a light hand on the bit, and for a moment we sat waiting in silence. Then her natural curiosity prompted a question.

My Lady of the North

"Why is it you seem so anxious to discover this cut-off?"

"We merely desire to take advantage of the more direct road," I replied somewhat shortly. "Besides, we are much farther to the east than I had supposed, and therefore too close to the lines of the enemy."

"How strange it is you should not have known!" she exclaimed in a voice of indignant wonder; but as I made no reply she did not venture to speak again.

My thoughts at that moment, indeed, were not with her, although I kept firm hold upon her rein. I was eager to be off, to make up by hard riding the tedious delay of this night's work, and constantly listening in dread for some sounds of struggle down the roadway. But all remained silent until I could dimly distinguish the returning hoof-beats of the Sergeant's horse; and so anxious was I to economize time that I was already urging our mounts forward when his shadow grew black in front, and he wheeled in at my side.

"No picket there, sir."

"Very well, Sergeant; when we come to the turn you are to ride a few rods in advance of us, and will set a good pace, for now we must make up for all this lost time."

I caught the motion of his hand as it was lifted in salute.

"Very well, sir; here is the turn — to your right."

I could dimly distinguish the opening designated, and as we wheeled into it he at once clapped spurs to his horse and forged ahead. In another moment he had totally disappeared, and as I urged our reluctant mounts to more rapid speed all sound of his progress was instantly lost in the pounding of our own hoofs on the hard road.

An Unwelcome Guest

It was like riding directly against a black wall, and far from comforting to the nerves, for the path was a strange one, and not too well made. Fortunately the horses followed the curves without mishap, save an occasional awkward stumble amid loose stones, while the high walls of rock on either hand made a somewhat denser shadow where they shut off the lower stars, and thus helped me to guide our progress.

But it was no time for conversation, even had the inclination been mine, for every nerve was now strained to intensity as I spurred on my horse and held tightly to the bridle of the other, almost cursing, as I rode, the unlucky chance which brought us such a burden on a night like this.

CHAPTER IV

A WOMAN WITH A TEMPER

I THOUGHT the stars grew somewhat brighter as we galloped on, the iron-shod hoofs now and then striking out sudden sparks of yellow flame from the flinty surface of the road; but this may have resulted from the lowering of the rocky barriers on either side, making the arch of sky more clearly visible. The air perceptibly freshened, with a chilly mountain wind beating against our faces and rustling the leaves of the phantom trees that lined the way. The woman rode silently and well. I could make out her figure now, dim and indistinct as the outlines were in that darkness and wrapped in the loose folds of an officer's cloak. She was sitting firm and upright in the saddle; I even marked how, with the ease and grace of a practical horsewoman, she held the reins.

I think we must have been fully an hour at it, riding at no mean pace, and with utter disregard of danger. Although I knew little of where we were, and nothing as to the condition of the path we traversed, yet so complete was my confidence in Craig that I felt no hesitancy in blindly following the pace he set. Then a black shape loomed up before us so suddenly that it was only by a quick effort I prevented a collision. Even as I held my horse poised half in air, I perceived it was Craig himself who blocked the way.

"What is it, Sergeant?"

A Woman with a Temper

"A picket, sir, at the end of the road," he said quietly. "I kinder reckoned they'd hev some sort o' guard thar, so I crept up on the quiet ter be sure. The feller helped me out a bit by strikin' a match ter see what time 't was, or I reckon I'd a walked over him in ther dark."

"Had we better ride him down?" I asked, thinking only how rapidly the night hours were speeding and of the importance of the duty pressing upon us.

"Not with ther woman, sir," he answered in a low, reproachful voice. "Besides, we never could git through without a shot, an' if by any dern luck it should turn out ter be a cavalry outpost,—an' I sorter reckon that's what it is,—why, our horses are in no shape fer a hard run. You uns better wait here, sir, an' let me tend ter that soger man quiet like, an' then p'raps we uns kin all slip by without a stirrin' up ther patrol."

"Well," I said, reluctantly yielding to what I felt was doubtless the wiser course, and mechanically grasping the rein he held out to me, "go ahead. But be careful, and don't waste any time. If we hear the sound of a shot we shall ride forward under spur."

"All right, sir, but there'll be no fuss, fer I know just whar ther fellar is."

Time seems criminally long when one is compelled to wait in helpless uncertainty, every nerve on strain.

"Hold yourself ready for a sudden start," I said warningly to my companion. "If there is any noise of a struggle yonder I shall drive in the spurs."

As I spoke I swung the Sergeant's horse around to my side, where I could control him more readily.

There was no reply from the woman, but I noticed she endeavored to draw together the flapping cape of her cloak, as though she felt chilled by the wind, and her figure seemed to stiffen in the saddle.

"Are you cold?" I questioned, more perhaps to throttle my own nervousness by speech than from better motive.

She shook her head; then, as if thinking better of it, answered lightly:

"The wind appears to find no obstacle in this cloak, but I am not suffering."

I wrapped the loose rein of Craig's horse about the pommel of my saddle and bent toward her.

"Permit me," I said; "you probably do not comprehend the intricacies of a cavalry cloak. If I fasten these upper frogs I think it will help to keep out the night air."

Without protest she permitted me to draw the flapping cloth together and fasten it closer about her throat; but whatever tantalizing curiosity I may have felt to view her face was effectually blocked by the high collar behind which she immediately took refuge.

"I am sure that will be much better; you are very kind." The words were pleasant enough, yet there was something in both tone and manner that piqued me, and I turned away without speaking.

It came at last — not the sharp flash of a musket cleaving the night in twain, but merely the tall figure of the Sergeant, stealing silently out of the gloom, like a black ghost, and standing at our very horses' heads.

"All clear, sir," he reported in a matter-of-fact tone. "But we shall hev ter move mighty quiet, fer ther main picket post ain't more nor a hundred yards ter the right o' ther crossin'."

He did not remount, but, with reins flung loosely over his arm, led the way slowly forward, and carefully we followed him.

34

A Woman with a Temper

What had become of the sentinel I did not know, respecting Craig's evident desire for silence; but as we drew nearer the White Briar road I sought in vain to pierce the dense gloom and note some sign of a struggle, some darker shadow where a body might be lying. There was nothing visible to tell the story.

The Sergeant walked without the least hesitation across the open space, directly into the deep shadows opposite, where the cross-road continued to hold way. Crouching low in the saddle, we followed him as silently as though we were but spirits of the night. Up the road I caught the red gleam of a fire almost spent, and a black figure crossed between us, casting an odd shadow against the face of the rock where it was lighted by the flickering red blaze. It was all over in a moment, a mere glimpse, but it formed one of those sudden pictures which paint themselves on the brain and can never after be effaced. I recall yet the long shade cast by the man's gun, the grotesque shape of his flapping army overcoat, the quick change in the silhouette as he wheeled to retrace his beat. But there was no noise, not even the sound of his footsteps reaching us. Even as I gazed, lying nearly full length upon my horse, we had crossed the open, and a perfect tangle of low bushes hid us as completely as if we had entered the yawning mouth of a cavern.

A hundred yards or more of sharply curving road densely lined with shrubbery on either hand, and then Craig swung into saddle and again gave spur to his horse.

"We must ride for it now," he said tersely. "When thet patrol makes their round, them fellers will be after us hot."

I urged my tired horse to a gallop, pressing upon Craig's heels as closely as I dared; nor did I glance back, for I knew well that a dead picket was lying somewhere by the cross-roads, and that his comrades would be heard from before the dawn.

We were moving bravely now; for the road under foot grew better as we advanced, and gave back the dull thud of soft earth instead of the rattling clang of the rocks we had been so long accustomed to. I forced the scabbard of my sabre beneath the bend of my knee to keep it from clanging against the iron stirrup, and only the breathing of the horses, and their heavy pounding on the earth, broke the night silence. Craig was riding directly in my front, sitting erect as if on parade, and the woman's horse kept up the pace without apparent effort. Surely we had already covered a good safe mile from where we had left the dead soldier to tell his speechless story, and the way ahead was clear. My spirits rose buoyantly with every stride of the horse, and my faith, never long dormant, already saw my task accomplished, my pledge to Lee fulfilled.

But it is the unexpected which masters us in the end. I had all but completely shut the dark night from my thoughts. I suppose, in truth, I was as keenly observant as ever, but it now seems to me that I was riding that black road with closed eyes, so busy were my thoughts elsewhere. Then, suddenly, my horse was jerked almost to a standstill, the hand upon his bit seemingly as hard as my own, and I wheeled in the saddle, pressing my knees tightly to prevent being thrown, only to perceive the woman tugging desperately at the lines.

"What now?" I asked sharply, and in sudden anger I forced her to release her grasp. "We must ride, and ride hard, madam, to be out of this cordon by daylight."

"Ride where?"

A Woman with a Temper

She faced me stiffly, and there was a slight sting in her voice, I felt.

"Where?" I repeated; then partially gathering my scattered wits: "Why, to the camp we are seeking, of course."

I was conscious that her eyes were striving anxiously to see my face in the darkness, — that her suspicions were now fully aroused; yet her quick retort surprised me.

"You lie!" she said coldly. "That was a Federal picket he killed."

It was no time for argument, and I knew it. Any moment might bring to us the sound of hoof-beats in pursuit; more, I realized that anything I might hope to say would only tend to make matters worse. There was but one course open. She must be compelled to ride, by force if necessary. Why should I hesitate? She had no claim on my consideration, and I hardened my heart to make her comprehend, once and for all, that I was the master. Even as I reached this decision, Craig, noting our pause, had ridden back, and reined in beside us without a word.

"You are right," I said tersely. "In one sense of the word you are prisoner, for the time being at least, but not through any wish of mine. We do not make war on women, and your being in this situation is altogether an accident. However, be that as it may, we must, first of all, protect ourselves. I would very gladly leave you with your friends, if possible, but as things have shaped themselves there remains but one alternative — *you must ride as I order.*"

I could mark her quick breathing while I spoke, and when I concluded one hand went up to her throat as if she choked.

My Lady of the North

"You — you are not Major Brennan's friend then? You were not sent by Frank to meet me?" The questions burst from her lips so rapidly that I scarcely caught their import.

"I am Captain Philip Wayne, —th Virginia Cavalry, at your service, madam," I said calmly, "and to the best of my knowledge I have not the pleasure of Major Brennan's acquaintance."

She seemed not to know what to say, and sat there staring at me through the darkness, as she might have gazed in speechless horror at some wild animal she expected would spring upon her.

"A Rebel!" The hated word hissed from her lips as if the utterance burned them.

"Yes, madam," I said, somewhat coldly, for I was not especially fond of the term, "that is what they call us on your side, but also an officer and a gentleman."

I doubt if she even heard me. All I know is she suddenly lifted the heavy riding whip that was clinched in her right hand, struck me with it full across the face, and then, as I quickly flung up my own arm to ward off a second blow, she sent the lash swirling down upon the flank of her horse. With one bound the maddened animal wrenched the reins from out my hands, nearly dragging me from the saddle, and swerved sharply to the left. There was a shock, a smothered oath, a moment's fierce struggle in the darkness, the sharp ping of the whip as it came down once, twice — then silence, broken only by deep breathing.

"I've got her, Captain," chuckled the Sergeant, softly, "but dog-gone if I know what to do with her."

There was small sentiment of mercy in my heart as I drew up toward them, for my cheek burned where the

38

A Woman with a Temper

lash had struck as though scorched with fire. For the moment I felt utterly indifferent to all claims of her womanhood. She had unsexed herself, and deserved treatment accordingly. It was thus I felt as I clinched my teeth in pain; but when I saw her leaning helplessly forward on her horse's neck, all bravado gone, her hands pinioned behind her in the iron grip of the Sergeant, my fierce resentment died away within me.

"Let go her hands, Craig," I commanded briefly.

She lifted her body slightly from its cramped, uncomfortable posture, but her head remained bowed.

"Madam," — I spoke sternly, for moments were of value now, — "listen to what I say. We are Confederate soldiers passing through the Federal lines with despatches. In order to save ourselves from discovery and capture we were compelled to take you in charge. It was the fortune of war. If now we could honorably leave you here we would most gladly do so, for having you with us adds vastly to our own danger; but these mountains are simply overrun with wandering guerillas who would show you neither respect nor mercy. We simply dare not, as honorable men, leave you here unprotected, and consequently you must continue to ride in our company. Now answer me plainly, will you proceed quietly, or shall we be compelled to tie you to your horse?"

I knew she was crying; but with an effort she succeeded in steadying her voice sufficiently to reply.

"I will go," she said.

"Thank you," and I gravely lifted my hat as I spoke. "You have saved me a most unpleasant duty. You may ride on, Sergeant; this lady and I will follow, as before."

She scarcely changed her posture as I spurred forward, riding now so close to her side that I could feel the flap of her saddle rise and fall against my knee. Whatever of evil she may have thought of us, I felt that she was sorry enough now for her hasty action, and I forgave the pain that yet stung me, and longed, without well knowing how, to tell her so.

CHAPTER V

A DISASTER ON THE ROAD

TO me she was merely a woman whom it had become my duty to protect, and whatever of chivalrous feeling I may have held toward her was based upon nothing deeper than this knowledge. She had come to us undesired and in darkness, her form enveloped in a cavalry cloak, her face shrouded by the night. As to whether she was young or old I had scarce means of knowing, saving only that the tone of her voice and the graceful manner of her riding made me confident that she had not lost the agility of youth. But beyond this vague impression (it was little more), and a fleeting gleam of the starlight in her eyes as she faced me in anger, I was as totally unaware of how she really looked as though we had never met. Her very name was unknown to me. Who was this Major Brennan? Was he father, brother, or husband? and was her name Brennan also? For some reason this last possibility was repugnant to me. Yet I knew not why.

I turned these thoughts over in my mind, speculating idly upon them, not because I felt any interest in their solution, or in the woman riding at my side, but because they seemed to fall into order to the steady music of my horse's feet and the darkness of the night. " No," I said to myself, " there is certainly no leaving her except in a disciplined camp; young or old, Yankee or what not, she is in our care, and we'll keep her out of the hands of those cut-throats between the lines."

I glanced toward her, wondering what the morning light might reveal as to her appearance. She was sitting erect and easy in the saddle, yet seemed to ride with her face averted from me.

"You ride as though born to the saddle," I said pleasantly; and although I spoke low, we were so close together that my voice carried distinctly to her ears. "We have been sufficiently conceited to suppose that to be an accomplishment peculiar to our Southern women."

"I have been accustomed to ride since childhood," she replied rather shortly, and I was conscious of a restraint in her manner far from pleasing. Yet I ventured upon one more effort at conversation.

"Is Major Brennan an officer on Sheridan's staff?"

"I was not aware" — and I could not mistake the accent of vindictiveness in her voice — "that prisoners were obliged to converse against their will."

My lady certainly possessed a temper of her own, and I was obliged to smile there in the dark at her high head and quick retort.

"I ask your pardon, I am sure," I returned soberly. "But my question was not altogether an idle one. I have chanced to meet several of General Sheridan's staff, and thought possibly Major Brennan might have been of their number. Seeing that we must associate for a time, I naturally felt it would prove pleasanter for both of us if we might discover some mutual tie."

There was no response. Her eyes were fastened upon the road ahead, and evidently my lady possessed no desire for the discovery of any such tie. Watching her, I pressed my lips together, and held her as a proud and silly fool.

A Disaster on the Road

I would perform my full duty toward her, of course, but beyond that I would go no further.

The pace we were travelling had already told severely on the horses, although hers was by far the best and freshest of the three. My own brave sorrel had stumbled several times already in a way that gave me no small uneasiness, yet I durst not venture to draw rein or even slacken speed. Already, beyond a doubt, the patrol in our rear had missed the picket stationed at the cross-roads, had searched until they found the lifeless body where Craig had hidden it, and were now hot upon our trail. Hard, continuous riding alone could save us — riding with a thoroughly aroused enemy at our heels, and yet another picket line to pass before we could even hope for a clear sweep into safety.

The road we were following here took a sudden trend downward, and we could tell from the sharper ring of the hoofs, and the spitting of flinty sparks beneath us, that we were among rocks once more. Then our horses suddenly splashed into water, and I held them up long enough to drink. I felt thirst strongly myself, and slipping out of the saddle, filled my canteen.

" Would you care for a drink? " I asked, stemming the stream to reach her side, and holding the vessel within easy grasp of her hand.

I actually believe her first impulse was to refuse haughtily this proffered civility from an enemy of her country, but the deep sense of need conquered foolish pride and caused her to accept the offering.

" I am very thankful to you," she said, handing back the canteen; yet the words were spoken in mockery. I ignored them, and swung into my saddle without response.

Another hill followed, and then another, and finally we

43

swept swiftly down a long slope densely bordered by trees and with irregular piles of rock uprearing ugly heads on either hand. A little edge of the waning moon began to peep over the ridge of the hill, and yielded sufficient light to enable our eyes to discern dimly the faint track we followed. I remember remarking the blacker figure of the Sergeant ahead of us, and already halfway down the long decline. I caught a swift glimpse of a rough log house on the right, so set back among trees that I half doubted its real existence, when — there was a slip, the crunching of a stone, a long stumble forward that fairly wrenched my hand loose from the woman's rein, and then, hopelessly struggling to regain his feet, my horse went down with a crash, head under, and I was hurled heavily forward upon my face.

Severely bruised by the shock, but fortunately without broken bones, I recall half-wheeling even as I fell, wondering if my prisoner would grasp this opportunity for escape. Quite probably the thought never occurred to her; perhaps her woman's heart, in the stress of such accident, held her motionless. But Craig, startled at the sudden crash behind him, spurred back to learn the full extent of my disaster. By this time I had regained my feet.

"I'm all right, I think, Sergeant," I said hastily, " but the sorrel has broken her neck."

He began to swear at our ill luck, but I stopped him with a gesture he knew better than to ignore.

"Enough of that," I commanded sternly. " Bad fortune is seldom bettered by hard words. First of all, help me to drag this dead body out of sight."

On one side of us the bank fell away with such precipitancy that when we once succeeded in dragging our load

44

A Disaster on the Road

to the edge, we experienced no difficulty in sending it crashing downward. The body plunged through the thick underbrush at the bottom of the gorge, where I knew it would be completely hidden, even in the glare of daylight, from the prying eyes of any troopers riding hard upon our track. With a branch, hastily wrenched from a near-by tree, I carefully raked over the track, so that, as far as I could determine in the dim light, all outward trace of my accident had been fairly obliterated.

As we rapidly worked on this disagreeable task, I thought and planned: two horses and three riders, — one of these latter a woman in need of protection,—a despatch to be delivered by daylight, at all hazards. It was indeed a difficult proposition, and I saw only a single possible solution. One of our number must press on; two of us must remain behind. Which one? what two? If I rode with the despatch (and how eagerly I longed to do so!), and succeeded in bringing Lee's message safe to Longstreet, it meant much to me — promotion, distinction, honor. On the other hand, if I remained behind, and Craig successfully carried out the duty which had been especially intrusted to me, I should be fortunate indeed to escape with a reprimand instead of more serious consequences. If failure resulted, it meant certain and deserved disgrace. Yet I could absolutely trust him with the despatch; he was a soldier, and would faithfully perform a soldier's duty. More, he would carry the message with even greater certainty than I, for he knew the roads much better, and — I write the words hesitatingly — I could not trust him there alone with the woman.

I glanced aside at him as I thus turned the perplexing situation over in my mind, — a tall, gaunt mountaineer, whose sole discipline of mind and body had been the army; hardened by service until every muscle in his lean, sinewy frame was like steel, a cavalryman who would follow his leader into the very jaws of hell, but whose morals were those of the camp, and whose face revealed audacious deviltry such as no man would care to see in one to whom he intrusted the welfare of sister or wife. Recalling to mind certain idle stories that circulated through the camp from time to time, in which his name had figured, I glanced backward to where the woman sat her horse in silence and loneliness, and made my resolve: I would risk the censure; if there must be sacrifice it should be mine.

"Sergeant," I asked, flinging aside the improvised brush, "how far do you suppose we are from Longstreet's picket line?"

"Ten miles at the very best, sir," he answered promptly, "an' I reckon with another Yankee outpost atween."

"With fair luck and good riding it might be made by daylight?"

"I reckon as how it might, Captain, if we only hed sum fresh hosses," he said glumly; "but it's bin mighty hard on my nag; I've looked fer him to roll over like yer sorrel did fer the las' two mile."

"Well, Craig, you shall have both horses. Ride the woman's, it is the fresher of the two; but you are to get through if you kill them both and then walk."

His face brightened, and he raised his hand in salute.

"And you?" he asked wonderingly.

"I remain with the woman; there is no other way. Wait here a moment while I speak with her."

I left him standing there, and moved back to where she waited. As I came up she faced me, and for the first time (for the night had lightened somewhat) I could see her

46

A Disaster on the Road

eyes and discern some faint outline of her face where the night wind flung back the upturned cape. It was a winsome sight to soldier vision, but with a certain semblance of pride and reserve about it that caused a hesitancy in my speech strange enough to me. I felt oddly like a bashful boy, and involuntarily lifted my hat as I approached, to cover my confusion. Some trick of the dancing moon shadows made me imagine that she smiled, and the sight nerved me instantly to speak bluntly the words I came to say.

"Madam," — I rested my hand upon her horse's mane and looked up at her with a glance as proud as her own, — "it might be as well for you to draw the cape closer about your face at present. There are rough men in all armies who would consider your beauty a lawful prize. The life we lead is not conducive to gentleness; virtue is not born in camps, and it would be better not to provoke a danger which may be so easily avoided."

A wave of sudden color swept her cheeks at my plain speech, and her hand sought the collar of the cloak, yet paused there irresolute.

"You claimed, I believe, to be an officer and a gentleman," she said coldly.

I smiled, even as I felt the full chill of her words, and my purpose stiffened within me.

"Even as I yet claim, and trust to be able to prove to your satisfaction," — my eyes looked unfalteringly into hers, — "but, unfortunately, I have one with me to-night who is neither. I would that he were for my own sake. However, madam, let that pass. The fact is here, and we have no time to argue or quarrel. I have already told you that we ride with despatches for Longstreet. These must go forward at all hazards, for thousands of human lives depend upon them; yet I dare not leave you here alone and unprotected to the mercies of the wolves who haunt these hills."

"You are exceedingly kind."

The tone in which she spoke was most sarcastic.

"I thank you for your approbation," and I bowed again; "but I venture to tell you this merely because I have already fully determined to despatch the Sergeant forward with the message, and remain behind myself to render you every protection possible."

"Do you mean that we are to remain here alone?"

"There is no other way."

She made no reply, but her proud unbelieving eyes were no longer upon my face.

"I beg you to believe, madam," I pleaded gently, for I confess my interest in her good opinion was growing stronger, "that I do this only because I believe it to be a duty, and not that I desire in any way to distress you with my presence."

She swept my upturned face suddenly with questioning eyes.

"As your prisoner I presume I have no choice in the matter."

"I should prefer that you took a different view, but in a measure you are right."

"Very well, sir; I simply yield to what I am powerless to avoid, and will obey your orders however distasteful they may be. What is your first command?"

"That you dismount. The Sergeant must ride your horse, as he is the more fit of the two."

Greatly to my surprise and relief she placed her gauntleted hand in mine, and, without so much as a word of protest, permitted me to swing her lightly from the saddle to the ground.

"Craig," I called, "come here"; and turning to her, added quietly, "Kindly draw up your cape for a moment."

I noticed her hands fasten the clasps, which had become loosened, and that she turned partially so as to look backward up the road as the Sergeant drew near.

"You know your work," I said to him briefly. "And now the sooner you are at it the better. Ride this horse and lead your own. As soon as you deliver Lee's message at headquarters, hunt up the cavalry brigade commander and report to him my position. Get a detail, insist upon one, and be back here by to-morrow without fail. That is all."

He saluted, wheeled about, swung lightly into saddle, and rode off on a rapid trot, grasping, as he passed down the hill, the rein of his own mount, and leading it, lagging, behind him, until the night swallowed the figures, and even the sound of the hoof-beats could be no longer heard. We were alone.

CHAPTER VI

A STRUGGLE IN THE DARK

I HAVE seldom been more deeply embarrassed than at that moment. I knew not what to say or how best to approach this young woman left so strangely to my protection. The very fact, which I now realized, that she was both young and fair added some indefinite burden and complicated the delicate situation. I saw no safety for us but in careful hiding until Craig could return, a squad of hard-riding troopers at his back. To permit the girl to venture forward alone through the desolate country we were in, overrun as I knew it to be by irregular bands whose sole purpose was plunder, and whose treatment of women had made my blood run cold as I listened to its recital, was not to be so much as thought of. Even if, by rare good fortune, she should succeed in safely reaching the Federal picket post in our front, the men on duty there were just as likely as not to prove of the same desperate stamp, and every indignity might be offered her were she to appear alone. Nor could I venture to accompany her on such a trip, for to do so would but assure my own capture, and involve months of confinement in Northern prisons, even were I fortunate enough to escape with life. Wearing as I did the full field uniform of my rank, it was hardly probable that regular troops would treat me as a spy, even though caught within

A Struggle in the Dark

their lines; but if we fell into the hands of guerillas it would be a short shrift indeed.

There was no help for it, and but one way out, disagreeable as that might prove to my lady. She stood there before me, motionless and silent as a statue, exactly where she had alighted when the Sergeant took her horse, and it seemed to me I could plainly read righteous indignation in the indistinct outline of her figure and the haughty pose of her head. To her at that moment I was evidently a most disagreeable and even hated companion, a " Rebel," the being of all others she had been taught to despise, the enemy of all she held sacred. " Could any good thing come out of Nazareth? "

Well, unpleasant as was the task, it had to be done, so, mustering my courage for the ordeal as I never had to do in time of battle, I advanced toward her, hat in hand. She never so much as glanced about at the sound of my footsteps, nor deigned by the slightest motion to acknowledge my presence. So intense, indeed, was her evident sense of indignity that it awoke within me something akin to anger at her unreasonableness, and for the moment I clinched my teeth to keep back the hot words burning upon my tongue. Then I smiled grimly with the rare humor of it, and became myself once more.

" The time has come when it becomes my duty to look after your comfort and safety," I said, striving to disguise all self-consciousness. " Every moment we delay now merely increases the danger of our remaining here."

" I imagine I might very easily dispense with any further care on your part."

Her reply nettled me, and I answered with an earnestness which she could neither ignore nor check: " Possibly you may think so, but if you do it is merely because of

51

your utter ignorance of the disorganized conditions which
prevail in these mountains. Your pride is almost ridiculous under all the circumstances. You have no just cause
to feel that I am forcing myself unnecessarily upon you.
Our being compelled to take you in charge has proven as
disastrous to us as to you. Personally I can say that
nothing will relieve me more than to be able to place you
uninjured into the care of your own people. I would
willingly assume great risks to that end. But while you
remain here and in my care, I shall perform my full duty
toward you as though you were my own sister. Now
please listen to me, and I assure you I shall speak nothing
for the mere purpose of alarming you, but simply that you
may better comprehend the facts which must influence
our present relationship. I have sent forward Sergeant
Craig with the message especially intrusted to me for de-
livery, and thus, if it fail to reach its destination, I have
laid myself open to the charge of a grave military crime.
In doing this I have not only perilled my own future, but
the lives of my comrades and the faith of my commander.
Yet I have deliberately chosen to do so because I feel the
impossibility of leaving you here unprotected, and because
I was unwilling to trust you alone with my companion.
I made this choice, remember, without in the least knowing whether you were young or old, worthy of respect or
unworthy. I did it because you were a woman, alone and
without friends. Whether you spurn my protection or
not will make no difference; I shall simply continue to
do what I may on your behalf until you are again in the
hands of those you trust."

" But why may I not go to them now? "

The question was impetuous, but the voice sounded
more gentle. My words had at least pierced her armor.

A Struggle in the Dark

"Simply because I dare not permit you to traverse these roads alone," I said soberly. "The mountains all about us, deserted as they now appear, are filled with wandering bands of desperate and hunted men whose tenderest mercy is death. Any rock may be the hiding-place of an outlaw, any dark ravine the rendezvous of as wild a gang as ever murdered for plunder. For months past — yes, for years — the two great armies have scouted these hills, have battled for them, and every forward or backward movement of the contesting lines has left its worthless horde of stragglers behind, until with guerilla and bushwhacker, fleeing conscript and deserter, it has become such a meeting-place of rascality and crime as to be a veritable hell on earth."

"But the Sergeant said there was a Federal picket post at the crossing of the White Briar."

Her voice trembled as she spoke.

"He merely supposed there would be; but even if it were true, we have no positive means of knowing that the men stationed there would be of the regular service. Doubtless these thieving, murdering bands — such as that headed by Red Lowrie, of whom you may have heard — are sufficiently organized to keep patrols posted, and may, indeed, be utilized at times by both armies for that purpose. Were you to go to them you might be simply walking into a den of wolves."

"But could you not go with me?"

I smiled at the naive innocence of her query.

"I wish you to feel that I have never thought so much about my own danger as about yours," I returned quietly. "But would it be a pleasure even to you to behold me swinging from the limb of a tree, hung as a spy without

53

trial, merely because I ventured to walk with you into a Federal camp?"

I could see her eyes now resting full upon me, and much of the hardness and doubt seemed to have gone out of them as she scanned my uncovered features in the dim light. I scarcely think I was ever considered a handsome man even by my friends, but I was young then, frank of face, with that about me which easily inspired confidence, and it did me good to note how her eyes softened, and to mark the perceptible tremor in her voice as she cried impulsively:

"Oh, no! Not that!"

"Your words yield me new heart," I replied fervently, determined, now that the ice was partially broken, to permit no excuse for its again forming, " for if you but once fully realize our situation you will certainly feel that I am merely endeavoring to perform my plain duty. I know not how I could do less without forfeiting entirely your respect. Now one thing more — please banish from your thought the idea that you are in any way a prisoner; forget, if possible, the color of my uniform, and think of me simply as an officer of equal rank and standing with those you know in your own army, — one who stands ready, if need arise, to protect you with his life; as glad to serve you as if he wore the blue instead of the gray."

I believed for a moment my words had appealed to her nobler nature; that she would outstretch to me her slightly uplifted hand and surrender utterly. But it was only for the moment; whatever wave of emotion may have moved her to the gesture, it was as suddenly swept aside by a return of the old proud, impetuous spirit.

"I will, of course, bow to the inevitable, sir," she said, " and shall endeavor to adapt myself to the requirements

A Struggle in the Dark

of my unfortunate situation. May I venture to inquire
what you now propose to do?"

I confess to experiencing a quick feeling of resentment
as I turned to scan the dim surroundings, not knowing
at the moment how best to answer her. Who was this
girl, that she should continue to bear herself as a disdainful queen might toward the very meanest of her sub-
jects? Was I so far beneath her, even in the social scale,
as to warrant such assumption of superiority? No, I felt
that this was not the cause of her cold suspicion, her
proud, unapproachable bearing. Undoubtedly it arose
from the manner in which she had fallen into our hands,
the strangeness and delicacy of our situation, the knowledge that I was a " Rebel " in arms against her people.
These were the things which had reared such a barrier
between us. She but resorted to what was apparently
her only available weapon of defence. Well, of one thing,
and that the most important, I was now assured — there
would occur no further struggle on her part; if not fully
resigned to the situation, she at least realized the necessity
of obedience to my will. This was much; but now what
could I do with her?

To the right of where we stood the ground sloped
rapidly downward until the dense darkness at the foot of
the steep defile shrouded everything from view. The de-
scent appeared rocky and impracticable, and I could distinguish the sound of rapid water far below. On the
opposite side stood a dense wood, the outer fringe of
trees overhanging the road, and through the waving leaves
the moonlight checkered the ground with silver, while the
dense mass beyond seemed to flow back up the steep side
of the mountain, thick with underbrush. Just below us,
and possibly fifty feet from the highway, I could perceive

55

a small one-story log cabin, as silent, gloomy, and deserted to all outward appearance as were the sombre woods of which it formed a part.

"There seems small choice," I said, speaking as cheerfully as possible. "But I propose to investigate the log hut yonder, and learn if it may not afford some degree of shelter."

She glanced furtively in the direction pointed out, and her eyes mirrored the sudden fear that swept into them.

"Oh, no!" she cried impulsively, "I could never venture into that horrible place."

It did, indeed, look uncanny enough in its black loneliness, a fit abiding place for ghost and goblin damned; but I was not inclined to yield to superstitious dread.

"Certainly not," I answered, "until after I have investigated it. Perhaps it may prove more attractive within than without, although, I confess, from here it appears gloomy enough to discourage any one. However, if you will rest here, in the shadow of these trees, I will soon discover whether it has inmates or not."

She followed me in silence across the road to the spot designated, but as I turned to leave her seated upon the grass, and well protected from prying eyes, she hurried quickly after me, and in her agitation so far forgot herself as to touch my sleeve with her hand.

"Oh, please do not leave me here alone. I am not naturally timid, yet everything is so gloomy I cannot stand it. Let me go with you, if you must go!"

"Most assuredly you shall if you desire," I returned heartily. "But really there is not a particle of danger in this, for if the house were inhabited its occupants would have been aroused long ago. Follow just behind me, and we shall soon solve the mystery."

A Struggle in the Dark

There appeared before us a dim, little-used path leading in among the trees, and following its erratic curves we were soon before the cabin, which grew ever more uninviting as we drew near. As I paused a moment before the closed door, in order that I might listen for any possible sound within, I could hear her quick breathing, as though the terror of the moment had driven all else from her mind.

"Do not feel frightened," I said, seeking to reassure her. "There is nothing here more terrifying than a vacant house, doubtless long since deserted. We shall discover nothing more formidable within than a rat or two."

The wooden latch yielded readily enough to my pressure, and pushing wide open the door, which creaked slightly upon its rusty hinges, I stepped across the puncheon threshold onto the hard earthen floor. There was no window visible, and the slight reflection of moonlight which crept in through the doorway scarcely revealed the nature of that dark interior. I could dimly perceive what I believed to be a table directly in front of me, while certain other indistinct and ill defined shadows might be chairs pushed back against the wall. At least this room was without occupants; yet it was with every sense alert that I entered, pressing slowly past the table toward where I felt the fireplace would naturally be, knowing that my companion was yet with me, her hand clutching my arm.

"Oh!" she cried sharply in terror, "what was that?"

It was something certainly, — a deadened, muffled, shuffling sound directly in our front, followed by a strange noise of scraping, as if with a dull knife on wood.

"Wait here," I said sternly. "Probably it is nothing more dangerous than a rat."

57

My Lady of the North

I felt my way carefully around the table, a revolver ready in my hand. There was nothing to be found there, —nothing, indeed, in the room; for from my new position I could look backward and distinguish in the moonlight the details of that simple, squalid interior. I ran my hand along the rough logs of the further wall. Ay! here was a break, doubtless a door; and groping along the crack I found the latch.

There was no longer any noise audible, and I drew the door inward, never dreaming of danger. Suddenly, with a fierce, wild spring out of the dark, a huge body hurled itself directly at my throat, striking with such headlong impetus that I went backward as if shot, crashing against the table, then to the floor, dropping my weapon as I fell. There was no noise, no sound, while for an instant, with strength of sheer desperation, I held back the snapping jaws that breathed hot fire into my very face. With a bound backward of its great body the beast jerked free from my grip, and the next instant had sunk its dripping fangs, deep and hard, into the flesh of my shoulder. As the intense pain shot through me, my right hand, driven with all the force I could muster, caught the monster once, twice, full in the throat, but tighter and tighter those clinched jaws locked, until it seemed as if every bone between them must be ground to powder. Even as I grasped the lower jaw, seeking vainly to wrench it loose, I heard the girl scream in sudden affright.

"Quick!" I gasped desperately. "Get my revolver there on the floor, and use it — but for God's sake keep down; don't let the brute see you."

She must have heard, but there was no response, although her crying ceased. Yet my own struggle to rid myself of that crushing weight and those iron

58

A Struggle in the Dark

jaws drowned all other sounds, drove all other thoughts from me. I doubt if what I now record occupied a minute; but God protect me from ever having to experience such another minute! I continued to struggle in desperate hopelessness with single hand, in vain endeavor to wrench loose that awful grip upon my shoulder. Every movement I made was an agony, an inexpressible torture, but the very intensity of pain kept me from faintness, as the maddened beast tore deeper and deeper into the quivering flesh. With knee bent double beneath me I succeeded in turning partially upon one side, lifting the entire weight of the animal as I did so; but no degree of force I could exert would loosen those set jaws. There was no growling, no savage snarling, no sound of any kind,—just that fierce, desperate, silent struggle for life in the darkness. Every muscle of my body began to weaken from the strain, my eyes blurred, faintness swept over me, I felt my brain reeling, when there burst a vivid flash of flame within a foot of my face, singeing my forehead; then followed a deafening report, and the huge brute sprang backward with a snarl of pain, his teeth clicking together like cogs of steel. Then he stiffened and fell prone across me, a dead, inert weight, pinning me breathless to the floor.

For the moment I could do no more than lie there helpless, gasping for breath, scarce conscious even of my deliverance. Then, as sufficient strength returned for action, I rolled the body of the dead brute off me, and lifting myself by aid of the wall against which my head rested, looked about. Two broken chairs overturned upon the floor, and the shapeless, huddled body of my late assailant, alone spoke of the violence of that deadly struggle; but the cabin was yet full of smoke, and I could perceive the figure of the girl leaning against the frame of the open door, the revolver still grasped in her hand. Her posture was that of a frightened deer, as her terror-filled eyes sought the dark interior.

"It is safely over," I said weakly, for my breath yet came to me in gasps. "The brute is dead."

"And you are not killed!" Shall I ever forget the glad ring in her voice? — "Oh, thank God! thank God!"

The sound of these eager words yielded me a fresh measure of life.

"Believe me, I certainly do," I said as cheerfully as possible, "and I thank you also as His instrument; but if you would keep me from fainting away like a nerveless woman, I beg you come here."

I could mark her coming across the narrow streak of moonlight, moving toward me as a frightened bird might, startled at everything, and passing as far from the lifeless mass on the floor as the small space would allow. As she bent anxiously over me her face was so in shadow that I could distinguish nothing of its features.

"What is it? Are you indeed severely hurt?"

"Not seriously, I think, yet I have lost some blood, and am in great pain. There is brandy in the inner pocket of my jacket, but I am unable to move my arm in order to reach it. Would you endeavor to draw the flask out?"

I felt her bend over me, her soft breath coming almost in sobs upon my face, as with trembling fingers she undid the buttons of my trooper's jacket and extracted the small flat flask I had been thoughtful enough to store away there.

The fiery liquid seemed to put new blood into my veins, and with it there returned all my old-time audacity, with that intense hopefulness in which I had been trained by years of war and self-reliance.

A Struggle in the Dark

"Ah! now I feel I am myself once more," I exclaimed cheerily. "Things are surely not so bad after all. At least we have a roof over our heads, and another day in which to live."

I felt her shudder.

"Oh, please do not make light of it," she whispered. "It is so like some horrid dream, and I am trembling yet." I put my hand upon hers, and it was not withdrawn.

"I trust you realize," I said, "that I am neither thoughtless nor ungrateful. Years of war service make one careless of life, but I know it was your shot that saved me. You are a brave girl."

Her overtaxed nerves gave way at my words, and I knew she was crying softly. The sobbing was in her voice as she strove to speak.

"Oh, no, I am not; you do not guess how great a coward I am. I scarcely knew what I was doing when I fired. That horrid thing — what was it?"

"A huge mastiff, I imagine; one of the largest of his breed. But whatever it may have been, the beast is dead, and we have nothing more to fear from him."

"Yet I tremble so," she confessed, almost hysterically. "Every shadow frightens me."

I realized that no amount of conversation would quiet her nerves so effectively as some positive action; besides, I felt the hot blood constantly trickling down my arm, and realized that something needed to be done at once to stanch its flow, before weakness should render me equally useless.

"Do you think you could build a fire on the hearth yonder?" I asked. "I am afraid I am hardly capable of helping you as yet; but we must have light in this gloomy old hole, or it is bound to craze us both. Take those broken chairs if you find nothing better."

She instantly did as I bade her, moving here and there about the room until she gathered together the materials necessary, but keeping carefully away from where the dead dog lay, until in a brief space of time the welcome flame leaped up in the wide black chimney, and cast its red glare all over the little room. The activity did her good, the light flooding the gloomy apartment yielded renewed courage, and there was a cheerier sound in her voice as she came back to me.

" The great ugly brute!" she exclaimed, looking at the form in the centre of the floor.

" He was certainly heavy enough to have been a bear," I replied, clinching my teeth in pain, " and sufficiently savage."

I viewed her now for the first time clearly, and the memory will remain with me till I die. How distinctly that entire picture stands forth with the mist of all these years between! The low-ceiled room, devoid of all furniture save of the rudest and most primitive kind; the bare logs forming the walls, unrelieved in their rough ugliness, except as here and there sundry unshapely garments dangled from wooden pegs; the rough deal table, with a few cheap dishes piled upon one end of it; the dead dog lying across the earthen floor; and over all the leap of ruddy flame as the newly kindled fire gathered way, leaving weird shadows here and there, yet steadily forcing them back, and flooding the whole interior with a cheery glow.

She had flung aside the blue and yellow cloak which, during the long hours of our night ride had so completely shrouded her, and stood before me dressed in some

A Struggle in the Dark

soft clinging stuff of a delicate brown color, so cut and
fashioned as to most become her rounded, graceful form.
About her neck a narrow strip of creamy lace was fitted,
the full throat rendered whiter by the contrast, while at
her wrists a similar ornament alone served to relieve the
simple plainness of her attire. The flaming fire lighted
up her face, making it seem to flush with the dancing
glow, which sparkled like diamonds in her eyes, and
touched with ruddy light the dark, dishevelled hair. Hers
was a young, fair face, — a face to love and trust forever,
yet with a pride in it, and a certain firmness also that
somehow was good to see. All this I noted with one quick
upward glance, and with a sudden thrill of the heart such
as I had never known before.

CHAPTER VII

A DISCIPLE OF SIR WALTER

I HAVE no doubt she wished me to see her thus. Every woman worth the winning is a bit of a coquette, and none can be utterly disdainful of the lesson their mirror tells. But even as I gazed upon her, my admiration deeper than my pain, the arch expression of her face changed; there came a sudden rush of pity, of anxiety into those clear, challenging eyes, and with one quick step she drew nearer and bent above me.

"Oh, Captain Wayne," she cried, her warm, womanly heart conquering all prejudice, "you are badly hurt and bleeding. Why did you not tell me? Please let me aid you."

"I fear I must," I replied grimly. "I would gladly spare you, for indeed I do not believe my injury sufficiently serious to cause alarm, but I find I have only one arm I can use at present; the brute got his teeth into the other."

The tender compassion within her eyes was most pleasant to see.

"Oh, believe me, I can do it." She spoke bravely, a sturdy ring of confidence in the voice, although at the thought her face paled. "I have been in the hospitals at Baltimore, and taken care of wounded soldiers. If there was only some water here!"

A Disciple of Sir Walter

She glanced about, dreading the possibility of having to go forth into the night alone in search of a spring or well.

"I think you will find a pail on the bench yonder," I said, for from where I leaned against the wall I could see out into the shed. "It was doubtless left for the dog to drink from."

She came back with it, tearing down a cloth from off a peg in the wall as she passed, and then, wearing a resolute air of authority, knelt beside me, and with rapid fingers flung back my jacket, unfastening the rough army shirt, and laid bare, so far as was possible, the lacerated shoulder.

It gave me intense pain, for the shirt had become matted to the wound by drying blood, so that in spite of her soft touch and my own clinched teeth a slight groan broke from my lips.

"Forgive me," she said anxiously, "but I fear I can never dress it in this way. We must remove your jacket and cut away the sleeve of your shirt."

It was an agonizing operation, for it has often seemed to me that the more superficial the wound the greater the pain experienced in dealing with it, and the perspiration stood in beads upon my forehead as she worked quickly and with skill. At last the disagreeable task was accomplished, the wounded shoulder completely bared. Her face was deathly white now, and she shielded her eyes with her hand.

"Oh, what a horrible wound!" she exclaimed, almost sobbing. "How that great brute must have hurt you!"

"The wound is not so serious as it appears," I replied reassuringly, and glad myself to feel that I spoke the truth, "but I confess the pain is intense, and makes me feel somewhat faint. It was not so much the mere bite

5   65

of the dog, but unfortunately he got his teeth into an old wound and tore it open."

"An old wound?"

"Yes; I received a Minié ball there at Gettysburg, and although the bullet was extracted, the wound never properly healed."

These words served to recall to her instantly the fact that I was not of her own people; there appeared to come again into her manner that marked restraint which had almost totally disappeared during the last few minutes. Not that she failed in any kindness or consideration, but a growing reserve put check upon what was fast becoming the intimacy of friendship. Yet she performed her disagreeable task with all the tenderness of a sympathetic woman, and as she worked swiftly and deftly, made no attempt to conceal the tears clinging to her long lashes. Skilfully the deep, jagged gash was bathed out, and then as carefully bound up with the softest cloths she could find at hand. The relief was great, and I felt, as I moved the shoulder, that saving the soreness it would probably not greatly bother me.

"Now you must lie back and rest," she said commandingly, as I attempted to thank her. "Here, put your head on this cloak. But first it will do you good to have more of the brandy, for you are as white as death."

"Merely a slight faintness; and I will only consent to indulge provided you partake first, for I know you require the stimulant as much as I," I retorted doggedly, gazing up into her face with an admiration she could scarcely fail to perceive.

She lifted the flask to her lips and did not answer, but when she handed it back to me there was a new flush upon her cheeks.

A Disciple of Sir Walter

" And now as your nurse I command absolute quiet," striving to speak gaily. " See, the daylight is already here, and I mean to discover if this lone cabin contains anything which human beings can eat; I confess that I am nearly famished."

" A most excellent symptom, and I imagine your quest will not be wholly vain. To my eye that greatly resembles a slab of bacon hanging beside the chimney."

" It indeed is," she exclaimed, " and I feel as a ship-wrecked seaman must on first beholding land.".

However my naturally energetic spirit revolted at in-activity, for the time being my faintness precluded any thought of doing other than obeying her orders, and I lay there silent, propped up against the logs, my eager eyes following her rapid, graceful movements with a constantly increasing interest. As she worked, the reflection of the red flames became mingled with the gray dawn, until the bare and cheerless interior grew more and more visible. Her search was far from unsuccessful, while her resource-fulness astonished me, old campaigner as I was; for it was scarcely more than full daylight before she had me at the table, and I was doing full justice to such coarse food as the larder furnished. A Confederate soldier in those days could not well afford to affect delicacy in matters of the cuisine, and indeed our long fast had left us both where any kind of food was most welcome.

The eating helped me greatly; but for some time so busy were we that neither of us spoke. On my own part I experienced a strange hesitancy in addressing her upon terms of equality. Ordinarily not easily embar-rassed in feminine society, I felt in this instance a definite barrier between us, which prevented my feeling at ease. Now and then as we sat opposite each other, eating amid a silence most unpleasant, I would catch her eyes glancing across at me, but they were lowered instantly whenever I ventured to meet them. Finally I broke the stillness with a commonplace remark:

"I presume your people will be greatly worried by this time over your mysterious disappearance."

A flush swept her throat and cheeks, but she did not lift her eyes from the plate. "Yes," she answered slowly, "Frank is doubtless searching for me long before this."

"Frank?" I asked, feeling glad of this opportunity to learn more of her relationships. "You forget, possibly, that your friends are strange to me. You refer to the gentleman who expected to meet you on the road?"

"To Major Brennan, yes."

There was nothing about the tone of her reply that invited me to press the inquiry further. One thing, however, was reasonably certain, — the man she called "Frank" could not be her father. I longed to ask if he was a brother, but the restraint of her whole manner repelled the suggestion.

"Did I understand that you have nursed in the Federal hospitals at Baltimore?" I questioned, more to continue the conversation than from any deep interest.

"Merely as a volunteer, and when the regular nurses were especially busy. Major Brennan was stationed there for some time when I first visited him, and I felt it my duty as a loyal woman to aid the poor fellows."

"It was surely far from being an agreeable task to one of your refinement."

"Oh, it was not that that made it so hard," and her eyes were upon me now unflinchingly. "It was the constant sight of so much misery one was unable to relieve. Besides, that was nearly a year ago; I was very young, just from school, and every form of suffering was new and terrible to me."

" I greatly wonder you were permitted to go there at all."

" The Major did object. He insisted it was no fit place for me, and that I ran the risk of contracting disease. But I generally have my own way, even with him, and in this case I felt it a duty to my country, and that I was right in my decision."

I remained silent, striving vainly to frame some innocent question which should solve for me the problem of who and what she was. Suddenly she spoke softly:

" Captain Wayne, I feel I owe you an apology for my unwarranted and unladylike conduct last night. I am very sure now that you are a gentleman, and will appreciate how bitterly I was tried, how deeply I have ever since regretted it."

It hurt her pride to say even this much, as I could tell by her downcast eyes and heaving bosom, and I hastened to relieve her embarrassment.

" You have nothing whatever to ask forgiveness for," I said earnestly. " Rather such a request should come from me. I only trust, Miss Brennan, that you will excuse my part in this extremely unfortunate affair."

She sat looking down upon her plate, her fingers nervously crumbling a bit of corn bread.

" You do not even know who I am," she said slowly. " I am not Miss, but Mrs. Brennan."

I felt as if a dash of cold water had been suddenly thrown in my face.

" Indeed? " I stammered, scarcely knowing what I said. " You appear so young a girl that I never once thought of you as being a married woman."

My Lady of the North

"I was married very early; indeed, before I was seventeen. My husband — "

What she was about to add I could but conjecture, for a quick change in the expression of her face startled me.

"What is it?" I questioned, half rising to my feet, and glancing over my shoulder toward the wall where her eyes were riveted.

"Something resembling a hand pushed aside the coat hanging yonder," she explained in low trembling tone, "and I thought I saw a face."

With one stride I was across the narrow room, and tore the garment from its wooden hook. The log wall where it hung was blank. I struck it here and there with the steel hilt of my sabre, but it returned a perfectly solid sound, and I glanced about bewildered. The woman was watching me with affrighted eyes.

"This entire house is uncanny," she exclaimed. "The very being in it makes my flesh creep. It may have been a den of murderers. Captain, let us get outside into the sunshine."

Believing it to be merely her overwrought nerves which were at fault, I sought to soothe her. "It was probably no more than a shadow," I said, crossing to her side of the table, to enable her better to feel the influence of my presence. "Let us be content to sit here by the door, for we should be taking too great a risk of discovery if we ventured into the open."

I had barely spoken these words and placed my fingers on her hand to lead her forward when the small door which opened into the shed was thrown back noisily, and two great shaggy dogs, the evident mates of the dead brute at our feet, leaped fiercely in. She shrank toward me with a sob of terror; but even as I drew a revolver from my belt, a man and a woman appeared almost simultaneously in that same opening.

"Down, Douglas! down, Roderick! Ha! 'There lies Red Murdoch, stark and stiff!' — down, you brutes; you'll be dead yourselves sometime."

The man strode forward as he spoke, clubbing the frenzied brutes with the stock of the long rifle he carried.

"'Yelled on the view the opening pack,'" he quoted, as he distributed his blows impartially to right and left; "'rock, glen, and cavern paid them back.' Them thar be Scott's words, stranger, an' I reckon as how ol' Sir Walter knew whut he wus writin' 'bout. Stop thet blame youlin', you Roderick, er I'll take t' other end o' this gun ter ye."

He redoubled his efforts for peace, finally driving the rebellious beasts back into one corner, where they sat upon their haunches and eyed us wistfully.

"'Two dogs of black Saint Hubert's breed, unmatched for courage, breath, and speed,'" he exclaimed, wiping the perspiration from his face with the back of one hand and staring at us, "specially the breath."

He was a fierce-looking little fellow, scarcely more than a half-grown boy in size, with round, red face full of strange wrinkles, and head as oddly peak-shaped as I ever looked upon. It went up exactly like the apex of a pear, while the upper portion was utterly bald. He formed a most remarkable contrast to the tall, raw-boned, angular female who loomed up like a small mountain just behind him.

"I reckon as how you uns hed quite a bit of a scrap afore ye laid thet thar dorg out, stranger," he said, a half-angry tone lurking in his deep voice. "'The fleetest hound in all the North,' an' I 'm durned if I jist likes ther way you uns makes yerselves et hum in this yere cabin."

"Shet up, Jed Bungay," cut in his better-half, sharply, and as she spoke she caught the little man unceremoniously by one arm, and thrusting him roughly to one side strode heavily forward until she paused in the centre of the room, facing us with her arms akimbo.

"Now I 'd jist like ter know," she said savagely, "who you uns be, a breakin' into a house, and a killin' a dorg, an' a eatin' up everything we uns got without so much as a sayin' 'by yer leave' er nuthin'. I reckon as how you uns don't take this yere cabin fer no tavern?"

The wrinkled red face peering cautiously around her ample waist line made me wish to laugh, but an earnest desire to placate the irate female, who was evidently the real head of this household, enabled me to conquer the inclination and answer gravely.

"Madam," I said with a low bow, "it is misfortune, not desire, which has caused us to trespass upon your hospitality. We will very gladly pay you liberally for any damage done. I am an officer in the Confederate service, and the breaking down of our horses compelled us to take refuge here in order that this lady might not be exposed to danger from roving gangs of guerillas. The dog attacked us in the dark, and we killed him in order to save our lives."

"'The deep-mouthed bloodhound's heavy bay resounded up the rocky way,'" ejaculated Bungay with dancing eyes.

"Drat yer potry, Jed Bungay! ye dew make me tired fer suah." She turned back to us, and from her first words it was plainly evident she had been impressed with but one sentence of my labored explanation.

A Disciple of Sir Walter

"Did you uns say as how ye'd pay fer whut ye et and fer thet truck ye busted?" she asked doubtfully.

"Certainly, madam," and I took some money from my pocket as evidence of good faith. "What would you consider due you?"

The grim, set face relaxed slightly, while she permitted her husband to edge his way a little more into the foreground.

"Wal, stranger, I sorter reckon as how 'bout four bits 'ill squar' things — dorgs is mighty durn cheap hereabout enyhow."

"'But Lufra, — whom from Douglas' side nor bribe nor threat could e'er divide,'" he protested. "Not that its name was Lufra, but he was a blame fine dorg."

The woman turned on him like a flash, and he crept subdued back into his corner. The incipient rebellion had been ended by a glance.

"Durn ye, Jed Bungay, why, thet's more money thin ye've airned in six months, an' ye've got more measly, flea-bit dorgs 'round yere now then ye kin ever feed. Give me ther four bits, mister, an' I reckon as how it'll be all right."

The little man balanced himself on one foot, and cocked up his eye in an abortive attempt to wink.

"Yas, don't ye ever mind me, Mariar," he said humbly. "'Whom ther Lord hath jined tergether let no man put asunder.' Thet thar ain't Scott, Cap, but I reckon it's out of another book mighty nigh es good. Hes you uns got all ther victuals ye want? 'He gave him of his Highland cheer, the hardened flesh of mountain deer.' This yere is slab bacon, but it smells purty durn good.'"

I glanced at Mrs. Brennan, and the amused twinkle

73

in her eyes led me to say heartily, " We had not entirely completed our meal, but imagined we saw ghosts."

" Ghosts ! " He glanced around apprehensively, — " ' On Heaven and on thy lady call, and enter the enchanted hall ! ' Wus ther ghosts ye saw over thar? " And he pointed toward the wall opposite.

I nodded.

" Then I sorter reckon as how Mariar and me wus them ghosts," he continued, grinning. " We sorter reckoned as how we wanted ter see who wus yere afore we come in. ' I 'll listen till my fancy hears the clang of swords, the crash of spears.' These yere is tough times, stranger, in these parts, an' a man whut has ter pertect a lovely female hes got ter keep his eye skinned."

Maria sniffed contemptuously.

" Ye 're no great shakes at a pertectin' o' me, Jed Bungay. Now you sit down thar an' begin ter fill up. I reckon as how ther Cap an' his gal will kinder jine with us fer manners."

She seated Jed with such extreme vigor that I looked for the chair to collapse beneath him as he came down, but the little man, not in the least daunted, picked up his knife and fork with a sigh of relief.

" ' O woman ! in our hours of ease uncertain, coy, and hard to please,' " he murmured. " Come, sit down, stranger; ' Sit down an' share a soldier's couch, a soldier's fare.' Not as I 'm a sojer," he hastened to explain, " but thet 's how it is in ther book. Say, old woman, kint ye kinder sker up some coffee fer we uns — leastwise whut us Confeds call coffee? "

Without much difficulty I induced Mrs. Brennan to draw her chair once more to the table, and I sat down beside her.

A Disciple of Sir Walter

" You are Confederate, then? " I asked, curious to know upon which side his sympathies were enlisted in the struggle.

He glanced warily at my gray jacket, then his shrewd, shifty eyes wandered to the blue and yellow cavalry cloak lying on the floor.

" Wal, I jist don't know, Cap," he said cautiously, continuing to eat as he talked, " as I 'm much o' enything in this yere row. First ther durned gray-backs they come snoopin' up yere, an' run off all my horgs; then ther blame blue-bellies come 'long an' cut down every lick o' my corn fodder, so thet I 'll be cussed if I ain't 'bout ready ter fight either side. Anyhow I ain't did no fightin' yit worth talkin' 'bout, fer Mariar is pow'ful feared I 'd git hurt."

Maria regarded him scornfully.

" Hiding out, I suppose? "

" Wal, 't ain't very healthful fer us ter be stayin' et hum much o' ther time, long with that thar Red Lowrie, an' Jim Hale, an' the rest o' thet cattle 'round yere."

" Guerillas pretty thick now in the mountains? "

He glanced up quickly, his shrewd gray eyes on my face, and Maria turned about as she stood beside the fireplace.

" Wal, I dunno; I heerd as they wus doin' somethin' down by ther brick church, but thar 's no great shakes of 'em jist 'round yere. I reckon as how they knows 'nough ter keep 'way from Jed Bungay — I 'd pitch 'em ' far as ever peasant pitched a bar.' "

" You have no fear of them, then? "

" Whut, me? " The little man sat bolt upright, and glared fiercely across the table as though he would resent an insult.

75

My Lady of the North

" Stranger, I have fit them ar fellers night an' day in these yere mountings fer nigh onter three year — me an' Mariar.

> " ' For love-lorn swain in lady's bower
> Ne'er panted for the appointed hour
> As I, until before me stand
> This rebel chieftain and his band.'

I jist tell ye, Cap, I reckon thar ain't no guerilla a goin' ter poke his nose 'round yere 'less he's a lookin' fer sudden death; thar's mighty few o' 'em ain't heerd o' Jed Bungay — Whut in thunder's ther matter with yer gal? "

He stopped suddenly, and stared at her;. but before I could turn about in my chair one of the great dogs began to growl savagely, and Maria sprang forward and cuffed the surly brutes into rebellious silence.

" It's hosses," she said harshly. " Likely as not it's Red's gang. Now, Jed Bungay, yere's two lovely females fer ye ter pertect."

As I hastily sprang to my feet I caught a fleeting glimpse out of the partially opened door. Down the steep of the hill road there was slowly moving toward us on foot a small party of perhaps a dozen men, so variously clothed as to make it evident they were irregulars. Just ahead of them, but on horseback, two others were even then turning into the narrow path that led to the house, attracted probably by the smoke which streamed from the chimney-top.

CHAPTER VIII

MRS. BUNGAY DEFENDS HER HEARTHSTONE

A HAND pressing hard upon my arm brought back my scattered senses with a rush. It was Mrs. Brennan who stood there, her face whitened by anxiety, her eyes peering anxiously through the opening of the door. Imminent danger may startle even a trained soldier, but any necessity for action always recalls him to duty, and that one glance at her sufficed to make me myself again.

"Surely those men are not soldiers, Captain Wayne!" she exclaimed. "They wear uniforms of both armies."

"No doubt they are guerillas," I answered, drawing her back from where she might be seen in their approach. "We must find hiding if possible, for you shall never fall into such hands. Bungay!"

I turned toward where the little giant had been sitting, but he was not to be seen. However, the sound of my voice aroused Maria to a full sense of our danger, nor was she a woman to hesitate in such emergency. With a single stride she crossed the narrow room, caught the white-faced hero by the collar of his shirt, dragged him ignominiously forth from beneath the table where he had sought refuge, shook him as she would shake a toy dog, until his teeth rattled, and then flung him out of the door leading into the back shed. It was done so expeditiously that I could only gasp.

77

My Lady of the North

"Now inter ther hole with ye, Jed Bungay — you an' yer dorgs," she panted furiously. "An' you uns foller him. I reckon I'm able ter handle thet lot out thar, even if it should be Red Lowrie an' his gang."

Catching firm hold of Mrs. Brennan's hand I sprang down the single step and closed the door tight behind us. Jed had scrambled to his feet, and rubbing himself vigorously with one hand, utilized the other to drag outward a rough cupboard, which appeared to be a portion of the house itself. As it swung open there was revealed behind it a fair-sized opening extending into the face of the hill. It was a most ingenious arrangement, doubtless finding frequent use in those troublesome times. Its presence partially explained how Jed had thus far escaped the conscription officer. Into this hole we entered one at a time, and when the heavy cupboard had been silently drawn back into place, found ourselves enveloped in such total darkness as to make any movement a dangerous operation. I felt the clasp of my companion's hand tighten, and knew that her whole form was trembling from intense excitement.

"Do not permit the darkness to alarm you," I whispered softly, bending down as I spoke until I could feel her quick breathing against my cheek. "Our visitors are not likely to remain longer than will be necessary to get something to eat. They need never suspect our presence, and all we have to do is to wait patiently until they move on. I only wish I could discover something upon which you might sit down."

"Pray do not think me a coward," she answered, "but I have heard of this man Lowrie in the Federal camps, and I would rather die than fall into his hands."

I had heard of him also, and of his outrageous treatment of women. The memory caused me to clasp my hand warmly over hers, and set my teeth hard.

"It may not prove to be Lowrie at all," I said soberly; "but all these gentry are pretty much alike, I fear. However, I promise that you shall never fall alive into the hands of any of their breed."

Before she could answer me other than by a slight nestling closer in the darkness, Bungay whispered: "This yere hole, Cap, leads down ter the right, an' comes out in a sort o' gully 'bout a hundred feet back. Thar 's light 'nough ter see ter walk by a'ter ye turn ther corner 'bout twenty feet er so. You uns kin go on down thar if ye 'd rather, follerin' ther dorgs, but I reckon as how I 'll stay right yere an' sorter see how ther ol' woman comes out.

> "'Where, where was Roderick then?
> One blast upon his bugle horn
> Were worth a thousand men.'

If you uns like ter see a durned good fight maybe ye better stay tew — ther ol' woman is pisen if she once gits her dander up."

His voice was expressive of great expectations, and I had reason to believe his faith in Maria would be justified. Before any of us, however, had time to change our positions we heard the fellows come stamping roughly into the cabin. The thin slabs which divided us scarcely muffled their loud voices.

"Well, old woman," exclaimed one in voice so gruff as to seem almost assumed, "pretending to be alone, are you, with all those dishes sitting out on the table; just been eaten off, too. Have n't seen no strange party along the road this morning, have ye?"

"Nary a one," said Maria, and I knew from her voice she was standing close beside the fireplace.

"Are you Mrs. Bungay?"

"I reckon I am, if it 's any o' yer business."

"Don't git hifty, old woman, or we 're liable to give you a lesson in politeness before we leave." The leader dropped the butt of his gun with a crash on the floor. "Where is the little sneak, anyhow?"

"What do you want of him?"

"Want him to go 'long with us; we 're hunting some parties, and need a guide. They tol' us up the road a bit he knew every inch o' these yere mountings."

There was a pause, as if Maria was endeavoring to decide as to the honesty of the speaker. Her final answer proved the mental survey had not proven satisfactory.

"Wal, I reckon," she said calmly, "as you uns 'll be more likely ter find him down 'bout Connersville."

"Then whut 's all these yere dirty dishes doing on the table?"

"Hed sum Yankee officers yere; they just rode on down ther trail as you uns cum up."

"Like hell!" ejaculated the fellow with complete loss of temper. "See here, old woman, we 're too old birds to be caught with any such chaff. We 'll take a look around the old shebang anyhow, and while we 're at it you put something on the table for me and my mates to eat."

The voice and manner were rough, but I was impressed with a certain accent creeping into the man's speech bespeaking education. More, in spite of an apparent effort to make it so, his dialect was not that of those mountains.

Even as he uttered these last words, throwing into them a threat more in the tone than the language, I

Mrs. Bungay Defends Her Hearthstone

became aware of a thin ray of light penetrating the seemingly solid wall just in front of me, and bending silently
forward could dimly distinguish the elliptical head of
Bungay as he applied one eye to a small opening he had
industriously made between the logs. Grasping Mrs.
Brennan firmly by the hand so that we should not become
separated, I crept across the intervening blackness, and
reached his side.

"Holy smoke, Cap," the little man muttered in suppressed excitement, as he realized my presence, "it's
a goin' ter be b'ilin' hot in thar mighty soon. Mariar's
steam is a risin'."

He silently made room for me, and bending down so
as to bring my eye upon a level with his, I managed to
gain some slight glimpse of the scene within the cabin.

Mrs. Bungay stood with her back to the fireplace, an
iron skillet firmly gripped in one hand. Her face was red
with indignation, and there was a look in her eyes,
together with a defiant set to her chin, which promised
trouble. In front of her, carelessly resting on the table,
his feet dangling in the air, was a sturdy-looking fellow
of forty or so, with red, straggling beard covering all
the lower half of his face, and a weather-worn black hat
pulled so low as almost to conceal his eyes. His attire
was nondescript, as though he had patronized the junk-
shop of both armies. In his belt were thrust a revolver
and a knife, while within easy reach of his hand a musket
leaned against a chair. Two others of the party, younger
men, but even more roughly dressed than their leader,
were lounging between him and the door.

Bungay chuckled expectantly.

"O Lord! if they only git the ol' gal just a little more
riled," he whispered hoarsely, jumping up and down

6   81

on one foot in his excitement, " they 'll hev ther fight of their life."

" Do you know the fellows? " I asked. " Is that Red Lowrie? "

He shook his head.

" Never laid eyes on any of 'em afore, but ye bet they 're no good. Reckon they 're a part o' his crowd."

The man who posed as the leader of the party picked up the empty coffee-pot beside him and shook it.

" Come, now, Mrs. Bungay," he commanded, " I tell you we 're hungry, so trot out some hoecake and fill up this pot, unless you want to reckon with Red Lowrie."

The woman stood facing him, yet never moved. I could see a red spot begin to glow in either cheek. If I had ever doubted it, I knew now that Maria possessed a temper of her own.

" You ain't no Red Lowrie," she retorted.

The fellow laughed easily.

" No more I ain't, old woman, but I reckon we ain't so durn far apart when it comes to getting what we go after. Come, honest now, where is the little white-livered cur that runs this shebang? "

Whatever Maria might venture to call her lord and master in the privacy of home, it evidently did not soothe her spirit to hear him thus spoken of by another.

" If Jed Bungay wus hum," she answered fiercely, her eyes fairly blazing, " I reckon you would n't be sprawlin' on thet thar table fer long."

" Would n't I, now? Well, old hen, we 've fooled here with you about as long as I care to. Bill, go over there and put some of that bacon on to fry. If she does n't get out of the way I 'll give her something to jump for." And he patted the stock of his gun.

Mrs. Bungay Defends Her Hearthstone

Instinctively I drew my revolver, and pushed its black muzzle into the light under Jed's nose.

"Shall I give him a dose?" I asked eagerly.

"Not yit; O Lord, not yit!" he exclaimed, dancing from one foot to the other in excitement. "Let ther ol' gal hev a show. I reckon she's good fer ther whole three of 'em, 'less they shoot."

Bill came up grinning. He evidently anticipated some fun, and as he reached out a grimy hand for the slab of bacon, took occasion to make some remark. What it was I could not hear, but I noted the quick responsive flash in the woman's eyes, and the next instant with a crash she brought the iron skillet down with all her strength on top of the fellow's head. Without even a groan he went plunging down, face foremost, in front of the fire. In another moment she was battling like a wild fury with the other two.

It was a quick, intense struggle. The man near the door chanced to be the first in, and he received a blow from the skillet that most assuredly would have crushed his skull had he not dodged; as it was it landed upon his shoulder and he reeled back sick and helpless. By this time the fellow with the red beard had closed upon her, and wrested the skillet from her hand. Struggling fiercely back and forth across the floor, Maria tripped over the body of the dead dog and fell, but as she did so her fingers grasped the red beard of her antagonist. It yielded to her hand, and bare of face, save for a dark moustache, the man stood there, panting for breath, above her. Then suddenly, almost at my very ear, a voice cried,

"Frank! Frank! I am here!"

83

CHAPTER IX

IN THE HANDS OF THE ENEMY

IN the first surprise of that unexpected joyful cry ringing at my very ears all my senses seemed confused, and I stood motionless. Then I heard Bungay utter a smothered oath, and knew he had wheeled about in the darkness. Unable to distinguish the slightest outline of his figure, I was yet impressed with the thought that he was endeavoring to muffle the girl, to prevent her uttering a second cry. Impelled by this intuition I flung out my arm hastily, and by rare good luck it came in contact with his hand.

"None of that, you little cur!" I muttered sternly, unmindful of his efforts to break away. "No hand on her, mind you! Mrs. Brennan, what does this mean?"

She made no attempt to answer, but I could hear her now groping her way through the darkness toward the place of our entrance. Bungay detected the movement also, and made a violent effort to break loose from my grip, that he might hurry after her.

"You lit go o' me," he cried excitedly, "er, by goll', I'll use a knife. She'll give this whole thing away if she ever gits out."

For answer I hurled him backward with all my strength and sprang after the fleeing woman. But I was already too late to stop her, even had that been my intention. With strength yielded her by desperation, she thrust aside

84

In the Hands of the Enemy

the heavy cupboard, and as the light swept in, sprang forward into the rude shed. With another bound, gathering her skirts as she ran, she was up the steps and had burst into the outer room. A moment later I also stood in the doorway, gazing upon a scene that made my blood like fire.

The fighting had evidently ceased suddenly with her first cry. Maria stood panting in one corner, the deadly skillet again in her hand, her hair hanging in wisps down her back. Still unconscious from the blow he had received, one fellow lay outstretched on the floor, his head barely missing the hot ashes of the fireplace; while his companion nursed his bruises and scowled from a safe refuge behind the table. The unshaven faces of several others of the gang were peering curiously in through the open door. I know now I saw all this, for the picture of it is upon the retina of memory, but at the moment everything I appeared to perceive or hear occurred in the centre of the room.

The man who had posed as the leader stood there alone facing us, his expression a strange mixture of amazement and delight. He was a powerfully built man, with keen gray eyes deeply set in their sockets. His right hand rested heavily upon the hilt of a cavalry sabre, the scabbard of which was concealed beneath the folds of the long brown coat he wore. As Mrs. Brennan burst through the doorway he stepped eagerly forward, his eyes brightening, and they met with clasped hands.

"Is it possible — Edith?" he cried, as if the recognition could scarcely be credited.

"Oh, Frank!" she exclaimed, eagerly, "it seems all too good to be true. How came you here?"

"Hunting after you, my fair lady. Did you suppose you could disappear as mysteriously as you did last night without my being early on the trail? Have these people injured you in any way?" And he glanced about him with a threat in his gesture.

"Oh, no, Frank," hastily; "every one has been most kind. It was a mere mistake. But how strangely you are dressed! how very rough you look!"

He laughed, but still retained his warm clasp of her hands.

"Not the pomp and circumstance of glorious war which you expected, girl?" he asked lightly. "But we have all sorts of conditions to meet down here, and soon learn in Rome to do as the Romans do."

As he finished speaking he perceived me for the first time, and his face changed instantly into cold sternness. I saw him sweep one hasty glance around, as though he suspected that I might not be alone, and his hand fell once more upon his sword hilt, in posture suggestive of readiness for action.

"Who have we here?" he asked, staring at me in amazement. "A Johnny Reb?"

"Whatever I am," I retorted, my gorge rising suddenly at his contemptuous term, and stepping out into the room before him, "I at least wear the uniform of my service and rank, and not the nondescript garments of a guerilla."

The scornful words stung him; I noticed the quick flush of anger in his eyes, and was not sorry.

"You are insolent, sir. Moreover, you go too far, for as it chances you are well within our lines, and we will see to what extent honor is consistent with the work of a spy. The uniform of your service, indeed!" he echoed hotly, pointing as he spoke across the room; "that cavalry cloak over yonder tells its own story. Peters, Steele, arrest this fellow."

In the Hands of the Enemy

"Frank, don't do that," she urged earnestly. "You mistake; that was the cloak I wore."

If he heard her he gave no sign.

"Bind him," was the stern order, as the two men advanced. "Use your belts if you have nothing else handy."

Angry as I most assuredly was, swept also by a new emotion which I did not in the least comprehend, I yet fully realized the utter helplessness of my position in point of resistance. They were twenty to one. However much I longed to grapple with him who mocked me, the very thought was insanity; my only possible chance of escape lay in flight. To realize this was to act. I leaped backward, trusting for a clear field in my rear, and an opportunity to run for it, but the door by which I had just entered was now closed and barred — Bungay had made sure his retreat. The man, watching my every movement, with sword half drawn in his hand, saw instantly that I was securely trapped, and laughed in scorn.

"You are not making war on women now," he said with a cutting sneer. "You will not find me so easy a victim."

The taunt stung me, but more the tone and manner of the speaker, and the hot blood of youth cast all caution to the winds. With a single spring, forgetful of my own wound, I was at his throat, dashed aside his uplifted hand, and by the sheer audacity of my sudden, unexpected onset, bore him back crashing to the floor. He struggled gamely, yet I possessed the advantage of position, and would have punished him severely, but for the dozen strong hands which instantly laid hold upon me, and dragged me off, still fighting madly, although as helpless as a child.

My Lady of the North

My opponent instantly leaped to his feet and started forward, drawing a revolver as he came. His face was deathly white from passion, and there was a look in his eyes which told me he would be restrained now by no rule of war.

"You cowardly spy!" he cried, and my ears caught the sharp click as he drew back the hammer. "Do you think I will let that blow go unavenged?"

"I assuredly trust not," I answered, gazing up at him from behind the gun muzzles with which I was yet securely pinned to the floor. "But if you are, as I am led to believe, a Federal officer, with some pretensions to being also a gentleman, and not the outlaw your clothes proclaim, you will at least permit me to stand upon my feet and face you as a man. If I am a spy, as you seem inclined to claim, there are army courts to try me; if not, then I am your equal in standing and rank, and have every right of a prisoner of war."

"This has become personal," hoarsely. "Your blow, as well as your connection with the forcible abduction of this young lady, whose legal protector I am, are not matters to be settled by an army court."

"Then permit me to meet you in any satisfactory way. The murder of a helpless man will scarcely clarify your honor."

I knew from the unrelenting expression upon his face that my plea was likely to prove a perfectly useless one, but before I had ended it Mrs. Brennan stood between us.

"Frank," she said calmly, "you shall not. This man is a Confederate officer; he is no spy; and during all the events of last night he has proven himself a friend rather than an enemy. Only for my sake is he here now."

88

In the Hands of the Enemy

Ignoring the look upon his face she turned toward me, impetuously waved aside the fellows who yet held me prostrate, and extending her hand lifted me to my feet. For an instant, as if by accident, our eyes met, and a sudden flush swept across her throat and cheeks.

"It is my turn now," she whispered softly, so softly the words did not carry beyond my own ears. Then she stood erect between us, as though in her own drawing-room, and gravely presented us to each other, as if she dared either to quarrel longer in her presence.

"Major Brennan, Captain Wayne."

We bowed to each other as men salute on the duelling field. In his eyes I read an unforgiveness, a bitter personal enmity, which I returned with interest, and secretly rejoiced over.

"The lady seems to be in control at present," he said shortly, shoving back the revolver into his belt. "Nevertheless I shall do my military duty, and hold you as a prisoner. May I inquire your full name and rank?"

"Philip Wayne, Captain —th Virginia Cavalry, Shirtley's Brigade."

"Why are you within our lines?"

"I attempted to pass through them last night with despatches, but was prevented by my desire to be of assistance to this lady."

"Indeed?" He smiled incredulously. "Your tale is quite interesting and rather romantic. I presume you yet carry the papers with you as evidence of its truth?"

"If you refer to the despatches, I do not. I sincerely trust they are already safely deposited in the hands of the one for whom they were intended."

A malignant look crept into Brennan's face, and his jaws set ominously.

My Lady of the North

" You will have to concoct a far better story than that, my friend, before you face Sheridan," he said insolently, " or you will be very apt to learn how a rope feels. He is not inclined to parley long with such fellows as you. Bind his hands, men, and take him out with you into the road."

The two soldiers grasped me instantly at the word of command. For a single moment I braced myself to resist, but even as I did so my eyes fell upon a slight opening in the wall, and I caught a quick glimpse of Bungay's face, his finger to his lips. Even as I gazed in astonishment at this sudden apparition, a lighter touch rested pleadingly on my arm.

" Do not struggle any longer, Captain Wayne," spoke Mrs. Brennan's voice, gently. " I will go to General Sheridan myself, and tell him the entire story."

I bowed to her, and held out my hands to be bound.

" I yield myself your prisoner, madam," I said meaningly, and not unconscious that her glance sank before mine. " I even imagine the bonds may prove not altogether unpleasant."

Brennan strode between us hastily, and with quick gesture to his men.

" Bind the fellow," he said sternly. " And mind you, sir, one word more, and they shall buck you as well. It may be valuable for you to remember that I am in command here, however I may seem to yield to the wish of Mrs. Brennan."

CHAPTER X

A WOMAN'S TENDERNESS

YOUTH is never largely given to reflection, which is the gift of years; and although my life had in a measure rendered me more thoughtful than I might have proven under ordinary conditions, yet it is to be frankly confessed, by one desirous of writing merely the truth, that I generally acted more upon impulse than reason. As I stood forth in the sunlight of that lonely mountain road, my hands securely bound behind my back, the end of the rope held by one of my captors, while his fellow leaned lazily upon his gun and watched us, I thought somewhat deeply over the situation and those peculiar circumstances leading up to it.

Under other conditions I might have felt tempted to enter into conversation with my guards, who, as I now perceived, were far from being the rough banditti I had at first imagined. Judging from their faces and language they were intelligent enough young fellows, such as I had often found in the ranks of the Federal army. But I realized they could aid me little, if any, in the one thing I most desired to know, and even if they could, a sense of delicacy would have caused me to hesitate in asking those personal questions that burned upon my lips. My deep and abiding respect for this woman whom I had so strangely met, and with whom I had attained some degree of intimacy, would never permit of my discussing her, even indirectly, with private soldiers behind the back of their officer. Every sense of honor revolted at such a thought. Not through any curiosity of mine, however justified by the depth of my own feeling, should she be made the subject of idle gossip about the camp-fire.

For, in truth, at this time, unhappy as my own situation undeniably was, — and as a soldier I realized all its dangers, — I gave it but little consideration. Usually quick of wit, fertile in expedients, ever ready to take advantage of each opportunity, I had taken stock of all my surroundings, yet discovered nowhere the slightest opening for escape. The vigilance of the guard, as well as the thorough manner in which I was bound, rendered any such attempt the merest madness. Realizing this, with the fatalism of a veteran I resigned myself in all patience to what must be.

Then it was that other thoughts came surging upon me in a series of interrogatories, which no knowledge I possessed could possibly answer. Who was this proud, womanly woman who called herself Edith Brennan? She had been at some pains to inform me that she was married, yet there was that about her — her bearing, her manner — which I could not in the least reconcile with that thought. Her extreme youthfulness made me feel it improbable, and the impression remained with me that she intended to make some explanation of her words, when the coming of Bungay interrupted us. How they might be explained I could not imagine; I merely struggled against accepting what I longed to believe untrue. And this man? this Federal major, bearing the same name, whom she called Frank, who was he? What manner of relationship existed between them? In their meet-

A Woman's Tenderness

ing and short intercourse I had noted several things which told me much — that she feared, respected, valued him, and that he was not only swayed by, but intensely jealous of any rival in, her good opinion. Yet their unexpected meeting was scarcely that of husband and wife. Was he the one she sought in her night ride from one Federal camp to another? If so, was he brother, friend, or husband? What was the bond of union existing between these two? Every word spoken made me fear the last must be the true solution.

Such were some of the queries I silently struggled with, and they were rendered more acute by that deepening interest which I now confessed to myself I was feeling toward her who inspired them. It may be fashionable nowadays to sneer at love, yet certain it is, the rare personality of this Edith Brennan had reached and influenced me in those few hours we had been thrown together as that of no other woman had ever done. Possibly this was so because the long years in camp and field had kept me isolated from all cultured and refined womanhood. This may, indeed, have caused me to be peculiarly susceptible to the beauty and purity of this one. I know not; I am content to give facts, and leave philosophy to others. My life has ever been one of action, of intense feeling; and there in the road that day, standing bareheaded in the sun, I was clearly conscious of but one changeless fact, that I loved Edith Brennan with every throb of my heart, and that there was enmity, bitter and unforgiving, between me and the man within who bore her name. Whatever he might be to her I rejoiced to know that he hated me with all the unreasoning hatred of jealousy. I had read it in his eyes, in his words, in his manner; and the memory of its open manifestation caused me to smile, as I hoped for an hour when we should meet alone and face to face. How she regarded him I was unable as yet to tell, but his love for her was plainly apparent in every glance and word.

As I was thus thinking, half in despair and half in hope, the two came out from the house together; and it pleased me to note how immediately her eyes sought for me, and how she lifted her hand to shade them from the glare of the sun, so that she might see more clearly. Her companion appeared to ignore my presence utterly, and gazed anxiously up and down the road as though searching for something.

"Peters," he asked sharply of the fellow on guard, "where are Sergeant Steele and the rest of the squad?"

The soldier addressed saluted in a manner that convinced me he was of the regular service.

"They are resting out of the sun in that clump of bushes down the hill, sir."

Brennan glanced in the direction indicated.

"Very well," he said. "Take your prisoner down there, and tell the Sergeant to press on at once toward the lower road. We shall follow you, and the lady will ride his horse."

The man turned, and with peremptory gesture ordered me forward. As I drew closer to where the two waited beside the open door, I lifted my head proudly, determined that neither should perceive how deeply I felt the humiliation of my position. As I thus passed them, my eyes fixed upon the shining road ahead, my ears caught a word or two of indignant expostulation from her lips.

"But, Frank, it is positively shameful in this sun."

He laughed lightly, yet his answer came to me in all clearness of utterance. I believed he wished me to over-

A Woman's Tenderness

hear the words. "Oh, it will only prove of benefit to his brains, if by rare chance he possesses any."

I glanced aside, and saw her turn instantly and face him, her eyes aflame with indignation. "Then I will!"

As she spoke, her voice fairly trembling with intense feeling, she stepped backward out of sight into the house.

Another instant and she reappeared, sweeping past him without so much as a word, and bearing in her hand my old campaign hat, came directly up to us.

"Sentry," she said in her old imperious manner, "I desire to place this hat on the head of your prisoner."

The fellow glanced uneasily over his shoulder at the seemingly unconscious officer, not knowing whether it were better to permit the act or not, but she waited for no permission.

"Captain Wayne," she said, her voice grown kindly in a moment, and her eyes frankly meeting mine, "you will pardon such liberty, I am sure, but it is not right that you should be compelled to march uncovered in this sun."

She placed the hat in position, asking as she did so:

"Does that feel comfortable?"

"The memory of your thoughtfulness," I replied warmly, bowing as best I might, "will make the march pleasant, no matter what its end may mean to me."

Her eyes darkened with sudden emotion.

"Do not deem me wholly ungrateful," she said quickly and in a low tone. "The conditions are such that I am utterly helpless now to aid you. Major Brennan is a man not to be lightly disobeyed, but I shall tell my story to General Sheridan so soon as we reach his camp."

I would have spoken again, but at this moment Brennan came striding toward us.

95

My Lady of the North

" Come, Edith," he cried, almost roughly, " this foolishness has surely gone far enough. Peters, what are you waiting here for? I told you to take your prisoner down the road."

A few moments later, the centre of a little squad of heavily armed men, I was tramping along the rocky pathway, and when once I attempted to glance back to discover if the others followed us, the sergeant advised me, with an oath, to keep my eyes to the front. I obeyed him.

It was a most tiresome march in the hot sun over the rough mountain roads. There were times when we left these altogether, and crept along half-obliterated trails leading through the dense woods and among the rocks. I learned from scraps of conversation floating about me as we struggled onward, that these precautions were not taken out of any fear of meeting with Confederate troops, whose nearest commands were supposed to be considerably to the westward of where we were, but because of a desire to avoid all possibility of conflict with those armed and irresponsible bands that ranged at will between the lines of the two great armies. Already they had become sufficiently strong to make trouble for small detachments.

It must have been nearly the end of the afternoon. We had certainly traversed several miles, and were then moving almost directly south upon a well-defined pike, the name of which I never knew. All the party were travelling close together, when the scout, who throughout the day had been kept a few hundred yards in advance, came back toward us on a run, his hand flung up in an urgent warning to halt.

" What is it, Steele?" Brennan questioned, spurring forward to meet him. " Come, speak up, man!"

" A squad of cavalry has just swung onto the pike, sir,

96

A Woman's Tenderness

from the dirt road that leads toward the White Briar,"
was the soldier's panting reply. "And I could get a
glimpse through the trees down the valley, and there's
a heavy infantry column just behind them. They're
Rebs, sir, or I don't know them."

"Rebs?" with an incredulous laugh. "Why, man,
we've got the only Reb here who is east of the Briar."

"Well," returned the scout, sullenly, "they're coming
from the west, and I know they ain't our fellows."

He was too old a soldier to have his judgment doubted,
and he was evidently convinced. Brennan glanced quickly
about. However he may have sneered at the report, he
was not rash enough to chance so grave a mistake.

"Get back into those rocks there on the right," he
commanded sharply. "Hustle your prisoner along lively,
men, and one of you stand over him with a cocked gun;
if he so much as opens his mouth, let him have it."

Rapidly as we moved, we were scarcely all under cover
before the advance cavalry guard came in sight, the light
fringe of troopers, dust-begrimed and weary, resting
heavily in their saddles, and apparently thoughtless as
to any possibility of meeting with the enemy. There
were not more than a troop of them all told, yet their
short gray jackets and wide-brimmed light hats instantly
told the story of their service. Their rear rank was yet
in sight when we heard the heavy tread of the approaching column, together with the dull tinkle of steel which
always accompanies marching troops. Peering forth as
much as I dared from behind the thick brush where I had
been roughly thrown face downward, I saw the head of
that solid, sturdy column swing around the sharp bend
in the road, and in double front, spreading from rock to
rock, come sweeping down toward us.

My Lady of the North

The command was moving forward rapidly at the rout step, that long, easy, swinging stride so peculiar to the Southern infantry, with the merest semblance of order in formation, which is the inevitable result of hard, rapid marching. Every movement bespoke them veteran troops. They were covered with dust, their faces fairly caked with it, their uniforms almost indistinguishable; their drums silent, their colors cased, their wide-brimmed hats pulled low over their eyes, their guns held in any position most convenient for carrying, and with stern, wearied faces set doggedly upon the road in their front. No pomp and circumstance of glorious war was here, but these were fighting men. Never before, save as I watched Pickett's charging line sweep on to death at Gettysburg, did I feel the stern manliness of war as now.

File upon file, company after company, regiment following regiment, they swung sternly by. Scarcely so much as a word reached us, excepting now and then some briefly muttered command to close up, or a half-inaudible curse as a shuffling foot stumbled. I could distinguish no badge, no insignia of either corps or division; the circling dust enveloped them in a choking, disfiguring cloud. But they were Confederates! I marked them well; here and there along the toiling ranks I even noted a familiar face, and there could be no mistaking the gaunt North Carolina mountaineer, the sallow Georgian, or the jaunty Louisiana creole. They were Confederates — Packer's Division of Hill's corps, I could have almost sworn — east-bound on forced march, and I doubted not that each cross-road to left and right of us would likewise show its hurrying gray column, sturdily pressing forward. The veteran fighting men of the left wing of

A Woman's Tenderness

the Army of Northern Virginia were boldly pushing eastward to keep their tryst with Lee. The despatch intrusted to my care had been borne safely to Longstreet.

The keen joy of it lighted up my face, and Brennan turning toward me as the last limping straggler disappeared over the ridge, saw it, and grew white with anger.

"You Rebel cur!" he cried fiercely, in his sudden outburst of passion, "what does all this mean? Where is that division bound?"

"Some change in Longstreet's front, I should judge," I answered coolly, too happy even to note his slur.

"You know better," he retorted hotly. "The way those fellows march tells plainly enough that they have covered all of fifteen miles since daybreak. It is a general movement, and, by Heaven! you shall answer Sheridan, even if you won't me."

CHAPTER XI

IT had been dark for nearly an hour before we entered what was from all appearances a large and populous camp. Hurried forward constantly, closely surrounded by my guard, I was enabled to gain but an inadequate conception of either its situation or extent. Yet the distance traversed by our party after passing the outer sentries and before we made final halt, taken in connection with evidence on every side of the presence in considerable numbers of all the varied branches of the service, convinced me we were within no mere brigade encampment, but had doubtless arrived at the main headquarters of this department.

Although I noted all this in a vague way, so as to recall it afterwards, yet I was too thoroughly fatigued to care where I was or what became of me. Hardened as I had grown through experience to exposure and weariness, the continuous strain undergone since I had ridden westward from General Lee's tent had completely unnerved me. No sooner was I thrust into the unknown darkness of a hut by the not unkindly sergeant, than I threw myself prone on the floor, and was sound asleep before the door had fairly closed behind him.

My rest was not destined to be a long one. It seemed I had barely closed my eyes when a rough hand shook me again into consciousness. The flaming glare of an

100

In the Presence of Sheridan

uplifted pine-knot flung its radiance over half-a-dozen figures grouped in the open doorway. A corporal, with a white chin beard, was bending over me.

"Come, Johnny," he said tersely, "get up — you 're wanted."

The instinct of soldierly obedience in which I had been so long trained caused me to grope my way to my feet.

"What time is it, Corporal?" I asked sleepily.

"After midnight."

"Who wishes me?"

"Headquarters," he returned brusquely. "Come, move on. Fall in, men."

A moment later we were off, passing between long lines of dying fires, tramping rapidly along a rough road which seemed to incline sharply upward, our single torch throwing grotesque shadows on either side. The swift movement and the crisp night air swept the vestiges of slumber from my brain, and I began instinctively to gather together my scattered wits for whatever new experience confronted me.

Our march was a short one, and we soon turned abruptly in at a wide-open gateway. High pillars of brick stood upon either hand, and the passage was well lighted by a brightly blazing fire of logs. Two sentries stood there, and our party passed between them without uttering a word. As we moved beyond the radiance I noted a little knot of cavalrymen silently sitting their horses in the shadow of the high wall. A wide gravelled walk, bordered, I thought, with flowers, led toward the front door of a commodious house built after the colonial type. The lower story seemed fairly ablaze with lights, and at the head of the steps as we ascended a young officer came quickly forward.

My Lady of the North

"Is this the prisoner brought in to-night?"

The corporal pushed me forward.

"This is the man, sir."

"Very well; hold your command here until I send other orders."

He rested one hand, not unkindly, upon my arm, and his tone instantly changed from that of command to generous courtesy.

"You will accompany me, and permit me to advise you, for your own sake, to be as civil as possible in your answers to-night, for the 'old man' is in one of his tantrums."

We crossed the rather dimly lighted hall, which had a sentry posted at either end of it, and then my conductor threw open a side door, and silently motioned for me to enter in advance of him. It was a spacious room, elegant in all its appointments, but my hasty glance revealed only three occupants. Sitting at a handsomely polished mahogany writing-table near the centre of the apartment was a short, stoutly built man, with straggly beard and fierce, stern eyes. I recognized him at once, although he wore neither uniform nor other insignia of rank. Close beside him stood a colonel of engineers, possibly his chief of staff, while to the right, leaning negligently with one arm on the mantel-shelf above the fireplace, and smiling insolently at me, was Brennan.

The sight of him stiffened me like a drink of brandy, and as the young aide closed the door in my rear, I stepped instantly forward to the table, facing him who I knew must be in command, and removing my hat, saluted.

"This is the prisoner you sent for, sir," announced the aide.

In the Presence of Sheridan

The officer, who remained seated, looked at me intently.

" Have I ever met you before? " he questioned, as though doubting his memory.

" You have, General Sheridan," I replied. " I was with General Early during your conference at White Horse Tavern. I also bore a flag to you after the cavalry skirmish at Wilson's Ford."

" I remember," shortly, and as he spoke he wheeled in his chair to face Brennan.

" I thought you reported this officer as a spy? " he said sternly. " He is in uniform, and doubtless told you his name and rank."

" I certainly had every reason to believe he penetrated our lines in disguise," was the instant reply. " This cavalry cloak was found with him, and consequently I naturally supposed his claim of rank to be false."

Sheridan looked annoyed, yet turned back to me without administering the sharp rebuke which seemed burning upon his lips.

" Were you wearing that cavalry cloak within our lines? " he questioned sternly.

" I was not, sir; it was indeed lying upon the floor of the hut when Major Brennan entered, but I had nothing to do with it."

He gazed at me searchingly for a moment in silence.

" I regret we have treated you with so little consideration," he said apologetically, " but you were supposed to be merely a spy. May I ask your name and rank? "

" Captain Wayne, —th Virginia Cavalry."

" Why were you within our lines? "

" I was passing through them with despatches."

" For whom? "

My Lady of the North

" You certainly realize that I must decline to answer."

" Major Brennan," he asked, turning aside again, " was this officer searched by your party? "

" He was, sir, but no papers were found. He stated to me later that his despatch was verbal."

" Had it been delivered? "

" I so understood him."

" Well, how did he account to you for being where he was found? "

Brennan hesitated, and glanced uneasily toward me. Like a flash the thought came that the man was striving to keep her name entirely out of sight: he did not wish her presence mentioned.

" There was no explanation attempted," he said finally. " He seemed simply to be hiding there."

" Alone? "

Again I caught his eyes, and it almost seemed that I read entreaty in them.

" Excepting the wife of the mountaineer," he answered hoarsely.

" Is this true? " asked Sheridan, his stern face fronting me.

I made my decision instantly. There might be some reason, possibly her own request, whereby her being alone with me that night should remain untold. Very well, it would never be borne to other ears through any failure of my lips to guard the secret. She had voluntarily pledged herself to go to Sheridan in my defence; until she did so, her secret, if secret indeed it was, should remain safe with me. I could do no less in honor.

" It is not altogether true," I said firmly, " and no one knows this better than Major Brennan. I was there, as I told him, wholly because of an accident upon the road, but as to its particulars I must most respectfully decline to answer."

"You realize what such a refusal may mean to you?"

"I understand fully the construction which may unjustly be placed upon it by those who desire to condemn me, but at present I can make no more definite reply. I have reason to believe the full facts will be presented to you by one in whose word you will have confidence."

I caught a gleam of positive delight in Brennan's eyes, and instantly wondered if this seeming reluctance upon his part was not merely a clever mode of tricking me into silence, — into what might seem an insolent contempt of Federal authority. I would wait and see. There would surely be ample time for her to act if she desired to do so. Anyway, I was little disposed to find shelter behind a woman's skirts.

Sheridan straightened in his chair, and looked across the table at me almost angrily.

"Very well, sir," he said gravely. "Your fate is in your own hands, and will depend very largely upon your replies to my questions. You claim to have been the bearer of despatches, and hence no spy, yet you possess nothing to substantiate your claim. As your regiment is with Lee, I presume you were seeking Longstreet. Were your despatches delivered?"

"I have reason to believe so."

"By yourself?"

"By the sergeant who accompanied me, and who continued the journey after I was detained."

"Is Lee contemplating an immediate movement?"

"General Sheridan," I exclaimed indignantly, "you must surely forget that I am an officer of the Confederate Army. You certainly have no reason to expect that I will so far disregard my obvious duty as to answer such a question."

"Your refusal to explain why you were hiding within our lines is ample reason for my insistence," he said tartly, "and I am not accustomed to treating spies with any great consideration, even when they claim Rebel commissions. You are not the first to seek escape in that way. Was your despatch the cause of the hurried departure of Longstreet's troops eastward?"

This last question was hurled directly at me, and I noticed that every eye in the room was eagerly scanning my face. I had the quick, fiery temper of a boy then, and my cheeks flushed.

"I positively decline to answer one word relative to the despatches intrusted to me," I said deliberately, and my voice shook with sudden rush of anger. "And no officer who did not dishonor the uniform he wore would insult me with the question."

A bombshell exploding in the room could not have astonished them as did my answer. I realized to the full the probable result, but my spirit was high, and I felt the utter uselessness of prolonging the interview. Sooner or later the same end must come.

Sheridan's face, naturally flushed, instantly grew crimson, and a dangerous light flamed into his fierce eyes. For a moment he seemed unable to speak; then he thundered forth:

"You young fool! I can tell you that you will speak before another twenty-four hours, or I 'll hang you for a spy if it cost me my command. Major Brennan, take this young popinjay to the Mansion House under guard."

Brennan stepped forward, smiling as if he enjoyed the part assigned to him.

In the Presence of Sheridan

"Come on, you Johnny," he said coarsely, his hand closing heavily on my arm. Then, seeming unable to repress his pleasure at the ending of the interview, and his present sense of power, he bent lower, so that his insolent words should not reach the others, and hissed hotly:

"Stealing women is probably more in your line than this."

At the sneering words, and the insulting look which accompanied them, my blood, already boiling, leaped into sudden fire. All the fierce hatred engendered within me by his past treatment, his cowardly insinuations, his unknown yet intimate relationship to the woman I loved, flamed up in irresistible power, and I struck him with my open hand across the lips.

"You miserable hound!" I cried madly. "None but a coward would taunt a helpless prisoner. I only hope I may yet be free long enough to write the lie with steel across your heart."

Before he could move Sheridan was upon his feet and between us.

"Back, both of you!" he ordered sharply. "There shall be no brawling here. Major Brennan, you will remain; I would speak with you further regarding this matter. Lieutenant Caton, take charge of the prisoner."

CHAPTER XII

UNDER SENTENCE OF DEATH

AT this late date I doubt greatly if my situation at that time was so desperate as I then conceived it. I question now whether the death sentence would ever have been executed. But then, with the memory of Sheridan's rage and my own hot-headed retort, I fully believed my fate was destined to be that of the condemned spy, unless she who alone might tell the whole truth should voluntarily do so. That circumstances had left me in the power of one whose fierce dislike was already evident was beyond question, and I had yielded to his goading to such an extent as to give those in authority every excuse for the exercise of extreme military power. Yet of one thing I was firmly resolved — no thoughtless word of mine should ever endanger the reputation of Edith Brennan. Right or wrong, I would go to a death of dishonor before I would speak without her authority. Love and pride conspired to make this decision adamant.

There might, indeed, be no reason why I should not speak with utmost freedom; but as to this I could not judge, and therefore preferred the safer side of silence. The action of Brennan had impressed this upon me as a duty; had caused me to feel that I could best serve her by blotting out the adventures of the night before. Seemingly it was her own desire, and as a gentleman, an officer, a man of honor, I might not even question that decree.

Under Sentence of Death

Deeply as these considerations would have affected me under ordinary conditions, one doubt now overshadowed them all. Was the man I struck the husband of the woman I loved? This was what I desired to know even above my own fate. I scarcely doubted, yet would not yield the slight hope I retained that it might prove otherwise. A trick of chance speech seemed to solve the problem, to answer that question which I durst not ask directly.

" Come," said Caton, briefly, and I turned and accompanied him without thought of resistance. At the front door he ordered the little squad of waiting soldiers to fall in, and taking me by the arm, led the way down the gravelled path to the road. I was impressed by his seeming carelessness, but as we cleared the gateway he spoke, and his words helped me to comprehend.

" Captain Wayne," he said quietly, so that the words could not be overheard, " you do not recognize me, but I was the officer who conducted you to headquarters when you brought the flag in at Wilson Creek. Of course I must perform the duty given me, but I wish you to understand that I wholly believe your word."

He stopped, extended his hand, and I accepted it silently.

" There must surely be some grave personal reason, which seals your lips? " he questioned.

" There is."

" I thought as much. I chanced to overhear the words, or rather a portion of them, which Brennan whispered, and have no doubt if they were explained to the General he would feel more kindly disposed toward you."

It was asked as a question, and I felt obliged to reply.

109

My Lady of the North

"I appreciate deeply your desire to aid me, but there are circumstances involving others which compel me for the present to silence. Indeed my possible fate does not so greatly trouble me, only that I possess a strong desire to have freedom long enough to cross swords with this major of yours. The quarrel between us has become bitterly personal, and I hunger for a chance to have it out. Do you know, is he a man who would fight?"

The young fellow stiffened slightly.

"We are serving upon the same staff," he said more abruptly, "and while we have never been close friends, yet I cannot honorably take sides against him. He has been out twice within the last three years to my knowledge, and is not devoid either of courage or skill. Possibly, however, the arrival of his wife may make him less a fire-eater."

"His wife?"

I stopped so suddenly that he involuntarily tightened his grip upon my arm as though suspicious of an attempt to escape.

"Do you," I asked, gaining some slight control over myself, "refer to the lady who came in with his party last evening?"

"Most certainly; she was presented to all of us as Mrs. Brennan, she has been assigned rooms at his quarters, and she wears a wedding-ring. Far too fine a woman in my judgment for such a master, but then that is not so uncommon a mistake in marriage. Why, come to think about it, you must have met her yourself. Have you reason to suspect this is not their relationship?"

"Not in the least," I hastened to answer, fearful lest my thoughtless exclamation might become the basis for camp gossip. "Indeed I was scarcely in the lady's presence at all coming in, as I was left in charge of the sergeant."

He looked at me keenly through the darkness.

"It seems somewhat curious to me that such deep enmity has grown up between you two in so short a time. One almost suspects, as in most cases, there may be a woman at the bottom of it."

I laughed carelessly.

"Not in the least, my friend. But there are indignities a captor can show to his prisoner which no true gentleman would ever be guilty of and no soldier would forgive."

I could see in the torch-light his face flush with sudden indignation.

"You are right," he returned heartily, "and from my knowledge of Brennan I can understand your meaning. What business has such a man to possess a wife?"

Perhaps he felt that he had already said too much, for we tramped on in silence until we drew near a large, square white building standing directly beside the road.

"This is the old Culverton tavern, known as the Mansion House," he said. "It is a tremendous big building for this country, with as fine a ballroom in it as I have seen since leaving New York. We utilize it for almost every military purpose, and among others some of the strong rooms in the basement are found valuable for the safe-keeping of important prisoners."

We mounted the front steps as he was speaking, passing through a cordon of guards, and in the wide hallway I was turned over to the officer in charge.

"Good-night, Captain," said Caton, kindly extending his hand. "You may rest assured that I shall say all I can in your favor, but it is to be regretted that Brennan has great influence just now at headquarters, and Sheridan is not a man to lightly overlook those hasty words you spoke to him."

I could only thank him most warmly for his interest, realizing fully from his grave manner my desperate situation, and follow my silent conductor down some narrow and steep stairs until we stood upon the cemented floor of the basement. Here a heavy door in the stone division wall was opened; I was pushed forward into the dense darkness within, and the lock clicked dully behind me. So thick was the wall I could not even distinguish the retreating steps of the jailer.

Tired as I was from the intense strain of the past thirty-six hours, even my anxious thoughts were insufficient to keep me awake. Feeling my way cautiously along the wall, I came at last to a wide wooden bench, and stretching my form at full length upon it, pillowed my head on one arm, and almost instantly was sound asleep.

When I awoke, sore from my hard bed and stiffened by the uncomfortable position in which I lay, it was broad daylight. That the morning was, indeed, well advanced I knew from the single ray of sunlight which streamed in through a grated window high up in the wall opposite me and fell like a bar of gold across the rough stone floor. I was alone. Even in the dark of the previous night I had discovered the sole pretence to furniture in the place. The room itself proved to be a large and almost square apartment, probably during the ordinary occupancy of the house a receptacle for wood or garden produce, but now peculiarly well adapted to the safeguarding of prisoners.

The solid stone walls were of sufficient height to afford

no chance of reaching the great oak girders that sup-
ported the floor above, even had the doing so offered a
favorable opening for escape. There were, apparently,
but three openings of any kind, — the outside window
through which the sunlight streamed, protected by thick
bars of iron; a second opening, quite narrow, and likewise protected by a heavy metal grating; and the tightly
locked door by means of which I had entered. The
second, I concluded, after inspecting it closely, was a
mere air passage leading into some other division of the
cellar. I noted these openings idly, and with scarcely
a thought as to the possibility of escape. I had awakened
with strange indifference as to what my fate might be.
Such a feeling was not natural to me, but the fierce emotions of the preceding night had seemingly robbed me
of all my usual buoyancy of hope. In one sense I yet
trusted that Mrs. Brennan would keep her pledge and
tell her story to Sheridan; if she failed to do this, and
left me to face the rifles or the rope, then it made but
small odds how soon it should be over. If she cared for
me in the slightest degree she would not let me die unjustly, and to my mind then she had become the centre
of all life.

Despondency is largely a matter of physical condition,
and I was still sufficiently fagged to be in the depths, when
the door opened suddenly, and an ordinary army ration
was placed within. The soldier who brought it did not
speak, nor did I attempt to address him; but after he
retired, the appetizing smell of the bacon, together with
the unmistakable flavor of real coffee, drew me irrresistibly
that way, and I made a hearty meal. The food put new
life into me, and I fell to pacing back and forth between
the corners of the cell, my mind full of questioning, yet

8   113

with a fresh measure of confidence that all would still be well.

I was yet at it when, without warning, the door once again opened, and Lieutenant Caton entered. He advanced toward me with outstretched hand, which I grasped warmly, for I felt how much depended on his friendship, and resolved to ask him some questions which should solve my last remaining doubts.

"Captain Wayne," he began soberly, looking about him, "you are in even worse stress here than I had supposed, but I shall see to it that you are furnished with blankets before I leave."

"You have nothing new, then, to communicate regarding the possibility of release?" I asked anxiously.

"Alas, no; Brennan appears to hate you with all the animosity of his strange nature, and his influence is so much stronger than mine that I have almost been commanded not to mention your name again."

"But surely," I urged, "I am to receive the ordinary privilege of a prisoner of war? General Sheridan will not condemn me without evidence or trial, merely because in a moment of sudden anger I used hasty words, which I have ever since regretted?"

Caton shook his head.

"My dear fellow, it is not that. Sheridan is hasty himself, and his temper often leads him to rash language. No, I am sure he bears you no malice for what you said. But Brennan has his ear, and has whispered something to him in confidence — what, I have been unable to ascertain — which has convinced him that you are deserving of death under martial law."

"Without trial?"

"The opportunity of furnishing the information desired

will be again offered you; but, as near as I can learn, the charge preferred against you is of such a private nature that it is deemed best not to make it matter for camp talk. Whatever it may be, Sheridan evidently feels justified in taking the case out from the usual channels, and in using most drastic measures. I am sorry to bring you such news, especially as I believe the charges are largely concocted in the brain of him who makes them, and have but the thinnest circumstantial evidence to sustain them. Yet Sheridan is thoroughly convinced, and will brook no interference. The discussion of the case has already led to his using extremely harsh words to his chief of staff."

"I am to be shot, then?"

His hand closed warmly over mine. "While there is life there is always hope," he answered. "Surely it must be in your power to prove the nature of your mission within our lines, and the delay thus gained will enable us to learn and meet these more serious allegations."

"If I but had time to communicate with General Lee."

"But now — is there no one, no way by which such representation can be given this very day? If not full proof of your innocence, then sufficient, at least, to cause the necessary delay?"

I shook my head. "I know of nothing other than my own unsupported word," I answered shortly, "and that is evidently of no value as against Major Brennan's secret insinuations. When is the hour set?"

"I am not positive that final decision has yet been reached, but I heard daybreak to-morrow mentioned. The probability of an early movement of our troops is the excuse urged for such unseemly haste."

I remained silent for a moment, conscious only of his kindly eyes reading my face.

" Mrs. Brennan," I asked finally, recurring to the one thought in which I retained deep interest, — " does she still remain in the camp? "

" She was with the Major at headquarters this morning. I believe they breakfasted with the General, but I was on duty so late last night that I overslept, and thus missed the pleasure of meeting her again."

We talked for some time longer, and he continued to urge me for some further word, but I could give him none, and finally the kindly fellow departed, promising to see me again within a few hours. Greatly as I now valued his friendship, it was, nevertheless, a relief to be alone with my thoughts once more.

CHAPTER XIII

CATON came in once more about the middle of the afternoon, bringing me some blankets; but he had no news, and his boyish face was a picture of pathos as he wrung my hand good-bye. Sheridan, he said, had gone down the lines, and both Brennan and himself were under orders to follow in another hour. What instructions, if any, had been left regarding my case he could not say, but he feared the worst from the unusual secrecy. Sheridan expected to return to his headquarters that same evening, as the officers of his staff were to give a grand ball.

I felt no inclination to partake of the rude supper left me, and just before dark I was lying upon the bench idly wondering if that was to prove the last vestige of daylight I should ever behold in this world, when, without slightest warning, the heavy iron grating in the wall directly above me fell suddenly, striking the edge of the bench, and clattered noisily to the floor. The fall was so unexpected, and my escape from injury so narrow, that I lay almost stunned, staring up helplessly at the dark hole thus left bare. As I gazed, a face framed itself in this narrow opening, and two wary eyes peered cautiously down at me. There was no mistaking that countenance even in the fast waning light, and I instantly sat up with an exclamation of surprise.

My Lady of the North

"Jed Bungay, as I live!"

The puzzled face broke into a grin of delight.

"Holy smoke, Cap," he ejaculated, with a deep sigh of relief, "is thet you, suah? I wus so durned skeered I'd made a mess o' it whin thet thar iron drapped thet I near died. 'He crossed the threshold — and a clang of angry steel that instant rang.'"

He peered around cautiously, screwing up his little eyes as though transforming them into miniature telescopes.

"'If thou wouldst view fair Melrose aright, go visit it by the pale moonlight.' Be ye all alone, Cap?"

"With the exception of a few rats, yes."

"Whut be they a goin' ter dew with ye?"

"I have every reason to believe it is their purpose to shoot me at daybreak to-morrow."

"Shoot? — Hell!" He stared at me as if he had just heard his own death sentence pronounced, and his little peaked face looked ghastly in the dim light. "Shoot ye? Good Lord, Cap, whut fer? Ye ain't done nothin' as I knows on, 'cept ter scrap a bit with thet blasted Yank, an' sure thet's no shootin' matter, er else I'd a bin a goner long ago."

"That 'Yank' has seen fit to charge me with being a spy; and as I was foolish enough to insult General Sheridan last night, my fate is probably sealed."

This somewhat complex statement seemed to be too much for Jed to grasp promptly.

"Gosh, ye don't say!" he muttered. "Then, durn it, I'm in luck, fer all they've got agin me is pot-shootin' at a nigger soger up in ther mountings; en thet ain't much, 'cause I did n't hit ther durned cuss. Blame sorry tew, fer 'Who spills the foremost foeman's life, his party conquers in the strife.' Thet's Scott agin, Cap.

A Strange Way Out

Dew ye ever read Sir Walter? I tell ye, he's a poet, suah."

Without pausing for a reply, or even noting that none had been given, Jed was carefully covering every inch of exposed wall with his little shrewd, glinting eyes.

"Ain't much show ter work out o' yere, is thar, Cap?" he asked at last reflectively; "leastwise I don't see none, 'less them thar dark corners hes got holes in 'em."

"The wall is entirely solid."

"So I sorter reckoned. But if ye'll crawl through yere inter my boodour, thar's a place whar I reckon ther tew of us tergether mought make a try fer it. It's too durn high up fer me ter git at alone."

I rose to my feet slowly, wondering at the strange lassitude which made me so indifferent to that life I had always before so highly valued. Bungay noticed my hopelessness.

"Durned if prison life don't take all the sand out o' a feller," he said cheerfully. "Blame me, but ye move as if ye wus 'bout half dead. But I reckon, Cap, if ye cud manage ter git out o' yere ternight, an' take some news ter Lee thet I've picked up, he'd 'bout make both of us ginerals. 'Speed, Malise, speed! The dun deer's hide on fleeter foot was never tied.'"

These words brought back to me in an instantaneous flash the old dominant military spirit. For Lee! Yes, for Lee I would yet take chances, undergo fatigue, brave death. If life must be given up, let it be yielded gallantly in the open, and on behalf of my distant comrades.

"News for Lee?" I exclaimed, staring eagerly at him through the now darkened room. "Do you mean it? What news?"

"Thought maybe thet wud wake ye up," he chuckled.

My Lady of the North

" 'Speed on the signal, clansman, speed!' Stan' up on ther bench, Cap, an' put yer ear up yere an' I 'll tell ye. This yere's gospel truth: Sheridan hes started his infantry on a half-circle march fer Minersville. Ther first division left et three o'clock, an' thar won't be nary Yank loafin' en ther valley by noon termorrow. An' more,'' he added rapidly, his eyes dancing wildly with suppressed excitement, — " Hancock is a swingin' of his corps west ter meet 'em thar, an' I reckon, as how thar 'll be hell fer sartain up ther Shenandoah in less ner a week — es Scott ses, ' the wild sounds of border war.' ''

" But how do you know all this?" I questioned incredulously, as the whole scene and its dread possibilities unrolled before my mental vision.

" Ther nigger I held up hed a despatch fer Heintzelman over on ther left, an' then Mariar she sorter pumped a young fule staff officer fer ther rest o' it," he replied promptly. " Oh, it 's a sure go, Cap, an' I reckon as how maybe Lee's whole army hangs on one of us gittin' out o' yere ternight.

" ' Where, where was Roderick then?
One blast upon his bugle horn
Were worth a thousand men.' "

That he meant every word he spoke I felt convinced, and his enthusiasm was contagious. My blood leaped within me at this call to action; all lethargy fled, and with it every deadening thought of her who had so suddenly woven about me the meshes of her power. False or true, maid, wife, or widow, my duty as a soldier to my commander and the army to which I belonged, blotted out all else. Even as this new rush of determination swept over me, above us there sounded clearly the dashing music

120

A Strange Way Out

of a military band in the strains of a Strauss's waltz, and we could distinguish the muffled shuffling of many feet on the oaken floor overhead. Caton's chance remark about the great ball to be given that evening by officers of the headquarters staff recurred to my memory.

"That dancing up there will help us, Jed," I said quickly, my mind now active to grasp every detail. "You say there is a chance for escape from your cell? Then give me your hand, and help me to crawl through that hole."

It was a narrow squeeze for a man of my size, yet I crept through without great difficulty, and found myself in the dense darkness of a room which, as I judged hastily from feeling about me, was similar in shape and extent to the one in which I had been confined.

Bungay, however, permitted me little time for exploration. Grasping me firmly by one arm, and feeling his way along the wall, he groped across to the other side.

"There 's a mighty big stone chimbly comes down yere, Cap," he whispered, his lips close to my ears, although the noise above made conversation in an ordinary tone perfectly safe. "An' ther openin' ter take out soot an' ashes is up thar, jist b'low ther fluer. It 's a sheet-iron pan, I reckon, ther way it feels; an' it must be thar they put a nigger in ter clean ther chimbly whin it gits stuffed up. I could git up thar alone, but I could n't do no work, but thet thar pan ought ter cum out all right. Dew ye think ye cud hol' me up, Cap? I 'm purty durn heavy."

I smiled in the darkness at the little fellow's egotism, and lifting him as I might a child, poised him lightly upon my shoulder. He struggled a moment to steady himself against the wall, and then I could feel him tugging eagerly at something which appeared to yield slowly to his

121

efforts. As he worked, a dense shower of dust and soot caused me to close my eyes.

"She's a comin' all right," he said cheerfully, puffing with his exertions, "but I reckon as how this chimbly ain't bin cleaned out since ther war begun. Hold up yer right han', Cap, an' git a blame good grip on her, fer she's almighty full, an 'll wanter go down sorter easy like."

I did as he suggested, bracing myself to meet his movements, as he stood straining on my shoulders, and in another moment I had succeeded in lowering the large sheet-iron pan silently to the floor.

"Room 'nough yere fer two men ter oncet," chuckled my companion, in rare delight. "'The chief in silence strode before.' Yere goes."

His weight left my shoulders; there was a slight scramble, another shower of dirt, then the sound of his voice once more.

"Lift up yer han's, Cap; dig in yer toes on ther stones, an' we'll begin our vi'ge."

He grasped my wrists with a strength which I had no conception the little fellow possessed. There was a moment's breathless struggle, and I squirmed through the opening, and lay panting on the flat slabs which composed the foot of the great funnel. To afford me more room Bungay had gone up a little, finding foot-lodgment upon the uneven stones of which the chimney was constructed. For a moment we rested thus motionless, both breathing heavily and listening to the music and shuffling of feet now almost upon a level with our heads.

The noise, which was strong and continuous, rendered discovery from any misstep highly improbable, and as delay was dangerous neither of us was disposed to linger long.

A Strange Way Out

"Be ye all ready, Cap?" questioned Bungay, bending his head down. "Fer if ye be, I 'm a goin' up."

"All right," I answered, struggling to my knees in the narrow space; "only take it slow, Jed. I 'm a trifle bigger man than you, and this is rather close quarters."

"Wal, yes, maybe a matter of a poun' er two," he retorted, and the next moment I could hear him scraping his way upward, feeling for foothold upon the irregular layers of stone. I followed, pressing my knees firmly against the rough wall, and trusting more to my hands than feet for security against falling. There was evidently a fireplace of some kind on the first floor, with a considerable opening leading from it into the chimney we were scaling, for as Jed slowly passed, I could perceive a sudden gleam of light streaming across his face from the glare of the lamps within. He glanced anxiously that way, but did not pause in his steady climb upward.

A moment later I came opposite that same beam of radiance, and cautiously peered down the sloped opening that led to the disused fireplace. All I could perceive was a pair of legs, evidently those of a cavalry officer, judging from the broad yellow stripe down the seam of the light-blue trousers, and the high boots ornamented with rowel spurs. He stood leaning carelessly against the mantel, talking with some one just beyond the range of my vision.

At that moment the music ceased suddenly, and afraid to proceed until it should strike up again, I braced myself securely on a projecting stone and bent my head over the orifice until I could catch a portion of the conversation being carried on by my unconscious neighbors.

"No," said the cavalryman, gruffly, and apparently in reply to some previous question, "the fellow was most devilish obstinate; would n't tell the first thing; even a threat of treating him as a spy and hanging him outright proved of no avail. But Sheridan's theory is that Lee has ordered Longstreet to hit our rear, while he makes a direct attack in front. That 's why the ' old man ' proposes to get in his work first, and we march at daylight to form connection with Hancock. By Jove, Chesley, but that woman in black over there with Follansbee is the handsomest picture I 've seen south of the line. Mark how her eyes sparkle, and how prettily the light gleams in her hair. Who is she, do you chance to know ? "

" Yes," lisped the other, languidly, " met her at breakfast, headquarters, this morning. Deuced pretty and all that, mighty good style, too, but taken, old man. She 's Brennan's."

" What! not Major Brennan ? " in surprise. " Why, he 's always posed as a bachelor among our fellows."

" Don't know anything about that, dear boy," indifferently, " but the lady came in with him yesterday, was introduced to the crowd of us as Mrs. Brennan, and he called her Edith. Deuced nice name, Edith. As Brennan has shown such poor taste as to be absent to-night, I 'm inclined to give a little of my time to his lady. Far and away the prettiest thing here."

Just at this moment I heard Bungay speaking to me agonizingly down the chimney:

" Durn it all, Cap, I 've — I 've got ter sneeze."

There was a smothered struggle in the darkness above me, then a muffled explosion that showered me with soot, and sounded to my startled nerves like the report of a gun. I drew up my legs hastily, and had barely done so when a heavily whiskered face peered up at me through the open fireplace. It appeared so close I had no doubt he saw me, but his eyes were unable to penetrate the darkness.

"Sounded devilishly like a sneeze," he said suspiciously, as he straightened up again. "Must have been wind in the chimney."

"More likely bats," returned the other. "Well, so' long, Somers; see you in the morning. I'm going to give the fair Edith a whirl."

The cavalry legs shifted their position; the band resumed its functions, and in the renewed activity and noise I began again the toilsome climb, my mind now a bewildered chaos between my plain duty to Lee and my nearly uncontrollable desire to meet once more the woman who was dancing in the room below.

The little mountaineer, as active as a cat, and not especially hampered by lack of room in which to work, was well above me by this time. The chimney, acting as a tube, brought down to me from time to time the slight noise of his climbing, varied by an occasional exclamation or comment, but I could perceive no other evidence of his presence. Above, all was as black as the grave.

"Holy smoke!" he ejaculated, probably unaware that he was giving utterance to his thoughts. "That was a sharp rock! Durn if thar's a inch o' skin left on my knee. Whut is it Scott ses? 'An' broken arms and disarray marked the fell havoc of the day.' Gee! if Mariar cud only see me now, maybe she would n't be proud —

"'Sweet *Maria*, dear my life must be
Since it is worthy care from thee;
Yet life I hold but idle breath,
When love or honor's weighed with death!'—

Ough! stop thet! who's got hold o' my fut?"

"Hush your racket, you little fool," I said angrily. "Do you want the whole Yankee army to trap us here like rats? I cannot get up this chimney any farther; it is growing too small to permit my body to pass."

"Is thet so, Cap?" he asked anxiously. "Whut be ye goin' ter dew 'bout it?"

I made no answer for a moment; I was groping about in the darkness of our narrow quarters to see if I could determine exactly where we were.

"How high is this house, Jed, do you know?"

"Three stories an' attic."

"How far up are we?"

"'Bout halfway 'long ther third story, I reckon; must be jist b'low whar ye are thet I stuck my fut down an openin'. Reckon 't was 'nother fireplace, like thet one on ther first flure."

I lowered myself silently, and felt along the stones until I located the opening, and roughly measured its dimensions.

"I shall have to risk crawling out here, Jed," I said finally, "for I shall surely stick fast if I go up another ten feet. Do you suppose you can squeeze through to the top?"

"I reckon I kin," he returned calmly. "'Just as the minstrel's sounds were stayed, a stranger climbed the steepy glade.' But had n't we better stick tergether, Cap?"

"No," I answered firmly. "You go on, and one of us must get through to Lee. Don't mind me at all; get down from the roof as best you can. If I am caught it will be all the more important that you should succeed."

"'T is done — 'I thank thee, Roderick, for the word; it nerves my heart, it steels my sword.'"

A Strange Way Out

Even as he spoke I could hear him creeping steadily upward. It soon became evident that his progress was growing slower, more difficult. Then all sounds above me ceased, and I knew he must have attained the roof in safety.

CHAPTER XIV

I BECOME A COLONEL OF ARTILLERY

MY own situation at this moment was too critical, too full of peril and uncertainty, to afford opportunity for moralizing over Bungay's chances of escape. Only one possibility lay before me — there remained no choice, no necessity for planning. It is pure luck which pries open most doors of life, and it was upon luck alone I must rely now. I have often wondered since how I ever succeeded in squeezing my body through that narrow opening into the empty fireplace without at least knocking over something during the difficult passage. But I did manage, working my way down slowly, creeping inch by inch like a snake, carefully testing each object I touched in the darkness for fear of its proving loose, until I finally lay stretched at full length upon what was evidently, from its feeling, a carpet of unusually fine texture.

The room proved to be an inner one and unlighted, a bedchamber, as I soon determined, for my outstretched hands encountered the posts of a bed. Then a slight gust of air partially swept aside a hanging curtain, which rustled like silk, and I caught a brief glimpse of the adjacent parlor. It was likewise unillumined, but the door leading into the front hall stood ajar, and through that opening there poured a stream of radiance, together with the incessant hum of many voices in animated con-

I Become a Colonel of Artillery

versation, the deep blare of the band, with the ceaseless movement of dancing feet.

Satisfying myself by sense of touch that the bed was unoccupied, for I was far too experienced a soldier to leave an enemy in my rear, I crept cautiously forward to the intercepting curtain, and drawing it aside took careful survey of the outer apartment. It was a large and handsomely furnished room, a polished mahogany writing-table littered with papers occupying a prominent position against the farther wall. A swivel chair stood beside it, and across its back hung what appeared to be a suit of clothing. I saw no other signs of human occupancy.

Convinced that the apartment was deserted, and discovering no different means of egress, I crossed the room on tiptoe, and peered cautiously out into the hall. It was not a pleasing prospect to one in my predicament. The lower portion, judging from the incessant hum of voices, was filled with people, who were either unable to find place within the crowded ballroom, or else preferred greater retirement for conversation. Even the wide stairway had been partially pre-empted, a young lieutenant, as I judged from his shoulder-straps, sitting just beneath the landing, whispering eagerly into the attentive ear of a pronounced blonde who shared the broad carpeted step with him.

I drew back noiselessly, to figure out the situation and determine what was best for me to attempt. It would be sheer madness to venture upon a passage to the front door, clad as I was in travel-worn gray uniform; to rush through that jam was impossible. If I were to wait until the dance was concluded the later hours of the night might indeed yield me somewhat clearer passage, yet it was hardly probable that the house, used as I knew it to be for a military prison, would be left unguarded. Besides, such delay must absolutely prevent my getting beyond the Federal picket lines before daybreak, and would hence render valueless the news I sought to bear to Lee.

I moved to the only window and glanced out; it opened upon the back of the house and presented a sheer drop to the ground. At the slight noise of the moving sash a sentry standing at the corner glanced up suspiciously. Evidently each side of the great building was abundantly protected by patrols.

Something had to be attempted, and at once. The room I was in bore unquestionable evidence of recent occupancy, and at any moment might be re-entered. My searching eyes fell upon the articles of clothing carelessly folded over the chair-back. I picked up the garments one by one and shook them out; they composed the new uniform of a colonel of artillery, and were resplendent with bright red facings and a profusion of gold braid. With all my soul I loathed the thought of disguise, and especially the hated uniform of the enemy. It was repugnant to every instinct of my being, and would certainly mean added degradation and danger in the event of capture.

Yet I saw no other way. Sheridan, Brennan, Caton, the three who would certainly recognize me on sight, I was assured were absent, although they might return at any moment. The greater reason for haste, the less excuse for delay. But if I should chance to run foul of the rightful owner of the garments amid that crush below, and he should recognize them, what then? I stood close beside the writing-table as I revolved these considerations rapidly in mind, and my eye chanced to fall upon an open

I Become a Colonel of Artillery

paper. It was an official order, bearing date at 5 P. M. that same day, commanding Colonel Culbertson to move his battery at once down the Kendallville pike, and report to Brigadier-General Knowls for assignment to his brigade. Evidently the new dress uniform had been carefully brushed and laid out to be worn at the ball that evening; the sudden receipt of this order had caused the owner to depart hastily in his service dress, vigorously expressing his feelings, no doubt, while his servant, now enjoying liberty below stairs, had neglected to pack up his master's things.

This knowledge was the straw which decided me; I would chance it. Hastily I drew on the rich blue and red over my old gray, adding the dress sword I had discovered in a closet, and then, wondering curiously what sort of figure I might cut in all these fine habiliments, sought a glance at myself within a mirror hanging upon the bedroom wall. Faith! but it was God's mercy that I did!

Such a face as grinned at me from that glass, peering over the high-cut, decorated collar, would surely have created a genuine sensation in those rooms below. Serious as my situation was, I laughed at the thought of it until tears ran down my cheeks, leaving white streaks the full length of them; for no chimney-sweep in the full tide of his glorious career was ever worse sooted and begrimed. I thought of the elegantly dressed lieutenant and the blonde young lady upon the stairs — surely they would have supposed the very devil himself was coming down.

It took me nearly a quarter of an hour to get myself tolerably clean, and I could not have done that had I not used some grease that was upon the stand. At the end, however, I stepped back from the glass confident that with good luck I should run the gantlet safely.

Just as I prepared to step forth a new thought occurred to me — who was I? If questioned, as was highly probable, how could I account for my presence? Who should I pretend to be? I turned over the mass of papers lying before me on the table. They were mostly accounts and detailed orders about which I cared nothing, but finally my search was rewarded by the discovery of a recent army list. I ran my eyes hastily down the artillery assignments — Barry, Sommers, Fitzmorris, Sloan, Reilly. Ah, there at last was exactly what I wanted — " Patrick L. Curran, Colonel Sixth Ohio Light Artillery, McRoberts's Division, Thomas's Corps, assigned special service, staff Major-General Halleck, Washington, D. C."

" Curran, Sixth Ohio " — good; and the other? I glanced again at the open order. " Culbertson, Fourteenth Pennsylvania." I would remember those names, and with a jaunty confidence in my success, born of thorough preparation, I stepped to the open door and strode forth into the brilliantly lighted hall. Barring the single accident of encountering a possible acquaintance in the throng below, I felt fully capable of deceiving his Satanic Majesty himself.

CHAPTER XV

THE young officer glanced up hastily at sound of approaching footsteps, and rose to his feet to permit of my passage. He wore the full dress uniform of an artilleryman, and his evident surprise at my presence made me realize the necessity of addressing him.

"Lieutenant," I asked courteously, resting one hand easily upon the balustrade, "could you inform me if General Sheridan and those members of the staff who accompanied him down the lines this afternoon have yet returned?"

"They have not, sir."

"Ah, I was in hopes they might have arrived by this time. I see that you belong to my branch of the service. May I inquire your battery?"

He flushed with pleasure at the delicate flattery of my tone, and in true soldierly pride of his corps.

"B, Fifth New Jersey, sir."

"I think I remember them in action — no better command in the service. You were at Gettysburg?"

"On Seminary Ridge, sir. It was my first battle."

"A hard baptism of fire, indeed, yet a remembrance you will long be proud to recall. I thank you for your courtesy."

133

My Lady of the North

I bowed to them both, and passed slowly down the wide stairway, several couples rising as I drew near to permit of my passage. The intense excitement of the strange adventure had by this time become a positive delight. My cheek flushed, my eyes kindled as though new blood flowed in my veins.

"Ah!" I thought to myself proudly, "what a story it will all make for the camp-fire, and if I reach Lee in time the tale of this night will be upon the lips of all the army."

The lower hall was very comfortably filled with figures moving here and there in converse, or occupying seats pressed close against the walls. The greater portion were attired in uniforms of the various branches of service, yet I observed not a few civilian suits, and a considerable number of women, some wearing the neat dress of the army nurse, others much more elaborately attired—daughters of the neighborhood, probably, with a sprinkling of wives and sisters of the soldiery. Guards, leaning upon their muskets, stood in statuesque poses on either side of the main entrance, while the wide archway, draped with flags, opening into the ballroom, revealed an inspiring glimpse of swiftly revolving figures in gay uniforms and flashing skirts. Over all floated the low, swinging music of the band.

All this I noted as I paused irresolutely on the lower stair, wondering if I could safely walk directly out of that front door, ignoring the sentries by right of the uniform I wore, and thus attain the open air. The constant haunting fear of the early return of Sheridan and his aides, or a possible encounter with some former acquaintance in that crushing throng, almost decided me upon venturing the passage. But already I had hesitated

134

At the Staff Officers' Ball

too long. A fat, good-natured-looking man of forty, an infantry major, but wearing staff decorations, and evidently officiating in the capacity of floor-manager, after whispering a word in the ear of another of the same kind beside the ballroom door, hastily pushed his way through the laughing throng directly toward me.

"Good-evening, Colonel," he said, bowing deeply. "Your face is not familiar to me, but you will permit me to introduce myself — Major Monsoon, of General Sheridan's staff."

I accepted the fat, shapeless hand he extended, and pressed it warmly.

"I was just meditating a retreat, Major, when you appeared," I replied frankly. "For I fear my face is equally unknown to all others present. Indeed, I feel like a cat in a strange garret, and hesitated to appear at all. My only excuse for doing so was a promise made Colonel Culbertson previous to his being ordered out on duty. I am Colonel Curran, of the Sixth Ohio, but at present serving on the staff of General Halleck at Washington."

The Major's round, red face glowed with welcome.

"Extremely pleased to meet you, indeed," he exclaimed eagerly, "and you may be sure of a most cordial greeting. Will you kindly step this way?"

As we slowly elbowed our way forward, all desire to escape from the ordeal fled, and I assumed the risks of the masquerade with the reckless audacity of my years. Before we reached the ballroom my conductor, his fat countenance fairly beaming with cordiality, had stopped at least twenty times to present me to various military titles, and I had accepted innumerable invitations without in the least knowing who gave them, or where they were to be fulfilled. Finally, however, we broke through the massed ring, and succeeded in reaching the tall individual in spectacles to whom the Major had spoken previous to seeking me, and I learned through the introduction which followed that I was in the presence of Brigadier-General Carlton, chief of staff.

For a moment, as I responded to the hearty cordiality of his welcome, I was enabled to take my first glance at the ballroom, and found it to my unaccustomed soldier eyes an inspiring spectacle. The room was magnificently large, — a surprising apartment, indeed, even in so superb a Southern home as this had evidently been, and its proportions were magnified by numerous mirrors extending from floor to ceiling, causing the more distant dancers to appear circling in space. Brilliantly illumined by means of hanging chandeliers that oscillated slightly to the merry feet; decorated lavishly everywhere with festooned flags and tastefully arranged munitions of war; gay with the dress uniforms of the men and the handsome gowns of the women, it composed a scene so different from any I had looked upon in years as to hold me fascinated. The constant clatter of tongues, the merry laughter, the flashing of bright eyes, and the gleam of snowy shoulders, the good-humored repartees caught as the various couples circled swiftly past, the quick, musical gliding of flying feet over the waxen floor, the continuous whirl of the intoxicating waltz, and over all the inspiring strains of Strauss, caused my heart to bound, and brought with it an insane desire to participate.

Yet gazing, entranced, upon the animated scene, and feeling deeply the intoxication of the moment, my eyes were eagerly searching that happy throng for sight of one fair woman's face. Strange as it must seem to others, in spite of the fact that to meet her might mean betrayal

and death — ay! might even result in the destruction of
an army — in my weakness I secretly longed for just such
a happening; felt, indeed, that I must again see her, have
speech with her, before I went forth alone into the mani-
fold dangers of the night. It was foolhardiness, — insanity in very truth, — yet such was the secret yearning of
my heart. If I could only once know, know from her own
truthful lips, that she already belonged to another, I
could, I believed, tear her image from my memory; but
while I yet doubted (and in spite of all I had heard I
doubted still), no desperate case should ever prevent my
seeking her with all the mad ardor of love, no faintness of
heart should intervene between us. That she was present
I knew from those chance words overheard in the chimney,
and my one deep hope ever since I donned that Federal
uniform and ventured down the stairs (a hope most oddly
mingled with dread) was that we might in some manner
be brought together. I was yet vainly seeking a glimpse
of her among the many who circled past, when I was suddenly recalled to the extreme delicacy of my situation by
the deep voice of the Major asking me a direct question:

"Do you ever dance, Colonel?"

Exactly what I may have replied I know not, but it was
evidently translated as an affirmative, for in another moment I was being piloted down the side of the long room,
while he gossiped in my rather inattentive ear.

"As you have doubtless remarked, Colonel, we are
extremely fortunate in our ladies to-night. By Jove,
they would grace an inauguration ball at Washington.
So many officers' wives have joined us lately, supposing
we would make permanent camp here, and besides there
are more loyal families in this neighborhood than we find
usually. At least their loyalty is quite apparent while

137

we remain. Then the General Hospital nurses are not especially busy, — no battle lately, you know, — and there are some deuced pretty girls among them. Ballroom looks nice, don't you think?"

"Extremely well; the decorations are in most excellent taste."

"Entirely the work of the staff. Great pity so many were compelled to be absent, but a soldier can never tell. Here upon special duty, Colonel?"

"I brought despatches from the President to General Sheridan."

"Wish you might remain with us permanently. Your command, I believe, is not connected with our Eastern army?"

"No, with Thomas in the Cumberland."

"Ah, yes; had some very pretty fighting out there, I understand — oh, pardon me, Miss Minor, permit me to present to you Colonel Curran, of General Halleck's staff. The Colonel, I believe, is as able a dancer as he is a soldier, and no higher compliment to his abilities could possibly be paid. Miss Minor, Colonel, is a native Virginian, who is present under protest, hoping doubtless to capture some young officer, and thus weaken the enemy."

I bowed pleasantly to the bright-eyed young woman facing me, and not sorry to escape the Major's inquisitiveness, at once begged for the remainder of the waltz. The request was laughingly granted, and in another moment we were threading our way amid the numerous couples upon the floor. She proved so delightful a dancer that I simply yielded myself up to full enjoyment of the measure, and conversation lapsed, until a sudden cessation of the music left us stranded so close to the

At the Staff Officers' Ball

fireplace that the very sight of it brought a vivid realization of my perilous position. If it had not, my companion's chance remark most assuredly would.

"How easily you waltz!" she said enthusiastically, her sparkling eyes and flushed cheeks testifying to her keen enjoyment. "So many find me difficult to keep step with that I have become fearful of venturing upon the floor with a stranger. However, I shall always be glad to give you a character to any of my friends."

"I sincerely thank you," I returned in the same spirit, "and I can certainly return the compliment most heartily. It is so long since I was privileged to dance with a lady that I confess to having felt decidedly awkward at the start, but your step proved so accommodating that I became at once at home, and enjoyed the waltz immensely. I fail to discover any seats in the room, or I should endeavor to find one vacant for you."

"Oh, I am not in the least tired." She was looking at me with so deep an expression of interest in her eyes that I dimly wondered at it.

"Did I understand rightly," she asked, playing idly with her fan, "that Major Monsoon introduced you to me as Colonel Curran of General Halleck's staff?"

What the deuce am I up against now? I thought, and my heart beat quickly. Yet retreat was impossible, and I answered with assumed carelessness:

"I am, most assuredly, Colonel Curran."

"From Ohio?"

This was certainly coming after me with a vengeance, and I stole one quick glance at the girl's face. It was devoid of suspicion, merely evincing a polite interest.

"I have the honor of commanding the Sixth Artillery Regiment from that State."

My Lady of the North

"You must pardon me, Colonel, for my seeming inquisitiveness," and her eyes sparkled with demure mischief. "Yet I cannot quite understand. I was at school in Connecticut with a Miss Curran whose father was an officer of artillery from Ohio, and, naturally, I at once thought of her when the Major pronounced your name; yet it certainly cannot be you — you are altogether too young, for Myrtle must be eighteen."

I laughed, decidedly relieved from what I feared might prove a most awkward situation.

"Well, yes, Miss Minor, I am indeed somewhat youthful to be Myrtle's father," I said at a venture, "but I might serve as her brother, you know, and not stretch the point of age over-much."

She clasped her hands on my arm with a gesture of delight.

"Oh, I am so glad; I knew Myrtle had a brother, but never heard he also was in the army. Did you know, Colonel, she was intending to come down here with me when I returned South, at the close of our school year, but from some cause was disappointed. How delighted she would have been to meet you! I shall certainly write and tell her what a splendidly romantic time we had together. You look so much like Myrtle I wonder I failed to recognize you at once."

She was rattling on without affording me the slightest opportunity to slip in a word explanatory, when her glance chanced to fall upon some one who was approaching us through the throng.

"Oh, by the way, Colonel, there is another of Myrtle's old schoolmates present to-night — a most intimate friend, indeed, who would never forgive me if I permitted you to go without meeting her."

At the Staff Officers' Ball

She drew me back hastily.

"Edith," she said, touching the sleeve of a young woman who was slowly passing, "Edith, wait just a moment, dear; this is Colonel Curran — Myrtle Curran's brother, you know. Colonel Curran, Mrs. Brennan."

CHAPTER XVI

THE WOMAN I LOVED

THE crucial moment had arrived, and I think my heart actually stopped beating as I stood gazing helplessly into her face. I saw her eyes open wide in astonished recognition, and then a deep flush swept over throat and cheek. For the instant I believed she would not speak, or that she would give way to her excitement and betray everything. I durst give no signal of warning, for there existed no tie between us to warrant my expecting any consideration from her. It was an instant so tense that her silence seemed like a blow. Yet it was only an instant. Then her eyes smiled into mine most frankly, and her hand was extended.

"I am more than delighted to meet you, Colonel Curran," she said calmly, although I could feel her lips tremble to the words, while the fingers I held were like ice. "Myrtle was one of my dearest friends, and she chanced to be in my mind even as we met. That was why," she added, turning toward Miss Minor, as though she felt her momentary agitation had not passed unobserved, "I was so surprised when you first presented Colonel Curran."

"I confess to having felt strangely myself," returned the other, archly, "although I believe I concealed my feelings far better than you did, Edith. Really, I thought you were going to faint. It must be that Colonel Curran exercises some strange occult influence over the weaker sex. Perhaps he is the seventh son of a seventh son; are you, Colonel? However, dear, I am safe for the present from his mysterious spell, and you will be compelled to face the danger alone, as here comes Lieutenant Hammersmith to claim the dance I 've promised him."

Before Mrs. Brennan could interfere, the laughing girl had placed her hand on the Lieutenant's blue sleeve, and, with a mocking good-bye flung backward over her shoulder, vanished in the crowd, leaving us standing there alone.

The lady waited in such apparent indifference, gently tapping the floor with her neatly shod foot, her eyes wandering carelessly over the throng in our front, that I felt utterly at sea. Evidently she had no intention of addressing me, yet I could not continue to stand there beside her in silence like a fool. That she possessed a pretty temper I already knew, but better a touch of that than this silent disdain.

"Would you be exceedingly angry if I were to ask you to dance?" I questioned, stealing surreptitiously a glance at her proudly averted face.

"Angry? Most assuredly not," in apparent surprise. "Yet I trust you will not ask me. I have been upon the floor only once to-night. I am not at all in the mood."

The words were not encouraging, yet they served to break the ice, and I was never easily daunted.

"If there were chairs here I should venture to ask even a greater favor — that you would consent to sit out this set with me."

She turned slightly, lifted her eyes inquiringly to mine, and her face lightened.

"No doubt we might discover seats without difficulty,

143

in the anteroom," she answered, indicating the direction by a glance. "There do not appear to be many 'sitters-out' at this ball, and the few who do are not crowded."

If the pendulum of hope and despair swings one way, the unalterable laws of mental gravitation compel it to go just as far the other, and although I do not remember uttering so much as a word while we traversed the crowded floor and gained entrance to the smaller room beyond, yet my heart was singing a song of the deepest hope. The apartment contained, as she prophesied, but few occupants, and I conducted her to the farther end of it, where we found a comfortable divan and no troublesome neighbors.

As I glanced at her now, I marked a distinct change in her face. The old indifference, so well assumed while we were in the presence of others, had utterly vanished as by magic, and she sat looking at me in anxious yet impetuous questioning.

"Captain Wayne," she exclaimed, her eyes never once leaving my face, "what does this mean? this masquerade? this wearing of the Federal uniform? this taking of another's name? this being here at all?"

"If I should say that I came hoping to see you again," I answered, scarce knowing how best to proceed or how far to put confidence in her, "what would you think?"

The color flamed quickly into her cheeks, but the clear eyes never faltered. They seemed to read my very soul.

"If that is true, that you were extremely foolish to take such a risk for so small a reward," she returned calmly. "Nor, under these circumstances, would I remain here so much as a moment to encourage you. But it is not true. This is no light act; your very life must lie in the balance, or you could never assume such risk. Doubtless you hesitate to trust me fully, but I assure you you need not, for you have placed me under certain personal obligations which I have no desire to ignore. Captain Wayne, you are in trouble, in danger — will you not tell me all, and permit me to aid you by every means in my power?"

"I would trust you gladly with my life or my honor," I replied soberly. "If I had less faith in you I should not be here now."

She started slightly at the words, and for an instant her eyes fell. "Your life?" she questioned, "do you mean that is in the balance?"

"I understand that I am condemned to be shot as a spy at daybreak."

"Shot? On what authority? Who told you?"

"On the order of General Sheridan. My informant was Lieutenant Caton, of his staff."

"Shot? As a spy? Why, it surely cannot be! Frank said — Captain Wayne, believe me, I knew absolutely nothing of all this. Do not think I should ever have rested if I had dreamed that you were held under so false a charge. I promised you I would see General Sheridan on your behalf."

"Yes," I assented hastily, for her agitation was so great I feared it might attract the attention of others. "I remember you said so at the time of my arrest, but supposed you had either forgotten or had found your intercession fruitless."

"Why, how you must have despised me! Forgotten?" —her eyes filled instantly with tears. "Not for an hour, Captain Wayne, but Frank —" she bit her lip impatiently — "I was told, that is, I was led to believe that you were — had been sent North as a prisoner of war late last night. Otherwise I should have insisted upon seeing you — on pleading your cause with the General himself. The Major and I breakfasted with him this morning, but your name was not mentioned, for I believed you safe."

She did not appear to realize, so deep was her present indignation and regret, that my hand had found a resting-place upon her own.

" You must believe me, Captain Wayne; I could not bear to have you feel that I could prove such an ingrate."

" You need never suppose I should think that," I replied, with an earnestness of manner that caused her to glance at me in surprise. " I confidently expected to hear from you all day, and finally when no word came I became convinced some such misconception as you have mentioned must have occurred. Then it became my turn to act upon my own behalf if I would preserve my life; yet never for one moment have I doubted you or the sincerity of your pledge to me."

She drew her hand away from my clasp, gently and not unkindly, then passed it through the masses of her dark, shining hair, but her face remained turned aside from me. Oh, how I longed at that moment to pour forth in fervent words the affection that burned within my heart! But irrespective of the doubt as to her being free to listen to such a declaration, there was a pride about her manner, a certain restraint which she ever seemed to exercise over me, that effectually sealed my lips. Her very presence was a moral tonic, and I felt it would be easier to tear out my tongue than to utter anything which she could construe into possible insult. The very depth of her perfect womanhood was itself protection, and, until the veil was finally lifted, my lips were vowed to silence.

146

The Woman I Loved

She waited quietly while a couple passed us and sought seats nearer the door.

"Tell me the entire story," she said gently.

As quickly as possible I reviewed the salient events which had occurred since our last meeting. Without denying the presence of Major Brennan during my stormy meeting with General Sheridan, I did not dwell upon it, nor mention the personal affray that had occurred between us. Even had I not supposed the man to be her husband I should never have taken advantage of his treachery to advance my own cause. God knows I have enough failings to account for, but I have never done my fighting in the dark. Neither did I speak of the information I now sought to bring to Lee, for her sympathy, her interest, her loyalty, were all with the opposing army. She followed my narrative eagerly, her eyes growing darker with intensity of interest as I depicted our eventful climb up the black chimney, and my venture down the stairs into the crowded ballroom. As I concluded there was a tear glistening on her long lashes, but she seemed unconscious of it, and made no attempt to dash it away.

"You have not told me all," she commented quietly. "But I can understand and appreciate the reason for your silence. I know Frank's impetuosity, and you are very kind, Captain Wayne, to spare my feelings, but you must not remain here; every moment of delay increases your danger. Sheridan and those of his staff who would surely recognize you were expected back before this, and may appear at any moment — yet how can you get away? how is it possible for me to assist you?"

There was an eager anxiety in her face that piqued me. Like most lovers I chose to give it a wrong interpretation.

My Lady of the North

" You are anxious to be rid of me? " I asked, ashamed of the words even as I uttered them.

" That remark is unworthy of you," and she arose to her feet almost haughtily. " My sole thought in this is the terrible risk you incur in remaining here."

" Your interest then is personal to me, may I believe? "

" I am a loyal woman," proudly, " and would do nothing whatever to imperil the cause of my country; but your condemnation is unjust, and I am, in a measure, responsible for it. I assist you, Captain Wayne, for your own sake, and in response to my individual sense of honor."

God knows I could not speak, although my heart seemed bursting within my bosom. By sheer power of her will, her pride, her perfect womanhood, she held me from her as though a wall divided us. Not for an instant did she permit me to forget that she was the wife of another.

" Have you formulated any plan? " she asked quickly, and her rising color made me feel that she had deciphered my struggle in my eyes.

" Only to walk out under protection of this uniform, and when once safe in the open to trust that same good fortune which has thus far befriended me."

She shook her head doubtfully, and stood a moment in silence, looking thoughtfully at the moving figures in the room beyond.

" I fear it cannot be done without arousing suspicion," she said at last, slowly. " I chance to know there are unusual precautions being taken to-night, and the entire camp is doubly patrolled. Even this house has a cordon of guards about it, but for what reason I have not learned. No," she spoke decisively, " there is no other way. Captain Wayne, I am going to try to save you to-night, but in doing so I must trust my reputation in your keeping."

The Woman I Loved

" I will protect it with my life."

" Protect it with your silence, rather. I know you to be a gentleman, or I should never attempt to carry out the only means of escape which seems at all feasible. Discovery would place me in an extremely embarrassing position, and I must rely upon you to protect me from such a possibility."

" I beg you," I began, " do not compromise yourself in any way for my sake."

" But I am myself already deeply involved in this," she interrupted, " and I could retain no peace of mind were I to do otherwise. Now listen. Make your way back to the ballroom, and in fifteen minutes from now be engaged in conversation with General Carlton near the main entrance. I shall join you there, and you will take your cue from me. You understand?"

" Perfectly, but — "

" There is no ' but,' Captain Wayne, only do not fail me."

Our eyes met for an instant; what she read in mine God knows — in hers was determination, with a daring strange to woman. The next moment she had vanished through a side door, and I was alone.

CHAPTER XVII

THROUGH THE CAMP OF THE ENEMY

A GLANCE at my watch told me that it was already within a few moments of midnight. There was, however, no diminution in the festivities, and I waited in silence until I heard the sentries calling the hour, and then pressed my way back into the noisy, crowded ballroom. I was stopped twice by well-meaning officers whom I had met earlier in the evening, but breaking away from them after the exchange of a sentence or two, I urged my course as directly as possible toward where the spectacled brigadier yet held his post as master of ceremonies.

We had been conversing pleasantly for several minutes when Mrs. Brennan appeared. Standing so as to face the stairs, I saw her first coming down, and noted that she wore her hat, and had a light walking-cloak thrown over her shoulders. My heart beat faster as I realized for the first time that she intended to be my companion.

"Oh, General, I am exceedingly glad to find you yet here," she exclaimed as she came up, and extended a neatly gloved hand to him. "I have a favor to ask which I am told you alone have the authority to grant."

He bowed gallantly.

"I am very sure," he returned smilingly, "that Mrs. Brennan will never request anything which I would not gladly yield."

Through the Camp of the Enemy

She flashed her eyes brightly into his face.

" Most assuredly not. The fact is, General, Colonel Curran, with whom I see you are already acquainted, was to pass the night at the Major's quarters, and as he has not yet returned, the duty has naturally devolved upon me to see our guest safely deposited. ,We are a· the Mitchell House, you remember, which is beyond the inner lines; and while, of course, I have been furnished with a pass," she held up the paper for his inspection, " and have been also instructed as to the countersign, I fear this will scarcely suffice for the safe passage of the Colonel."

The General laughed good-humoredly, evidently pleased with her assumption of military knowledge.

" Colonel Curran is certainly to be congratulated upon having found so charming a guide, madam, and I can assure you I shall most gladly do my part toward the success of the expedition. The Major was expected back before this, I believe?"

" He left word that if he had not returned by twelve I was to wait for him no longer, as he should go directly to his quarters. I find the life of a soldier to be extremely uncertain."

" We are our country's servants, madam," he replied proudly, and then taking out a pad of blanks from his pocket, turned to me.

" May I ask your full name and rank, Colonel?"

" Patrick L. Curran, Colonel, Sixth Ohio Light Artillery."

He wrote it down rapidly, tore off the paper, and handed it to me.

" That will take you safely through our inner guard lines," he said gravely, " that being as far as my jurisdiction extends. Good-night, Colonel; good-night, Mrs. Brennan."

She smiled her good-bye to him, and placed a gloved hand confidingly on my arm.

" I believe I recall the road and shall find no difficulty in guiding you," she said. " At least we cannot go so very far astray."

How cool and self-possessed she appeared — no hurry, no outward nervousness marred a single action. I felt my heart throb with new-born pride of her as I marked the marvellous self-control which characterized every movement, for I realized now that her risk in the adventure was scarcely second to my own. As I ventured life, she ventured honor, and I doubted not hers was the harder task of the two. Yet she gave no outward sign of struggle; as we crossed the crowded hall I could note no lack of resolution, no faltering of purpose in either step or voice.

At the door an officer spoke to her.

" Surely you are not leaving us so early, Mrs. Brennan?" he questioned anxiously. " Why, supper has not even been announced."

I felt her hand close more tightly upon my arm.

" Unfortunately we must," she replied, in a tone expressive of deep regret. " The Major was to go directly to his quarters if he was not here by midnight, and would surely worry were I still absent. Have you ever met my friend? Pardon me — Captain Burns, Colonel Curran."

We bowed ceremoniously, and the next moment Mrs. Brennan and I were out upon the steps, breathing the cool night air. I glanced curiously at her face as the gleam of light fell upon it — how calm and reserved she appeared, and yet her eyes were aglow with intense

152

excitement. At the foot of the steps she glanced up at the dark, projecting roof far above us.

"Do you suppose he can possibly be up there yet?" she asked, in a tone so low as to be inaudible to the ears of the sentry.

"Who? Bungay?" I questioned in surprise, for my thoughts were elsewhere. "Oh, he was like a cat, and there are trees at the rear. Probably he is safe long ago, or else a prisoner once more."

Beyond the gleam of the uncovered windows all was wrapped in complete darkness, save that here and there we could distinguish the dull red glare of camp-fires where the company cooks were yet at work, or some sentry post had been established. All the varied sounds of a congested camp at night were in the air — the champing and pounding of horses, the murmur of men's voices, the distant rumbling of heavy wagons, with an occasional shout, and the noise of axes. It was also evident, from the numerous flitting lanterns, like so many glow-worms, the late labors of the cooks, and other unmistakable signs, that active preparations for an early movement were already well under way.

We turned sharply to the left, and proceeded down a comparatively smooth road, which seemed to me to possess a rock basis, it felt so hard. From the position of the stars I judged our course to be eastward, but the night was sufficiently obscured to shroud all objects more than a few yards distant. Except for the varied camp noises on either side of us the evening was oppressively still, and the air had the late chill of high altitudes. Mrs. Brennan pressed more closely to me as we passed beyond the narrow zone of light, and unconsciously we fell into step together.

My Lady of the North

"Are you chilled?" I asked, bending my head toward her.

"Not in the least; but I must confess to nervousness."

I think we both recalled my wrapping her in the flapping cavalry cloak the night we were first alone together, for she added quickly: "I am quite warmly clothed, and have not far to go."

One often receives certain impressions without in the least knowing by what means they are conveyed — some peculiar trick of tone or manner teaching a lesson the lips refrain from expressing. Some such influence now, unconsciously exerted possibly, made me feel that my companion preferred to remain silent; that I could best prove my respect for her by quietly accepting her guidance without attempting converse. We walked slowly so as not to attract attention, as it was impossible to say that we were unobserved. Once she slipped upon a stone and I caught her, but neither spoke. Then there came the sudden clatter of hoofs on the rocky road behind us. I drew her swiftly aside within the protecting shadow of a tree, while a mounted officer rode by us at a slashing gait, his cavalry cape pulled high over his head, and the iron shoes of his horse striking fire from the flinty rocks. I could feel the heart of the girl beating wildly against my arm, but without exchanging so much as a word we crept back into the dark road and pressed on.

A few hundred yards farther a fire burned redly against a pile of logs. The forms of several men lay outstretched beside it, while a sentry paced back and forth, in and out of the range of light. We were almost upon him before he noted our approach, and in his haste he swung his musket down from his shoulder until the point of its bayonet nearly touched my breast.

Through the Camp of the Enemy

"Halt!" he cried sternly, peering at us in evident surprise. "Halt! this road is closed."

"Valley Forge," whispered the girl, and I noticed how white her face appeared in the flaming of the fire.

"The word is all right, Miss," returned the fellow, stoutly, yet without lowering his obstructing gun. "But we cannot pass any one out on the countersign alone. If you was going the other way it would answer."

"But we are returning from the officers' ball," she urged anxiously, "and are on our way to Major Brennan's quarters. We have passes."

As she drew the paper from out her glove one of the men at the fire sprang to his feet and strode across the narrow road toward us. He was smooth of face and boyish looking, but wore corporal's stripes.

"What is it, Mapes?" he asked sharply.

Without waiting an answer he took the paper she held out and scanned it rapidly.

"This is all right," he said, handing it back, and lifting his cap in salute. "You may pass, madam. You must pardon us, but the orders are exceedingly strict to-night. Have you a pass also, Colonel?" I handed it to him, and after a single glance it was returned.

"Pass them, guard," he said curtly, standing aside.

Beyond the radiance of the fire she broke the silence.

"I shall only be able to go with you so far as the summit of the hill yonder, for our quarters are just to the right, and I could furnish no excuse for being found beyond that point," she said. "Do you know enough of the country to make the lines of your army?"

"If this is the Kendallville pike we are on," I answered, "I have a pretty clear conception of what lies ahead,

155

but I should be very glad to know where I am to look for the outer picket."

"There is one post at the ford over the White Briar," she replied. "I chance to know this because Major Brennan selected the station, and remarked that the stream was so high and rapid as to be impassable at any other point for miles. But I regret this is as far as my information extends."

There was a moment of silence.

"But how may I ever sufficiently thank you for all you have done for me to-night?" I exclaimed warmly, pressing her arm to my side as I spoke, with the intensity of feeling which possessed me.

"I require no thanks, save as expressed by your silence," she returned, almost coldly, and slightly withdrawing herself. "I have merely repaid my indebtedness to you."

I started to say something — what I hardly know — when, almost without sound of warning, a little squad of horsemen swept over the brow of the hill in our front, their forms darkly outlined against the starlit sky, and rode down toward us at a sharp trot. I had barely time to swing my companion out of the track when they clattered by, their heads bent low to the wind, and seemingly oblivious to all save the movements of their leader.

"Sheridan!" I whispered, for even in that dimness I had not failed to recognize the short, erect figure which rode in front.

The woman shuddered, and drew closer within my protecting shadow. Then out of the darkness there burst a solitary rider, his horse limping as if crippled, and would have ridden us down, had I not flung up one hand and grasped his bridle-rein.

Through the Camp of the Enemy

"Great Scott! what have we here?" he cried roughly, peering down at us. "By all the gods, a woman!"

The hand upon my arm clutched me desperately, and my own heart seemed to choke back every utterance. The voice was Brennan's.

CHAPTER XVIII

THE REPUTATION OF A WOMAN

LIKE a flash occurred to me the only possible means by which we might escape open discovery — an instant disclosure of my supposed rank, coupled with indignant protest. Already, believing me merely some private soldier straying out of bounds with a woman of the camp as companion, he had thrown himself from the saddle to investigate. Whatever was to be done must be accomplished quickly, or it would prove all too late. To think was to act. Stepping instantly in front of the shrinking girl and facing him, I said sternly:

"I do not know who you may chance to be, sir, nor greatly care, yet your words and actions imply an insult to this lady which I am little disposed to overlook. For your information permit me to state, I am Colonel Curran, Sixth Ohio Light Artillery, and am not accustomed to being halted on the road by every drunken fool who sports a uniform."

He stopped short in complete surprise, staring at me through the darkness, and I doubted not was perfectly able to distinguish the glint of buttons and gleam of braid.

"Your pardon, sir," he ejaculated at last. "I mistook you for some runaway soldier. But I failed to catch your words; how did you name yourself?"

"Colonel Curran, of Major-General Halleck's staff."

"The hell you are! Curran had a full gray beard a month ago."

The Reputation of a Woman

He took a step forward, and before I could recover from the first numbing shock of surprise was peering intently into my face.

"Damn it!" he cried, tugging viciously at a revolver in his belt, "I know that face! You are the measly Johnny Reb I brought in day before yesterday."

I could mark the flash of the stars on the blue steel of his pistol barrel, and knew from the eager ring of his voice he exulted in the hope that I would give him excuse to fire. Yet I thought in that moment of but one thing — the woman who had compromised her name to help me to attain freedom. I would have died a thousand deaths if it might only be with my hands at his throat, her story unknown. Yet even as I braced my body for the leap, gazing straight into that deadly barrel, there came a quick flutter of drapery at my side, and she, pressing me firmly backward, faced him without a word.

The man's extended arm dropped to his side as though pierced by a bullet, and he took one step backward, shrinking as if his startled eyes beheld a ghost.

"Edith?" he cried, as though doubting his own vision, and the ring of agony in his voice was almost piteous. "Edith! My God! You here, at midnight, alone with this man?"

However the words, the tone, the gesture may have stung her, her face remained proudly calm, her voice cold and clear.

"I certainly am, Major Brennan," she answered, her eyes never once leaving his face. "And may I ask what reason you can have to object?"

"Reason?" His voice had grown hoarse with passion and surprise. "My God, how can you ask? How can you even face me? Why do you not sink down

159

in shame? Alone here," — he looked about him into the darkness, — "at such an hour, in company with a Rebel, a sneaking, cowardly spy, already condemned to be shot. By Heaven! he shall never live to boast of it!"

He flung up his revolver barrel to prove the truth of his threat, but she stepped directly between us, and shielded me with her form.

"Put down your pistol," she ordered coldly. "I assure you my reputation is in no immediate danger unless you shoot me, and your bullet shall certainly find my heart before it ever reaches Captain Wayne."

"Truly, you must indeed love him," he sneered.

So close to me was she standing that I could feel her form tremble at this insult, yet her voice remained emotionless.

"Your uncalled-for words shame me, not my actions. In being here with Captain Wayne to-night I am merely paying a simple debt of honor — a double debt, indeed, considering that he was condemned to death by your lie, while you deceived me by another."

"Did he tell you that?"

"He did not. Like the true gentleman he has ever shown himself to be, he endeavored to disguise the facts, to withhold from me all knowledge of your dastardly action. I know it by the infamous sentence pronounced against him and by your falsehood to me."

"Edith, you mistake," he urged anxiously. "I — I was told that he had been sent North."

She drew a deep breath, as though she could scarcely grasp the full audacity of his pretence to ignorance.

"You appeared to be fully informed but now as to his death sentence."

The Reputation of a Woman

" Yes, I heard of it while away, and intended telling you as soon as I reached our quarters."

I could feel the scorn of his miserable deception as it curled her lip, and her figure seemed to straighten between us.

" Then," she said slowly, " you will doubtless agree that I have done no more than was right, and will there-fore permit him this chance of escape from so unmerited a fate; for you know as well as I do that he has been wrongly condemned."

He stepped forward with a half-smothered oath, and rested one hand heavily upon her shoulder.

" An exceedingly neat trap," he said, with a grim laugh, " a most ingenious snare; yet hardly one I am likely to be caught in. I am not quite so green, my lady. What! let that fellow go? become the laughing stock of you and your Johnny Reb lover? I rather guess not, madam. Damn him! I will hang him now higher than Haman, just to show Queen Esther that it can be done. Out of the way, madam!"

Rendered desperate by her slight resistance and his own jealous hatred, he thrust the woman aside so rudely that she fell forward upon one knee. His revolver was yet in his right hand, gleaming in the starlight, but before he could raise or fire it I had grasped the steel barrel firmly, and the hammer came down noiselessly upon the flesh of my thumb. The next instant we were locked close together in fierce struggle for the mastery. He was the heavier, stronger man; I the younger and quicker. From the first every effort on both sides was put forth solely to gain command of the weapon, — his to fire, mine to prevent, for I knew well at the sound of the discharge there would come a rush of blue-coats to his rescue. My first fierce onset had put him on the defensive, but as we tugged and strained his superiority in weight began to tell, and slowly he bore me backward, desperately contesting every inch I was thus compelled to yield.

We struggled voiceless, neither having breath for useless speech, and each realizing that the end would probably mean death either to the one or the other. Only our heavy breathing, the quick shuffling of feet on the stony road, and an occasional rending of cloth, evinced the desperation in which we strove. Once, as we turned partially in the struggle, I caught a passing glimpse of the woman standing helpless, her face buried in her hands, and the sight yielded me new strength and determination. For her sake I must win! Even as this thought came, my burly antagonist pressed me backward until all the weight of my body rested upon my right leg. Then there occurred to me like a flash a wrestler's trick taught me years before by an old negro on my father's plantation. Instantly I appeared to yield to the force against which I contended with simulated weakness, sinking lower and lower, until, I doubt not, Brennan felt convinced I must go over backward. But as I thus sank, my left foot found steady support farther back, while my free hand sank slowly down his straining body until my groping fingers grasped firmly the broad belt about his waist. I yielded yet another inch, until he leaned so far over me as to be out of all balance, and then, with sudden straightening of my left leg, at the same time forcing my head beneath his chest in leverage, with one tremendous effort I flung him, head under, crashing down upon the hard road.

Trembling like a reed from the exertion, I stood there

The Reputation of a Woman

looking down upon the dark form lying huddled at my feet. He rested motionless, and I bent over, placing my hand upon his heart, horrified at the mere thought that he might be dead. But the heart beat, and with a prayer of thankfulness I looked up. She stood beside me.

"Tell me, Captain Wayne," she exclaimed anxiously, "he is not — not seriously hurt?"

The words thoroughly aroused me, and I recalled instantly her probable relationship to this man, her delicate position now.

"I believe not," I answered soberly. "He is a heavy man, and fell hard, yet his heart beats strong. He must have cut his head upon a stone, however, for he is bleeding."

She knelt beside him, and I caught the whiteness of a handkerchief within her hand.

"Believe me, Mrs. Brennan," I faltered lamely, "I regret this far more than I can tell. Nothing has ever occurred to me to give greater pain than the thought that I have brought you so much of sorrow and trouble."

She held up her hand to me, and I took it humbly.

"It was in no way your fault; pray do not consider that I can ever blame you for the outcome."

Her eyes were upon me; I could view her face in the starlight, and for the moment I utterly forgot the man who rested there between us.

"If you could only know," I exclaimed eagerly, "how sincerely I long to serve you, — to atone in some small way for all the difficulty I have brought into your life; how my heart throbs to your presence as to that of no other living woman —"

She hushed my impetuous words with the gesture of a queen, and rose to her feet facing me. Under the stars

163

our eyes looked into each other, and her face was very white.

"You must not," she said firmly, and I thought she glanced down upon the motionless figure at her feet. "I have trusted you; do not cause me to regret it now."

I bowed, humiliated to the very depths of my soul.

"Your rebuke is perfectly just," I answered slowly. "God knows I shall never be guilty again. You will have faith in me?"

"Always, everywhere — whether it ever be our fate to meet again or not. But now you must go."

"Go? And leave you here alone? Are you not afraid?"

"Afraid?" she looked about her into the darkness. "Of what? Surely you do not mean of Frank — of Major Brennan? And as to my being alone, our quarters are within a scant hundred yards from here, and a single cry will bring me aid in plenty. Hush! what was that?"

It was the shuffling tread of many feet, the sturdy tramp of a body of infantry on the march.

"Go!" she cried hurriedly. "If you would truly serve me, if you care at all for me, do not longer delay and be discovered here. It is the grand rounds. I beg of you, go!"

I grasped her outstretched hand, pressed my lips hotly upon it, and sped with noiseless footsteps down the black, deserted road.

CHAPTER XIX

THE CAVALRY OUTPOST

I LINGERED merely long enough to feel assured as to her safety, creeping closer until I heard her simple story of the Major's fall from his horse, and then watched through the night shadows while the little squad bore his unconscious form over the crest of the low hill toward their quarters. Then I turned my face eastward and tramped resolutely on.

The excitement of the night, and especially the sharp, fierce struggle with Brennan, had reawakened all my old military enthusiasm, and I felt every nerve tingling anew as I breasted the long slope before me. Even the depression naturally resulting from my unhappy parting with Edith Brennan gave way for the time being to this sense of surrounding danger, while the ardor of youth responded joyfully to the spirit of adventure. I simply would not think of what I had lost; certainly would not permit its memory to depress me. I was, first of all, a soldier, and nothing short of death or capture should prevent me reaching Lee with my message. Let what would happen, all else could wait!

The gleam of the stars fell upon the double row of buttons down the breast of the coat I wore, and I stopped suddenly with an exclamation of disgust. Nothing could be gained by longer masquerade, and I felt inexpressible shame at being thus attired. Neither pass nor uniform would suffice to get me safe through those outer picket lines, and if I should fall in the attempt, or be again made prisoner, I vastly preferred meeting my fate clad in the faded gray of my own regiment. With odd sense of relief I hastily stripped off the gorgeous trappings, flung them in the ditch beside the road, and pressed on, feeling like a new man.

There was small need for caution here, and for more than an hour I tramped steadily along, never meeting a person or being startled by a suspicious sound. Then, as I rounded a low eminence I perceived before me the dark outline of trees which marked the course of the White Briar, while directly in my front, and half obscured by thick leaves of the underbrush, blazed the red glare of a fire. I knew the stream well, its steep banks of precipitate rock, its rapid, swirling current which, I was well aware, I was not a sufficiently expert swimmer to cross. Once upon the other bank I should be comparatively safe, but to pass that picket post and attain the ford was certain to require all the good fortune I could ever hope for.

But despair was never for long my comrade, and I had learned how determination opens doors to the courageous — it is ever he who tries that enters in. It took me ten minutes, possibly, creeping much of the way like a wild animal over the rocks, but at the end of that time I had attained a position well within the dense thicket, and could observe clearly the ground before me and some of the obstacles to be overcome.

As I supposed, it was a cavalry outpost; I could distinguish the crossed sabres on the caps of the men, although it was some time before I was able to determine positively where their horses were picketed. There must

The Cavalry Outpost

have been all of twenty in the party, and I could distinguish the lieutenant in command, a middle-aged man
with light-colored chin beard, seated by himself against
the wall of a small shanty of logs, a pipe in his mouth
and an open book upon his knee. His men were gathered
close about the blazing fire, for the night air was decidedly
chill as it swept down the valley; a number were sleeping, a few at cards, while a little group, sitting with their
backs toward me, yet almost within reach of my hand,
were idly smoking and discussing the floating rumors
of the camp. I managed to make out dimly the figure
of a man on horseback beyond the range of flame, and
apparently upon the very bank of the stream, when some
words spoken by an old gray-bearded sergeant interested
me.

"Bob," he said to the soldier lounging next him, "whut
wus it thet staff officer sed ter ther leftenant? I did n't
just git ther straight of it."

The man, a debonair young fellow, stroked his little
black moustache reflectively.

"Ther cove sed as how Cole's division wud be along
here afore daylight, an' thet our fellers wud likely be
sent out ahead of 'em."

"Whar be they a goin'?"

"The leftenant asked him, an' the cove sed as it wus
a gineral advance to meet ol' Hancock at Minersville."

"Thet 's good 'nough, lads," chimed in the sergeant,
slapping his knee. "It means a dance down the valley
after Early. I 'm a guessin' we 'll have a bang-up ol'
fight 'fore three days more."

"Pervidin' allers thet ther Johnnies don't skedaddle
fust," commented another, tartly. "Whut in thunder is
ther matter with them hosses?" he asked suddenly, rising

and peering over into the bushes beyond the hut, where a noise of squealing and kicking had arisen.

"Oh, the bay filly is probably over the rope agin," returned the sergeant, lazily. "Sit down, Sims, an' be easy; you 're not on hoss guard ternight."

"I know thet," growled the soldier, doubtfully, "but thet thar kid is no good, an' I don't want my hoss all banged up jist as we 're goin' on campaign. 'T ain't no sorter way ter hitch 'em anyhow, to a picket rope; ruins more hosses than ther Rebs dew."

This gave me inspiration, and before the speaker's sullen growl had wholly ceased I was again upon hands and knees, silently groping my way along the bank toward the rear of the hut. It proved to be a tiny structure, containing but a single room — probably a mere fisherman's shack, without windows, but possessing a door at either end. Meeting no opposition I crept within, where I felt somewhat safer from observation, and then peered warily forth into the darkness extending between it and the river. The picket-rope stretched from one corner of the hut, where it seemed to be secured around the end of a projecting log, out into the night, evidently finding its other terminus at a big tree whose spreading top I could dimly perceive shadowed against the sky. Along it were tethered the horses, a few impatiently champing their bits and pounding with their hoofs on the trampled ground, but the majority resting quietly, their heads hanging sleepily down. The one nearest me appeared a finely proportioned animal of a dark color, and was equipped with both saddle and bridle. Of the soldier in charge I could distinguish nothing — doubtless he was lounging on his back, half asleep upon some soft patch of grass.

The Cavalry Outpost

My plan was conceived instantly. It was a desperate one, yet it alone seemed in the least feasible. If by chance it succeeded it would place me in saddle once more, and to a cavalryman that means everything; while if it failed — ah, well, it was merely a toss-up of the coin. I turned, impatient for the trial, when it suddenly occurred to me that the deserted hut might contain something I could use to advantage, — a firearm, perhaps, or even a stray box of matches. I felt about me cautiously, creeping along the hard earthen floor until I had nearly reached the opposite entrance. The light from the fire without leaped up, and its glow revealed a saddle, with leather holster attached, hanging to a nail just within the doorway. Moving noiselessly I managed to extract a revolver, but could discover no cartridges.

I was yet fumbling in the holster pocket when the lieutenant rose from his seat without, knocked the ashes from his pipe, yawned sleepily, standing directly between me and the fire, and then, turning sharply, walked slowly into the open door of the hut. I sprang to my feet, or he would certainly have stepped upon me, and before he could realize the situation I had him by the collar, with the cold muzzle of my stolen revolver pressed hard against his cheek.

"A single word or sound, and I fire!" I said sternly.

I have no recollection of ever seeing any man more completely astounded. He gasped like a fish newly landed, and I doubt if he could have made utterance even had he dared.

"Come in a little farther," I commanded. "Now look here, Lieutenant, you do exactly as I tell you and you will get out of this affair with a whole skin; otherwise — well, I'm playing this game to the limit."

My Lady of the North

"Who in hell are you?" he gasped finally, recovering some slight power of expression.

"Never mind, friend. I am simply a man with a gun at your head, and sufficiently desperate to use it if necessary; that's enough for you to know and reflect over. Now answer me: How many men have you mounted this side the ford?"

He glared at me sullenly, and I drew back the hammer with an ominous click, eying him fiercely.

"Well," I said shortly, "do you choose to answer, or die?"

"Two."

"On the other bank?"

"None."

Standing thus, covering him with the gun, and marking his slightest movement, I thought quickly. Years of danger teach concentrated thought, prompt decision, and I soon chose my course. To kill in battle is soldierly, but, if possible to avoid it, there should be no killing here.

"Lieutenant," I said, speaking low, but in a tone which left no doubt as to my exact meaning, "I am an escaped prisoner, and shall not hesitate to kill rather than be recaptured. It is your life or mine to-night, and I naturally prefer my own; but I'll give you one chance, and only one — obey my orders and I will leave you here unhurt: disobey, and your life is not worth the snap of a finger. Move back now until you face the door, and don't forget my pistol is within an inch of your ear, and this is a hair trigger. What is your sergeant's name?"

"Handley."

"Order him to take ten men on foot one hundred yards west on the pike, and wait further orders."

The Cavalry Outpost

The lieutenant twisted his head about and looked at me, his eyes stubborn with anger.

"If you have a wife up North, and care anything about seeing her again," I said coolly, "you will do exactly as I say."

"Handley," he called out, his voice so choked with rage as to make me fearful it might arouse suspicion, "take ten men on foot to the cross-roads, and wait there until you hear from me."

I could plainly note the dark shadows of the fellows as they filed out past the fire, but I never ventured to take eye or gun off the man I watched.

"How many remain there now?"

"Seven."

"Any non-com. among them?"

"A corporal."

"Have him take them all south on the cross-roads."

The man squirmed like an eel, and I was soldier enough to sympathize with him; yet every time he turned his head he looked death squarely in the face, and I doubt not thought of some one he loved in that distant North. I clicked the hammer suggestively.

"Come, friend," I said meaningly, "time flies."

"Jones," he called out huskily.

"Yes, sir?"

"Take what men you have left a hundred yards south on the cross-road."

We could hear them crunching their way through the bushes, until the sound finally died out in the distance.

"Now, Lieutenant, you come with me — softly, and keep your distance."

We moved back slowly, step by step, until we came to the rear door of the shed. I reached out into the darkness, but without turning my face away from him, and silently severed the picket-rope, retaining the loosened end in my grasp. It was so intensely dark where we stood that I slipped the pistol unobserved into my belt.

" Face to the rear," I said sternly.

As he turned to obey this order, with quick movement I tripped him, sprang backward, and shut the door.

In a single bound I was upon the back of the black, and had flung the severed rope's end at the flank of the next horse in line. There was a rush of feet, a sharp snapping of cords, a wild scurrying through the bushes, as twenty frightened horses stampeded up the bank, and then, lying face down over the saddle pommel, I sent the startled black crashing down into the shallows of the ford. The fellow on guard tried his best to stop us, but we were past him like the wind. He did not fire, and doubtless in the darkness saw merely a stray horse broken from the picket-rope. The other fellow took one swift shot, but it went wild, and I heard the voice of the enraged lieutenant damning in the distance. Then with a rush we went up the steep bank on the eastern shore, and I sat upright in the saddle and gave the black his rein.

CHAPTER XX

A DEMON ON HORSEBACK

I FELT positively happy then. The thrill of successful achievement was mine, and with the exultation of a soldier in having surmounted obstacles and peril, I nearly forgot for the moment the heart tragedy left behind. The swift impetus of the ride, the keen night air sweeping past me, the fresh sense of freedom and power engendered by that reckless dash through the darkness, all conspired to render me neglectful of everything save the joy of present victory. The spirit of wild adventure was in my blood.

A dozen spits of fire cleaved the intense blackness behind, and I knew the widely scattered patrol were sending chance shots across the stream. A clang of hoofs rang out upon the rocks, but I could distinguish nothing indicating a large pursuing party — probably the two who were mounted at the ford, with possibly others following when they caught their strayed horses. I had little to fear from such half-hearted pursuit as this was sure to be. The swift, powerful stride of the animal I rode assured me that I was not ill mounted, and there was small chance of contact with Federal outriders before I should reach the protecting picket lines of our own army. I laughed grimly as I leaned slightly back in saddle and listened; it was like a play, so swift and exciting had been the passing events, so unexpected their ending. I wondered what plausible story the discomfited lieutenant would concoct to account for his predicament, and whether the others had yet missed me back at the Mansion House.

The stars appeared to be paling somewhat down in the east, for the coming day-dawn was already whitening the horizon. I glanced at my watch, venturing to strike a match for the purpose, and found the hour after three o'clock. Early, I knew, was at Sowder Church, and his advance cavalry pickets ought to be as far west as the Warrentown road. The distance between, by hard riding, might be covered in three hours. My horse seemed fresh, his breath came naturally and without effort, and I pressed him along rapidly, for my whole ambition now centred upon bringing the information I possessed within our own lines. Bungay, beyond doubt, had been recaptured long since, for my own experience told me how extremely vigilant were the Federal guards. To one unacquainted as he was with military customs it would prove impossible to penetrate their lines; hence, everything must depend upon my getting through in safety.

Then my thoughts drifted to the one I had left in such serious predicament. If I had loved her before, I loved her doubly now, for she had proven herself a woman among women in time of danger and trial. How clearly her face, with those dark sweet eyes and the wealth of crowning hair, rose before me, while word by word I reviewed all that had passed between us, dwelling upon each look or accent that could evince her possible interest in me. Then reason returned to my aid, and resolutely, determinedly, inspired by every instinct of soldierly honor, I resolved that I would put her from my thoughts for ever. She was not mine either to love or possess, unless the uncertain fate of war should chance to set her free. Even to dream of her, to cherish her in memory while she

A Demon on Horseback

remained the wife of another, was but an affront to her purity and womanhood. I would prove myself a man entitled to her respect, a soldier worthy my service and corps; if ever again my name chanced to find mention in her presence it should be spoken with honor.

I was musing thus, lulled by the steady lope of my horse, and totally insensible to any possibility of peril, when clear upon my ears, instantly awakening me from such reverie, there rang through the night silence the sharp clang of iron on the road behind me. All sound of pursuit had long since died away, and I supposed the effort to recapture me had been abandoned. But there was no mistaking now — at least one horseman, riding recklessly through the black night, was pressing hot upon my trail.

"The lieutenant," I thought, "the lieutenant, burning with anger at the trick played upon him, has pushed far ahead of his troop, doubtless mounted upon a better horse, determined to risk everything if he may only bring me back dead or alive."

This thought awoke me in an instant from my dreaming, and I spurred my horse furiously, glancing anxiously backward as I rode, but unable through that dense gloom to distinguish the form of my pursuer. Yet the fellow was coming, coming faster than any speed I could possibly conjure out of the weary black I bestrode, either by whip or spur. Closer and closer upon me came rushing down that pounding of iron hoofs on the hard path. Heavens! how like a very demon the man rode! As a trooper I could not withhold admiration from the reckless audacity with which the vengeful fellow bore down upon me. In spite of my utmost efforts it almost seemed as if we were standing still. Surely nothing less than hate, and a thirst for vengeance bitter as death, implacable as fate, could ride like that through the black night on the track of a hunted man!

I was able to trace dimly his outlines now as he rose on an eminence in my rear, his horse looming dark against the sky, like those giant steeds that snorted fire in my child's picture-books at home, and then, with increasingly loud thunder of hoof-beats, he came charging straight down toward me. In sheer desperation I glanced on either side, seeking some avenue of escape, but the high banks were unscalable; my sole remaining hope lay in a shot which should drop that crazed brute before he struck and crushed me. Riding my best, with all the practised skill of the service, I swung my body sideways, bracing myself firmly in the deep saddle, and took steady aim. The hammer came down with a dull, dead click, the revolver was chargeless, and with an exclamation of baffled rage I hurled the useless weapon full at the advancing brute. Almost at the instant we struck, my horse went down with the impetus, while over us both, as if shot from a cannon, plunged our pursuer, his horse turning a complete somersault, the rider falling so close that I was upon him almost as soon as he struck the ground.

A dip of the flying hoof had cut a shallow gash across my forehead, and my hair was wet with blood, yet bruised and half stunned as I was from the hard fall, my sole longing was to reach and throttle that madman who had ridden me down in such demon style.

"You unchained devil!" I cried savagely, whirling him over upon his back, "I spared your life once to-night, but, by all the gods, I'll not do it again!"

"Gosh, Cap, is thet you?" asked the voice of the other, feebly.

A Demon on Horseback

I started back, and lost my hold upon him.

"Bungay?" in an astonishment that nearly robbed me of utterance. "Good God, man! is this really you?"

"It's whut's left o' me," he answered solemnly, sitting up and feeling his head as if expecting to find it gone. "Thet wus 'bout ther worst ride ever I took."

"I should think it likely," I exclaimed, my anger rising again as I thought of it. "What, in Heaven's name, do you mean by riding down on me like that?"

"Holy Gee, Cap," he explained penitently, "ye don't go ter think I ever did it a purpose, do ye? Why, ther gosh-durned old thing run away."

"Ran away?"

"Sure; I've bin a hangin' on ter ther mane o' thet critter fer nigh 'pon three mile, an' a prayin' fer a feather bed ter light on. It's my last 'listment en ther cavalry, ye bet. I never seed none o' yer steam keers, but I reckon they don't go no faster ner thet blame hoss. Gosh, Cap, ye ain't got no call fer ter git mad; I couldn't a stopped her with a yoke o' steers, durned if I cud. I sorter reckon I know now 'bout whut Scott meant when he said, 'The turf the flying courser spurn'd,' — you bet this en did."

Jed rubbed his cheek as if it stung him, and I looked at him in the faint dawning light of day, and laughed. His peaked head and weazen face looked piteous enough, decorated as they were with the black loam through which he had ploughed; his coat was ripped from tail to collar, while one of his eyes was nearly closed where the bruised flesh had puffed up over it.

"'It is a fearful strife, for man endowed with mortal life,'" he quoted mournfully.

My Lady of the North

"You 're right," I assented. " No doubt you had the worst of it. But how came you here?"

"Why, I wus a huntin' fer a hoss thar et ther picket post whin ye scared up ther bunch, an' by some sort a fule luck I got hole o' thet one, an' tuke arter ye, tho' in course I did n't know who it wus raised sich a rumpus, it wus so durned dark. Ther whole blame Yankee caboodle tuke a blaze et me, I reckon, leastwise they wus most durn keerless with ther shootin' irons, an' I rode one feller over, knocked him plum off his hoss down ther bank, kerslush inter ther water, by thunder, an' then ther derned critter I wus a straddlin' bolted. Thet 's 'bout all I know, Cap, till I lit yere."

There was no doubting the truth of his story, and I held out my hand. "You 're a good man, Jed," I said heartily, "and so long as we are both alive, a few hard jolts won't hurt us. Let 's see if the horses are in any condition for service."

A single glance told the story. The black mare was browsing by the roadside, apparently little the worse for the shock, although a thin line of blood trickled slowly down her flank. But the big roan had not been so fortunate, and lay, head under, stone dead in the middle of the narrow road. Bungay gazed at the motionless figure mournfully.

" 'Woe worth the chase, woe worth the day, that cost thy life, my gallant gray,'" he recited solemnly, " only it 's a roan, an' I ain't so durn sorry either."

Regrets of any nature, however, were vain, and as the little man positively refused to ride, I mounted again. He trudging along manfully beside me, the two of us set forth once more, our faces turned toward the red dawn.

CHAPTER XXI

REINFORCEMENTS FOR EARLY

"COME, Wayne, wake up, man! Captain, I say, you must turn out of this."

I opened my eyes with a struggle and looked up. The golden glow of sunlight along the white wall told me the day must be already well advanced, and I saw the lieutenant of my troop, Colgate, bending over me, attired in service uniform.

"What is it, Jack?"

"We have been ordered north on forced march to join Early, and the command has already started. I have delayed calling you until the final moment, but knew you would never forgive being left behind."

Before he had finished I was upon the floor, dressing with that rapidity acquired by years of practice, my mind thoroughly aroused to the thought of active service once more.

"Was it the news I brought in yesterday, Colgate, which has stirred this up?" I questioned, hastily dipping into a basin of water.

"I imagine it must have been, sir," replied the Lieutenant, leaning back comfortably upon a cracker-box, which formed our solitary chair. "Things have been on the move ever since, and it certainly resembles an advance of some importance. Staff officers at it all night long,

179

My Lady of the North

McDaniel's division off at daylight, while we go out ahead of Slayton's troops. Reede was in beastly good humor when he brought the orders; that usually means a fight."

"Any artillery?"

"Sloan's and Rocke's batteries are with us; did not learn who went out with McDaniel's. Longstreet has crossed the White Briar."

"Yes, I know," I said, drawing on the last of my equipments, and quickly glancing about to assure myself I had overlooked nothing likely to be of value. "All ready, Jack, and now for another ' dance of death.' "

Our regiment was drawn up in the square of the little town, and as we came forth into the glorious sunlight, the stentorian voice of the Colonel called them into column of fours. Staff officers, gray with dust from their all-night service, were riding madly along the curb, while at the rear of our men, just debouching from one of the side streets, appeared the solid front of a division of infantry. We had barely time to swing into the saddles of the two horses awaiting us, and ride swiftly to the head of our command, when the short, stern orders rolled along the motionless line of troopers, and the long, silent column swung out to the northward, the feet of the horses raising a thick cloud of red dust which fairly enveloped us in its choking folds.

With the ardor of young manhood I looked forward to the coming battle, when I knew the mighty armies of North and South would once again contest for the fertile Shenandoah. It was to be American pitted against American, a struggle ever worthy of the gods. Slowly I rode back down the files of my men, marking their alignment and accoutrements with practised eye, smiling grimly as I noted their eager faces, war-worn and bronzed by exposure, yet reanimated by hope of active service. Boys half of them appeared to be, yet I knew them as fire-tested veterans of many hard-fought fields, lads who would die without a murmur beneath their beloved Southern flag, as undaunted in hour of peril as were the Old Guard at Waterloo. In spite of frayed and ragged uniforms, tarnished, battered facings, dingy, flapping hats, they looked stanch and true, soldiers every inch of them, and I marked with the jealous pride of command their evenly closed ranks and upright carriage. How like some giant machine they moved — horses and men — in trained and disciplined power!

As I watched them thus, I thought again of those many other faces who once rode as these men did now, but who had died for duty even as these also might yet be called upon to die. One hundred and three strong, gay in bright new uniforms, with unstained banner kissing the breeze above our proud young heads, we rode hopefully forth from Charlottesville scarce three years before, untried, undisciplined, unknown, to place our lives willingly upon the sacred altar of our native State. What speechless years of horror those had been; what history we had written with our naked steel; what scenes of suffering and death lay along that bloody path we travelled! To-day, down the same red road, our eyes still set grimly to the northward, our flag a torn and ragged remnant, barely forty men wore the " D " between the crossed sabres on their slouched brown hats, in spite of all recruiting. The cheer in my heart was for the living; the tear in my eye was for the dead.

" Colgate," I said gravely, as I ranged up beside him at the rear of the troop, " the men look exceedingly well, and do not appear to have suffered greatly because of short rations."

"Oh, the lads are always in fine fettle when they expect a fight," he answered, his own eyes dancing as he swept them over that straight line of backs in his front. "They'll scrap the better for being a bit hungry, — it makes them savage. Beats all, Captain, what foolish notions some of those people on the other side have of us Southerners. They seem to think we are entirely different from themselves; yet I reckon it would puzzle any recruiting officer up yonder to show a finer lot of fighting men than those fellows ahead there. 'Food for powder?' Why, there is n't a lad among them unfit for command."

In spite of the indignation in his tone, his voice had the lazy, Southern drawl, and somehow, as he spoke, I thought of my fair prisoner in the mountains, and of how disdainfully she treated me on the occasion of our first meeting. I sincerely hoped her conception of the Southerner had received partial revision since.

"Well, yes," I answered thoughtfully. "Doubtless those who have never visited the South, and who form their conception of us from Northern newspapers and abolition orators, get hold of our worst characteristics, and judge accordingly. I sometimes feel that the whole trouble between the sections is merely such a misunderstanding on a large scale, and that had we only intermingled more freely, many of our differences would have disappeared. In this we are fully as wrong as those of the other side — narrowness of thought and life has been the secret force behind this war. Partisans upon both sides have ignored the fact that we are all of one blood and one history. But in this respect the tendency of the conflict has been to broaden out the actual participants, and teach them mutual respect. I imagine women are at present more apt to retain this prejudice, women whose loved ones are in arms against us."

"I was thinking about a woman when I spoke," he explained gravely. "She was certainly a beauty, and nursed me in the hospital at Baltimore. Oh, you need n't smile; she was married, — her husband was on Sheridan's staff; I saw him once, a big fellow with a black moustache. Of course we all looked alike lying there in those cots, and she very naturally supposed I was one of their wounded, until after the fever left me, and I became able to converse a bit, and then you ought to have seen the expression in her eyes when I confessed the truth. Actually she cried out, 'You a Rebel?' and gazed at me as if I had been some dangerous wild animal. Truly I believe she nearly looked upon herself as a traitress because she had nursed me and saved my life. Yet she was wonderfully tender-hearted and kind. You see she was n't a regular army nurse, and I was probably the first Confederate soldier she had ever come in close contact with."

"Did you become friends?"

"Most certainly; at least in a way, for she undertook my conversion. Frankly, if it had n't been for that inconvenient husband in the path, I am not so certain you would n't have lost a lieutenant. The fact that the lady was already Mrs. Brennan alone saved me."

"Mrs. Brennan!" Although the disclosure was not altogether unexpected, I could not help echoing the name.

"Certainly," in sudden surprise, and glancing aside at my face. "Can it be possible that you know her? Not more than twenty, I should say, with great clear, honest eyes, and a perfect wealth of hair that appears auburn in the sun."

"I had the privilege of meeting her once or twice briefly while in Sheridan's lines," I answered hurriedly, "and have reason to indorse all you say regarding the lady, especially as to her dislike of everything clad in gray uniform. But the men appear to be straggling somewhat, Lieutenant; perhaps it would be as well to brace them up a bit."

I rode slowly forward to my own position at the head of the troop, wondering at the strange coincidence which had placed Edith Brennan's name upon Colgate's lips. Her memory had been brought back to me with renewed freshness by his chance words, and so strongly did it haunt me as to be almost a visible presence. As I swung my horse into our accustomed position I was too deeply buried in reflection to be clearly conscious of much that was occurring about me. Suddenly, however, I became aware that some one, nearly obscured by the enveloping cloud of dust, was riding without the column, in an independence of military discipline not to be permitted. In the state of mind I was then in this discovery strangely irritated me.

"Sergeant," I questioned sharply, of the raw-boned trooper at the end of the first platoon, "what fellow is that riding out yonder?"

"It's ther pesky little cuss as come in with ye yesterday, sir," he returned with a grin. "He's confiscated a muel somewhar an' says he's a goin' back hum 'long o' we uns."

Curious to learn how Jed had emerged from his arduous adventures, I spurred my horse alongside of him.

Reinforcements for Early

The little man, bending forward dubiously, as if fearful of accident, was riding bareback on a gaunt, long-legged mule, which, judging from all outward appearances, must have been some discarded asset of the quarter-master's department. The animal was evidently a complete wreck, and drooped along, dragging one foot heavily after the other as if every move were liable to be the last, his head hanging dejectedly, while his long ears flopped solemnly over the half-closed eyes at each step. Altogether the two composed so melancholy a picture it was with difficulty I suppressed my strong inclination to laugh.

"Going home, Jed?" I asked, as he glanced up and saw me.

"Jist as durn quick as I kin git thar," he returned emphatically. "By gum, Cap, I ain't bin 'way from Mariar long as this afore in twelve year. Reckon she thinks I've skedaddled fer good this time, an' 'ill be a takin' up with some other male critter lest I git back thar mighty sudden. Women's odd, Cap, durn nigh as ornary 'bout some things as a muel."

"I have never enjoyed much experience with them," I said, "but I confess to knowing something about mules. Now that seems to be rather an extraordinary specimen you are riding."

He eyed his mount critically.

"Durned if ever I thought I'd git astraddle o' any four-legged critter agin," he said, rubbing himself as if in sudden and painful recollection of the past. "But I sorter picked up this yere muel down et ther corral, an' he's tew durn wore out a totin' things fer you uns ter ever move offen a walk. I sorter reckon it's a heap easier a sittin' yere than ter take it afut all ther way ter ther mountings."

My Lady of the North

"He certainly has the appearance of being perfectly safe, but you know a mule is always full of tricks."

"Oh, this en ain't," confidently. "Why, he's so durn wore out a yankin' things 'round thet he's bin plum asleep all ther way out yere. Say, Cap, be it true thet a muel will wake up an' git a move on itself if ye blow in his ear?"

"Who told you that?"

"The feller down et ther quartermaster's corral. He said as how thet wus ther way ther niggers got 'em ter go 'long whin they got tew durn lazy. Blamed if I don't b'lieve I'll try it jist fer onst, fer I'd like durn well ter git ahead out o' this pesky dust."

I had never before seen such an experiment tried, but a slight knowledge of the nature of the animal involved induced me to rein back my horse, and to that precaution I have no doubt I owe my life. Jed blew only once; he lacked opportunity to do more, for a shock of electricity could never have more quickly aroused that mule. His long ears were erected with a snap, his short, spike tail shot out straight, while his heels cut the air in furious semicircles, as he backed viciously. I heard a yell from Jed, saw him clasp his arms lovingly about the animal's neck, caught a confused glimpse of the wildly cavorting figure amid the red dust cloud, and then, rear on, and lashing out crazily, that juggernaut of a mule struck the unsuspecting advancing column of troopers, and plunged half through their close-set ranks before they even realized what had happened. Horses plunged wildly to escape; here and there a man went down in the crush; oaths, blows, shouts of anger rang out, while beneath the dense dust cloud frightened horses and startled riders struggled fiercely to escape. For the

186

moment it was pandemonium in earnest, and I could only trace the disastrous passage of Bungay by the shouts of angry men and the sharp cries of injured horses.

"Captain Wayne, what does all this mean, sir? What is the cause of the disorder in your troop?"

It was the Major's voice, stern, indignant, commanding. I dashed the tears of laughter from my eyes, and strove to face him decorously.

"A mule, sir, which has taken a fit of kicking. I will straighten them out in a moment."

I wheeled, and peered into the rolling, surging mass of dust, out of which there arose such a hubbub of sounds as to make the noise of battle tame by comparison.

"Catch the brute by the bridle, two of you," I roared stoutly. "Craig, Whortley, what are you hanging back for? Go in there! Take hold of the devil from in front; there is no danger at that end."

The stern words of command, the return of discipline, seemed to steady that seething, fighting mass in an instant; there was a squeal, a curse, a slight settling down of the dust cloud, and two red-faced, perspiring troopers emerged from the jam, dragging the yet reluctant mule by main strength behind them. As they cleared the line of the column, Bungay rolled off the animal's back, and, in his eagerness, came down on all fours.

"Well," I said sarcastically, "what do you think of your mule now?"

"By Jinks, Cap," and his face lit up with intense admiration as he surveyed the animal, "durned if I don't take him hum. Gee! whut a scrap Mariar an' thet muel kin have!"

The Major pushed through the curious line of troopers and faced him angrily.

187

My Lady of the North

"What do you mean by running your dod-gasted old mule into this column?" he thundered. "Who are you, anyhow? Blamed if the little fool has n't done more damage than a Yankee battery."

Jed faced him ruefully.

"I did n't go ter dew it, mister," he explained. "Ther muel wus jist pinted ther wrong way. I never knowed ther mean ol' cuss wint back'ards like thet."

The wrath on the Major's face caused me to interfere. In a few words I made everything clear, and substantial justice was attained by an order for Jed to move on with his animated battering ram. He disappeared dolefully in the dust cloud, the mule, once more asleep, trailing lazily behind him. The troop, slightly disfigured, closed up their broken ranks, and the weary march was resumed.

It was long after dark the second day when, thoroughly wearied, we turned into an old tobacco field and made camp for the night. To right and left of our position glowed the cheery fires, telling where Early's command bivouacked in line of battle. From the low range of hills in front of where we rested one could look across an intervening valley, and see far off to the northward the dim flames which marked the position of the enemy. Down in the mysterious darkness between, divided only by a swift and narrow stream, were the blue and gray pickets. The opposing forces were sleeping on their arms, making ready for the death grip on the morrow.

As I lay there thinking, wondering what might be my fate before another nightfall, seeing constantly in my half-dreams the fair face of a woman, which made me more of a coward than I had ever felt myself before, I was partially aroused by the droning tones of a voice close at hand. Lifting myself on one elbow I glanced curiously around to see where it originated, what was occurring. Clustered about a roaring fire of rails were a dozen troopers, and in the midst of them, occupying the post of honor upon an empty powder keg, was Bungay, enthusiastically reciting Scott. I caught a line or two:

> " ' At once there rose so wild a yell
> Within that dark and narrow dell,
> As all the fiends from heaven that fell
> Had pealed the battle-cry of hell.' "

and then the drowsy god pressed down my heavy eyelids, and I fell asleep.

CHAPTER XXII

THE BATTLE IN THE SHENANDOAH

TO me it has always seemed remarkable that after all my other battle experiences — Antietam, Gettysburg, the Wilderness, ay! even including that first fierce baptism of fire at Manassas — no action in which I ever participated should remain so clearly photographed upon memory as this last desperate struggle for supremacy in the Shenandoah. Every minute detail of the conflict, at least so far as I chanced to be a personal participant, rises before me as I write, and I doubt not I could trace to-day each step taken upon that stricken field.

The reveille had not sounded when I first awoke and, rolling from my blanket, looked about me. Already a faint, dim line of gray, heralding the dawn, was growing clearly defined in the east, and making manifest those heavy fog-banks which, hanging dank and low, obscured the valley. The tired men of my troop were yet lying upon the ground, wrapped tightly in their blankets, oblivious of the deadly work before them; but I could hear the horses already moving uneasily at their picket-ropes, and observed here and there the chilled figure of a sentry leaning upon his gun, oddly distorted in form by the enveloping mist.

Directly in advance of where we rested, a long hill sloped gently upward for perhaps a hundred yards, its

The Battle in the Shenandoah

crest topped with a thick growth of young oak-trees, yet seemingly devoid of underbrush. No troops were camped in our immediate front, and feeling curious to ascertain something of our formation, as well as to examine the lay of the land between us and the position occupied by the enemy, I walked slowly forward, unhindered, until I attained the crest. Numberless birds were singing amid the branches overhead, while the leaves of the low bushes I passed on my way were glistening with dew. Except for those long rows of sleeping soldiers, I seemed utterly alone within some rural solitude upon a quiet Sabbath morning. Not an unwonted sound reached me to make discord; so quiet, indeed, was all the earth that I became startled by the sudden chatter of a squirrel disturbed at my approach, and unthinkingly I stooped to pluck a delicate pink flower blooming in the grass, and placed it in a ragged buttonhole of my old gray jacket.

The fog yet held the secrets of the valley safely locked within its brown hand, and I could penetrate none of its mysteries. It was like gazing down from some headland into a silent, unvexed sea. But directly across from where I stood, apparently along the summit of another chain of low hills similar to those we occupied, I could perceive the flames of numerous camp-fires leaping up into sudden radiance, while against the brightening sky a great flag lazily flapped its folds to the freshening breeze. Evidently our opponents were first astir, and the headquarters of some division of the enemy must be across yonder. As I gazed, other fires burst forth to left and right, as far as the unaided eye could carry through the gloom, and I was thus enabled to trace distinctly those advanced lines opposing us. Experience told me their position must be a strong one, and their force heavy.

As I turned to mark our own formation, the roll of drums rang out, while the quickening notes of the reveille sounded down the long lines of slumbering men. Life returned, as if by magic, to those motionless forms, and almost in a moment all below me became astir, and I could clearly distinguish the various branches of the service, as they stretched away commingled upon either hand. We were evidently stationed close to the centre of our own position. Our battle-line was not so extended as the one across the valley; apparently there were fewer troops along our front than theirs, nor could I perceive to the southward, now that dawning day somewhat clarified the scene, any evidence of reserve force; yet what I saw looked extremely well, and my heart bounded proudly at the sturdy promise of our fighting men. The cavalry appeared to be principally concentrated at the foot of the hill upon which I stood, although at the distant wings I was able to perceive some flying guidons that told me of the presence of numerous troops of horse. I marked it all with eager, kindling eyes, for it was a sight to cheer the heart of any soldier — those dark, dense squares where the infantry were massed, and battery after battery of flying artillery ranged along the ridge. But it seemed to me the larger, heavier force had been concentrated upon our left, massed there in deeper lines, as if that were the point selected from whence the attacking wedge was to be driven. The intervening ground sloped so gently forward, while the hill crest was so thickly crowned with trees, it looked an ideal position from which to advance in line of attack. Upon my right there appeared a break in the solidity

The Battle in the Shenandoah

of our line, but even as I noted it, wondering at the oversight, the dense front of an infantry column debouched from a ravine and, marching steadily forward, filled the gap. I could distinctly mark the wearied manner in which the men composing it flung themselves prostrate on the hard ground the moment they were halted — doubtless all through the long hours of the black night they had been toiling on to be in time.

Aides were galloping furiously now among the scattered commands. The obscuring fog slowly rose from off the face of the valley, but all the central portion remained veiled from view. Suddenly, as I watched, the brown cloud beneath me was rent asunder here and there by little spits of fire, and it was curious to observe how those quick, spiteful darts of flame swept the full length of my vista. I could distinguish no reports, — it was too far away, — but realized that the opposing pickets had caught sight of each other through the gloom. Then a big gun boomed almost directly opposite me, its flame seeming like a red-hot knife rending the mist. This had barely vanished when a sudden cheer rang out upon my left, and I turned in time to behold a thin, scattered line of gray-clad infantrymen swarm down the steep slope into the valley. With hats drawn low, and guns advanced, they plunged at a run into the mist and disappeared. Our skirmishers had gone in; the ball had opened.

I had tarried long enough; any moment now might bring " boots and saddles," and if I possessed the slightest desire for a breakfast to fight on, it behooved me to get back within our lines. The memory of that animated scene in front still fresh upon me, how quiet and commonplace everything appeared down there in the hill shadow. No one would have dreamed it to be a battle-line. The fires crackled gayly, while the men lounged about them, smoking or eating. There was no sound save the gentle rustling of leaves overhead, or the light laughter of some group of story-tellers. Horses munched their grain just at our rear, and now and then some careful trooper sauntered back to make sure his mount was not neglected. One or two of the men were cleaning their revolvers, and an old corporal was polishing his sabre where a spot of rust disfigured its gleaming blade. You might have dreamed it a picnic, a military review, possibly, were it not for the travel-soiled and ragged uniforms, but a line held there for the stern purpose of deadly conflict — it scarcely seemed credible.

"Captain," said a white-faced lad of seventeen, as I sat down on the ground to my coffee and corn bread, "did you see anything of the blue-bellies out there?"

"Plenty of them, my boy," I answered, noting the curls that clustered upon his forehead, and wondering what mother prayed for him. "We have plenty of hot work cut out for us to-day."

"I hope they 'll give us a charge before it 's all over." His blue eyes danced as he strode off, whistling gayly.

"What has become of Bungay?" I questioned of Colgate, who was lying upon his back with eyes fastened on a floating cloud.

"Do you mean the little mountaineer who came in with us last night?"

I nodded.

"Oh, his mule bolted at the first shot over yonder, and the little fellow is after it. He 's down the field there somewhere."

How time dragged! The battery to left of us went

The Battle in the Shenandoah

into action, and began firing rapidly; we could mark the black figures of the cannoneers at the nearer guns, outlined against the sky over the crest, as they moved quickly back and forth. Twice they bore motionless bodies to the rear, and laid them down tenderly beyond the fierce zone of fire. Then the heavier pieces of artillery farther down the line burst into thunder, and we silently watched a large force of infantry move slowly past us up the long slope until they halted in line of battle just behind its summit, the advanced files lying flat upon their faces and peering over. But no orders came for us.

The eagerly expectant men moved back toward their picketed horses in anticipation of a hurried call, but as the minutes slowly passed and none came, they broke into little groups, sitting about on the ground, seemingly careless as to the dread rumbling in front, and the continuous zip of Minié bullets through the trees overhead. One or two, I noticed as I walked about, were writing what, possibly they dreamed, might be final words of love to dear ones far away; one more careless group were playing poker upon an outspread blanket; while a grizzled old sergeant, a God-fearing man, had drawn forth his well-worn pocket Testament, and was reading over again the familiar story of the Nazarene. The sullen boom of the great guns, deep, ominous, began to blend with the sustained rattle of musketry, telling plainly of heavy fighting by massed infantry; the smoke clouds, obscuring the blue sky, rolled high above the fringe of trees; the battle-line lying along the crest at our front swept down the hill out of our sight into that hail of death below; but we seemed to be forgotten.

Nearly noon by the red sun hiding behind the drifting powder cloud. The ever-deepening roar of ceaseless

195

contest had moved westward down the valley, when an aide wheeled his smoking horse in front of the Colonel, spoke a dozen hasty words, pointed impetuously to the left, and dashed off down the line. The men leaped to their feet in eager expectancy, and as the " Fall in, fall in there, lads," echoed joyously from lip to lip, the kindling eyes and rapid movements voiced unmistakably the soldier spirit. We moved westward down the long, bare slope in the sunshine, through a half-dozen deserted, desolate fields, and along a narrow, rocky defile leading into a deep ravine. Every step of our horses brought us closer to that deep roar of surging battle; the air we breathed became pungent with powder smoke, and once or twice we heard the deep hurrah of the North, the wild answering yell of the South, as victory rolled from flag to flag. Streams of wearied and wounded men began to pass us, white-faced and terror-stricken, or haggard and silent, but all alike seeking the rear. The head of our advancing column pushed them sternly aside, the troopers chaffing the uninjured without mercy, but tender as women to those who suffered. Back among the rocks, out of reach from plunging shells, a field hospital had been hastily set up; the ground was already thickly strewn with bodies, while surgeons labored above them, elbow-deep in blood. With averted, stern, set faces, paling to the cries of agony, we rode past, more eager than ever to strike the enemy.

At the mouth of the ravine we came forth into the broad valley, and halted. Just in front of us, scarcely a half-mile distant, were the fighting lines, partially enveloped in dense smoke, out from which broke patches of blue or gray, as charge succeeded charge, or the wind swept aside the fog of battle. The firing was one continuous crash, while plunging bullets, overreaching their mark, began to chug into our own ranks, dealing death impartially to horse and man. The captain of the troop next mine wheeled suddenly, a look of surprise upon his face, and fell backward into the arms of one of his men; with an intense scream of agony, almost human, the horse of my first sergeant reared and came over, crushing the rider before he could loosen foot from stirrup; the Lieutenant-Colonel rode slowly past us to the rear, his face deathly white, one arm, dripping blood, dangling helpless at his side. This was the hardest work of war, that silent agony which tried men in helpless bondage to unyielding discipline. I glanced anxiously along the front of my troop, but they required no word from me; with tightly set lips, and pale, stern faces, they held their line steady as granite, closing up silently the ragged gaps torn by plunging balls.

"Captain," said Colgate, riding to where I sat my horse, "you will see that the paper I gave you reaches home safe if I fail to come out of this?"

I reached over and gripped his hand hard.

"It will be the first thing I shall remember, Jack," I answered earnestly. "But we may have it easy enough after all — it seems to be an infantry affair."

He shook his head gravely.

"No," he said, pointing forward, "they will need us now."

As he spoke it seemed as though the sharp firing upon both sides suddenly ceased by mutual consent. The terrible roar of small arms, which had mingled with the continuous thunder of great guns, died away into an intermittent rattling of musketry, and as the heavy smoke slowly drifted upward in a great white cloud, we could

197

plainly distinguish the advancing Federal lines, three ranks deep, stretching to left and right in one vast, impenetrable blue wall, sweeping toward us upon a run. Where but a brief moment before the plain appeared deserted, it was now fairly alive with soldiery, the sun gleaming on fixed bayonets, and faces aglow with the ardor of surprise. Some one had blundered! The thin, unsupported line of gray infantry directly in our front closed up their shattered ranks hastily in desperate effort to stay the rush. We could see them jamming their muskets for volley fire, and then, with clash and clatter that drowned all other sounds, a battery of six black guns came flying madly past us, every horse on the run, lashed into frenzy by his wild rider. With carriage and caisson leaping at every jump, the half-naked, smoke-begrimed cannoneers clinging to their seats like monkeys, they dashed recklessly forward, swung about into position, and almost before the muzzles had been well pointed, were hurling canister into that blue, victorious advance. How those gallant fellows worked! their guns leaping into air at each discharge, their movements clockwork! **Tense,** eager, expectant, every hand among us hard gripped on sabre hilt, we waited that word which surely could not be delayed, while from end to end, down the full length of our straining line, rang out the yell of exultant pride.

"Steady, men; steady there, lads!" called the old Colonel, sternly, his own eyes filled with tears. "Our turn will come."

Torn, rent, shattered, bleeding, treading upon the dead and mangled in rows, those iron men in blue came on. They were as demons laughing at death. No rain of lead, no hail of canister, no certainty of destruction could check

The Battle in the Shenandoah

now the fierce impetus of that forward rush. God knows it was magnificent; the supreme effort of men intoxicated with the enthusiasm of war! Even where we were we could see and feel the giant power in those grim ranks of steel — the tattered flags, the stern, set faces, the deep-toned chorus of " Glory, glory, hallelujah," that echoed to their tread. Those men meant to win or die, and they rolled on as Cromwell's Ironsides at Marston Moor. Twice they staggered, when the mad volleys ploughed ragged red lanes through them, but only to rally and press sternly on. They struck that crouching gray line of infantry, fairly buried it within their dense blue folds, and, with one fierce hurrah of triumph, closed down upon the guns. Even as they blotted them from sight, an aide, hatless and bleeding, his horse wounded and staggering from weakness, tore down toward us along the crest. A hundred feet away his mount fell headlong, but on foot and dying he reached our front.

" Colonel Carter," he panted, pressing one hand upon his breast to keep back the welling blood, " charge, and hold that battery until we can bring infantry to your support."

No man among us doubted the full meaning of it — *we were to save the army!* The very horses seemed to feel a sense of relief, hands clinched more tightly on taut reins to hold them in check; under the old battered hats the eyes of the troopers gleamed hungrily.

" Virginians! " and the old Colonel's voice rang like a clarion down the breathless line, " there is where you die! Follow me! "

Slowly, like some mighty mountain torrent gaining force, we rode forth at a walk, each trooper lined to precision of review, yet instinctively taking distance for sword-play. Halfway down the slight slope our line broke into a sharp trot, then, as the thrilling notes of the charge sounded above us, we swept forward in wild, impetuous tumult.

Who can tell the story of those seconds that so swiftly followed? Surely not one who saw but the vivid flash of steel, the agonized faces, the flame of belching fire. I recall the frenzied leap of my horse as we struck the line ere it could form into square; the blows dealt savagely to right and left; the blaze of a volley scorching our faces; the look of the big infantryman I rode down; the sudden thrust that saved me from a levelled gun; the quick swerving of our horses as they came in contact with the cannon; the shouts of rage; the blows; the screams of pain; the white face of Colgate as he reeled and fell. These are all in my memory, blurred, commingled, indistinct, yet distressful as any nightmare. In some way, how I know not, I realized that we had hurled them back, shattered them by our first fierce blow; that the guns were once again ours; that fifty dismounted troopers were tugging desperately at their wheels. Then that dense blue mass surged forward once again, engulfed us in its deadly folds, and with steel and bullet, sword and clubbed musket, ploughed through our broken ranks, rending us in twain, fairly smothering us by sheer force of numbers. I saw the old Colonel plunge headdown into the ruck beneath the horses' feet; the Major riding stone dead in his saddle, a ghastly red stain in the centre of his forehead; then Hunter, of E, went down screaming, and I knew I was the senior captain left. About me scarce a hundred men battled like demons for their lives in the midst of the guns. Even as I glanced aside at them, shielding my head with uplifted sabre from

The Battle in the Shenandoah

the blows rained upon me, the color-sergeant flung up his hand, and grasped his saddle pommel to keep from falling. Out of his opening fingers I snatched the splintered staff, lifted it high up, until the rent folds of the old flag caught the dull glow of the sunlight.

"—th Virginia!" I shouted. "Rally on the colors!"

I could see them coming — all that was left of them — fighting their way through the press, cleaving the mass with their blows as the prow of a ship cuts the sea. With one vicious jab of the spur I led them, a thin wedge of tempered gray steel, battering, gouging, rending a passage into that solid blue wall. Inch by inch, foot by foot, yard by yard, slashing madly with our broken sabres, battling as men crazed with lust of blood, our very horses fighting for us with teeth and hoofs, we ploughed a lane of death through a dozen files. Then the vast mass closed in upon us, rolled completely over us. There was a flash, a vision of frenzied faces, and I knew no more.

CHAPTER XXIII

FIELD HOSPITAL, SIXTH CORPS

MY head ached so abominably when I first opened my eyes that I was compelled to close them again, merely realizing dimly that I looked up at something white above me, which appeared to sway as though blown gently by the wind. My groping hand, the only one I appeared able to move, told me I was lying upon a camp-cot, with soft sheets about me, and that my head rested upon a pillow. Then I passed once more into unconsciousness, but this time it was sleep.

When I once more awakened the throbbing pain had largely left my hot temples, and I saw that the swaying white canopy composed the roof of a large tent, upon which the golden sunlight now lay in checkered masses, telling me the canvas had been erected among trees. A faint moan caused me to move my head slightly on the gratefully soft pillow, and I could perceive a long row of cots, exactly similar to the one I occupied, each apparently filled, stretching away toward an opening that looked forth into the open air. A man was moving slowly down the narrow aisle toward me, stopping here and there to bend over some sufferer with medicine or a cheery word. He wore a short white jacket, and was without a cap, his head of heavy red hair a most conspicuous object. As he approached I endeavored to speak, but for the moment my throat refused response to the effort. Then I managed to ask feebly: "Where am I?"

The blue eyes in the freckled, boyish face danced good-humoredly, and he laid a big red hand gently upon my forehead.

"Field hospital, Sixth Corps," he said, with a strong Hibernian accent. "An' how de ye loike it, Johnny?"

"Better than some others I've seen," I managed to articulate faintly. "Who won?"

"Divil a wan of us knows," he admitted frankly, "but your fellows did the retratin'."

It was an old, old story to all of us by that time, and I closed my eyes wearily, content to ask no more.

I have no way of knowing how long I rested there motionless although awake, my eyes closed to keep out the painful glare, my sad thoughts busied with memory of those men whom I had seen reel and fall upon that stricken field we had battled so vainly to save. Once I wondered, with sudden start of fear, if I had lost a limb, if I was to be crippled for life, the one thing I dreaded above all else. Feeling feebly beneath my bed-clothing I tested, as best I could, each limb. All were apparently intact, although my left arm seemed useless and devoid of feeling, broken no doubt, and I heaved a sigh of genuine relief. Then I became partially aroused to my surroundings by a voice speaking from the cot next mine.

"You lazy Irish marine!" it cried petulantly, "that beef stew was to have been given me an hour ago."

"Sure, sor," was the soothing reply, "it was n't to be given yer honor till two o'clock."

"Well, it's all of three now."

My Lady of the North

"Wan-thirty, on me sowl, sor."

That first voice sounded oddly familiar, and I turned my face that way, but was unable to perceive the speaker.

"Is that Lieutenant Caton?" I asked doubtfully.

"Most assuredly it is," quickly. "And who are you?"

"Captain Wayne, of the Confederate Army."

"Oh, Wayne? Glad you spoke, but extremely sorry to have you here. Badly hurt?"

"Not seriously, I think. No limbs missing, anyhow, but exceedingly weak. Where did they get you?"

"In the side, a musket ball, but extracted. I would be all right if that lazy Irish scamp would only give me half enough to eat. By the way, Wayne, of course I never got the straight of it, for there are half-a-dozen stories about the affair flying around, and those most interested will not talk, but one of your special friends, and to my notion a most charming young woman, will be in here to see me sometime this afternoon. She will be delighted to meet you again, I'm sure."

"One of my friends?" I questioned incredulously, yet instantly thinking of Edith Brennan. "A young woman?"

"Sure; at least she has confessed enough to me regarding that night's work to make me strongly suspicion that Captain Wayne, of the Confederate Army, and Colonel Curran, late of Major-General Halleck's staff, are one and the same person. A mighty neat trick, by Jove, and it would have done you good to see Sheridan's face when they told him. But about the young lady — she claims great friendship with the gallant Colonel of light artillery, and her description of his appearance at the ball is assuredly a masterpiece of romantic fiction. Come, Captain, surely you are not the kind of man to forget a pretty face like that? I can assure you, you made a deep impression. There are times when I am almost jealous of you."

"But," I protested, my heart beating rapidly, "I met several that evening, and you have mentioned no name."

"Well, to me it chances there is but one worthy of mention," he said earnestly, "and that one is Celia Minor."

"Miss Minor!" I felt a strange sense of disappointment. "Does she come alone?"

"Most certainly; do you suppose she would expose me in my present weak state to the fascinations of any one else?"

"Oh, so the wind lies in that quarter, does it, old fellow? I congratulate you, I'm sure."

My recollection of Miss Minor was certainly a most pleasant one, and I recalled to memory the attractive picture of her glossy black hair and flashing brown eyes, yet I felt exceedingly small interest in again meeting her. Indeed I was asleep when she finally entered, and it was the sound of Caton's voice that aroused me and made me conscious of the presence of others.

"I shall share these grapes with my cot-mate over yonder," he said laughingly. "By the way, Celia, his voice sounded strangely familiar to me a short time ago. Just glance over there and see if he is any one you know."

I heard the soft rustle of skirts, and, without a smile, looked up into her dark eyes. There was a sudden start of pleased surprise.

"Why," she exclaimed eagerly, "it is Colonel Curran! Edith, dear, here is the Rebel who pretended to be Myrtle Curran's brother."

How the hot blood leaped within my veins at mention of that name; but before I could lift my head she had swept across the narrow aisle, and was standing beside me. Wife, or what, there was that within her eyes which told me a wondrous story. For the instant, in her surprise and agitation, she forgot herself, and lost that marvellous self-restraint which had held us so far apart.

"Captain Wayne!" she cried, and her gloved hands fell instantly upon my own, where it rested without the coverlet. "You here, and wounded?"

I smiled up at her, feeling now that my injuries were indeed trivial.

"Somewhat weakened by loss of blood, Mrs. Brennan, but not dangerously hurt." Then I could not forbear asking softly, "Is it possible you can feel regret over injuries inflicted upon a Rebel?"

Her cheeks flamed, and the audacious words served to recall her to our surroundings.

"Even although I love my country, and sincerely hope for the downfall of her enemies," she answered soberly, "I do not delight in suffering. Were you in that terrible cavalry charge? They tell me scarcely a man among them survived."

"I rode with my regiment."

"I knew it was your regiment — the name was upon every lip, and even our own men unite in declaring it a magnificent sacrifice, a most gallant deed. You must know I thought instantly of you when I was told it was the act of the —th Virginia."

There were tears in my eyes, I know, as I listened to her, and my heart warmed at this frank confession of her remembrance.

"I am glad you cared sufficiently for me," I said gravely, "to hold me in your thought at such a time.

Field Hospital, Sixth Corps

Our command merely performed the work given it, but the necessity has cost us dearly. You are yet at General Sheridan's headquarters?"

"Only temporarily, and simply because there has been no opportunity to get away, the movements of the army have been so hurried and uncertain. Since the battle Miss Minor has desired to remain until assured of Lieutenant Caton's permanent recovery. He was most severely wounded, and of course I could not well leave her here alone. Indeed I am her guest, as we depart tomorrow for her home, to remain indefinitely."

"But Miss Minor is, I understand, a native of this State?"

"Her home is in the foot-hills of the Blue Ridge, along the valley of the Cowskin, — a most delightful old Southern mansion. I passed one summer there when a mere girl, previous to the war."

"But will it prove safe for you now?"

"Oh, indeed, yes; everybody says so. It is entirely out of the track of both armies, and has completely escaped despoliation."

"I was not thinking of the main combatants, but rather of those irregulars who will be most certain to invade promptly any section not patrolled by disciplined troops. I confess to fearing greatly that there will be an early outpouring of these rascals from the mountains into the adjacent lowlands the moment we are compelled to fall back and let loose the iron grip with which we have held them thus far partially in check. Yet I do not say this to frighten you, or in any way spoil the pleasure of your contemplated visit."

"Indeed I shall not permit it. So many have assured me it would be perfectly safe that I do not mean to worry. I expect to be very happy there until the war is over. Surely, Captain Wayne, it cannot long continue now?"

Her voice was low, earnest, almost supplicating.

"It looks hopeless, even from our standpoint, I admit," I returned, watching the straying sunlight play amid the dusky coils of her hair. "Yet we are not likely to yield until we must."

"But you, Captain Wayne; surely you have already risked enough?"

"I presume I am a prisoner," I answered, smiling, "and therefore unable at present to choose my future; but were I free to do so, I should return to my command to-morrow."

"Yet surely you do not consider that this terrible rebellion is justified, is right?"

"I think there is, undoubtedly, much wrong upon both sides, Mrs. Brennan; but I am a soldier, and my duty is very simple — I follow my flag and, as a Virginian, am loyal to my State and to the principles taught me in my childhood."

Her beautiful eyes filled with tears, and as she bent down her head that the others might not perceive her agitation, one salty drop fell upon my hand.

"It is all so very, very sad," she said softly.

"There is much suffering upon both sides, but surely even you would not wish me to be other than true to what I look upon as a duty?"

"No; I — I think I — I respect you the more."

"Then you do respect me?"

Another word, a far stronger one, trembled upon my lips, yet I restrained it sternly, and asked all I dared.

"I do," earnestly, her eyes dwelling upon my face.

Field Hospital, Sixth Corps

"I may not comprehend how you can view matters from your standpoint, for I am in full sympathy with the Union, and am a woman. But I believe you to be honest, and I know you to be a gallant soldier."

I clasped her hand close within my own.

"Your words encourage me greatly," I said earnestly. "I have done so much to bring you trouble and sorrow that I have been fearful lest it had cost me what I value more highly than you can ever know."

These words were unfortunate, and instantly brought back to her a memory which seemed a barrier between us. I read the change in her averted face.

"That can never be, Captain Wayne," she returned calmly, yet rising even as she spoke. "You have come into my life under circumstances so peculiar as to make me always your friend. Celia," and she turned toward the others, "is it not time we were going? I am very sure the doctor said you were to remain with Lieutenant Caton but a brief time."

"Why, Edith," retorted the other, gayly, "I have been ready for half an hour — have n't I, Arthur? — but you were so deeply engrossed with your Rebel I had n't the heart to interrupt."

I could see the quick color as it mounted over Mrs. Brennan's throat.

"Nonsense," she answered; "we have not been here that length of time."

"Did the Major emerge from out the late entanglement unhurt?" It was Caton's voice that spoke.

"Much to his regret, I believe, he was not even under fire." The tone was cool and collected again. "I will say good-bye, Lieutenant; doubtless we shall see you at Mountain View so soon as you are able to take the journey. And, Captain Wayne, I trust I shall soon learn of your complete recovery."

My eyes followed them down the long aisle. At the entrance she glanced back, and I lifted my hand. Whether she marked the gesture I do not know, for the next instant both ladies had disappeared without.

Caton endeavored to talk with me, but I answered him so briefly, and with such vague knowledge of what had been said, that he soon desisted. I could see only the face that had so lately bent above me, and reflect upon the fate which held me helpless in its grasp. I felt that had circumstances been other than they were, this proudly tender woman might have learned from me the lesson of love, and in my weakness, both of spirit and body, I rebelled against the impassable barrier holding us apart. She was the wife of another, yet, in spite of every determination, I loved her with all my soul.

The night drew slowly down, and as it darkened, only one miserable lamp shed its dim rays throughout the great tent; nurses moved noiselessly from cot to cot, and I learned something of the nature of my own injuries from the gruff old surgeon who dressed the wound in my chest and refastened the splints along my arm. Then silence followed, excepting for the heavy breathing of the sleepers and the restless tossing of sufferers on their narrow cots. Here and there echoed wild words of delirium, but soon even these faint sounds died away in slumber, while the drowsy night-watch dozed in a chair. I could see from where I lay a blazing fire without, while in its glow along the side of the tent there was cast the black shadow of a sentinel, as he paced back and forth along his beat. So clear were the shaded lines I was able to trace his gun, and even the peculiar turn-up

Field Hospital, Sixth Corps

to the visor of his forage-cap. The pain I had experienced earlier in the day grew less acute, and at last I also fell asleep.

It must have been midnight, possibly even later, when a number of rapid shots fired outside the tent aroused me, and I heard many voices shouting, mingled with the tread of horses' feet. The night-watch had already disappeared, and the startled inmates of the tent were in a state of intense confusion. As I lifted myself slightly, dazed by the sudden uproar and eager to learn its cause, the tent-flap, which had been lowered to exclude the cold night air, was hastily jerked aside, and a man stepped within, casting one rapid glance about that dim interior. The flaring lamp overhead revealed to me a short, heavy-set figure, clad in a gray uniform.

"No one here need feel alarm," he said quietly. "We are not making war upon the wounded. Are there any Confederates present able to travel?"

A dozen eager voices answered him, and men began to crawl out of their cots onto the floor.

He started down the aisle.

"We can be burdened with no helpless or badly wounded men," he said sternly. "Only those able to ride. No, my man, you are in too bad shape to travel. Very sorry, my boy, but it can't be done. Only your left arm, you say? Very well, move out in front there. No, lad, it would be the death of you, for we must ride fast and hard."

He came to a pause a half-dozen cots away from me, and seemed about to retrace his steps. Dim as the light was, I felt convinced I had formerly seen that short figure and stern face with its closely cropped beard.

"Mosby," I called out, resolved to risk his remembrance, "Colonel Mosby, is n't it possible to take me?"

"Who are you?" he questioned sharply, turning in the direction of my voice.

"Wayne," I answered eagerly, "Wayne, of the —th Virginia."

In an instant he was standing beside my cot, his eyes filled with anxious interest.

"Phil Wayne, of Charlottesville? You here? Not badly hurt, my boy?"

"Shot and bruised, Colonel, but I 'd stand a good deal to get out of this."

"And, by the Eternal, you shall; that is, if you can travel in a wagon. Here, Sims, Thomas; two of you carry this officer out. Take bed-clothes and all — easy now."

The fellows picked me up tenderly, and bore me slowly down the central aisle. Mosby walked beside us as far as the outer opening.

"Put him down there by the fire," he ordered, "until I look over the rest of these chaps and divide the wheat from the chaff."

CHAPTER XXIV

A NIGHT RIDE OF THE WOUNDED

IT was a wild, rude scene without, yet in its way typical of a little-understood chapter of Civil War. Moreover it was one with which I was not entirely unacquainted. Years of cavalry scouting, bearing me beyond the patrol lines of the two great armies, had frequently brought me into contact with those various independent, irregular forces which, co-operating with us, often rendered most efficient service by preying on the scattered Federal camps and piercing their lines of communication. Seldom risking an engagement in the open, their policy was rather to dash down upon some outpost or poorly guarded wagon train, and retreat with a rapidity rendering pursuit hopeless. It was partisan warfare, and appealed to many ill-adapted to abide the stricter discipline of regular service. These border rangers would rendezvous under some chosen leader, strike an unexpected blow where weakness had been discovered, then disappear as quickly as they came, oftentimes scattering widely until the call went forth for some fresh assault. It was service not dissimilar to that performed during the Revolutionary struggle by Sumter and Marion in the Carolinas, and added in the aggregate many a day to the contest of the Confederacy.

Among these wild, rough riders between the lines no leader was more favorably known of our army, nor more

dreaded by the enemy, than Mosby. Daring to the point
of recklessness, yet wary as a fox, counting opposing numbers nothing when weighed against the advantage of surprise, tireless in saddle, audacious in resource, quick to
plan and equally quick to execute, he was always where
least expected, and it was seldom he failed to win reward
for those who rode at his back. Possessing regular rank
in the Confederate Army, making report of his operations
to the commander-in-chief, his peculiar talent as a partisan
leader had won him what was practically an independent
command. Knowing him as I did, I was not surprised
that he should now have swept suddenly out of the black
night upon the very verge of the battle to drive his irri-
tating sting into the hard-earned Federal victory.

An empty army wagon, the " U. S. A." yet conspicuous
upon its canvas cover, had been overturned and fired in
front of the hospital tent to give light to the raiders.
Grouped about beneath the trees, and within the glow
of the flames, was a picturesque squad of horsemen, hardy,
tough-looking fellows the most of them, their clothing an
odd mixture of uniforms, but every man heavily armed
and admirably equipped for service. Some remained
mounted, lounging carelessly in their saddles, but far the
larger number were on foot, their bridle-reins wound
about their wrists. All alike appeared alert and ready
for any emergency. How many composed the party I
was unable to judge with accuracy, as they constantly came
and went from out the shadows beyond the circumference
of the fire. As all sounds of firing had ceased, I concluded that the work planned had been already accomplished. Undoubtedly, surprised as they were, the small
Federal force left to guard this point had been quickly
overwhelmed and scattered.

A Night Ride of the Wounded

The excitement attendant upon my release had left me for the time being utterly forgetful as to the pain of my wounds, so that weakness alone held me to the blanket upon which I had been left. The night was decidedly chilly, yet I had scarcely begun to feel its discomfort, when a man strode forward from out the nearer group and stood looking down upon me. He was a young fellow, wearing a gray artillery jacket, with high cavalry boots coming above the knees. I noticed his firm-set jaw, and a pearl-handled revolver stuck carelessly in his belt, but observed no symbol of rank about him.

"Is this Captain Wayne?" he asked, not unpleasantly.

I answered by an inclination of the head, and he turned at once toward the others.

"Cass, bring three men over here, and carry this officer to the same wagon you did the others," he commanded briefly. "Fix him comfortably, but be in a hurry about it."

They lifted me in the blanket, one holding tightly at either corner, and bore me tenderly out into the night. Once one of them tripped over a projecting root, and the sudden jar of his stumble shot a spasm of pain through me, which caused me to cry out even through my clinched teeth.

"Pardon me, lads," I panted, ashamed of the weakness, "but it slipped out before I could help it."

"Don't be after a mentionin' av it, yer honor," returned a rich brogue. "Sure an me feet got so mixed oup that I wondher I did n't drap ye entoirely."

"If ye had, Clancy," said the man named Cass, grimly, "I reckon as how the Colonel would have drapped you."

At the foot of a narrow ravine, leading forth into the broader valley, we came to a covered army wagon, to

215

which four mules had been already attached. The canvas was drawn aside, and I was lifted up and carefully deposited in the hay that thickly covered the bottom. It was so intensely dark within I could see nothing of my immediate surroundings, but a low moan told me there must be at least one other wounded man present. Outside I heard the tread of horses' hoofs, and then the sound of Mosby's voice.

"Jake," he said, "drive rapidly, but with as much care as possible. Take the lower road after you cross the bridge, and you will meet with no patrols. We will ride beside you for a couple of miles."

Then a hand thrust aside the canvas, and a face peered in. I caught a faint glimmer of stars, but could distinguish little else.

"Boys," said the leader, kindly, "I wish I might give you better transportation, but this is the only form of vehicle we can find. I reckon you 'll get pretty badly bumped over the road you are going, but I 'm furnishing you all the chance to get away in my power."

"For one I am grateful enough," I answered, after waiting for some one else to speak. "A little pain is preferable to imprisonment."

"After you pass the bridge you will be perfectly safe on that score," he said heartily. "Anything more I can do for any of you?"

"How many of us are there?" asked some one faintly from out the darkness.

"Oh, yes," returned Mosby, with a laugh, "I forgot; you will want to know each other. There are three of you — Colonel Colby of North Carolina, Major Wilkins of Thome's Battery, and Captain Wayne, —th Virginia. Let that answer for an introduction, gentle-

A Night Ride of the Wounded

men, and now good-night. We shall guard you as long as necessary, and then must leave you to the kindly ministrations of the driver."

He reached in, leaning down from his saddle to do so, drew the blanket somewhat closer about me, and was gone. I caught the words of a sharp, short order, and the heavy wagon lurched forward, its wheels bumping over the irregularities in the road, each jolt sending a fresh spasm of pain through my tortured body.

May the merciful God ever protect me from such a ride again! It seemed interminable, while each long mile we travelled brought with it new and greater agony of mind and body. That I did not suffer alone was early evident from the low moans borne to me from out the darkness. Once a weak, trembling voice prayed for release, — a short, fervent prayer, which so impressed me in the weakness of my own anguish that I added to it "Amen," spoken unconsciously aloud.

"Who spoke?" asked the same voice, faintly.

"I am Captain Wayne," I answered, almost glad to break the terrible silence by speech of any kind; "and I merely echoed your prayer. Death would indeed prove a welcome relief from such intensity of suffering."

"Yes," he acquiesced gently. "I fear I have not sufficient strength to bear mine for long; yet I am a Christian, and there are wife and child waiting for me at home. God knows I am ready when He calls, but my duty is to live, if possible, for their sake. They will have nothing left if I pass on."

"The road must grow smoother as we come down into the valley. Are your wounds serious?"

"I was struck by fragments of a shell," he answered, and I could tell he spoke the words through his clinched

teeth, " and am wounded in the head as well as the body
— oh, my God!" The cry was wrung from him by
a sudden tilting of the wagon, and for a moment my
own pain prevented utterance.

" I hear nothing from the other man," I managed to
say at last. "Colonel Mosby said there were three of
us; surely the third man cannot be already dead?"

"Mercifully unconscious, I think; at least he has made
no sound since I was placed in here."

"No, friends," spoke another and deeper voice from
farther back within the jolting wagon, "I am not unconscious, but less noticeably in pain. I have lost a leg, yet
the stump seems seared and dead, hurting me little unless I touch it."

We lapsed into solemn silence, it was such an effort
to talk, and we had so little to say. Each man, no doubt,
was struggling, as I know I was, to withhold expression
of his agony for the sake of the others. I lay racked in
every nerve, my teeth tightly clinched, my temples beaded
with perspiration. I could hear the troopers riding without, the jingling of their accoutrements, and the steady
beat of their horses' feet being easily distinguishable above
the deeper rumble of the wheels. Then there came a
quick order in Mosby's familiar voice, a calling aloud of
some further directions to the driver, and afterwards
nothing was distinguishable excepting the noise of our
own rapid progress.

Jake drove, it seemed to me, most recklessly. I could
hear the almost constant crack of his lash and the rough
words of goading hurled at the straining mules. The
road appeared to be filled with roots, while occasionally
the wheels would strike a stone, coming down again with
a jar that nearly drove me frantic. The chill night air

A Night Ride of the Wounded

swept in through the open front of the hood, and made me
feel as if my veins were filled with ice, even while the
inflammation of my wounds burned and throbbed as with
fire. The pitiful moaning of the man who lay next me
grew gradually fainter, and finally ceased altogether.
Tortured as I was, yet I could not but think of the wife
and child far away praying for his safe return. For
their sake I forced back the intensity of my own sufferings and spoke into the darkness.

"The man who prayed," I said, not knowing which of
my two companions it might be. "Are you suffering
less, that you have ceased to moan?"

There was no answer. Then the loose hay rustled, as
though some one was slowly dragging his helpless body
through it. A moment later the deep voice spoke:

"He is dead," solemnly. "God has answered his
prayer. His hand already begins to feel cold."

"Dead?" I echoed, inexpressibly shocked. "Do you
know his name?"

"As I am Major Wilkins, it must be Colonel Colby
who has died. May God be merciful to the widow and
the orphan."

The hours that followed were all but endless. I knew
we had reached the lower valley, for the road became
more level, yet the slightest jolting now was sufficient to
render me crazed with pain, and I had lost all power of
restraint. My tortured nerves throbbed; the fever gripped
me, and my mind began to wander. Visions of delirium
came, and I dreamed dreams too terrible for record:
demons danced on the drifting clouds before me, while
whirling savages chanting in horrid discord stuck my
frenzied body full of blazing brands. At times I was
awake, calling in vain for water to quench a thirst which

grew maddening, then I lapsed into a semi-consciousness that drove me wild with its delirious fancies. I knew vaguely that the Major had crept back through the darkness and passed his strong arm gently beneath my head. I heard him shouting in his deep voice to the driver for something to drink, but was unaware of any response. All became blurred, confused, bewildering. I thought it was my mother comforting me. The faint gray daylight stole in at last through the cracks of the wagon cover; I could dimly distinguish a dark face bending over me, framed by a heavy gray beard, and then, merciful unconsciousness came, and I rested as one dead beside the corpse of the Colonel.

CHAPTER XXV

A LOST REGIMENT

IT was a bright, sunshiny day in early spring. Birds were sweetly singing in the trees lining the road I was travelling, the grass on either side was softly green, and beautified by countless wild-flowers blooming in great variety of coloring. Nothing seemed to speak of war, although I was amid the very heart of its desolation, save the deserted houses I was continually passing, and the fenceless, untilled fields. I must have shown my late illness greatly, for the few I met, as I tramped slowly onward, mostly soldiers, gazed at me curiously, as if they mistook me for the ghost of some dead comrade; and I doubt not my pale face, yet bearing the deep imprint of pain, with the long untrimmed hair framing it, and the blood-stained, ragged uniform, the same I wore that fierce day of battle, rendered me an object of wonder.

All through those long, weary winter weeks I had been hovering between life and death in an obscure hospital at Richmond. How I first came there I know not, but when at length I struggled back to recollection and life, there I found myself, and there I remained, slowly convalescing, a prisoner to weakness, until finally discharged but two days before. During those months little that related to the progress of the war reached me. My nurses were black-robed nuns, kind-hearted and tender of touch, but feeling slight interest in affairs of the world without. I saw no old-time familiar faces, while the few wounded about me were fully as ignorant of passing events as myself. The moment the door was opened to permit of my passing forth into the world again, I sought eagerly to discover the present station of my old comrades in arms, yet could learn only that the cavalry brigade with which I had formerly served was in camp somewhere near Appomattox Court House. On foot and moneyless, I set off alone, my sole anxiety to be once more with friends; and now, at the beginning of the second day, I was already beyond Petersburg, and sturdily pushing westward.

A battery of light artillery was parked in a field upon my right, but so far away from the road that I hesitated to travel that distance simply to ask a question which it was extremely doubtful if they would be able to answer. Instead I pushed on grimly, and as the road swerved slightly to the left, passing through a grove of handsome trees, I came suddenly opposite a large house of imposing aspect. A group of Confederate officers stood in converse beside the gate leading into the open driveway, and as I paused a moment, gazing at them and wondering whom I had better address, — for I recognized none of the faces fronting me, — one among the group turned suddenly, and took a hurried step in my direction, as though despatched upon an errand of importance. He was a tall, slender man, wearing a long gray moustache, and I no sooner viewed his face than I recognized him as having been one of those officers present in General Lee's tent the day I was sent out with despatches. He glanced at me curiously, yet with no sign of recognition, but before he could pass I accosted him.

"Colonel Maitland," I said, "you doubtless remember me. I am seeking my old command; would you kindly inform me where it may be found?"

A Lost Regiment

He stopped instantly at sound of my voice, and stared at me in odd bewilderment; but my words had already reached the ears of the others, and before he had found an answer another voice spoke sternly: "What is all this? Who are you, sir? What masquerade puts you into that parody of a captain's uniform?"

I turned and looked into the flushed, indignant face of General Lee.

"It is no masquerade, sir," I answered, instantly removing my hat; "it is the rightful uniform of my rank, greatly as I regret its present condition."

He gazed at me keenly, evidently doubtful as to his best course of action, and I heard an officer behind him laugh.

"Where are you from?"

"I was discharged from St. Mary's Hospital in Richmond day before yesterday, and am now seeking to rejoin my regiment."

I almost imagined I was looked upon as a soldier crazed by his sufferings; I heard a whisper, "Out of his head," yet as I gazed earnestly into those stern gray eyes which fronted me, they suddenly grew moist.

"Surely," he said gravely, "I have seen your face before. To what regiment were you attached?"

"The —th Virginia Cavalry."

The buzzing of voices about me instantly ceased, and General Lee took a step nearer.

"The —th Virginia? You were a captain? Surely this is not Philip Wayne?"

So deeply surprised was his tone, so uncertain his recognition, I scarcely knew what to answer. Had I lost my very identity? was this all a dream?

"I am Captain Wayne, Troop D, —th Virginia."

My Lady of the North

He grasped my hand warmly between both his own, and his kindly face lit up instantly with a rare smile.

"Captain Wayne, I cannot tell you how greatly I rejoice at your safe return. We certainly owe you an apology for this poor reception, but you were reported as killed in action many months ago. I doubt not Colonel Maitland truly believed he looked upon a ghost when you first accosted him."

For the moment I was unable to speak, so deeply did his words affect me.

"I fear, Captain Wayne," he continued gravely, yet retaining my hand within his own, "that I must bring you sad news."

"Sad news?" Instantly there came to me the thought of my widowed mother. "Not from home, I trust, sir?"

"No," with great tenderness, "your mother, I believe, remains well; yet the words I must speak are nevertheless sad ones, and must prove a severe shock to you. There is no —th Virginia."

"No —th Virginia?" I echoed, scarce able to comprehend his meaning, "no —th Virginia? I beg you to explain, sir; surely"—and I looked about me upon the various uniforms of the service present—"the war has not yet ceased—we have not surrendered?"

"No, my boy," and the old hero reverently bared his gray head in the sunlight, "but the —th Virginia gave itself to the South that day in the Shenandoah."

I must have grown very white, for a young aide sprang hastily forward and passed his arm about me. Yet I scarcely realized the action, for my whole thought was with the dead.

"Do you mean they are *all* gone?" I questioned, tremblingly, hardly able to grasp the full dread import of

224

such ghastly tidings. " Surely, General Lee, some among them must have come back."

" So few," he responded soberly, his hat still retained in his hand, " so very few that we could only scatter them in other commands. But you have not yet fully recovered your strength. You must not remain longer standing here. Major Holmes, will you kindly conduct Captain Wayne to my headquarters, and see that he is furnished with a uniform suitable to his rank. For the present he will serve as extra aide upon my personal staff."

I turned away, the Major leading me as if I had been a child. I walked as a man stunned by some sudden, unexpected blow. Speech was impossible, for all sensation seemed dead within me, save the one vivid memory of those loved comrades who had perished on the field. I could not realize, even dimly, in that awful hour, that of all those gallant fellows who had ridden so often at my side not enough remained alive to retain the old regimental name and number. The officer with me, himself a tried, true soldier, comprehended something of the agitation which swayed me, and respecting my silence, made no attempt to break my sorrowful reverie by speech. At the door of the room assigned me for present quarters, he left me with a warm, sympathetic pressure of the hand, and feeling utterly worn out, disheartened to a degree I had never before known, I flung myself face downward upon the cot and burst into tears.

With true soldierly kindness they left me to conquer my own sorrow and depression, and when I finally joined the mess upon the following day, clad now in fit uniform, I had regained no small measure of self-restraint, and with it came likewise renewal of the military spirit. My welcome proved extremely cordial, and the conversation of the others present soon placed in my possession whatever of incident had occurred since that disastrous day of battle in the valley. It was not much, other than a variety of desultory skirmishing, together with the steady closing in upon our lines of the overwhelming masses of the enemy, but I noted that the officers of the staff no longer hesitated to voice frankly the prevailing sentiment that the vast and unequal struggle was now rapidly drawing to its close. No attempt was made to conceal our weakness, nor to disguise the fact that we were making a last desperate stand. It was evident to all that nothing now remained but to fold our tattered battle-flags with honor.

Directly opposite me, at the long and rather scantily furnished mess-table, was seated a captain of infantry, quite foreign in appearance, — a tall, slender man, wearing a light-colored moustache and goatee. His name, as I gathered from the conversation, was Carlson, and I was considerably surprised at the fixedness with which his eyes were fastened upon me during the earlier part of the meal. Thinking we might have met somewhere before, I ransacked my memory in vain for any recollection which would serve to account for his evident interest in me. Finally, not a little annoyed by the persistency of his stare, I ventured to ask, as pleasantly as possible:

" Captain Carlson, do I remind you of some one, since you regard me so intently?"

The man instantly flushed all over his fair face at this direct inquiry.

" It vas not dat " (he almost stammered in sudden confusion, speaking quite brokenly), " bot, sair, it haf come to me dat you vos an insulter of womens, an' had refuse to fight mit mens. I know not; it seems not so."

A Lost Regiment

I was upon my feet in an instant, scarcely crediting my own ears, yet on fire with indignation.

"I know not what you may mean," I said, white with anger. "But I hold you personally accountable for those words, and you shall discover that I will fight 'mit mens.'"

He pushed his chair hastily back, his face fairly crimson, and began to stammer an explanation; but Maitland interfered.

"What does all this mean, Carlson?" he exclaimed sternly. "Sit down, Wayne — there is some strange mistake here."

I resumed my chair, wondering if they had all gone crazy, yet resolved upon taking instant action if some satisfactory explanation were not at once forthcoming.

"Come, Carlson, what do you mean by addressing such language to Captain Wayne?"

"Vell," said the Swede, so agitated by the excitement about him he could scarcely find English in which to express himself intelligibly, "it vos dis vay. I vould not insult Captain Vayne; oh, no, bot it vos told to me, an' I vould haf him to know how it all vos. It vos two months ago I go mit de flag of truce into de Federal lines at Minersville. You know dat time? I vos vaitin' for answer ven a Yankee rides oop, an' looks me all ofer like I vos a hog. 'Vell,' I say, plain like, 'vot you vant?' He say, 'I heard der vos Reb officer come in der lines, an' I rides down to see if he vos der hound vot I vanted to horsevip.' 'Vell,' I say, for it made me much mad, 'maybe you like to horsevip me?' 'No,' he says, laughing, 'it vos a damn pup in der —th Virginia Cavalry, named Vayne, I am after.' I say, 'Vot has he done?' He says, 'He insult a voman, an' vould not fight mit me.'"

My Lady of the North

He looked about him anxiously to see if we comprehended his words.

"And what did you say?" from a dozen eager voices.

The Swede gazed at them in manifest astonishment.

"I say I knowed notting about der voman, but if he say dat an officer of der —th Virginia Cavalry vould not fight mit him he vos a damned liar. I vould have hit him, but I vos under der flag of truce."

I reached my hand out to him across the table.

"I thank you, Captain Carlson," I said, "for both your message and your answer. What did this man look like?"

"He vos a pig vellow, mit a black moustache and gray eyes."

"Do you know him?" questioned Maitland.

"His name is Brennan," I answered slowly, "a major in the Federal service. We have already met twice in rough and tumble contests, but the next time it will be with steel."

"There is a woman, then?"

"It seems from Captain Carlson's report he has seen fit to connect one with our difficulty."

There was a pause, as if they waited for me to add some further explanation, but I could not — her name should never be idly discussed about a mess-table through any word of mine.

"Gentlemen," said Maitland at last, gravely, "this is evidently a personal matter with which we have no direct concern. Captain Wayne's reputation is not one to be questioned, either as regards his chivalry toward women or his bravery in arms. I pledge you his early meeting with this major."

They drank the toast standing, and I read in each face before me a frank, soldierly confidence and comradeship which caused my heart to glow.

CHAPTER XXVI

THE SCOUTING DETAIL

THIS premeditated insult, which Brennan had evidently despatched broadcast in hope that through some unknown channel it might reach me, changed my entire relationship with the man. Heretofore, while feeling deep resentment toward him, I yet was strongly inclined to avoid any personal meeting. Fear had nothing whatever to do with this shrinking on my part, nor would I have deliberately avoided him, yet as the husband of Edith Brennan I realized that if he suffered seriously at my hands it must for ever separate us. I felt more and more deeply the shame of loving the wife of another, and certainly I could never bring myself to advertise her as in any way the cause of so disgraceful a brawl. Far better was it for me to suffer in silence any taunts and degradations he chose to place upon me. Surely I loved her well enough to remain patient for her sake.

But now all this had been changed by a word. His deliberate attempt to soil my reputation among officers of my own corps left me no choice but that of a resort to arms. I have never felt that Brennan was at heart a bad man; he was hard, stern, revengeful, yet I have no doubt under different circumstances I might even have valued him highly as a comrade or a friend. There is no demon like jealousy; and his early distrust of me, fostered by that mad disease, had apparently warped his entire nature. Yet not even for love could I consent to leave my honor undefended, and after those hateful words there could be no rest for me until our differences were settled by the stern arbitrament of the naked blade. All prudence to the winds, no opportunity of meeting him should now be cast aside.

I decided this carefully before falling asleep, and had almost determined upon seeking release from immediate duty that I might hunt him out even within the fancied security of his own camp. This latter plan, however, was instantly halted by those events which crowded swiftly upon me. The coming day was barely gray in the east when I was awakened by a heavy pounding upon the door. A smart-looking orderly stood without.

"Captain Wayne?" he asked.

"That is my name. What have you, my man?"

"Compliments of Colonel Maitland, chief of staff, sir," he said, handing me a folded paper.

I opened it eagerly, for I was more than ready to welcome any occurrence which would help to change the tenor of my thought.

"Dear Wayne:" the private note read, "Believing you would be glad to have the detail, I have just arranged to send you at once upon some active service. Please report at these quarters immediately, fully equipped for the field."

Glad! It was the very medicine I most needed, and within twenty minutes of my receipt of this communication I was with Maitland, thanking him warmly for his thoughtfulness.

"Not another word, Wayne," he insisted. "It is not much, a mere scouting detail over neutral territory, and will probably prove dull enough. I only hope it may

The Scouting Detail

help to divert your mind a trifle. Now listen — you are
to proceed with twenty mounted men of the escort west
as far as the foot-hills, and are expected to note carefully
three things: First, the condition of forage for the sus-
tenance of a wagon train; second, what forces of Federal troops, if any, are along the Honeywell; and third,
the gathering of all information obtainable as to the
reported consolidation of guerillas for purposes of
plunder between the lines. If time suffice, you might
cross over into the valley of the Cowskin and learn the
condition of forage there as well. A guide will accompany your party, and you are to avoid contact with the
enemy as far as possible. Your men carry five days'
rations. You understand fully?"

"I do, sir; I presume I am to start at once?"

"Your squad, under command of Sergeant Ebers, is
already waiting outside."

I found them a sturdy looking lot, but, as they composed
a portion of the commander's personal guard, somewhat
better attired than I was accustomed to seeing Confederate soldiers. I possessed a field officer's prejudice
relative to escort soldiery, yet their equipment looked
well, they sat their horses easily, and I could find nothing
worthy of criticism. I should have preferred riding at
the head of men from my old troop, but in all probability
we would none of us be called upon to draw a sabre.

"Are you all ready, Sergeant?" I asked of the rather
heavy-weight German who stood fronting me, his broad,
red face as impassive as though carved from stone.

"Ve vos, Captain."

"Where is the guide?"

"Dot is him, mit der mule, ain't it?" he answered,
pointing with one huge hand down the road.

231

My Lady of the North

"Very well, we will pick him up then as we go."

I cared so little as to whether or not he accompanied us at all, that we had advanced some distance before the thought of him again occurred to me. I knew the gentry fairly well, and had experienced in the past so many evidences of their stupidity, if not actual disloyalty, as to prefer my own knowledge of the country to theirs. My thought, indeed, for several miles was not at all with the little party of troopers jogging steadily at my heels, nor, in truth, was it greatly concerned with the fate of the expedition. That was but service routine, and I rode forward carelessly enough, never once dreaming that every hour of progress was bearing me toward the most important adventure of my life. So I feel we constantly advance into the future; and it is well that we do not know, for few would possess the necessary courage if beforehand we might perceive the sorrows and the dangers.

Outside my military duties I had but one thought in those days — Edith Brennan. The great struggle was rapidly drawing to its close; hope of future military preferment could no longer inspire a Confederate soldier, for we realized fully we were battling in a lost cause. All ambition which I might otherwise have experienced was therefore concentrated by this fate upon the woman I loved. And how earnestly I endeavored not to love her; how I sought to stifle such feeling, to remain true to what I deemed my highest duty to her and to my own honor! And yet she remained my constant dream. I thought of her now as I rode into the west. Somewhere out yonder, amid those distant blue hills — ay! even within the very zone of my present duty — it was possible she yet waited for the war to cease. I wished

232

in my heart I might again meet her, and then roundly denounced myself as a cur for having such a desire. Yet again and again would the fond hope recur, surging up unbidden into my brain as I rode steadily forward, oblivious of both distance and pace, the sinking sun full in my eyes, yet utterly forgetful of the hoof-beats pounding along behind me. It was the German sergeant who recalled me to the responsibilities of command.

"Captain," he exclaimed apologetically, riding up to my side, and wiping his round perspiring face with great energy, "ve are riding too hard, ain't ve? Mein Gott, but der horses vill give out ontirely, already."

"Is that so?" I asked in surprise at his words. A single swift glance around convinced me he was correct, for the mounts were exceedingly soft, and already looked nearly played out from our sharp pace. "Very well, Ebers, we will halt here."

With a sigh of relief he drew back, and as he did so my eyes fell for the first time upon the guide. As I live, it was Jed Bungay, and when I stared at him in sudden amazement he broke into a broad grin.

"'It trickled still, the starting tear,
    When light a footstep struck her ear,
    And Snowdoun's graceful knight was near,'"

he quoted gravely, his eyes brightening at my recognition. "Durn if I didn't begin ter think as how ye'd gone an' clar fergot me, Cap."

"Not a bit of it, Jed," and I rode up to him and extended my hand. "But how came you here? Are you the guide?"

"Sure thing, Cap; know this yere kintry like a buk. 'Jaded horsemen from the west, at evening to the castle pressed.' By gum, you put Beelzebub an' me through a blamed hard jolt of it so fur."

" Beelzebub? "

" Ye bet, ther muel; I reckon as how ye ain't gone an' fergot him, hev ye?" and the little man squirmed in the delight of his vivid recollection. " ' One blast upon his bugle horn is worth a thousand men.' But ye did ride like thunder, Cap, that 's a fac', an' I ain't ther only one done up, neither. Jist take a squint et thet fat Dutchman thar."

The fleshy Sergeant was undoubtedly fatigued, yet he was a thorough soldier, a strict disciplinarian, and although he moved as if his coarse army trousers were constant torture, he was not guilty of omitting any known requirement of his office.

" Chones," he shouted impressively, " dot is not a good vay to tie dot horse. By Chiminy, he vould break his neck mit der rope. Glen, vy you makes play mit der gun dot vay? Donnerwetter! ven I speak mit you, stand op mit der little finger to der seam of der pantaloons. You vill never be no good."

" Ebers," I interrupted, " let the men rest as they please. I regret having ridden so hard, but I am used to soldiers who are toughened in field work. Are you pretty sore, Sergeant?"

" By Chiminy, I am, Captain; der skin vos rubbed off me by der saddle," he answered, touching the afflicted part tenderly. " It vos der rackin' gait mit der horse vot did it. He is der vorst horse dot ever I ride."

" Well, get as comfortable as you can, and I 'll try to be more thoughtful in the future. Bungay, what has become of Maria?"

The little man's eyes suddenly filled with tears.

The Scouting Detail

"I jist don't know, Cap," he answered mournfully.

"'No more at dawning morn I rise
And sun myself in Ellen's eyes.
That life is lost to love and me.'

Whin I got hum ther ol' cabin hed bin plum burnt down, nary stick o' it left, by gum! an' Mariar she wus clean gone. Hain't seed neither hide ner hair o' her since, thet 's a fac'. An' I sorter drifted back ter you uns 'cause I did n't hev nowhar else ter go."

"Did you hunt for her among the old plantations along the valley?" I asked, deeply touched by his evident feeling. "She very likely sought refuge in some of those houses."

He looked at me in surprise. "I reckon, Cap, as how ye don't know much 'bout whut 's a goin' on in ther valley fer ther las' few months," he said soberly, rubbing down his mule as he spoke. "Tell ye whut, thar jist hain't no plantation houses left thar now, thet 's a fac', leastwise not north o' ther lines we uns sorter hol' onto yit. Sheridan he played hell with his cavalry raids, an' whut the blue-bellies left ther durned guerillas an' bushwhackers wiped up es clean es a slate. Durn if a crow wud n't starve ter deth in ther valley now. Why, Cap, them thar deserters an' sich truck is organized now till they 're mighty nigh an army, an' they don't skeer fer nuthin' les' ner a reg'ment. I see more ner a hundred an' fifty in one bunch up on ther White Briar two week ago, an' they 're worse ner a parcel er pirates. I reckon as how they got Mariar, but I 'll bet she giv 'em a hot ol' time afore she done quit."

Rumors of this state of affairs to north and west of our defending lines had already reached me, — indeed, the verification had formed part of my instructions; but Bungay's homely yet graphic description made the situation appear terribly real, and my thought went instantly forth to those I knew who might even then be exposed to this great and unexpected danger. That it was indeed menacing and constantly growing worse I could not doubt; the certainty of our early defeat was leading to almost wholesale desertions, and doubtless many of these went to swell those lawless ranks, whose sole purpose was plunder, and whose safe rendezvous was the inaccessible mountains. Wherever the guarding armies left neutral ground, there these bands overflowed and inaugurated a reign of terror. What they had been in their weakness I knew well through experiences of the past; what they might become in strength I could readily conjecture,—wild wolves of the hills, to whom human life was of no account, the fierce spawn of civil war. The very conception of Edith Brennan in such hands as these was agony. I felt I could never rest until assured of her safety, and since my orders granted me full authority to prolong my journey, I might ascertain whether or not she yet remained within the valley.

"Jed," I asked, my mind finally settled, "do you know the old Minor plantation?"

"Ol' Jedge Minor's place? Sure; it's up on ther south branch of ther Cowskin, an' used ter be quite a shebang afore ther war, an' afore ther ol' Jedge died. I reckon as how he hed ther biggest gang o' niggers in ther whole county, an' he wus allers durn gud ter 'em tew. Never no nigger ever run 'way from ol' Jedge Minor, ye bet. Mariar she used ter live thar whin Mis' Celie wus a baby."

"Have those fellows got down that far yet?"

The Scouting Detail

" Wal, I reckon not, but durn if I know fer sure, Cap. Ther whole valley is mighty bare north o' thar, fer I rid through it, an' Beelzebub hed ter live on clay, fer sure. Gee! but he wus hot. So them thar vultures hes got ter either work south er quit, an' I reckon as how they hain't likely ter quit till they hes tew. 'Sides, they're strong 'nough by now ter laugh et any sojers thar'bouts, an' ther ol' Minor place u'd make mighty gud pickin'. Thar hain't neither army ever bin up thar durin' ther war."

" How long would it take us to reach there? "

" 'Bout two days, I reckon, pervidin' ye shuck ther Dutchman."

I turned and looked at my men in some perplexity. They were scattered along the edge of the road, and only one group had taken the precaution to build a fire. The Sergeant lay flat upon his back on a grassy knoll, his stomach rising and falling with a regularity which convinced me he was sleeping.

" Ebers," I said sternly.

There was no response, and I could distinguish clearly his heavy breathing.

" One of you stir up the Sergeant, will you? I want to speak with him."

A young fellow came forward grinning, and laid one hand heavily on his officer's shoulder.

" Come, Dutchy," he said with easy familiarity, " get up ! "

The Sergeant shot to an upright position like a jack-in-the-box. " Mein Gott," he asked anxiously, " is it der Yanks vot come already? "

" Hell, no; but the Captain wants you."

" Der Captain? " He arose ponderously, and came forward with a decidedly halting gait.

237

"Vos I sent for?" he asked.

"Yes," I said; "I want you to have the men get their supper at once, as we shall be obliged to ride a good portion of the night."

"Ride?" and his face took on an expression of genuine horror. "By Chiminy, Captain, it vos impossible. Mein Gott! it could not be done."

"Why, what is the difficulty, Sergeant?"

"I am vounded vare I sets me down on der saddle. I am all — vot you calls it? — rare. Dunder, but it could not be."

"I am exceedingly sorry, Ebers, and if you are unable to travel we shall be compelled to leave you behind," I said, tired of it all by this time. "Get the men to their supper. We shall go on in an hour."

How often since have I smiled at the expression upon his solemn round face as he turned ruefully away!

CHAPTER XXVII

AN EMBARRASSING SITUATION

IT was well into the third day when we came down into the fertile valley of the Cowskin. It had proven an uneventful ride thus far, for we had met with no adventures and had observed little worthy of consideration from a military standpoint. We had travelled slowly, carefully watchful of our horses, not only because we felt they might be greatly needed farther on, but owing to the impoverished and almost deserted country through which we rode. Abandoned houses, many of them devastated by fire, deserted negro quarters, and uncultivated fields greeted our eyes constantly, and told us we were in the track of armies. Forage there was absolutely none, while even the pasture-land gave small return. The men had done well, however, and were stiffening nicely into field soldiers, while my Teutonic second in command had sufficiently recovered from his wounds to sit his saddle with some elephantine grace. He early proved himself a good soldier, and I learned he had seen considerable active service in Europe.

While constantly observant of those points regarding which I had been despatched, my one overmastering thought during all those hours was the possibility of again meeting with Edith Brennan and proving of some assistance to her. Her greeting of me in the Federal hospital had been so sweetly gracious, so marked with tender sympathy, while the memory of her words, and even more of the look which accompanied them, had so remained with me in encouragement that I longed to encounter her again. God knows what I hoped for, for I knew well it must all inevitably end in despair, yet like the moth I must continue to singe my wings until the flame devoured me. Now, however, as we actually drew near to where I supposed she might be, I felt my earlier courage fast deserting me. Nor was I furnished with even the slightest excuse for pressing on; my orders did not positively compel me to proceed, and nothing appeared along the way to lead me to suppose that harm of any kind threatened that peaceful valley. Everything meeting my eyes evidenced that here, at least, war with its attendant horrors had not come. Totally without the beaten track of those great armies which had battled so fiercely for the Shenandoah, it had been traversed only by a few scouting and foraging parties, and so short had been their stay that even the rail fences remained undisturbed to guard the fields, and nowhere did I note outward signs of devastation. It was Virginia as I recalled it in those old days of peace and plenty, before civil strife had sown the land with dead.

What possible excuse, then, had I for going there? In my own heart I knew I had none, or one so poor and selfish I scarcely durst whisper it even to myself; yet I rode steadily on. Impelled by my own weakness, or drawn irresistibly by fate, — whichever the real cause I know not, — I would at least look upon those walls that had once sheltered her, would learn if possible if she was yet there. Then — well, in the bondage of my passion I hoped for what might happen, as every lover does.

It must have been two o'clock; we had baited our

An Embarrassing Situation

horses, I remember, an hour previous; and the Sergeant
had enjoyed his noonday siesta beneath the shade of
a great bush bearing purple blossoms. The road we had
been travelling since early morning wound in and out
among great trees, and crossed and recrossed the little
stream called the Cowskin until I almost thought we had
lost our way. We met with no one in all the long day's
riding, not even a stray negro, and indeed it was some
hours since we had passed a house of any kind. Leaving
the brook behind us we toiled slowly up a long hill,
and at the top Bungay, riding beside me, pointed to
the westward.

"Cap," he said, "thar is ther Minor place."

The very sight of it in the distance was a thrill —
a great white house placed well back from the road and
almost hidden from sight by fine, large trees; an old-
fashioned, big-roomed house it looked to be, built after
the colonial type, a wide veranda upon three sides, with
fluted columns to support the overhanging roof.

"Hain't no signs es fer es I kin see of any trouble
havin' 'curred thar," Jed said slowly, his shrewd gray
eyes roaming over the peaceful scene. "Somebody ter
hum tew, fer ther chimley is a smokin'."

Of course, now I was there, the only sensible thing for
me to do would have been to ride openly to the front
door, and thus learn all I desired. But what man who
loves, who is continually swayed by hopes and fears, by
strength and weakness, ever does the sensible thing?
I had certainly intended doing so at the start, but now
my nerve failed me. She was the wife of another. I
could not confess I had ventured to come to her in love,
nor could I look into those clear, honest, questioning
eyes and lie.

16   241

My Lady of the North

"Halt!" I ordered. "Sergeant!"

"I am here, Captain."

"Take your men down into that hollow yonder, and remain there until I return. Better post a sentry on the hill here."

"It vill be done, Captain."

"I shall not, probably, be absent more than an hour, so don't permit the men to stray."

"Dot is it, Captain. I vill be mit dem all over."

I rode down alone into the thick woods at the foot of the hill, and dismounting, tied my horse to a sapling. Then on foot I struck across the fields, my intention being to come in by way of the negro quarters at the rear, in hope of meeting some one from whom I might inquire relative to the great house and its inmates.

It was a slight upward trend of land I had to traverse, and although the house was a most sightly object and stood upon the very summit of the elevation, yet so surrounded was it with trees, both fruit and ornamental, I was enabled to make but little of its situation until I approached the out-buildings. I met with no one, nor could I perceive any negroes about the slave quarters. Yet the place did not bear the appearance of desertion. There were horses in the stable, a cat was curled up on one of the cabin doorsteps, and smoke continued to pour in a dull yellow cloud from the kitchen chimney. Altogether there was much in the situation to puzzle over, and I no longer regretted that I had exercised some caution in my approach.

The orchard, with the remains of a garden, lay between the house and the stable, protected by a low fence of whitened pickets. So far as I could observe, it contained no occupant, and I pushed open the gate and started down

242

An Embarrassing Situation

a narrow cinder-path which led between two rows of low bushes. To right of me was an extensive grape-arbor completely covered with vines, the fresh green leaves forming a delightful contrast to the deep blue sky beyond. As I came opposite an opening leading into this arbor I suddenly caught the flutter of drapery and stopped instantly, my heart throbbing like a frightened girl's. It was quite dark beneath the vine shadow, and I could make out no more than that a woman stood there, her back toward me, busied at some task. Possibly she felt my presence, for all at once she glanced around, and upon perceiving me gave vent to a quick exclamation of terror.

"Pardon me," I said hastily, and removing my hat, "but you have nothing to fear."

There was a moment's hesitancy on her part, and I knew I was being scrutinized by a pair of bright eyes.

"Surely," said a familiar voice, "I cannot be mistaken —you are Captain Wayne."

Before I could even answer she stepped forth from her partial concealment and advanced toward me with cordially extended hands. It was Celia Minor.

"Well, of all men!" she cried gayly, her dark eyes smiling a most kindly welcome. "And Edith and I were speaking about you only yesterday. That is, I was, for really I do not recall now that Edith made any remark apropos of the subject. You have no idea, Captain Wayne, what a hero I have made you out to be. It would make you positively vain if I should confess; why, Arthur has actually become so jealous that he has almost forbidden me even to mention your name in his presence. So when I want to talk about you I am compelled to go to Edith. She has n't power to stop me, you know, but I'm sure I must bore her awfully. And then to

243

think that when you stood there just now, and I saw
your gray uniform, I actually thought the guerillas had
come. My heart beats so now I can hardly talk. But
how pale and haggard you look — is it that horrible
wound which troubles you still?"

"I have been discharged from the hospital only a short
time," I answered, as she paused to take breath. "Indeed, this is my first military service for several months,
yet I am feeling quite strong again. Mrs. Brennan, then,
is still with you?"

"Oh, yes; we have been here all winter long. It has
been so dull, for really nothing has happened, and the
valley is quite devoid of inhabitants — even the negroes
have gone hunting freedom. But Major Brennan and
Arthur are to be here this afternoon, and sometime to-
night we are all of us going away together. How glad
I am you arrived before we left! I would n't have missed
meeting you for worlds. Do you know, it is so hard
for me not to call you Colonel Curran, but Edith always
insists on my saying Captain Wayne, so that it comes
more natural now. Really, sometimes I actually believe
she has corrected me a dozen times a day, for you know
we have so little to talk about here that we are always
drifting back to what occurred to us while we were with
the army. I often wonder Edith can be contented here
at all, but she really seems to regret that we must leave.
I 'm sure I don't, even if I was born here; it 's an awful
poky old place."

I gave heed to but little of her good-humored chatter
after the first sentence. Eager as I was to meet Brennan,
I had no desire that we should meet in the presence of
his wife. Better, far better, would it be for me to leave
at once and without even seeing her.

An Embarrassing Situation

"You say you are about to depart?" I asked, determined to learn all possible regarding their plans. "Do you go North?"

"Yes, to Baltimore and Washington. The guerillas are becoming so desperate in this neighborhood that we are actually afraid to remain here longer. They attacked the Cuyler plantation, only ten miles from here, two weeks ago, killed old Mr. Cuyler, turned his wife out partially dressed in the middle of the night, looted the house of everything it contained of value, and then set it on fire. You see we have no men folks here, except two negroes, who have clung to us because they were so aged they were afraid to leave — just mamma, Edith, my old nurse, and myself. It seems so lonely, and Major Brennan and Arthur both insist it is no longer safe. So they are coming with a cavalry escort to take us all North. I am sure we shall have a splendid time."

"You have experienced no trouble, then, thus far?"

"Oh, none at all — we have not even been bothered by scouting parties. Oh, I do not mean you; you are no bother. But yesterday there was a horrible man here; he came to the kitchen door, and asked all sorts of impudent questions. Mrs. Bungay actually had to threaten him with a gun before he would leave."

"Is Maria Bungay here, then?"

"Why, certainly; do you know her? Isn't she a delightful old dear, — just as good as a man?"

"Her husband is with my party."

"Jed — really? Why, do you know, Maria has got it into her head that he had run away from her. I should so love to witness their meeting; it would be most interesting. But you must come into the house, Captain Wayne; Edith will be overjoyed to see you again, although you know she is never demonstrative, as I am. It must be awfully nice to be always cool and calm, don't you think?"

Determined that I would not be tempted, I yet hesitated, and my vivacious companion took everything for granted at once.

"Oh, before we go in, won't you do me a favor?" she asked. "But of course you will. I was trying to tie this grapevine into place when you surprised me, but I could not hold on with one hand and tie with the other. See what I mean?" And placing one slender foot upon a slat of the trellis she lifted herself up until she could barely reach the refractory branch. "Now," she said, smiling down upon me, "please just hold me here for a moment until I secure this end."

My hand was scarcely upon her in support when the slender slat snapped beneath her weight. As she fell I caught her with both arms. For a moment she lay, panting and startled, on my breast; then, as with a little laugh she disengaged herself from my embrace, we stood there hand in hand and face to face with Edith Brennan.

Shall I ever forget the look within her eyes? How plainly I saw it, although she stood half hidden beneath the shadow of the vines. Amazement, incredulity, scorn were expressed there, yet even as I marked them all became merged into proud unconsciousness. She would have turned away without a word, but my companion stopped her.

"Edith," she cried eagerly, "do you not see? This is Captain Wayne."

She turned toward me and slightly inclined her head.

"I recognized Captain Wayne," was her calm answer,

"and regret greatly having intruded upon him. It was entirely unintentional, and I have no desire to remain."

I could not have spoken at that moment to save my life. It fairly stunned me to realize the construction she so plainly placed upon the scene just enacted. Not so the girl at my side. Her cheeks flushed with indignation, and her audacity gave her speech which made matters even worse than before.

"You are exceedingly free with your criticisms, Edith," she exclaimed sharply, as the latter turned her back upon us. "Perhaps it would be as well for you first to ascertain the truth."

"You wholly mistake," was the calm reply. "I have not presumed to criticise. Why should I? It is not a matter which interests me in the least. I presume you have no further objection to my returning to the house?"

She did not so much as deign to look again at either of us, but as she moved slowly out of sight Miss Minor turned and looked into my face with questioning eyes. What she may have read there I know not, but she sank back upon a bench and burst into a merry peal of laughter.

"Isn't it perfectly ridiculous!" she cried, as soon as she was able to speak. "Only I do hope she won't tell Arthur."

CHAPTER XXVIII

WE CAPTURE A COURIER

THE girl's light burst of laughter aroused me thoroughly to a sense of our situation.

"You seem to derive much amusement from a condition of affairs almost intolerable to me," I said bitterly. "I have always valued most highly the friendship of Mrs. Brennan, but this unfortunate occurrence will doubtless end it."

She glanced up at me, her long lashes wet, but her dark eyes sparkling with mischief.

"Oh, she won't care so far as you are concerned," she exclaimed indifferently. "But I suppose she will think I am perfectly horrid. Well, I don't care if she does; she might have waited and learned the truth first. Was n't her face a study? And how shall I ever explain to Arthur so that he will understand? I 'm sure I have got the worst of it. Oh, Captain Wayne, is my hair all ruffled up? I know I look like a fright. You must come in now, and we will explain to Mrs. Brennan the whole matter. She cannot help believing us both, while I know she would be so cold and proud with me alone."

I shook my head decisively. Perhaps it was better ended so; at least I possessed no courage just then to face her indignation. She might but deem we had concocted our explanation, and would very likely receive it with all the scorn she felt it deserved. Besides, it was clear there was nothing I could do to aid them. I should be now merely an unwelcome intruder. An escort was to be there shortly to convoy them northward, and for me to be found in their company by Brennan would only inflame him and add greatly to the embarrassment of his wife's position. Much as I might long for immediate vindication in her sight, the plain duty of true love was to depart at once, and permit time to straighten out the tangle.

"You must pardon me," I hastened to say, standing hat in hand before her, "but it would not be best for me to intrude upon Mrs. Brennan after her late reception. I merely halted here in order to assure myself of your presence and safety. My men are even now waiting for me a few hundred yards away."

"But I wish you to meet Arthur."

"Oh, I think not, Miss Minor. I feel warm friendship for Lieutenant Caton, but we wear different uniforms, serve under different flags, and a meeting here, both with armed forces behind us, would naturally have to be a hostile one. However the Lieutenant and I might consent to a temporary truce, his superior officer, Major Brennan, would not likely prove of the same mind."

"Then you really must go?"

"Unless you specially desire to witness a cavalry skirmish in your front dooryard, I certainly consider it best," and I held out my hand. "Surely we part as friends, and I may hope that you will intercede in my behalf with Mrs. Brennan?"

She rose up impulsively.

"How ridiculous; how supremely ridiculous! Why, of course I will, though I don't suppose Edith really cares very much, but she believed it would be highly proper to be shocked. I don't think she likes you so very well anyway, Captain Wayne, for she never will talk about you."

With these cheering words ringing in my ears, and feeling thoroughly defeated in every cherished hope, I strode savagely down the long hill and mounted my horse. How roughly fortune had buffeted me, to be sure, and how extremely small the inspiration left. Well, perhaps I deserved it for ever permitting myself to love one whom I knew to be the wife of another. Doubtless she had seized upon this slight pretext to be rid of me, and was already rejoicing over its easy accomplishment.

In my agitation I forgot entirely the presence of Maria Bungay at the house, and ordering my men into saddle prepared for departure without giving a thought to the little fellow and his domestic troubles. I chose the road leading toward the northwest, for although I had not asked the question I conceived it highly probable that Brennan and his party would ride from the Federal cavalry quarters at Colter's Church, and I had no desire to meet them. They were upon an errand of mercy of far greater importance than my revenge.

As we swung along through the heavily timbered land fringing our road, Bungay pressed his mule into a trot and finally succeeded in ranging up at my side. Even in my disturbed mental condition I was amused at his unique style of riding, although I would not wound him by laughing.

"I say, Cap," he said, jerking the words out to the mule's hard trot, and grasping his saddle pommel desperately, "I sorter reckon as how ther'll be some fun back thar afore long, 'less all signs fail."

"Why?" I stared at him, now thoroughly aroused

to the thought that he had important news to communicate.

"Wal," he explained slowly, "whin ye wint off, I sorter tuk a notion ter look 'bout a bit. Used ter be an ol' stompin' ground o' mine. So Dutchy an' me clumb thet big hill back o' whar we halted, an' by gum, down thar in ther gully on t' other side thar 's a durned big camp o' fellers."

I reined up short, and with uplifted hand signalled the men behind to halt.

"Why did n't you tell me this before?" I questioned sternly. "How many were there? and what did they look like?"

He scratched the back of his head thoughtfully, and answered with careful deliberation. "Durn it, I did n't jine ye till after ye 'd started, an' I reckon as how it took me all o' tew mile ter git this yere blame muel up ter whar I cud talk. Thar 's quite a smart bunch, but they hed some pickets out, an' I cud n't git close 'nough ter tell zackly. Dutchy thought thar wus nigh onter two hunderd o' 'em, but I jist don't know. They wus n't dressed like sojers o' either army, an' I reckon they 're out o' ther hills."

I glanced at my little handful of men, scarcely knowing what decision it might be wise to make. Undoubtedly they would fight if occasion arose, but the odds were terribly heavy; besides, if Brennan came, and his party got away that same evening, as was planned for them to do, then it might not be necessary for us to strike a blow. I was certainly in no mood to expose my small command merely to save the empty house from destruction.

"Ebers," I said, turning toward the Sergeant, who sat

his horse with expressionless face, "you were with the guide when he discovered this camp. How many do you think it contained? and who were they?"

"Vel, dere vos more as two gompanies, Captain, und dere vos some horses, but dey vos dressed — vot you calls it? — all ober not der same."

"Not in uniform?"

"Dot vos it."

"Have any of the rest of you seen anything that looked suspicious?" I asked, glancing around into the different faces.

"Maybe I did," answered one of the troopers named Earl. "As we rode up the first hill after leaving the house my horse picked up a stone, and I had to stop and get it out. I reckon I fell behind a quarter of a mile or more, and just as I started I looked back, and a party of ten or twelve fellows was just riding in through them big gates onto the front lawn. But them fellows was soldiers for sure; they rode regular like, and all of them wore caps. It was so far off I could n't tell the color of their clothes, but them caps made me think they was Feds."

I chose my course at once. This undoubtedly must have been Brennan's party.

"Thank you, my man; it would have been better if you had reported that to me at once," I said. "However, I understand the situation much better now. Sergeant, we will go into camp here. Post pickets in both directions, but put your most careful men on that hill yonder. Let them report promptly any signs of fire to the southeast, or any sound of guns."

We completed all our cooking before dark, and when the night finally closed down about us it proved to be an exceedingly black one, although the skies were clear. Sleep was an impossibility for me, as my mind was in constant turmoil. I felt hampered, prisoned, shut in, unable to do what I most desired. I wondered where she was — probably riding northward beside her husband, and I bit my lip savagely at thought of it; possibly she was even then laughing merrily in memory of my unfortunate predicament in the garden. So she cared nothing for me, exhibited her indifference clearly in presence of others, disliked even to hear my name mentioned. Very well, I would take exceeding good care never again to intrude myself upon her. Then my thoughts swerved to the big house out yonder in the darkness. If signs of attack came to us, what should I do? The question truly puzzled me, for I was unwilling to expose the lives of my men merely to save property — Confederate soldiers were far too valuable at that stage of the war. If I only knew positively that the women were safely away, I would tarry no longer in the neighborhood. But I did not know; I merely hoped.

Ebers was lying next me upon the grass, solemnly puffing at his huge pipe, and I held my watch to the glow in its bowl in order to see the time. It was nearly midnight.

"Those fellows ought to be at it before this," I said to him, "if they intend to accomplish anything to-night."

"I dink so too," he answered slowly. "I vill see dot der guard is all right, an' den vill get some sleep, for I am pretty moch done op already."

He arose ponderously to his feet, and stretched out his short arms in a prodigious yawn. As he stood there, his pudgy figure outlined against the sky, there was borne to our ears the sound of a furious struggle on the

253

hilltop to the south — a shout, blows, a volley of cursing, then silence. An instant later we were both running through the darkness toward the scene of trouble.

"What is it, Sands?" I questioned breathlessly, as I came suddenly upon the little group.

"A fellar on hossback," was the answer. "He come up on us like a streak out o' thet black hollor, an' he'd a sure got away ef Mason hed n't clubbed him with his gun. I've got the cuss safe collared now."

"Who are you?" I asked sternly, striving in vain to see something of him through the darkness. "Where were you riding?"

He maintained a sullen silence, and Sands kicked him.

"None of that," I commanded. "Ebers, strike a match, will you, and let me see this chap."

I had scarcely spoken when our prisoner thrust Sands roughly aside and took one hasty step toward me.

"My God, Wayne! Is it possible this is you?" he cried excitedly.

"Caton?" I exclaimed, as surprised as himself. "Caton? What is it? What is wrong?"

"Am I to do dot?" asked the Sergeant, anxiously.

"No," I answered. "I know this man, and we shall need no fire. Caton, are you from the Minor house? Has it been attacked?"

"Yes," he answered, panting yet from his exertion and excitement. "We were to start North with the ladies at nine o'clock, but the house was surrounded as soon as it became dark. Those devils supposed it to be unguarded, and advanced without precautions. We fired and drove them back. We had repulsed three attacks when I left at eleven, but three of our men were already hit."

We Capture a Courier

"You were after aid?"

"I was striving to reach our advance pickets at McMillan. It seemed the only possible chance, and none of the men would volunteer to make the ride. One was killed trying it before I started. God knows how I hated to leave them, but it had to be done. How many have you?"

"Only twenty; but if we could once get inside along with your fellows, we might hold the house until reinforcements came."

"Thank God! I knew you would!" he cried joyfully, grasping me again fervently by the hand. "You are not one to hesitate over the color of a uniform at such a time as this. I have been proud all through this war to feel that we on both sides were of the same blood, and have felt like cheering your gray lines more than once. Only, Wayne," and he hesitated an instant, "it is right I should tell you that Brennan is there, and in command."

"I know it, but those women must be saved nevertheless," I answered firmly, my mind settled. "This is no time for personal quarrelling, and whatever color of cloth we wear those outlaws are our common enemies, to be hunted down like wild beasts. I have seen specimens of their fiendish cruelty that make my blood run cold to remember. The very thought of those who are now exposed falling into such hands is enough to craze one; death would be preferable a thousand times. How many fighting men have you?"

"Seven fit for duty."

"Will you ride forward, or go back with us?"

"We must send word,"—and the gallant fellow's voice shook,—"but God knows, Wayne, I want to go back. If we both live I am to marry Celia Minor."

255

"I understand," I said gravely. "Ebers, who is your best rider?"

"It vos dot funny leetle yellow Glen, Captain."

"Glen, come here."

The trooper, a mere boy, with freckled face and great honest gray eyes, but wiry and tough as steel, pushed his way through the group and faced me.

"Glen," I said, "your Sergeant tells me you are the best rider in the troop. I am going to intrust you with the most important duty of all. The lives of every one of us and of four helpless women depend entirely upon your riding. You will take two horses, kill both if necessary, but stop for nothing until your duty is done. You are to carry a note from me, and another from this gentleman, who is an officer in the Federal army, and deliver them both to the commandant of the first military post you find. Insist upon reaching him in person. It makes no difference which army the post belongs to, for this is a matter of humanity. The Federal outpost at McMillan is the nearest to us; make for there. You understand?"

The boy saluted gravely, all mischief gone from his face.

"I do, sir," he said. "But I 'd a darn sight rather stay here and fight."

"You will be back in plenty of time to take a hand, my lad. Now, men," — and I turned to the dark, expectant ring about me, — "this is no ordinary duty of your enlistment, and I wish no one to accompany me to-night who does not volunteer for the service. Seven Federal soldiers and four women, three of them Virginians, are attacked at the house we have just left by a large party of bushwhacking guerillas, the offscourings of hell. Every one of you knows what that means. Will you go with me to their rescue?"

No one seemed anxious to be first to speak. I could see them look aside uneasily at one another.

"Bungay," I said, "I feel sure you will go, for your wife is there."

"Mariar?"

"Yes; Miss Minor told me this afternoon, but I had forgotten to mention it."

The little man sprang into the air and came down with a whoop.

"The bloody devils!" he cried excitedly. "Ye bet I'll go."

"Come, Sergeant, speak up; what do you men say?"

"I like not to fight mit der Yankees," he admitted candidly, "but der vomens, py Chiminy, dot vos anoder ting. I vill go, Captain; mein Gott, yaw."

"We're with you, sir," spoke voice after voice gravely around the dark circle, and then Sands added: "We'll show them thar Yanks how the Johnny Rebs kin fight, sir."

Ten minutes later Glen, bearing his two messages to the Blue and Gray, was speeding recklessly through the black night northward, while my little squad was moving cautiously back over the road we had so lately traversed.

CHAPTER XXIX

A MISSION FOR BEELZEBUB

AS we picked our way slowly forward through the gloom I gleaned from Caton all he knew regarding the situation before us. My own knowledge of the environments of the Minor house helped me greatly to appreciate the difficulties to be surmounted. He had succeeded in his escape by dodging among the negro cabins where the attacking line appeared weakest, but expressed the conviction that even this slight gap would be securely closed long before we reached there.

" Have they sufficient men, then, to cover thoroughly all four sides ? " I asked.

" To the best of my judgment there must be fully two hundred and fifty in the gang, and apparently they operate under strict military discipline. It is a revelation to me, Wayne, of the growing power of these desperate fellows. I knew they were becoming numerous and bold, but this surpasses anything I could imagine. More, they are being constantly recruited by new arrivals. A party of at least a dozen came in while I was hiding behind the stables. I heard them asking for the leader."

" What did they call him? "

" Lory, or Laurie, something like that. They claimed to be deserters from Lee's army, but two or three of them wore our uniforms."

" It 's Red Lowrie," I said gravely, more impressed than

A Mission for Beelzebub

ever with the seriousness of the situation. "I heard of him two years ago — he killed a man in the Sixth North Carolina, and took to the hills. Since then he has developed into quite a leader for such scum, and has proven himself a merciless monster. You have no suggestion to offer as to how we had better attempt to get in?"

He shook his head despondingly.

"What station does Brennan defend?" I asked.

"The front of the house; the main point of attack has been there."

We could distinguish the sound of firing by this time, and its continuous volume convinced me that Caton's estimate of the number engaged was not greatly overdrawn. As we topped the summit of the hill a great burst of red fire leaped suddenly high into the sky.

"Great God, Wayne! we are too late!" he cried wildly. "Those devils have fired the house."

With fiercely throbbing heart I gazed down at the flames far below in the black valley.

"No," I said with eager relief. "It is the stable which is ablaze. See, the light falls full upon the white sides of the house. Thank Heaven, we are not too late."

As I sat my horse there, gazing down upon that scene of black rapine, unwilling to venture into its midst until I could formulate some definite plan of action, fully a dozen wild schemes thronged into my brain, only to be cast aside, one after another, as thoroughly impracticable.

"We shall have to make a dash for it, and trust in God," said Caton, guessing at my dilemma.

"No," I answered firmly, "there would be no possibility of success in such a course. Those fellows are old hands, and have pickets out. See, Caton, that is certainly a picket-fire yonder where the road dips. Every

man of us would be shot down before we penetrated
those guard lines and attained the house. We have got
to reach their inner line someway through strategy, and
even then must risk being fired upon by our own people
before we get within cover."

Even as I was speaking I evolved a plan of action —
desperate it certainly was, yet nothing better occurred to
me, and time was golden.

"Ebers," I said, "did n't I see an extra jacket strapped
back of your saddle?"

"It is no good," he protested vehemently. "It vos for
der rain come."

"All right; hand it over to the Lieutenant here. Caton,
throw that uniform coat of yours into the ditch, and don
honest gray for once. Sands, come here. Take your
knife and cut away every symbol of rank on my jacket;
tear it off, any way you can."

In another moment these necessary changes had been
accomplished.

"Now," I ordered, "pile your sabres there with mine
beside the road; then hobble your horses, all but the mule;
I shall want him."

"Does we go der rest of der vay on foot?" questioned
the Sergeant, anxiously.

"Certainly; and I desire you to remember one important thing: let me do the talking, but if any of you are
asked questions, we are deserters from Hills's corps, tired
of the war."

"Mein Gott!" muttered the German, disconsolately.
"I hope it vos not long off, Captain; I am no good on
foot in der dark, by Chiminy."

"You had better manage to keep up to-night, unless
you are seeking to commit suicide. Now, men, mark

A Mission for Beelzebub

me carefully! Load your carbines. Are you all ready? Sergeant, see that each man has his gun properly charged and capped. You are to carry your arms as thoroughly concealed as possible; keep close to me always; obey my orders instantly, and to the letter. We are but twenty men pitted against over two hundred, remember, and when we strike, it must be both quick and hard."

I mounted the mule, counted the dim figures in the darkness, and then gave the order to march. As we moved slowly down the hill I was aware that Caton walked upon one side of me, while Bungay plodded along upon the other; but my mind was so filled with the excitement of our adventure and all that depended upon its successful culmination, as scarcely to realize anything other than the part I must personally play. Good fortune and audacity alone could combine to win the game we were now engaged upon.

A tall, heavily bearded mountaineer stood squarely in the middle of the road to the north of the picket-fire. I could make but little of him as the light shone, excepting that he wore a high coonskin cap and bore a long rifle.

"Stop right thar!" he called out hoarsely, upon hearing us. "Who are you uns?"

As he challenged, a dozen others sprang up from about the flame and, guns in hand, came toward us on a run.

"We uns are doggoned tired o' soldierin', an' a gittin' nuthin' fer it," I said in the slow Southern drawl, "an' wanter jine yer gang, pervidin' thar 's any show fer it."

"How many are ye?" asked one of the newcomers, striding forward between us and the sentry.

"A right smart heap o' a bunch; bin a pickin' o' 'em up ever since we left Charlotte," I returned evasively.

My Lady of the North

" They be dandies ter fight, an' I reckon as how ye kin use 'em, can't ye? "

" Maybe; who did ye want ter see? "

" Wal, they sed as how a feller named Lowrie wus a runnin' this yere gang, an' if thet's ther way o' it, I reckon as how it's Lowrie we're after. Be you Lowrie? "

" Naw."

The answer was so gruff and short, and the fellow hesitated so long in adding anything to it, I began to think it was all off.

" Wal," he consented to say at last, ungraciously, " thar's a blame pile o' ye kim in lately, an' I calcalate we got 'bout 'nough fer our business, but I reckon as how Red will use ye somewhar. Anyhow you uns kin come 'long with me an' find out, but ye'll diskiver him 'bout ther ornerest man jist now ever ye run up agin. He's plum mad, Red is, fer sartain."

He turned and strode off, without so much as giving us a backward glance, and, with a hearty congratulatory kick to the mule, I and my company followed him. A hundred yards further in we passed through the fringe of trees and emerged into an open space from whence we could see plainly the great white house still illumined by the flames which continued to consume the stables. Shots were flashing like fireflies out of the darkness on every side of us, the smell of burning powder scented the air, and I could distinguish the black forms of men lying prone on the grass in something resembling a skirmish line.

" Makin' a fight o' it, ain't they? " I asked of our taciturn guide, as we picked our way carefully among the recumbent forms.

A Mission for Beelzebub

"Damn 'em, yes; a hell o' a fight," he admitted bitterly. "Reckoned we hed a soft job yere, an' lots o' ther stuff fer ther boys. They 've got some Yanks in thar with repeatin' rifles, but I reckon as whin Red once gits hold on 'em, they 'll dance ter another tune."

"Ye mean ter stick it out, then?"

"Stick it out? I reckon ye don't know Red, er ye would n't be askin' sich a fule question. He 'll hev them Yanks now, if it wur ter cost every man he 's got. He ain't no quitter, Red ain't."

Just beyond musket-shot from the house, and nearly opposite the front entrance, quite a group of men were standing beneath the black shadows of a grove of trees. In spite of the gleam from the fire I could make little of them, but as we approached from the direction of the rear, one of them exclaimed suddenly:

"Who comes thar? What body o' men is thet?"

"It 's 'nother party o' deserters, as wants ter jine us," said the guide, sourly. "They 's Johnnies from Lee's army."

"Oh, they dew, dew they? Hain't got 'nough o' fightin' yit, I reckon," and the speaker strode forward, with a rough, mirthless laugh. "Wal, damn 'em, they will yere 'fore I 'm done. We 're a goin' ter rush thet thar house 'fore long, an' hang 'bout a dozen Yanks, an' these yere lads will come in right handy ter go in first. If you uns like fightin' so durn well we 'll give ye your bellies full. Who 's ther boss o' this yere crowd?"

I swung down from my seat on the mule's back, and stood facing him.

"We uns hain't got no boss," I answered, "but they sorter fell in ahind o' me 'cause I wus astraddle o' this muel. Be you named Lowrie?"

My Lady of the North

"I reckon; I'm Red Lowrie," proudly. "'Spect, maybe, ye've heerd tell o' me, an' if ye hev, ye know ye've got ter step damn lively whin I howl. Whut wus ye in ther army?"

"Corporal."

The flames of the burning barn leaped suddenly upward, as if fed by some fresh combustion, and flung a brighter glare over the rough faces clustered about us. I saw Red Lowrie plainly enough now, as he peered eagerly forward to scan my face, a heavy-set, coarse-featured man, with prominent nose, and thick, matted red beard. He wore a wide-brimmed soft army hat, under which his eyes shone maliciously, and he grasped a long rifle in one big, hairy hand. As I gazed at him curiously, some one hastily pushed a way through the group at his back, and the next instant a tall figure stood at his side. I recognized the newcomer at a single glance, and for the moment my heart fairly choked me — it was Craig.

"Lowrie," he said, pointing straight at me, "thar's somethin' wrong yere. That feller thar is Captain Wayne, o' my ol' reg'ment."

All that occurred next was but the impulse of a second. I stood with hand resting lightly upon the mule's neck, his long head drooping sleepily beside my shoulder. I saw Red Lowrie throw up his gun, all his evil nature written in his face, his cruel eyes instantly aflame with anger, and, inspired by the desperation of our case, I stooped suddenly, and blew with all my force into that long, pendant ear. Beelzebub gave vent to one snort of mingled rage and terror, and then let drive, backing into that cluster of choice rascals like a very thunderbolt of wrath, cleaving his way by every lightning blow of those nimble legs, and tumbling men to right and left.

A Mission for Beelzebub

There was a yell of fright, a wild scramble for safety, a perfect volley of cursing — I saw Red Lowrie go tumbling backward, a heel planted fairly in the pit of his stomach, and the next instant Craig, swearing like a pirate, was jammed down on top of him, a red gash across his forehead. It was all accomplished so speedily, that it seemed but a medley of heels, of wildly cavorting mule, of scrambling, falling men.

"Fire!" I cried excitedly. "Sock it into them, lads, and follow me!"

There was a quick outburst of flame, a thunderous report, and, without waiting to see or hear more, I sprang forward through the dense smoke, and raced madly toward the front door. Caton panted at my side, and I could hear the heavy feet of a score of men pounding the turf behind us. The rush was so rapid, the noise so great and confusing, I could not distinguish whether we were even fired upon from the rear, but I marked a red flash at one of the windows in our front, and heard behind me a sharp wail of agony.

"If any man drops, pick him up!" I called, and at that moment we sprang up the steps, and began pounding loudly against the door.

"Open up!" shouted the Lieutenant, anxiously. "Brennan, open up, quick! It's Caton with help."

I thought it never would open. A volley crashed into us, and Sands pitched down upon his face, clutching at the man next him as he fell. I glanced back anxiously — a dark, confused mass of men, without military formation, were running across the open space toward us.

"'Bout face!" I shouted. "Load at will — fire!"

We poured one scattering volley into them. It halted

265

their movement for a moment, and then the door opened a scant crack.

" Is this you, Caton?"

" Yes; for God's sake, open up!"

The heavy door swung slowly inward, and with a wild rush to be first, we surged headlong into the hall.

CHAPTER XXX

A UNION OF YANK AND REB

AS the heavy door clanged behind us some one upon the outside began pounding upon it, while with deadly chug a bullet crashed into the oaken panel.

"Donnerwetter!" shouted a deep voice, wildly. "Captain, I am yet out mit der bullets."

With a crash I flung aside the thick iron bar which answered as a lock, and drew in the Sergeant, yet panting heavily from his hard run.

"By Chiminy, dot vas a narrow squeak," he exclaimed, as I released my grasp upon him and hurled the door back into its place.

A dim light swinging suspended from the ceiling of the great wide hall revealed clearly the scene within. As I turned I beheld Brennan for the first time, and his face remains a memory. Standing with his back to the stair-railing, a revolver grasped tightly in either hand, his eyes burning, his countenance flushed with anger, and clouded by doubt, he appeared almost like one distracted. At sight of me he gave up all attempt to control his raging temper.

"What does all this mean?" he demanded hoarsely. "Who are these men? Caton, if you have betrayed us, by God, I will shoot you dead."

"There is no betrayal," returned the Lieutenant, coolly. "These men are friends."

"Friends?" he laughed cynically. "Friends? in that uniform, and you attired in a Rebel cavalry jacket? Friends? that fellow over there?" and he pointed derisively at me with his pistol barrel. "Damn you, but I believe you are all a pack of lying thieves!"

Caton's face burned. He took one step toward him, his hands clinched, and when he spoke his clear voice shook with intense indignation.

"Major Brennan," he said, coldly deliberate, "you are my superior officer, but you go beyond all privilege of rank in those words. I say these men are friends; they have sunk the issues of war in order that they may answer the call of humanity. If you dare impeach my motives any further, I shall hurl back the cowardly insult in your face. I will take no such words, sir, from any living man."

Brennan looked at him, his lips struggling with the utterance that would not come. Knowing well the danger of such delay, I hastily pushed aside the ring of men, and fronted him, determined to end this foolishness then and there.

"Major Brennan," I said firmly, ignoring his efforts to silence me, "you must listen to reason whether you wish to do so or not. My troopers are all around you; I have two men to your one in this house, and can enforce my will if necessary. Now mark what I say — we are not here in anger or in war, but to help you in the protection of endangered women. We captured your courier, have despatched one of our own number into the Federal camp for aid, and have fought our way in here to stand beside you and your men in defence of this house against those ruffians without. You can use us or not, just as you please; it rests with you to say whether we shall be comrades in arms on this occasion, or whether I shall assume command by the power of force which I chance to control."

He seemed utterly unable to grasp my full meaning, to comprehend the situation.

"You mean, you would fight with us? under my command?" he asked incredulously.

"I offer my services under your orders," I replied clearly, "and these men in gray will obey mine."

I actually thought he would extend his hand, but some remembrance suddenly restrained him.

"I — of course, Captain Wayne," he stammered, at length, "I — I must accept your offer. I — I am grateful for it, but I shall insist upon one thing; there must be a final settlement of the personal matter existing between us. I am not willing to waive my rights in this."

"There is no occasion for your doing so, sir," I answered coldly, for I considered the reference at that moment in extremely ill taste. "When our work here has been accomplished, you will find me very much at your service."

He bowed gravely.

"I am exceedingly glad we understand each other," he said. "May I ask the size of your command?"

"Sergeant," I questioned, "whom have we lost?"

"Nelson vos kilt, I dinks; der Kid is not here yet, und Sands vos vounded bad."

"Very well; then, Major Brennan, I tender you sixteen men fit for duty, besides myself. You are doubtless acquainted with the house, and can assign us to positions where our services will prove of greatest value."

He had completely recovered his self-control by this time, and spoke now with the terse sentences of a tried soldier.

"I thank you, Captain Wayne, and will ask you to choose four men and assume command of the east side of the house. Caton, you will take the same number for defence of the rear. Captain, what is your sergeant's name?"

"Ebers, an experienced German soldier."

"I should have suspected his nationality. Let him have command of four more, and cover the west windows. I shall defend the front myself, as I have been doing."

"Very well," I answered shortly, for his eyes had remained fixed upon me all the time he was talking. "Take the positions assigned you, lads, and do not permit a man from without to put foot on the veranda. If they once succeed in getting under cover of the porch roof, they will give us plenty of trouble."

"They have remained remarkably quiet since you came in," interposed the Major. "Even my men seem to see nothing to shoot at."

"Probably they haven't recovered as yet from our little surprise party," I said, with a smile of remembrance. "We left a mule out there who will entertain them for some time, unless they adopt heroic measures."

The position for defence assigned to my care took me into the dining-room of the mansion, — a spacious, almost square apartment, containing three large windows reaching nearly to the floor. The outside blinds had been closed, but the glass in the panes was mostly broken, and there were other evidences that the firing had been both heavy and continuous. I found two soldiers of Brennan's party within, both lying upon the floor, and peering cautiously through the apertures of the blinds. They glanced up at us with undisguised amazement.

A Union of Yank and Reb

"It's all right, lads," I said heartily. "Never mind our colors to-night; we are all fighting the same way."

I had taken with me Bungay, together with three of my troopers, and after placing them as advantageously as possible, I stretched myself out on the floor, and applying an eye to a convenient opening took careful survey of the situation without. There was little to be observed, for darkness securely hid the movements of the enemy. Everything upon our side of the house, however, appeared comparatively quiet, yet it was clearly evident that the besiegers had no present intention of withdrawing from the attack; the flame of the stables had already largely died away, but what little light remained enabled me to perceive unmistakable signs of their presence. I could distinguish frequent moving figures in the background, but was unable to determine their distance from the house. Occasionally a flash out of the night would evidence the discharge of a gun, and I heard a gruff voice shouting forth an order. One shot struck the window just above me, showering my shoulders with fragments of broken glass, and I noticed one of the Federal soldiers in the room carried his arm in a rude sling.

This present cessation of activity was, I felt convinced, only temporary. I did not expect, from all I could now see, that the final assault would take place upon my side of the building. The massing of the main body of the besiegers before the front entrance, together with the presence there of their leaders, was sufficient to convince me that this was to prove the principal point of attack, and from my knowledge of such affairs I decided that probably the first signs of returning daylight would be the signal for a determined assault. The dark interior of such a house as this offered too many defensive advantages which the daylight would largely overcome.

"Have you had some hard fighting?" I asked of the man lying next me, a manly-looking fellow, wearing the yellow chevrons of a corporal of cavalry.

"They pitched in mighty strong at first, sir," he answered civilly. "An' we had so few men they pretty nearly rushed us, fer sure. It was our repeatin' rifles thet drove 'em back."

"You suffered to some extent?"

"Two killed, sir, and three or four wounded. It wus hot 'nough fer a while, I tell you; as lively a little jig as I 've ever bin in. McNeal, there, got a lump of lead in his arm. Would you mind explainin' 'bout you fellows comin' in here to help us, sir? It seems kinder odd to be fightin' longside of gray-backs."

I told him briefly the circumstances, and his eyes danced merrily at the recital.

"Be a rum story to tell if ever we get out of here, sir," he commented, patting his gun. "I 've mostly seen you fellows from the t'other side, but, dern it all, this is more the way it ought to be."

I agreed with him thoroughly as to that, and we relapsed into silence, each intent upon the uncertainty without.

As I lay there, gazing anxiously into the darkness, I could not forbear wondering where Brennan had concealed the women to keep them from harm. Would he inform them of our arrival? He could scarcely hope to keep the fact long hidden, for they would certainly see some of my gray-jackets, and ask questions. I doubted, however, if he would mention my name, yet Caton surely would, and Caton could not be kept long away from Miss Minor, unless serious attack was imminent. Unquestionably, I should be compelled to meet them before this duty was concluded; how should I be received, and how should I conduct myself? There was but one way — a dignified courtesy, seemingly ignoring all that had previously occurred. Any explanation at present was apparently out of the question, and I certainly could not venture to intrude after the coldness of my last reception. Besides, there was Brennan to be considered. He would make use of my services in this emergency, but I had been distinctly informed it could make no difference in the feud existing between us. I had no wish that it should, and I could consistently hope for very little consideration from the wife of a man whom I was destined to meet upon the field of honor. No, the far better way was to see as little of her as possible, to meet almost as strangers, and then **to part for ever.** Difficult as this programme assuredly **was,** it seemed the only honorable course left me. Even had she loved me as truly as I did her, I could yet do no less.

"They seem to be peckin' away pretty lively out in front," said the corporal, interrupting my reverie.

"Yes," I admitted. "In my judgment that will prove the main point of attack. How many men did the Major have there before we came?"

"Same as here, sir."

"And four of mine; that makes seven altogether, counting himself, and two of these ought to be posted in the upper story. He's bound to need more; that firing is very steady."

"He's got the women loadin' for him, and that helps some."

18   273

My Lady of the North

"The women?" I asked, staring at him in amazement. "Do you mean to say Mrs. Brennan and Celia Minor are there in that front room?"

"Don't know who they are, sir — two mighty fine lookin' young ladies, an old lady with white hair, an' a big, rough-lookin' female, sir. The last one wus handlin' a gun to beat the band just afore you came."

"And he keeps them there, exposed to all this heavy fire? What can the man mean? Why, Corporal, that constant shooting must have completely shattered the windows. There could be no safety for any one except lying flat upon the floor."

"Well, 't aint quite so bad as that, sir," he protested, seemingly anxious to shield his officer from adverse criticism. "You see it's a double parlor, with a wall an' foldin' doors atween, an' the women are all in the rear room. Of course, it's almighty dark back there, an' they has to lie pretty close, but blamed if I know of any better place for them. This house hain't got no cellar."

It certainly was not my place to interfere. Her husband was the one who should be most solicitous as to her safety, yet it worried me greatly to think of Edith Brennan lying helpless in the dark, exposed to constant danger, with the deadly rifles crackling all about her. Surely somewhere in this great house there would be an interior apartment where greater protection could be assured. Doubtless Brennan was unwilling to have them away from him; possibly he even continued to hold them where they were to prevent all possibility of their meeting with me. It was this last thought, improbable as it surely was, which put me on my mettle. If that was his little scheme, and to my suspicion it looked like it, I was not unwilling

274

to play a hand in the game. I might not hold trumps, yet I could bluff as well as any one.

I had barely arrived at this point in my musing when opportunity for action came. A man groped his way in from the lighted hall, but halted close beside the door, unable to perceive us in the darkness.

"Is Captain Wayne here?" he asked.

"Yes; what is it?"

"Major Brennan has had two of his men hit, sir, and wishes you to spare him three of yours, unless you are hotly pressed."

"All right; there's nothing doing here," I answered, instantly determining upon my course. "Corporal, I shall leave you in command of this side for a few minutes. I believe I can be of more immediate value elsewhere. Bungay, you and Elliott come with me."

The lower hall, having no windows in it, was the only safe place in the building, and here a light had been kept burning. The door which, as I judged, must lead into the back parlor, was closed, and fastened upon the inside. At least it refused to yield to my hand when tried. Another in front stood very slightly ajar.

"Report to Brennan," I whispered into Jed's ear, "and forget to mention I am with you. I desire to investigate matters for myself a few moments."

He nodded to intimate that he understood, and then we crept, one at a time, into the front apartment, hugging the floor closely to keep beneath the range of the bullets which swept every now and then through the broken windows, and chugged into the wall behind us. I was the last to wriggle in through the narrow opening, and rolling instantly out of the tiny bar of light, I lay silent for a moment, endeavoring to get my bearings. I was determined upon just one thing — to obtain speech with the women, learn, if possible, their exact situation, and, if I found it necessary, insist upon their better protection. An insane jealousy of me should not continue to expose them to unnecessary peril.

Brennan was directly across the room from where I lay. I could hear his voice issuing low, stern orders.

"If you 'll only keep down you 're safe enough," he said gruffly. "There has n't a shot come within a foot of the sill. The ground slopes out yonder, and those fellows can't fire low. Put the new men at the central window, and let them shoot at every flash they see. Bradley will pass back their empty guns."

I wondered how long our supply of ammunition would hold out with such a fusillade kept up, but ventured upon no protest, for I was already groping my way through the darkness along the inner wall. Furniture lay overturned in every direction, and I experienced considerable difficulty in making progress through the débris without attracting attention. A great square piano stood directly across the entrance to the back parlor, left by the drawing nearly together of the sliding doors. I waited until Bradley had crawled through with an armful of loaded guns, and then entered also, creeping silently between the piano legs. As I did so a bullet struck the case above me, and the whole instrument trembled to the impact, giving forth a strange moan, as if in pain.

Some one was groaning in the corner at my left, and supposing the wounded to be lying there, I turned more toward the right, keeping as close as possible to the wall, hopeful I might come in contact with one of the women. I do not honestly know why I did this — really I had no excuse, except my natural distrust of Brennan, coupled

A Union of Yank and Reb

with an eager desire to be of service to the woman of
my heart. There was little to guide me in the search,
as the flame of the discharging rifles did not penetrate
here. Once I heard the rustle of a skirt, while a faint
sound of whispering reached me from the rear of the
room. Then my hand, groping blindly along the wall,
touched the lower fold of a dress. It felt like coarse
calico to my fingers.

" Mrs. Bungay," I whispered cautiously, " is this you? "

The woman started at sound of my voice, but replied
in the same low tone: " Thet 's my name; who mought
ye be? "

" A friend of yours, and of your husband," I answered,
for I doubted if she would recall my name. " Did you
know Jed was here? "

" My man? Hiven be praised! But I 'll knock ther
head off ther little divil if ever I git my hand on him, I
will thet. Whar 's ther little imp bin all ther time? "

" Hunting for you, and crying his eyes out," I answered,
smiling to myself in the darkness. " Where is Mrs.
Brennan? "

" Jist beyond me, thar in ther corner."

As she spoke a bullet whizzed past us, having missed
the obstruction of the piano. I could feel the wind
stirred by its passage, while its peculiar hum told me it
was a Minié ball.

" You are too far out from the wall," I protested.
" You are in range."

" Can't help it if I be. I 'm yere ter take ther guns from
ther sojer, an' pass 'em back."

I crept slowly along beyond her, keeping close to the
wall, but had progressed hardly more than a couple of
yards, when I felt a hand lightly touch me.

277

My Lady of the North

" I recognize your voice," said a soft whisper, " and am so glad you are here."

Who can guess the motives that inspire a woman? This was my welcome, where I had anticipated coldness and repellant pride.

CHAPTER XXXI

A CONVERSATION IN THE DARK

IN my extreme surprise at the intimate cordiality expressed by her words and manner I failed in utterance. Anticipating coldness, indifference, possibly even resentment at my presuming to approach her, I was instead greeted by an unstudied warmth of welcome that made my heart beat fiercely.

"Surely I am not mistaken," she questioned, rendered doubtful by my silence. "Is not this Captain Wayne?"

"There is no mistake," I hastened to assure her, "but I had anticipated from our last meeting a far less cordial greeting."

"Oh," she exclaimed, with a light laugh, "and is that all? Yet surely, if I was to believe my own eyes I was perfectly justified in my actions then. However, Captain, I have been forced to realize the truth of that situation, and am now disposed to make up to you in kindness for all my unjust suspicions."

"I am more than delighted to learn that cloud is no longer to overshadow us. Miss Minor has made a full explanation, then?"

"You have been completely exonerated, and restored to my good graces."

As she spoke, I became aware that she was busily engaged upon some task, and when she ended I felt the steel of a gun-barrel touch my hand.

279

"Please pass this to Maria," she said calmly, "and hand me back the one she has."

"You are loading, then?" I asked, as I complied with her request.

"We have all been busy. Isn't it terrible? I was so frightened at first, but now they tell me that you and your men have come, there is no longer danger of those horrible creatures getting in here."

"You knew, then, that I was in the house?"

"I was told some noble Confederates had accompanied Lieutenant Caton back to aid us, but your name was not mentioned."

"Then my appearance must have proven a complete surprise?"

"Yes, and no," she answered frankly. "I was not sure it was you, of course, and I did not venture to ask, but I knew you were in the neighborhood, and that such an act would be in every way characteristic. I was certain you would come if you knew, and I — I, well really, I hoped it was."

In spite of a slight effort at restraint I groped in the darkness until I touched her hand. For the moment she permitted me to retain it, as if unconsciously, within my grasp.

"Why?" I questioned, scarcely relying upon my own voice.

"Oh, one always trusts friends more readily than strangers, and I have seen you in danger before, and possess such confidence in your courage and resource."

"But Miss Minor took particular care to inform me you felt little or no interest in me — that you never even spoke of me except as she compelled you to do so."

For a moment she did not answer, and then with a

light laugh said: " Did she, really? How very kind of her, and how extremely intimate you must have become to draw forth so frank a confession. However, Captain Wayne, you must not give credence to all you hear about me, even from Celia. You know one does not usually give public expression to one's more secret thoughts, and I can assure you I have always been most deeply interested whenever you were the subject of our conversations."

" Her words made me feel I might be an intruder on your privacy."

" You are never that. Cold as I appeared only a few hours ago, I was yet thinking of you as I entered the arbor. Perhaps that was why the sight meeting my eyes proved such a shock."

Possibly she felt our conversation growing dangerously intimate, for in the silence which ensued she gently withdrew her hand. As she did so my fingers chanced to touch the plain gold ring she wore. It was like a dash of water in my face, and instantly brought back to me our common danger.

" How constant the firing continues," she said at last, as I sat struggling dumbly with temptation.

" A mere waste of powder, I fear," was my reply, given thoughtlessly. " When the rush finally comes we are likely to be without sufficient ammunition to repel it."

" When the rush comes? " she echoed in startled tone. " Do you expect an assault? "

" I hardly expect those fellows out there will ever leave without a most determined effort to carry the house by storm. They are here for plunder, and will not be baffled easily, nor will the leaders hesitate to sacrifice any number of lives to gain their end, especially now that a desire for revenge has been added to the original lust for spoils. I have been among them, you know, and learned enough of their power, organization, and leadership to convince me they will never raise the siege until they exhaust every resource. I have no doubt they are simply drawing all this fire in the hope that our ammunition will thus be uselessly expended. It is an old army trick, and one I am surprised to see so experienced an officer as Major Brennan yield to. In my judgment they will make an effort to rush us as soon as there is sufficient light."

" But why not warn him? "

I smiled to myself at the naïve question. Surely it could not be possible she remained ignorant of the feud existing between us. She had twice witnessed our hostile meetings, and certainly could not forget how we had last parted.

" Major Brennan would scarcely welcome any interference on my part."

" But surely, as a soldier, he must value the advice of another soldier? "

" Possibly you forget," I explained, striving to speak as lightly of it as might be, " that there is a lack of friendship between Major Brennan and myself."

" Still? " she asked. " Truly I thought that might all be over. Even if it survived until now, this noble act of yours in coming to our defence should have earned you his gratitude. He — he has never once mentioned your name to me since that night."

" Not even when I came here with my troop, I believe? "

" No; yet I did not connect that fact with the other. I supposed it a mere oversight, or that he believed the mention of your name would not greatly interest me. Surely, Captain Wayne, you are not keeping open this unhappy wound?"

"On my word, no; but I regret to confess it is very far from being closed."

"He — Major Brennan does not know, then, that you are here now with me?" She evidently hesitated to ask this question.

"Certainly not," in surprise at her apparent innocence. "You cannot have supposed I had been sent here by him to talk with you?"

"I — I did not know. I do not think I realized," she stammered, vainly seeking for words with which to make clear her bewilderment. "I imagined you might have come at his suggestion to see that we were amply protected. This is all so very strange. He does not even know you are here with us?"

"No," I admitted reluctantly. "Perhaps I have no excuse even for being here at all. My duty as a soldier is certainly elsewhere, but I could not rest content until I knew you were in a position of safety. Believe me, Mrs. Brennan, I have intended no indiscretion, but I was informed by a soldier that you were being held here under fire. It would have been useless for me to appeal to the Major for information, and I felt I must know the truth. If I have erred in this I can only plead the deep interest I have always had in your welfare."

Her hand touched mine impulsively, and it was warm and throbbing.

"I can merely thank you with all my heart, Captain Wayne, and assure you I both understand and appreciate your purpose. But truly I do not wish any trouble to occur again — you will go back to your post, will you not? You can serve me best in that way, and retain the gratitude and admiration I have ever felt for you."

There was a pathetic pleading in her voice, low as she spoke, impossible to resist. It made me feel thoroughly ashamed of my impulsive, ill-considered action.

"At once, Mrs. Brennan," I returned earnestly. "I realize I have done wrong in ever coming here as I have. It is my first act of disobedience to orders in all my military life. But tell me first that I have forfeited neither your confidence nor your friendship?"

Her warm hand closed frankly over mine, and as I bent above it her hair softly brushed my cheek.

"You have not," she answered, so soft and low I could barely catch the words. "I appreciate your motive, and shall always respect and honor you." She paused a moment, then added quickly, as though in sudden rush of feeling: "No friend stands higher in my esteem than you — now please go, Captain Wayne."

As I crept back through the darkness, passing beneath the piano into the front room, which was filled with the choking fumes of powder, my mind was a chaos of emotions impossible to analyze. The touch of her soft hand was yet warm upon me, and her manner as well as her words caused my blood to leap riotously in my veins. What did this woman mean? Was it possible she loved me, and was fighting, even as I, to conquer a passion that could never be realized? which had no right to exist? Surely, young and fair as she was, she could be no vain and shallow coquette, venturing upon flirtation for the mere excitement of it? The calm self-possession of her nature, her marked pride and strength of character, stamped this as impossible. Honesty and pure, true

284

A Conversation in the Dark

womanhood were woven into her every word and act; that indefinable something which all men feel and respect was about her like an atmosphere; to doubt her for an instant was beyond my power. Yet she had made me feel I was more to her than a mere friend. I longed to go back, to pour forth those words I had struggled so hard not to speak, to urge the high law of mutual love as final arbiter of our destiny — but no! I simply could not. Honor chained me, and the depth of my respect would never permit of her humiliation. If she had become weak, all the more reason why I should remain strong. The very depth of love which drew me to her operated now in restraint. God alone knows the struggle in the darkness as I continued to move slowly away from her and toward the door.

So deep indeed was my agitation, so intense my thought, that I scarcely realized I was creeping along barely beneath the dead line of those bullets which constantly swept the apartment. Their crashing into the wall was almost meaningless, and I barely noted either the dense smoke or the fitful flashes of flame as the little garrison returned shot for shot. It was Brennan's voice — how hateful it sounded then — which recalled my attention.

" Mapes," he said, with the sharp tone of wearied command, " take a crack at that fellow over yonder by the big tree; he must be in range. You men, I verily believe, shut your eyes when you shoot, for there has n't a man dropped out there in the last half hour."

I had reached the door by this time, but paused now, determined to venture one word of expostulation at his recklessness.

" Major Brennan," I said, speaking sufficiently loud

to be audible above the uproar, " do you not think they will attempt to charge the house? "

" Not while we keep up this fire," he returned coldly, evidently recognizing my voice.

" I grant that, at least while darkness lasts. But you have just complained that your men were doing but small execution, and is there not danger of exhausting our stock of ammunition by such a useless fusillade? "

" It will last until our fellows get here — that is, if your man was ever really sent for aid, as you say."

There was a thinly veiled sneer in the words as he spoke them, but I curbed my temper.

" Well, in my judgment, sir, — and I tell it you because I deem it a duty, — " I retorted plainly, " you are making a grave mistake which you may realize when it becomes too late to rectify it. Possibly I have no right to criticise one who is technically in command; yet I am serving as a volunteer, and the conditions are peculiar. I not only remember the scene witnessed by me in the lines out yonder, but also recall the fact that we are here to fulfil a sacred duty — the defence of helpless women from outrage. A fatal mistake upon our part would be horrible."

" Your deep interest in the welfare of the ladies is purely chivalric, I presume? "

" It is merely the interest a true soldier must always feel," I responded, determined not to be goaded into quarrel. " I have neither wife nor sister, but I have a mother."

" Very well, sir," — and his tone was rough and overbearing, — " then kindly recall your soldierly instincts to another little matter. I chance to command here by authority of rank, and hold myself responsible for the proper defence of this portion of the house. I believe you have already been assigned your duties; if you will attend to them I shall be greatly obliged, and whenever I may desire your valuable advice I shall take pleasure in sending for you."

I have often wondered since how I controlled myself; yet I did, biting my lip till the blood came, a fair, reproachful face ever before my eyes.

"I shall obey your orders," I managed to say with calmness, so soon as I could control my voice to speak at all, "but shall hold myself, and my men, prepared for a call here at any moment."

"As you please," with an ill-suppressed sneer. "I have always found you exceedingly anxious to be with the ladies. Indeed I have wondered if you might not prove a modern illustration of that ancient worthy ' whose best boast was but to wear a braid of his fair lady's hair.' "

I turned away in silence and strode back to my post, white with anger. The dining-room remained as I had left it, and when I lay down in my old position and peered out throught the broken blind, I could mark no change in the appearance of our besiegers.

CHAPTER XXXII

HAND TO HAND

I HAVE never been willing to believe I slept during the next hour. Wearied as I have often been, duty has ever held my eyes wide open, and I prefer to think I merely plunged so deep in reflection as to become oblivious of all occurring about me. Surely I had sufficient excuse.

However this may be, when I once again aroused to observe my surroundings, the faint gray light of early dawn rested upon the outside world, and through the fleeting shadows of the mist I was able to distinguish much which before had been shrouded by the black curtain. In front of the window where I rested, the grass-covered lawn sloped gradually downward until it terminated at a low picket fence, thickly covered with vines. A great variety of shrubs, which during the night had doubtless afforded shelter for sharpshooters, dotted this grass plot, while beyond the fence boundary stood a double row of large trees. To the far left of our position the burnt stable yet smouldered dully, occasionally sending up a shower of sparks as a draught of air fanned the embers, but there were few signs of life visible. For the moment I even hoped our enemies might have grown discouraged and withdrawn.

" What has become of the guerillas? " I asked in wonderment, turning as I spoke to face the Federal corporal who lay on the other side of me. " Is it possible they have given up ? "

" I think not, Captain," he replied respectfully, saluting as he would one of his own officers. " They were there just before the light came, and I saw a dozen or more stealing along behind the fence not five minutes ago. See, there is a squad of them now, huddled together back of where the stable stood."

I noticed them as he spoke, and their movements instantly aroused my suspicion.

" Screw your eye close to the corner of the pane," I ordered hurriedly, " and see what you make out toward the front of the house."

He did as directed, and for a moment continued to gaze silently into the gray dawn.

" Well ? " I asked impatiently.

" There 's men out there sure, plenty of 'em," he reported slowly. " It looks to me mighty like the end of a line of battle, right there by that big magnolia-tree. Anyhow, there must be all of twenty fellows lying close together between there and where the corner of the house shuts off my view. I don't see none this side anywhere, unless it 's a shooter or two hiding along the fence where the vines are thick."

" That 's it, my lad," I exclaimed heartily, getting upon my feet as I spoke. " We can stand up now, there 's no danger here, but there will be music for all of us presently. Those fellows are getting ready to charge us front and rear."

There were five in the room. I could see them only indistinctly, as the morning light was not yet sufficiently strong to penetrate clearly to where we were,

19   289

but I was able to note those present — the corporal and his wounded companion, with Hollis and Call of my troop.

"Let the wounded man remain and guard these windows," I commanded. "He would prove of small value in a hand to hand struggle, but can probably do some shooting. The rest come with me."

I led them forth into the wide hallway, which extended the full length of the house, with a broad flight of stairs just forward of the centre, gradually curving and leading to the second story.

I was fully determined as to my duty — whether orders reached me or not, the moment an assault was launched I should throw all the force I commanded beside Brennan, and between our assailants and the imperilled women. The suspended light was yet burning as we came out, but flickered wildly as if in a strong draught of air, and I noticed that the constant rain of bullets during the night had badly splintered an upper panel of the door. Halfway down the broad hallway, and partially obscured by the turn of the stairs, a door stood slightly ajar upon the right hand. Conjecturing this might be where the defenders of the eastern exposure were lying, I peered within. The blinds were tightly drawn and I was able to perceive little of its interior, excepting that the walls were lined with books.

"Ebers," I called, thinking he must be there, "are you in charge here?"

"I vos, Captain," came the instant reply, and he at once emerged from the darkness, his honest face full of interest. "Is it der preakfast vot is already?"

"Hardly, my man. I imagine we may enjoy a fight first, to give us better appetites."

Hand to Hand

"Mein Gott, but I am vurnished mit der abbetite already. I vould fight mit more fun if I vos full."

"So no doubt would all of us; but I have no time for mere talk. Did you meet with any trouble during the night?"

"Troubles? By Chiminy, yes, Captain, I vos hongry for six hour. I have took der belt oop dree time already, an' I vos empty yet. Troubles? Donnerwetter, it is all troubles."

"Not that," sternly. "I mean, have the enemy kept you busy?"

"Der vos some shooting, und Hadley he got hurt bad, but der fellers is all gone. Dis is der right time to eat in der bantry, ain't it?"

"Bring your men fit for duty out here in the hall, and have them join my party," I said, ignoring his pathetic appeal. "How many have you?"

"Der is four, und, Captain, dey vos most as veak as I am mit notting to eat."

Seeing I was not to be moved by thought of their pitiable condition, he drew back with a profound sigh, and as he disappeared some one came hastily toward us along the hallway from the rear.

"What is it, Caton?" I asked anxiously, as I recognized him.

"They are forming to rush me, I think," he answered. "I need a few more men if I can get them."

"They are preparing to assault front and rear at the same time," I answered. "They are massing now, and in my judgment Brennan will have to face the brunt of it. The front of this house is greatly exposed, and will prove extremely difficult to defend if they come against it with any force. How many men do you absolutely require in order to hold your position? Remember, the women are all in the front part of the house, and we must protect them at all hazards."

"Good God, Wayne! Do you think I am likely to forget, with Celia Minor among them?" he exclaimed indignantly. "Nothing but a strict sense of duty holds me one moment where I am. Heaven knows I wish to be with her, and, by thunder, Brennan is aware of it."

"Then come with me," I cried. "There are times when a higher law than that of military despotism should control our actions. I am going there, orders or no orders. Ebers can command your detachment and accomplish all the service you possibly could. Your rightful place is between these ruffians and the woman you love. How many additional men will be required to make the back of the house secure?"

His face brightened as I was speaking, and the haggard look vanished from his eyes.

"I feel like a new man, Wayne," he said thankfully, "and I know you are right. Four more would be sufficient, besides the one in command. The wainscoting is high and of solid oak, the windows are small, there is no porch, while the guns have a perfectly clear range for nearly a hundred yards."

"Good! Ebers," I said, as my portly Sergeant again emerged from out the darkness, "take your four men back to the kitchen and assume command. The guerillas are preparing to make a rush there, and you must drive them back by rapid fire. Hurry along now."

"By Chiminy, but I vos glad to git in der kitchen, anyhow. Is der anyting cold to put in der stomach in dot bantry?" he asked anxiously.

Hand to Hand

"You will have something exceedingly hot in your stomach unless you move more lively," I said sternly.

The little group had barely vanished beyond the glow of the light when from without our ears were suddenly assailed by a wild, exulting yell that bespoke the charge.

"There they are!" I cried. "Now, lads, come with me!"

The dull, gray, chilling dawn revealed a room in utmost disorder, the windows shattered, the blinds cut and splintered, the walls scarred with bullets and disfigured with stains of blood, the furniture overturned and broken. A dead soldier in gray uniform lay in the centre of the floor, his life-blood a dark stain upon the rich carpet; a man with coat off, and blue shirt ripped wide open, was leaning against the further wall vainly endeavoring to stanch a wound in his chest. Brennan was upon one knee near the central window, a smoking gun in his hand, a red welt showing ghastly across his cheek. All this I saw in a single glance, and then, with the leap of a panther, I was beside him, gazing out into the morning mist, and firing as fast as I could handle my gun.

Through the shifting smoke clouds we could see them advancing on a run, — an ugly, motley line, part blue, part gray, part everything, — yelling as they swept forward like a pack of infuriated wolves, their fierce faces scowling savagely behind the rifles. It was half war, half riot — the reckless onslaught of outcasts bent on plunder, inspired by lust, yet guided by rude discipline.

I knew little of detail; faces were blurred, unrecognizable; all I seemed to note clearly was that solid, brutal, heartless, blaspheming line of desperate men sweeping toward us with a relentless fury our puny bullets could not check. Reckless ferocity was in that mad rush; they pressed on more like demons than human beings. I saw men fall; I saw the living stumble over the dead. I heard cries of agony, shouts, curses, but there was no pause. I could mark their faces now, cruel, angry, revengeful; the hands that grasped the veranda railings; the leaping bodies; the rifle-butts uplifted to batter down our frail defences.

As trapped tigers we fought, hurling them back from the windows, slashing, clubbing, striking with fist and steel. Two lay dead across the sill before me, cloven to the very chin, but their bleeding bodies were hurled remorselessly aside, while others clambered forward, mad from lust of blood, crazed with liquor. With clubbed guns we cleared it again and again, battering mercilessly at every head that fronted us. Then a great giant of a fellow — dead or alive I know not — was hurled headlong through the opening, an inert, limp weight, that bore the two soldiers beside me to the floor beneath his body. With wide sweep of my gun I struck him, shattering the stock into fragments, and swung back to meet the others, the hot barrel falling to right and left like a flail. They were through and on me! Wild as any sea-rover of the north I fought, crazed with blood, unconscious of injury, animated solely by desire to strike and slay! Back I had to go; back — I trod on dead bodies, on wounded shrieking in pain, yet no man who came within sweep of that iron bar lived. I loved to hear the thud of it, and I fronted those glaring eyes, my blood afire, my arms like steel. Through the red mist I beheld Caton for an instant as twenty brutal hands uplifted, and then hurled him into the ruck beneath their feet. Whether I fought alone I knew not, cared not. Then some one pressed next to me, facing as

Hand to Hand

I did, wielding a sword like a madman. We had our backs against the piano, our shoulders touched; before us that mob swayed, checked for the moment, held fast by sudden overpowering dread. I glanced aside. My companion was Brennan, hatless, his deep-set eyes aflame, his coat torn off, his shirt ripped open to the waist, his bare breast red with blood.

"No shootin', damn ye!" shouted a voice, hoarsely. "No shootin'; I want that Reb alive!"

Through the swirling smoke I recognized the malicious face of Red Lowrie as he pushed his way to the front. To me it was like a personal challenge to combat.

"Rush them!" I muttered into Brennan's ear. "Hurl them back a bit, and then dodge under into the next room."

I never waited to ascertain if he heard me. With one fierce spring I struck their stunned line, and my iron bar swept a clear space as it crashed remorselessly into them. The next instant Lowrie and I were seemingly alone and fronting each other. A wild cat enraged by pain looks as he did when he leaped to meet me. Hate, deadly, relentless, glared in his eyes, and with a yell of exultation he swung up his long rifle and struck savagely at my head with the stock. I caught it partially on my barrel, breaking its full force, and even as it descended upon my shoulder, jabbed the muzzle hard into his leering face. With a snarl of pain he dropped his gun and grappled with me, but as his fingers closed about my throat, something swirled down through the maze, and the maddened brute staggered back, his arms uplifted, his red beard cloven in twain.

"Now for it, Wayne!" shouted Brennan. "Back with you!"

My Lady of the North

With a dive I went under the piano. I heard the sliding doors shut behind us, and almost with the sound was again upon my feet.

" To the stairs ! " I panted. " Brennan, take the women to the stairs; those fellows are not in the hallway yet, and we can hold them there a while."

In our terrible need for haste, and amid the thick, swirling smoke filling that inner room almost to suffocation, I grasped the woman chancing to be nearest me, without knowing at the moment who she was. Already the rifle-butts were splintering the light wood behind us into staves, and I hastily dragged my dazed companion forward. The others were in advance, and we groped our way like blind persons out into the hall. By rare good fortune it was yet unoccupied, and as we took the few hurried steps toward the foot of the stairs I found my arm was encircling Celia Minor. The depth of despair within her dark eyes, and the speechless anguish of her white face, swept for an instant the fierce rage of battle from my brain.

" Do not fail us now, Miss Minor," I urged kindly, " we may yet hold out until help comes."

" Oh, it is not *that!* " she cried pitifully. " But Arthur; where is Arthur? "

" God knows," I was compelled to answer. " I saw him fronting the first rush when it struck us. I think he went down, yet he may not be seriously hurt."

She burst into tears, but I had no time to comfort her, for at that moment the mob, discovering our direction of escape, jammed both doorways and surged forth howling into the hall.

" Up! " I cried, forcing her forward. " Up with you; quick! "

296

Hand to Hand

I paused a scant second to pluck a sabre from beside a dead soldier on the floor, and then with a spring up the intervening steps, faced about at Brennan's side on the first landing.

"We ought to leave our mark on those incarnate devils here," he said grimly, wiping his red blade on the carpet.

"Unless they reach the second story from without, and take us in the rear," I answered, "we ought to hold back the whole cowardly crew, so long as they refuse to fire."

It was a scene to abide long with a man — a horrible nightmare, never to be forgotten. Above us, protected somewhat by the abrupt curve of the wide staircase, crouched the women. Two were sobbing, their heads buried in their hands, but Maria and Mrs. Brennan sat white of face and dry-eyed. I caught one quick glance at the fair face I loved, — my sweet lady of the North, — thinking, indeed, it might prove the last on earth, and knew her eyes were upon me. Then, stronger of heart than ever for the coming struggle, I fronted that scene below.

Through the rising haze of smoke I looked down into angry faces, unkempt beards, and brandished weapons. The baffled rascals poured out upon us from both doors, crowding into the narrow space, cursing, threatening, thirsting for revenge. Yet they were seemingly leaderless, and the boldest among them paused at the foot of the stairs. They had already felt our arms, had tested our steel, and knew well that grim death awaited their advance.

But they could not pause there long — the ever increasing rush of those behind pressed the earlier arrivals steadily forward. Grim necessity furnished a courage

297

naturally lacking, and suddenly, giving vent to a fierce shout, they were hurled upward, seeking to crush us at whatever sacrifice, by sheer force of numbers. We met them with the point, in the good old Roman way, thrusting home remorselessly, fighting with silent contempt for them which must have been maddening. I even heard Brennan laugh, as he pierced a huge ruffian through the shoulder and hurled him backward; but at that moment I saw Craig knock aside a levelled gun and press his way to the front of the seething mass to assume control. His face was inflamed, his eyes bloodshot; drink had changed him into a very demon.

"Damn ye, Red told you not to fire!" he yelled. "Come on, you dogs! You could eat 'em up if ye wasn't sich blamed cowards. There's only two, and we'll hang them yet."

He leaped straight up the broad steps, his long cavalry sabre in hand, while a dozen of the boldest followed him. Brennan swung his sword high over head, grasping it with both hands for a death-blow, even as I thrust directly at the fellow's throat. The uplifted blade struck the chain of the hanging lamp, snapped at the hilt, and losing his balance the Major plunged headlong into the ruck beneath. The downward fall of his body swept the stairs.

As I stood there, panting and breathless, a woman rushed downward. Believing she would throw herself into that tangled mass below, I instantly caught her to me.

"Don't," I cried anxiously. "You cannot help him. For God's sake go back where you were."

"It is not that," she exclaimed, her voice thrilling with excitement. "Oh, Captain Wayne, do you not hear the bugles?"

Hand to Hand

As by magic those hateful faces vanished, disappearing by means of every opening leading out from the hall, and when the cheering blue-coats surged in through the broken door, I was yet standing there, apparently alone but for the dead, leaning weak and breathless against the wall, my arm about Edith Brennan.

CHAPTER XXXIII

A BELLIGERENT GERMAN

A YOUNG officer, whose red face was rendered extremely conspicuous by the blue of his uniform, led the rush of his soldiers as they came tumbling gallantly into the hall.

"Up there, men!" he cried, catching instant sight of me, and pointing. "Get that Johnny with the girl."

As they sprang eagerly forward over the dead bodies littering the floor at the foot of the stairs, Brennan scrambled unsteadily to his feet, and halted them with imperious gesture.

"Leave him alone!" he commanded. "That is the commander of the Confederate detachment who came to our aid. The guerillas have fled down the hallway, and are most of them outside by now. Wayne," he turned and glanced up at us, his face instantly darkening at the tableau, "kindly assist the ladies to descend; we must get them out of this shambles."

He lifted them one by one and with ceremonious politeness across the ghastly pile of dead and wounded men.

"Escort them to the library," he suggested, as I hesitated. "That room will probably be found clear."

I was somewhat surprised that Brennan should not have come personally to the aid of his wife, but as he ignored her presence utterly, I at once offered her my arm, and silently led the way to the room designated, the others following as best they might. The apartment was unoccupied, exhibiting no signs of the late struggle, and I found comfortable resting places for all. Miss Minor was yet sobbing softly, her face hidden upon her mother's shoulder, and I felt constrained to speak with her.

"I shall go at once," I said kindly, "to ascertain all I can regarding Lieutenant Caton, and will bring you word."

She thanked me with a glance of her dark eyes clouded with tears, but as I turned hastily away to execute this errand, Mrs. Brennan laid restraining hand upon my arm.

"Captain Wayne," she said with much seriousness, "you are very unselfish, but you must not go until your own wounds have been attended to; they may be far more serious than you apprehend."

"My wounds?" I almost laughed at the gravity of her face, for although exhausted, I was unconscious of any injury. "They must be trivial indeed, for I was not even aware I had any."

"But you have!" she insisted, her eyes full upon me. "Your hair is fairly clotted with blood, while your shoulder is torn and bruised until it is horrible to look upon."

As I gazed at her, surprised by the anxiety she so openly displayed, I chanced to behold myself reflected within a large mirror directly across the room. One glance was sufficient to convince me her words were fully justified. My remains of uniform literally clung to me in rags, my bare shoulder looked a contused mass of battered flesh, my hair was matted, and my face blackened by powder stains and streaked with blood.

"I certainly do appear disreputable enough," I admitted; "but I can assure you it is nothing sufficiently serious to require immediate attention. Indeed a little water is probably all I need. Besides, why should I care — was it not all received for your sake?"

I spoke the pronoun so strongly she could not well ignore my obvious meaning, nor did she endeavor to escape the inference. Her face, yet white from the strain of the past few hours, became rosy in an instant, and her eyes fell.

"I know," she answered softly. "Perhaps that may be why I am so exceedingly anxious your injuries should be attended to."

As I stepped without, and closed the door behind me, I was at once startled by the rapid firing of shots from the rear of the house, and the next moment I encountered the young, red-faced officer hurrying along the hallway at the head of a squad of Federal cavalrymen. Recognizing me in the gloom of the passage he paused suddenly.

"I owe you a belated apology, Captain," he exclaimed cordially, "for having mistaken you for one of those miscreants, but really your appearance was not flattering."

"Having viewed myself since within a mirror," I replied, "I am prepared to acknowledge the mistake a most natural one. However, I am grateful to be out of the scrape, and can scarcely find fault with my rescuers. Five minutes more would have witnessed the end."

"We rode hard," he said, "and were in saddle within fifteen minutes after the arrival of your courier. You evidently made a hard fight of it; the house bears testi-

mony to a terrible struggle. We are rejoicing to learn
that Lieutenant Caton was merely stunned; we believed
him dead at first, and he is far too fine a fellow to go
in that way."

"He is truly living, then?" I exclaimed, greatly relieved. "Miss Minor, to whom he is engaged, is sor-
rowing over his possible fate in the library yonder. Could
not two of your men assist him to her? She would do
more to hasten his recovery than any one."

"Certainly," was the instant response. "Haines, you
and McDonald get the officer out of the front room;
carry him in there where the ladies are, and then rejoin
us."

His face darkened as the men designated departed on
their errand.

"I really require all the force I possess," he said
doubtfully. "It seems impossible to dislodge those rascals back yonder. What we need is a field howitzer."

"I have been wondering at the firing; pretty lively,
is n't it? Have some of those fellows made a stand?"

"Yes; quite a crowd of them have succeeded in bar-
ricading themselves in the kitchen, and it is so arranged
as to prove an exceedingly awkward place to attack.
We have had three men hit already, in spite of every
precaution, and I am seeking now to discover some
means of forcing their position from the hall. Their
leader appears to be a bullet-headed Dutchman about as
easy to manage as a mule."

The words aroused me to a possibility.

"A Dutchman, you say? and in the kitchen? Have
you had sight of the fellow?"

"Merely a glimpse, and that over a rifle-barrel. He
has a round, dull face, with a big flat nose."

My Lady of the North

"That idiot is my sergeant, Lieutenant, and supposes he is still fighting guerillas."

The Lieutenant looked at me in surprise, then burst into a peal of laughter. "Well, if that is true," he cried, "I most sincerely hope you will call him off before he succeeds in cleaning out our entire troop."

I started down the hallway toward the point of firing. There was a sharp jog in the wall leading to the kitchen door, and as I approached it some soldiers stationed there warned me to be careful.

"They 're perfect devils to shoot, sir," said one respectfully, "an' the Dutchman fetches his man every time."

"Oh, it will be all right, boys," I replied confidently. "He 'll know me."

Before me as I stepped forth was a double door of oak, the upper half partially open.

"Sergeant," I cried, "come out; the fight is all over."

For answer a bullet whizzed past me, chugging into the wall at my back, and I skipped around the corner with a celerity of movement which caused the fellows watching me to grin with delight.

"Find me a white cloth of some kind," I demanded as soon as I reached cover, and now thoroughly angered. "We shall see if that wooden-headed old fool knows the meaning of a flag of truce."

They succeeded in securing me a torn pillow-slip from somewhere, and sheltering my body as best I might behind the wall angle I waved it violently in full view of the kitchen door. For a few moments it remained apparently unnoted, and then Ebers's round, placid countenance looked suspiciously through the slight aperture.

"Did you give op?" he questioned anxiously.

A Belligerent German

"Give up nothing," I retorted, my temper thoroughly exhausted. "Come out of that! You are firing on your own friends."

He put his fat fingers to his nose and wiggled them derisively.

"Dot is too thin," he said meaningly. "You dink me von ol' fool, but I show you. By Chiminy, I want no friends — you shoot me der ear off, and I fights mit you good and blenty. Der is dings to eat in der bantry, and you be damned."

He drew back, leaving merely the black muzzle of his gun projecting across the top of the lower door.

"Ebers," I called out at the top of my voice, "unless you obey my orders I'll have you strung up by your own men. Open that door!"

The fat, puzzled face peered once more cautiously over the menacing gun-barrel.

"Is dot you, Captain?"

"Yes, come out; the fight is all over."

"No, vos it?" and he flung open the lower half of the door. "Vell, I vos not sorry. Have ve vipped dem already?"

"Yes, it's all done with. Take your men out of there, and go into camp somewhere in the yard. Seek out our wounded and attend to them as soon as possible. Are your men hungry?"

"Vell, maybe dey vos not quite full, but dere is a ham in der bantry dot vould pe bretty good mit der stomach."

"Take it along with you; only hurry up, and attend at once to what I have told you."

I watched closely until they had all passed out, and then turned to the highly amused Federal lieutenant.

"You surely have a character in that fellow," he said

good-humoredly, " and I can bear witness he is a fighter when the time comes."

I left them, remembering then my own need. By using the back stairway I avoided unpleasant contact with the traces of conflict yet visible at the front of the house, and finally discovered a bathroom which afforded facilities for cleansing my flesh wounds and making my general appearance more presentable. I found I could do little to improve the condition of my clothing, but after making such changes for the better as were possible, soaking the clotted blood from out my hair, and washing the powder stains from my face, I felt I should no longer prove an object of aversion even to the critical eyes of the women, who would fully realize the cause for my torn and begrimed uniform.

A glance from the window told me the Federal cavalrymen were bearing out the dead and depositing them beyond view of the house in the deserted negro cabins. Ebers and one or two of my own men were standing near, carefully scanning the uncovered faces as they were borne past, while scraps of conversation overheard brought the information that the long dining-room where I had passed the night on guard had been converted into a temporary hospital.

Irresolute as to my next action, I passed out into the upper hall. It was deserted and strangely silent, seemingly far removed from all those terrible scenes so lately enacted in the rooms beneath. My head by this time throbbed with pain; I desired to be alone, to think, to map out my future course before proceeding down the stairs to meet the others. With this in view I sank down in complete weariness upon a convenient settee. I could hear the sound of muffled voices below, while an occasional order was spoken loud enough to reach me; but I was utterly alone, and my thoughts wandered, as though the strain of the past few hours had completely wrecked all my mental faculties. It was Edith Brennan — Edith Brennan — who remained constantly before me, and wherever my eyes wandered they beheld the same fair face, which tantalized me by its presence and mocked me in every resolve I sought to form. There was no safety for me — and none for her, as I now verily believed — save in my immediate departure. We could be together no longer without my unlocking sealed lips and giving utterance to words she could not listen to, words she must never hear. I was yet struggling to force this decision into action when complete fatigue overcame me. My heavy head sank back upon the arm of the settee, and deep sleep closed my eyes.

CHAPTER XXXIV

IT was in my dreams I felt it first, — a light, moist touch upon my burning forehead, — and I imagined I was a child once more, back at the old home, caressed by the soft hand of my mother. But as consciousness slowly returned I began to realize dimly where I was, and that I was no longer alone. A gentle hand was stroking back the hair from off my temples, while the barest uplift of my eyelids revealed the folds of a dark blue skirt pressed close to my side. Instantly I realized who must be the wearer, and remained motionless until I could better control my first unwise impulse.

She spoke no word, and I cautiously opened my eyes and glanced up into her face. For a time she remained unaware of my awakening, and sat there silently stroking my forehead, her gaze fixed musingly upon the window at the farther end of the hall. Doubtless she had been sitting thus for some time, and had become absorbed in her own reflections, for I lay there drinking in her beauty for several moments before she chanced to glance downward and observe that I was awake. The evidences of past exposure and strain were not absent from her features, yet had not robbed her of that delicate charm which to my mind separated her so widely from all others, — her rounded cheek yet retained the fresh hue of perfect health, her clear, thoughtful eyes were soft and earnest, while the luxuriant hair, swept back from off the broad, low forehead, had been tastefully arranged and exhibited no signs of neglect. It was not a perfect face, for there was unmistakable pride in it, nor would I venture to term it faultless in contour or regularity of outline, but it was distinctly lovable, and the dearest face for ever in all this world to me. How regally was the proud head poised upon the round, swelling throat, and with what regularity her bosom rose and fell to her soft breathing. I think the very intensity of my gaze awakened her from reverie, for she turned almost with a start and looked down upon me. As our eyes met, a warm wave of color dyed her throat and cheeks crimson.

"Why," she exclaimed in momentary confusion, "I supposed I should know before you awoke, and have ample time to escape unobserved."

"Possibly if you had been noting the symptoms of your patient with greater care, you would."

"True, I was dreaming," she admitted, "and had almost forgotten where I was."

"Could I purchase your dream? I was intently studying your face as you sat there, yet was unable to determine whether your reflections were pleasant or unpleasant."

"They were merely foolish," was the frank response, "but such as they were they are certainly not for sale. You are better, Captain Wayne?"

"How could I fail to be better with so delightful a nurse? I confess I am tempted to say no, so as to regain the soft touch of your palm upon my temple; but it was really nothing more serious than fatigue that had overcome me. I scarcely know how I chanced to fall asleep. I merely sat down here for a rest; it was very quiet, and that was the last I remember. Have I been lying here long?"

"There is a rule of evidence, I believe, which protects a suspected person from incriminating himself, but I will acknowledge that I have been here all of half an hour," she answered, too proud to deny her part. "The people below were wondering where you could have gone, and I undertook a search upon my own account. Yes, sir," somewhat archly, "I was afraid lest your injuries were more serious than you believed them to be. I discovered you lying here. You were resting very uncomfortably when I first came, and I felt it my duty to render your position as easy as possible. I did not forget that your fatigue came in our defence."

"Could you not say in yours?" I corrected. "But I have already been more than repaid. Your hand upon my brow was far more restful than I can tell you — its soft stroking mingled in my dreams even before I awoke. It brought back to me the thought of my mother. I do not think I have had a woman's hand press back my hair since I was a child."

Her eyes fell slightly, and she moved uneasily.

"There was a look of pain upon your face as you lay sleeping, and I thought it might ease you somewhat. I have had some experience as a nurse, you know," she explained quietly. "You mentioned your mother; is she yet living?"

"She is in Richmond, stopping with friends, but since my capture we have lost all trace of each other. I was reported as having been killed in action, and I doubt if she even yet knows the truth. Everything is so confused in the capital that it is impossible to trace any one not directly connected with the army, once you lose exact knowledge of their whereabouts."

"Your father, then, is dead?"

"He yielded his life the first year of the war; and our plantation near Charlottesville has been constantly in the track of the armies. One rather important battle, indeed, was fought upon it, so you may realize that it is now desolate, and utterly unfit for habitation."

"The house yet stands?"

"The chimney and one wall alone remained when I was last there," I replied, glad of the interest she exhibited. "Fortunately two of the negro cabins were yet standing. Doubtless these will form the nucleus of our home when the war ceases; they will prove a trifle better than the mere sky."

"The South is certainly paying a terrible price for rebellion," she said soberly, her fine eyes filled with tears. "Only those of us who have beheld some portion of the sacrifice can ever realize how complete it is."

"The uselessness of it is what makes it seem now so unutterably sad."

"Yes," she assented, "and this the South is beginning to understand. But I cannot help thinking of the joy awaiting your mother when she learns that you are well, after she has mourned you as dead. It will almost repay her for all the rest. How I should love to be the bearer of such news."

As she spoke she quietly rose to her feet and smiled pleasantly as I took advantage of the opportunity to sit up.

"I thought you must be tired, lying in that position so long; besides, I am sure I have tarried here quite as long as I should, now that I can be of no further service."

My Lady of the North

As she gathered her skirts in her hand preparatory to descending the stairs, I yielded to temptation and stopped her. Right or wrong I must yet have one word more.

"I beg of you do not desert me so soon. This may prove our final meeting,—indeed, I fear it must be; surely, then, it need not be so brief a one?"

She paused irresolute, one white hand resting upon the dark stair-rail, her face turned partially aside so I could only guess at its expression.

"Our final meeting?"

She echoed my words as though scarcely comprehending their meaning.

"Yes," I said, rising and standing before her. "How can we well hope it shall be otherwise? I am not free to remain here, even were it best for other reasons, for I am a soldier under orders. You undoubtedly will proceed North at the earliest possible moment. There is scarcely a probability that in the great wide world we shall meet again."

"The war will soon be over; perhaps then you may come North also."

"I scarcely expect to do so. My work then will be to join with my comrades in an effort to rebuild the shattered fortunes of Virginia. When the lines of lives diverge so widely as ours must, the chances are indeed few that they ever meet again."

"Yes; yet we are free agents."

"Not always, nor under all circumstances — there are outside influences which cannot be ignored."

Her head was bowed slightly, but she lifted it now, and I dreamed I saw unshed tears in her eyes.

"But surely you can remain here until we leave?" she questioned, evidently striving not to reveal the depth

of interest she felt in the decision. " It will not be until
to-morrow that all details are arranged so as to permit of
our departure. I had supposed you would certainly be
with us until then."

" Mrs. Brennan!" I exclaimed almost passionately, "do
not tempt me! Your wish is a temptation most difficult
to resist."

" Why resist, then? "

She did not look at me, but stood twisting a handkerchief nervously through her fingers. The abrupt question startled me almost into full confession, but fortunately
my eyes chanced to fall upon her wedding-ring, and
instantly I crushed the mad words back into my throat.

" Because it is right," I replied slowly, feeling each
sentence as a death-blow. " For me to remain can mean
only one thing. For that I am ready enough, if I thought
you desired it, but I dare not choose such a course
myself."

" You speak in riddles. What is the one thing? "

" A personal meeting with Major Brennan."

The high color deserted her cheeks, and her eyes met
mine in sudden inquiry. " Oh, no, no!" she exclaimed
with energy. " You and Frank must never meet in that
way. You mean a duel? "

I bowed gravely. " I can assure you I earnestly desire
to avoid it for your sake, but am aware of no possibility
of escape except through my immediate departure."

" There has been no challenge then? "

" Not formally, yet almost an equivalent — I was permitted to aid in defence of this house only by pledging
myself to Major Brennan afterwards."

" But why need it be — at least now that you have stood
together as comrades? "

My Lady of the North

" I fear," I said quietly, " that fact will not count for much. We both fought inspired by your presence."

" Mine ! " I hardly knew how to interpret her tone.

" Certainly; you cannot be ignorant that Major Brennan's dislike is based upon your friendship for me."

" But there is no reason," she stammered. " He has no cause — "

" His reason I must leave him to explain," I interrupted, to relieve her evident embarrassment. " His words, however, were extremely explicit; and to ignore them by departure is to imperil my own reputation in both armies. I would do so for no one else in the world but you."

Her reception of this almost open avowal surprised me. For an instant she remained motionless, her eyes lowered upon the carpet, a flush on either cheek; then they were frankly lifted to mine, and she extended both hands.

" How can I ever thank you ? " she asked gravely. " Captain Wayne, you make me trust you utterly, and place me constantly in your debt."

Her words and manner combined to make me realize the depth of her feeling. But what did they really betoken ? Was it merely thankfulness at her husband's escape from peril, or a personal devotion toward myself ? I could not determine, but might only venture to believe the first more probable.

"Then you realize that I am right ? "

" Yes," slowly, but making no effort to release her hands. " Yet is no other escape possible ? "

" None within my knowledge."

" And you must go ? "

" I must go — unless you bid me stay."

" Oh, I cannot; I cannot at such a cost ! " she cried,

314

and I could feel her body tremble with the intensity of her emotion. "But, Captain Wayne, our friendship surely need not be severed now for ever? I cannot bear to think that it should be. I am no cold, heartless ingrate, and shall never forget what you have done to serve me. I value every sacrifice you have made on my behalf. Let us indeed part now if, as you say, it must be so; yet surely there are happier days in store for both of us — days when the men of this nation will not wear different uniforms and deem it manly to fight and kill each other."

"The great struggle will certainly cease, possibly within a very few weeks," I answered, greatly moved by her earnestness, "but I fear the men engaged in it will remain much the same in their natures however they may dress. I can only say this: Were the path clear I would surely find you, no matter where you were hidden."

She bowed her head against the post of the stair-rail and sobbed silently. I stood without speaking, knowing nothing I could hope to say which would in the least comfort her, for in my own heart abode the same dull despair. At last she looked up, making not the slightest attempt to disguise her emotion.

"How terrible it is that a woman must ever choose between such evils," she said almost bitterly. "The heart says one thing and duty another all through life, it seems to me. I have seen so much of suffering in these last few months, so much of heartless cruelty, that I cannot bear to be the cause of any more. You and Major Brennan must not meet; but, Captain Wayne, I will not believe that we are to part thus for ever."

"Do you mean that I am to seek you when the war closes?"

My Lady of the North

"There will be no time when I shall not most gladly welcome you."

"Your home?" I asked, wondering still if she could mean all that her words implied. "I have never known where you resided in the North."

"Stonington, Connecticut." She smiled at me through the tears yet clinging to her long lashes. "You may never come, of course, yet I shall always feel now that perhaps you will; and that is not like a final good-bye, is it?"

I bowed above the hands I held, and pressed my lips upon them. For the moment I durst not speak, and then — a voice suddenly sounded in the hall below:

"I am greatly obliged to you, Miss Minor; she is probably lying down. I will run up and call her."

We started as if rudely awakened from a dream, while a sudden expression of fright swept across her face.

"Oh, do not meet him," she begged piteously. "For my sake do not remain here."

"I will go down the back stairway," I returned hastily, "but do you indeed mean it? may I come to you?"

"Yes, yes; but pray go now!"

Unable longer to restrain myself, I clasped her to me, held her for one brief instant strained to my breast, kissed her twice upon lips which had no opportunity for refusal.

"This world is not so wide but that somewhere in it I shall again find the one woman of my heart," I whispered passionately, and was gone.

CHAPTER XXXV

A PLAN MISCARRIED

I REMEMBERED as I hurried down the back stairway her flushed face, but could recall no look of indignant pride in those clear eyes whose pleasant memory haunted me. She loved me; of this I now felt doubly assured, and the knowledge made my heart light, even while I dreaded the consequences to us both. To have won was much, even although hope of possession did not accompany the winning. Neither of us might ever again blot out those passionate words of love, nor forget the glad meeting of our lips.

I stepped out into the kitchen and came to a sudden pause, facing a table laden with such a variety and abundance of food as had been strange to me for many a long day. Directly opposite, a napkin tucked beneath his double chin, his plate piled high with good things, sat Ebers, while at either end I beheld Mr. and Mrs. Bungay similarly situated. The astonishment of our meeting seemed mutual. The Sergeant, apparently feeling the necessity of explanation, wiped his mouth soberly.

"I vos yoost goin' to fill me op mit der dings like a good soldier, Captain," he said in anxiety.

"So I perceive," I answered, my own spirits high. "The long night of fasting must have left quite a vacancy."

"I vos like a cistern in mein insides, by Chiminy."

317

My Lady of the North

"No doubt; well, I am rather hungry myself. Mrs. Bungay, in memory of old times cannot you spare me a plate? If so, I will take pleasure in joining your happy company. Thank you. I see you have found your man."

She glared down the table, and the little fellow visibly shrank.

"I have thet, sir," she answered grimly, "an' I reckon as how he's likely ter stay et hum arter this."

"But you forget he is my guide," I protested, not disinclined to test her temper. "Surely, Mrs. Bungay, you would not deprive the South of his valuable services?"

"An' wouldn't I, now? An' didn't thet little whiffit promise me long afore he ever did you uns? Ain't he my nat'ral pertecter? Whut's a lone female a goin' ter dew yere in ther mountings wi'out no man?" Her eyes flashed angrily at me. "Suah, an' if it's jist fightin' as he wants so bad I reckon as how he kin git it et hum wi'out goin' ter no war — anyhow ye kin bet I don't give him up, now I got my hand on him agin, fer ther whole kit an' caboodle of ye. He bean't much ter look et, likely, but he's my man, an' I reckon as how ther Lord giv' him ter me ter take keer of."

"Really, Mrs. Bungay," I insisted, "of course it will prove exceedingly disagreeable to me, and I shall greatly regret being compelled to do anything of the kind, but it is undoubtedly my duty to place Jed under guard and carry him back to camp with me."

"But suah, an' ye won't, Captain dear?" she pleaded, entirely changing her tone. "Whut good is thet little whiffit ter you uns? There's never so much as a decent fight in him thet I've found in twenty years. Maybe ye think as how I'm jist a bit hard on him; but he's thet gay at times thet he drives me fair crazy. Every

318

lick I ever give him wus fer his own good. Suah now, an' ye never would run off with my man?"

"Come, Jed, what do you say? Are you tired fighting the battles of the Confederacy, and prefer those of home?"

> "'Poor remnants of the Bleeding Heart,
>   Ellen and I will seek, apart,
>   The refuge of some forest cell,
>   There like the hunted quarry dwell,
>   Till on the mountain and the moor,
>   The stern pursuit be passed and o'er,'"

he quoted humbly. "I like ter read all 'bout fightin' well 'nough, but durn it, Cap, it kinder hurts whin they hits ye on ther head with a gun." His face lit up suddenly. "'Sides, I sorter wanter hev Mariar git 'quainted with thet thar muel o' mine, Beelzebub."

"But you've lost him."

"Nary a durn loss; ye jist can't lose thet muel, he's too blame ornary. He's out thar now, hitched ter a tree, an' a eatin' fit ter bust his biler — never a durn mark on his hide fer all he wint through."

"Well, I suppose I shall be compelled to let you and Beelzebub go, but it will prove a serious loss to the cause of the South," I said, my thoughts instantly turned by mention of the mule to matters of more importance. "I expect there will be lively times up your way."

"Ye kin jist bet thar will," enthusiastically. "It 'll be nip an' tuck, I reckon, but I'm mighty hopeful o' Mariar. Thet dern muel he needs ter be took down a peg."

Ebers was eating all this time with an eagerness which plainly exhibited his fear lest I should call him to halt before he had entirely filled the aching void in his interior department. I could not fail to note the deep anxiety in his eyes as he watched me furtively.

"Sergeant," I said, and he started perceptibly.

"I vos not yet done, Captain," he implored. "Mein Gott, but I vos so hongry as never vos."

"Oh, eat all you please; I merely wished to question you a little. Did you send out a party to bring in our horses and the sabres?"

"It vos all done already; der horses vos found und der swords. Yaw, I see to all dot; but I vos hongry, und vaited here to fill me op."

"How many men have we lost?"

He checked them off on the tines of his fork, occasionally pausing to take a bite from the meat held in his other hand.

"Der vos five kilt, Captain; dot vos it. I vos hit mit der ear off, und vos hongry as never vos; Sands is goin' to die, und maybe Elliott vill not get some better; some odders vos hurted, und der guide vos took brisoner."

"Taken prisoner?"

"Dot is it, Captain; by Chiminy, he vos took by der ear by his voman und led in der house. Vot you calls dot, if he vos not brisoner, hay?"

"Why, she is his wife."

"Vell, dot may be, too," he insisted stoutly. "His frau, yaw, dot is it, but by Chiminy, he fights mit her yoost der same, und vos brisoner; und I vos vounded mit der ear off, und vos hongry as never vos."

"How many men does that leave us fit for duty?" I asked decisively, pushing back my plate and rising from the table.

He counted them up with painful slowness, speaking each name deliberately, as if calling the roll.

A Plan Miscarried

"Dere vos twelve, Captain, mit me, but I am not fit for duty widout I eat somedings first."

"That will do," I said peremptorily. "You can have fifteen minutes more to complete filling up. In half an hour from now have the men ready for the road."

"But, Captain," he protested, "I vould rattle so mit my insides, by Chiminy, dot der horse vould scare."

"Do exactly as I say, and no more words, Sergeant," and I turned and left the room.

We must depart, and at once. More than ever now I realized the necessity for haste. I hoped to meet the officer commanding the Federal detachment who had come to our aid, pay him the customary marks of respect, and get away without again coming in contact with Major Brennan. I felt myself pledged to this course of action.

A sentry stationed in the lower hallway informed me the officers were messing together in the front parlor, and I at once headed that way. I paused, however, to visit the wounded for a moment, spoke cheerily to my own men, and then, opening the door quietly, entered the room which I had last left in possession of the guerillas. With the exception of broken windows and bullet-scarred walls little evidence remained of that contest which had raged here with such fury but a few hours previously. There were numerous dark stains upon the carpet, but much of the furniture had been restored to place, while a cheerful wood fire crackled in the open grate. Before it three men were sitting smoking, while upon a small table close at their elbows rested a flat bottle, flanked by several glasses. A single glance sufficed to tell me they were Federal cavalrymen, one being the red-faced lieutenant whom I had already met.

My Lady of the North

"I am seeking the commander of this detachment," I explained, as they glanced up in surprise at my entrance unannounced. "I am Captain Wayne, in charge of the Confederate troop which was engaged in defence of this house."

A portly man with a strong face, and wearing a closely clipped gray beard, arose from a comfortable armchair and advanced with hand extended.

"I am Captain Moorehouse, in command," he answered cordially, "and am very glad to meet you. Will you not join with us? My second lieutenant, who has positive genius in that line, has unearthed a few bottles of rather choice whiskey which we will divide most gladly."

"I thank you," I replied, anxious to meet him as pleasantly as possible, "but I am eager to get away upon my duty as early as may be, and have merely intruded upon you to explain my purpose."

"Nonsense," he insisted. "Duty is never quite so urgent as to require a waste of good liquor. Captain Wayne, permit me to present my officers — Lieutenants Warren and Starr, Second New Hampshire Cavalry. If by any luck you were at Gettysburg, you have met before."

I smiled and accepted the glass held out to me.

"I was certainly there," I replied in the same spirit with which he had spoken, "and now you recall it, retain a most vivid recollection of meeting several Federal cavalrymen on that occasion, but believe I did not linger to ascertain the number of their regiment. My curiosity was completely satisfied before I reached that point. However, I am far better pleased to renew the acquaintance in this manner."

The ice broken, we continued to converse freely for

322

A Plan Miscarried

several minutes regarding incidents of the war, and I described the peculiar conditions which had brought me to the relief of Brennan's party. Under other circumstances I should have greatly enjoyed this exchange of reminiscences, but the constant haunting fear of the Major's possible entrance at any moment rendered me extremely uneasy, and anxious to be away. Undoubtedly this feeling exhibited itself in my manner, for Captain Moorehouse said finally:

"I realize your natural anxiety to be off, Captain Wayne, and while we should be very glad to keep you with us indefinitely, yet I trust you will feel perfectly free in the matter."

"I thank you greatly," I answered, rising as I spoke. "My duty is of such a nature, and has already been so long neglected, that I feel every moment of unnecessary delay to be a crime. I wish you a pleasant return within your own lines, and an early cessation of hostilities."

I had shaken hands with them all, and turned toward the door, congratulating myself on escaping thus easily, when a new voice broke suddenly in upon my self-satisfaction:

"I trust Captain Wayne is not intending to depart without at least a word with me?"

It was Brennan. He had entered unobserved from the second parlor, and now stood leaning with an almost insolent assumption of languor against the sliding door, his eyes fastened upon me.

"Frankly," I responded, "I had hoped I might."

His brows contracted into a frown of anger that seemed to darken his entire face.

"Have you forgotten, then, our compact, or do you simply elect to ignore it?"

323

My Lady of the North

I saw the others exchange quick glances of amazement, but I answered coolly:

"The latter supposition is more nearly the truth, Major Brennan. I felt that after what we have just passed through together we could both afford to ignore the past, and consequently was hoping to escape without again encountering you."

"Indeed!" he exclaimed sarcastically. "But I might have expected it. Gentlemen," and he turned toward the expectant group, "this man and I have a personal grievance of long standing unsettled. I have sought him for months in vain. When he came last night to our assistance, before I even consented to accept his services I insisted that no occurrence of the defence should prevent our meeting if we both survived. Now he endeavors to sneak away like a whipped cur. I demand satisfaction at his hands, and if it is refused I shall denounce him in both armies."

My cheeks burned, but before I could control myself sufficiently for answer Moorehouse spoke.

"But, Brennan, see here," he said anxiously, "surely Captain Wayne has served you well. Is this trouble between you so serious that no amends are possible?"

"None, short of a personal meeting."

"Captain," and the perplexed Federal commander, turned toward me, "have you any word of explanation in this unfortunate affair?"

"Very little," I answered. "I am not even aware that I have done injury to Major Brennan, purposely or otherwise. He has not so much as honored me with information as to his cause for complaint. However, I care very little what it may be. As he has seen fit to denounce me before officers of my own corps, I should be extremely

A Plan Miscarried

glad to meet him upon that ground alone; but after what we have just passed through together, I felt ready to blot out these past differences. Whatever they may have been, they are not liable to occur again, nor we to meet."

"They have occurred again since you have been in this house!" Brennan broke forth excitedly. "You are not a coward, but I brand you here and now as sneak and liar! Now will you fight?"

We stood for a moment in utter silence, eye to eye, and I knew there was no help for it. These words, publicly spoken, left me no choice.

"I am at your service, Major Brennan," I returned sternly, "now, or at any time. But I am unfortunate here in having no officer of my army present, and hence can name no second."

"Doubtless one of these gentlemen will consent to serve," he said, his face brightening at my rejoinder.

There was a moment of hesitation, natural enough, for they could scarcely feel like pitting themselves against a brother officer in a quarrel the merits of which were so obscure. I was about to speak, volunteering to stand alone, when some one hastily pushed a way to the front, and Lieutenant Caton, pale but determined, stood at my shoulder.

"It will afford me pleasure to act for Captain Wayne," he said clearly, "if he will accept my services. Moreover," he added, with a significant glance at Brennan, "I do this as a friend, and with full confidence that I am upon the right side in the quarrel."

For a moment no one spoke, Brennan biting his moustache to keep back words he durst not utter. Then Caton turned to me.

"If you will retire to the library, Wayne, I will arrange this matter with whoever may represent Major Brennan."

With a slight formal bow to those present I quitted the room.

CHAPTER XXXVI

I FOUND the library deserted, and paced the floor for fully half an hour before Caton appeared. Stung as I had been by Brennan's harsh, uncalled-for words, I yet shrank from the thought that I must now meet him in deadly combat. It was no fear of personal injury that troubled me; indeed I do not recall giving this the slightest consideration, for my mind was altogether concentrated upon what such a meeting must necessarily mean to Edith Brennan, and how it would affect all our future relationship. This was the thought that swayed and mastered me. I had pledged myself to avoid him, and indeed had used every means possible to that end. I was even willing to go forth stamped by his denunciation rather than involve her in such contro- versy. But the effort was fruitless, and I must now stand before him, or else forever forfeit my manhood. Thus the die was already cast, yet in one point I might still prove true to the spirit of my pledge, and retain her approbation — I could permit my antagonist to leave the field unscathed.

One who does not realize my feelings toward this man, my fierce resentment of every indignity he had heaped upon me, my intense rivalry, and my burning desire to punish him for a hundred mental wounds, cannot com- prehend how difficult a battle I fought in those few

327

moments in order that I might conquer myself. The time was none too long, yet my mind once thoroughly settled as to my duty to her, I became calm again, and confident as to the outcome. When Caton entered, flushed and visibly excited from what had evidently proven an acrimonious controversy, I greeted him with a smile.

" You appear to have experienced difficulties in regard to details," I said curiously.

" There was much unnecessary talk," he admitted, " but matters have been at last arranged to the satisfaction of all concerned. You are to meet at once, in the rear of the big tobacco shed, a spot entirely removed from observation. I have been compelled to accept pistols as the weapons, as we have nothing else here at all suitable for the purpose — cavalry sabres being far too cumbersome. Lieutenant Starr chances to possess two derringers exactly alike which we have mutually agreed upon. I hope this is satisfactory to you, Wayne? "

" I am not precisely an expert, but that does not greatly matter. Who acts for Brennan? "

" Captain Moorehouse, rather against his will, I think."

" Very well, Caton; I am perfectly satisfied, and am, indeed, greatly obliged to you; yet before we go out I desire to speak a word or two with the utmost frankness." I stood facing him, my hand resting lightly upon the writing-table, my eyes reading his expressive face. " As my second I wish you to comprehend fully my actions, and the motives that inspire them. If they are in any way unsatisfactory to your mind, you may feel at perfect liberty to withhold your services. I am now, and always have been, opposed to duelling; I believe it wrong in principle, and a travesty upon justice; but it is a custom of the South, a requirement among officers

The Last Resort of Gentlemen

of our army, and after what has just occurred between Major Brennan and myself I cannot honorably refuse any longer to go out. Major Brennan has deliberately placed me in a position where I cannot avoid meeting him without losing all standing in my corps. I sought to escape, but was prevented by accident; now I simply yield to the inevitable. I feel confident you will not misconstrue these words; you surely know me sufficiently well so as not to attribute them to cowardice. I shall face him exactly in accordance with your arrangements, asking nothing upon my part, yielding him every satisfaction he can possibly desire — but I shall fire in the air."

He stared at me incredulously, his face a perfect picture of amazement. "But, Wayne," he stammered, "are you aware that Major Brennan is an expert with the pistol? that he holds the Sixth Corps trophy? Do you realize that he goes out deliberately intending to kill you?"

"I was not posted as to the first fact you mention, but have never entertained the slightest doubt as to the other. However, they do not in the least affect my decision."

"But, man, it will be murder! I should never forgive myself if I sanctioned it."

"That is exactly why I told you," I said calmly; "and I am perfectly willing to stand alone and absolve you from all responsibility. Yet I do not desire you to suppose that I am at all quixotic in this — there is a personal reason why I am perfectly willing to risk my life rather than injure Major Brennan."

His troubled eyes studied me intently, and then his face suddenly brightened with a new thought. "Wayne," he asked, placing his hand upon my arm familiarly, "is it Mrs. Brennan?"

My Lady of the North

For an instant I hesitated, but his manly, honest countenance reassured me. "Between us only, it is," I answered gravely; "but not the slightest blame attaches to her."

"I do not wholly understand," he said at last, "yet I do not doubt you may be perfectly right in your decision." He extended his hand impulsively. "I know you to be a good soldier and a true gentleman; I will stand with you, Wayne, but I pledge this — if he takes advantage treacherously, and you fall (as God forbid!), I will face him myself; and when I do, there shall be no firing in the air."

I wrung his hand silently, and my heart went out in unspeakable gratitude to this noble fellow, who, wearing the uniform of an enemy, had constantly proven himself my sincere friend. "Your words strengthen me greatly," I managed to say at last. "Now let us go, and not keep the others waiting."

I do not remember that we spoke, save once, while we passed out through the orchard into the field where the big tobacco shed stood. A group of soldiers were digging a grave behind one of the negro cabins, but other than these we saw no one. It was as we paused a moment to refasten the gate that I finally broke the silence between us.

"In the inner pocket of my shirt," I said, "you will find directions which will enable you to communicate with my people."

His eyes instantly filled with tears.

"Don't say that, Wayne," he protested. "I will not believe it is destined to end so."

"I certainly trust it is not," I answered, smiling at him, and deeply touched by his show of genuine feeling,

The Last Resort of Gentlemen

" but I have only you to rely upon in this matter if by any chance it does."

The deserted field we were compelled to cross had long been neglected, and was now thickly overgrown with weeds. Not until we turned the corner of the great ramshackle building, which in other and more prosperous days had been dedicated to the curing of the leaf, did we perceive any signs of the presence of our antagonists. They were standing upon the farther side, directly opposite the door, and both bowed slightly as we approached. The Captain came toward us slowly.

" It is to be greatly regretted, gentlemen," he said, with ceremonious politeness, " that we have no surgeon with us. However, neither contestant has any advantage in this respect. Lieutenant Caton, may I ask if the arrangements as already completed have proven satisfactory to your principal?"

" Entirely so."

" Then if you will kindly step this way a moment we will confer as to certain details."

Brennan was leaning in negligent attitude against the side of the building, his eyes fastened upon the ground, the blue smoke of a cigar curling lazily above his head. I glanced toward him, and then sought to amuse myself watching the queer antics of a gray squirrel on the rail fence beyond. I felt no desire for further thought, only an intense anxiety for them to hurry the preliminaries, and have the affair settled as speedily as possible. I was aroused by Moorehouse's rather nasal voice.

" Gentlemen, will you please take your positions. Major Brennan, you will stand three paces to the right of that sapling, facing directly south. Captain Wayne, kindly walk straight west from the shed door until you come opposite the Major's position."

I noted Brennan throw away the stump of his cigar, and then I walked slowly forward until I reached the point assigned me. My heart was beating fast now, for I fully realized the probabilities of the next few minutes, and felt little doubt that serious injury, if not death, was to be my portion. Yet my trained nerves did not fail me, and outwardly I appeared fully as cool and deliberate as my opponent. Years of constant exposure to peril in every form had yielded me a grim philosophy of fatalism that now stood me in most excellent stead. Indeed, I doubt not, had I chosen to put it to the test, my hand would have proven the steadier of the two, for Brennan's face was flushed, and he plainly exhibited the intense animosity with which he confronted me.

How peculiarly the mind often operates in such moments of exciting suspense! I recall remarking a very slight stoop in Brennan's shoulders which I had never perceived before, I remember wondering where Moorehouse had ever discovered a tailor to give so shocking a fit to his coat, and finally I grew almost interested in two birds perched upon the limb of a tree opposite where I stood. I even smiled to myself over a jest one of the young officers had made an hour before. Yet with it all I remained keenly observant, and fully aware of each movement made by the others on the field. I saw Caton accept the derringer handed him and test it carefully, the long, slim, blue barrel looking deadly enough as he held it up between me and the sky. Then Moorehouse approached Brennan with its fellow in his grasp, and the Lieutenant crossed over, and stood beside me.

" Here is the gun, Wayne," he said, " and I sincerely

332

hope you have changed your decision. There is no mercy in Brennan's eyes."

" So I notice," I answered, taking the derringer from him, and examining it with some curiosity, " but I shall do as I said, nevertheless. It is not any sentiment of mercy I feel which spares him, but a duty that appeals to me even more strongly than hate."

" By Heaven, I wish it were otherwise."

I remained silent, for I could not say in my heart that I echoed his wish, and I cared not to go down in another minute with a lie upon my lips. The love of Edith Brennan, which I now felt assured was mine, was sweeter far to me than life.

" Who gives the word? " I questioned.

" I do; are you ready? "

" Perfectly."

I held out my hand, and his fingers closed upon it with warm, friendly grip. The next moment Brennan and I stood, seemingly alone, facing each other, as motionless as two statues. His coat was buttoned to the throat, his cap-visor pulled low over his eyes, his pistol hand hanging straight down at his side, his gaze never wavering from me. I knew he was coolly, deliberately measuring the distance between us with as deadly a purpose as any murderer. The almost painful stillness was broken by Caton, and I marked the tremor in his voice.

" Are you both ready, gentlemen? "

" I am," said Brennan.

" Ready," I replied.

" The word will be one, two, three — fire; with a slight pause after the three. A report from either pistol before the final word is spoken I shall take personally. Be prepared now."

My Lady of the North

There was a moment's pause; so still was it I heard the chirping of birds overhead, and the flutter of a leaf as it fell swirling at my feet. I saw Brennan as through a mist, and in its undulations there seemed to be pictures of the face of his wife, as if her spirit hovered there between us. To have shot then would have been like piercing her before reaching him.

"Ready!" said the voice once more; and as I saw Brennan's arm slowly rise, I lifted mine also, and covered him, noting, as I did so, almost in wonder, with what steadiness of nerve and wrist I held the slender gauge just beneath the visor of his cap. Deliberately, as though he dreaded the necessity, Caton counted:

"One; two; three — fire!"

My pistol exploded, the charge striking the limb above him, and I staggered backward, my hat torn from my head, a white line cut through my hair, and a thin trickle of blood upon my temple. I saw Caton rushing toward me, his face filled with anxiety, and then Brennan hurled his yet smoking derringer into the dirt at his feet with an oath.

"Damn it, Moorehouse," he roared, fairly beside himself, "the charge was too heavy; it overshot."

"Are you much hurt?" panted Caton.

"Merely pricked the skin."

Then Brennan's angry voice rang out once more.

"I demand another shot," he insisted loudly. "I demand it, I tell you, Moorehouse. This settles nothing, and I will not be balked just because you don't know enough to load a gun."

Caton wheeled upon him, his blue eyes blazing dangerously.

"You demand a second shot?" he cried indignantly.

The Last Resort of Gentlemen

"Are you not aware, sir, that Captain Wayne fired in the air? It would be murder."

"Fired in the air!" he laughed, as if it was a most excellent joke. "Of course he did, but it was because my ball disconcerted his aim. I fired a second the first, but his derringer was covering me."

Caton strode toward him, his face white with passion.

"Let him have it his way," I called after him, for now my own blood was up. "I shall not be guilty of such neglect again."

He did not heed me, perhaps he did not hear.

"Major Brennan," he said, facing him, his voice trembling with feeling, "I tell you Captain Wayne purposely shot in the air. He informed me before coming upon the field that he should do so. I positively refuse to permit him to face your fire again."

Brennan's face blazed; chagrin, anger, disappointment fairly infuriated him, and he seemed to lose all self-control. "This is some cowardly trick!" he roared, glaring about him as if seeking some one upon whom he could vent his wrath. "Damn it, I believe my pistol was fixed to overshoot in order to save that fellow. I never missed such a shot before."

Moorehouse broke in upon his raving, so astounded at these intemperate words as to stutter in his speech.

"D-do you d-dare to in-insinuate, Major Brennan," he began, "that I have —" he paused, his mouth wide open, staring toward the shed. Involuntarily we glanced in that direction also, wondering what he saw. There, in the open doorway, as in a frame, dressed almost entirely in white, her graceful figure and fair young face clearly defined against the dark background, stood Edith Brennan.

CHAPTER XXXVII

THE LAST GOOD-BYE

SHE exhibited no outward sign of agitation as she left her position and slowly advanced toward us. However fiercely her heart may have beaten she remained apparently calm and composed. Never before had I felt so completely dominated by her womanly spirit, while her very presence upon the field hushed in an instant the breathings of dispute. She never so much as glanced at either Brennan or myself, but ignored us totally as she drew near. Daintily lifting her skirts to keep them from contact with the weeds under foot, her head poised proudly, her eyes a bit disdainful of it all, she paused before Caton.

"Lieutenant," she questioned in a clear tone which seemed to command an answer, "I have always found you an impartial friend. Will you kindly inform me as to the true meaning of all this?"

He hesitated, hardly knowing what to reply, but her imperious eyes were upon him — they insisted, and he stammered lamely:

"Two of the gentlemen, madam, were about to settle a slight disagreement by means of the code."

"Were about?" she echoed, scornful of all deceit. "Surely I heard shots as I came through the orchard?"

"One fire has been exchanged," he reluctantly admitted.

"And Captain Wayne has been wounded?"

The Last Good-Bye

I was not aware until that moment that she had even so much as noticed my presence.

"Very slightly, madam."

"His opponent escaped uninjured?"

Caton bowed, glanced uneasily toward me, and then blurted forth impulsively: "Captain Wayne fired in the air, madam."

She never glanced toward where I stood, yet I instantly marked the quick droop of her eyes, the faint pink that overspread her cheek. This slight confusion, unnoted save by eyes of love, was but momentary, still it was sufficient to apprise me that she both understood and approved my action.

"A most delightful situation, surely," she said clearly and sarcastically. "One would almost suppose we had wholly reverted to barbarism, and that our boasted civilization was but mockery. Think of it," and the proud disdain in her face held us silent, "not six hours ago that house yonder was the scene of a desperate battle. Within its blood-stained rooms men fought and died, cheering in their agony like heroes of romance. I saw there two men battling shoulder to shoulder against a host of infuriated ruffians, seeking to protect helpless women. They wore different uniforms, they followed different flags, by the fortune of war they were enemies, yet they could fight and die in defence of the weak. I thanked God upon my knees that I had been privileged to know such men and could call them friends. No nobler, truer, manlier deed at arms was ever done! Yet, mark you, no sooner is that duty over — scarcely are their dead comrades buried — when they forget every natural instinct of gratitude, of true manliness, and spring at each other's throat like two maddened beasts. I care not what the cause may be — the act is shameful, and an insult to every woman of this household. Even as I came upon the field voices were clamoring for another shot, in spite of the fact that one man stood already wounded. War may be excusable, but this is not war. Gentlemen, you have fired your last shot on this field, unless you choose to make me your target."

I would that I possessed a picture of that scene — a picture which would show the varied expressions of countenance as those scornful words lashed us. She stood there as a queen might, and commanded an obedience no man among us durst refuse. Brennan's flushed face paled, and his lips trembled as he sought to make excuse.

" But, Edith," he protested, " you do not know, you do not understand. There are wrongs which can be righted in no other way."

" I do not care to know," she answered coldly, " nor do I ever expect to learn that murder can right a wrong."

" Murder! You use strong terms. The code has been recognized for centuries as the last resort of gentlemen."

" The code! Has it, indeed? What gentlemen? Those of the South exclusively of late. That might possibly pardon your opponent, but not you, for you know very well that in the North no man of any standing would ever venture to resort to it. Moreover, even the code presupposes that men shall stand equal at its bar — I am informed that Captain Wayne fired in the air."

He hesitated, feeling doubtless the uselessness of further protest, yet she permitted him small opportunity for consideration. " Major," she said quietly but firmly, " I should be pleased to have you escort me to the house."

These words, gently as they were spoken, still constituted a command. Her eyes were upon his face, and I doubt not he read within them that he would forfeit all her respect if he failed to obey. Yet he yielded with exceeding poor grace.

"As it seems impossible to continue," he admitted bitterly, "I suppose I may as well go." He turned and fronted me, his eyes glowing. "But understand, sir, this is merely a cessation, not an ending."

I bowed gravely, not daring to trust my voice in speech, lest I should yield to the temptation of my own temper.

"Captain Wayne," she said, glancing back across his broad blue shoulder, and I thought there was a new quality in her voice, the sting had someway gone out of it, "I shall esteem it a kindness if you will call upon me before you depart."

"With pleasure," I hastened to reply, my surprise at the request almost robbing me of speech, "but I shall be compelled to leave at once, as my troop is already under orders."

"I shall detain you for only a moment, but after what you have passed through on our behalf I am unwilling you should depart without realizing our gratitude. You will find me in the library. Come, Frank, I am ready now."

We remained motionless, watching them until they disappeared around the corner of the shed. Brennan walked with stern face, his step heavy, she with averted eyes, a slight smile of triumph curling her lip. Then Moorehouse stooped and picked up the derringer the Major had thrown away.

"By thunder, but she's right!" he exclaimed emphatically. "I tell you that's a mighty fine woman. Blame me, if she didn't face us like a queen."

My Lady of the North

No one answered, and without exchanging another word we walked together to the house. There I found the remnant of my troop standing beside their horses, chaffing with a dozen idle Yankee cavalrymen who were lounging on the wide steps.

The time had come when I must say a final farewell and depart. Not the slightest excuse remained for further delay. I dreaded the ordeal, but no escape was possible, and I entered the house for what I well knew was to be the last time. My mind was gravely troubled; I knew not what to expect, how far I might venture to hope. Why had she desired to see me again? Surely the public reason she offered could not be the real one. Was it to confess that I had won her heart, or to show me by scornful words her indignation at my folly? What should I say, how could I act in her presence? These and a hundred other queries arose to perplex me.

Had she only been free, a maid whose hand remained her own to surrender as she pleased, I should never have hesitated, never have doubted her purpose; but now that could not be. I felt that every word and look between us already bordered upon sin, that danger to both alike lurked in each stolen glance and meeting. Better far we should have parted without further speech. I knew this, yet love constrained me, as it has constrained many another, and I lingered at her wish — a foolish moth fluttering to the flame.

As I knocked almost timidly at the closed library door a gentle voice said, "Come," and I entered, my heart throbbing like a frightened girl's. She stood waiting me nearly in the centre of that spacious apartment, dressed in the same light raiment she had worn without, and her greeting was calm and friendly, yet tinged by a proud

The Last Good-Bye

dignity I cannot describe. I believed for an instant that we were alone, and my blood raced through my veins in sudden expectancy; then my eyes fell upon Mrs. Minor comfortably seated in an armchair before the fire, and I realized that she was present to restrain me from forgetfulness. But in very truth my lady hardly needed such protection — her speech, her manner, her proud constraint told me at once most plainly that no existing tie between us had caused our meeting.

"Captain Wayne," she said softly, her high color alone giving evidence of any memory of the past, "I scarcely thought that we should meet again, yet was not willing to part with you under any misunderstanding. I have learned from Lieutenant Caton the full particulars of your action in connection with Major Brennan. I wish you to realize that I appreciate your efforts to escape a hostile meeting, and esteem you most highly for your forbearance on the field. It was indeed a noble proof of true courage. May I ask, why did you fire in the air?"

Had she not held me so away from her by her manner I should have then and there told her all the truth. As it was I durst not.

"I felt convinced that if my bullet reached Major Brennan it would injure you. I preferred not to do that."

She bowed gravely, while a kinder look, if I may use that expression, seemed to dominate her face.

"I believed it was for my sake you made the sacrifice." She paused; then asked in yet lower tones: "Was my name mentioned during your contention — I mean publicly?"

"It was not; Caton alone is aware I refrained because of the reason I have already given you."

"Your wound is not serious?"

341

My Lady of the North

"Too insignificant to be worthy of mention."

She was silent, her eyes upon the carpet, her bosom rising and falling with the emotion she sought in vain to suppress.

"I thank you for coming to me," she said finally. "I shall understand it all better, comprehend your motive better, for this brief talk. Whatever you may think of me in the future," and she held out her hand with something of the old frankness in the gesture, "do not hold me as ungrateful for a single kindness you have shown me. I have not fully understood you, Captain Wayne; indeed, I doubt if I do even now, yet I am under great obligations which I hope some day to be able to requite, at least in part."

"A thousand times they are already paid," I exclaimed eagerly, forgetting for the moment the presence of her silent chaperon. "You have given me that which is more than life — "

"Do not, Captain Wayne," she interrupted, her cheeks aflame. "I would rather forget. Please do not; I did not send to you for that, only to tell you I knew and understood. We must part now. Will you say good-bye?"

"If you bid me, yes, I will say good-bye," I answered, my own self-control brought back instantly by her words and manner, "but I retain that which I do not mean to forget — your gracious words of invitation to the North."

She stood with parted lips, as though she struggled to force back that which should not be uttered. Then she whispered swiftly:

"It is not my wish that you should."

Was there ever such another paradox of a woman?

The Last Good-Bye

I knew not how to read her aright, for I scarce ever found her twice the same. Which represented the truth of her character — her cool dignity, her impetuous pride, or that gentle tenderness whch befitted her so well? Which was the armor, which the heart of this fair lady of the North?

As we rode down the path to the eastward, a snowy handkerchief fluttered for an instant at the library window. I raised my hat in silent greeting, and we were gone.

CHAPTER XXXVIII

THE FURLING OF THE FLAGS

THE close of the long and bitter struggle had come; to those who had cast their fortunes with the South it seemed almost as the end of the world. I had thought to write of those last sad days, to picture them in all their contrasting light and shadow, but now I cannot. There are thoughts too deep for human utterance, memories too sacred for the pen. I rejoice that I was a part of it; that to the lowering of the last tattered battle-flag I remained constant to the best traditions of my house. I cannot sit here now, beneath the protecting shadow of a flag for which my son fought and died, and write that I regret the ending, for years of peace have taught us of the South lessons no less valuable than did the war; yet do I rejoice to-day that, having once donned the gray, I wore it until the last shotted gun voiced its grim message to the North.

It is hardly more than a dream now, sometimes vague and shadowy, again distinct with living figures and historic scenes. I require but to close my eyes to behold once more those slender lines of ragged, weary, hungry men, to whom fighting had become synonymous with life. I pass again through the fiery rain of those last fierce battles, when in desperation we sought to check the un-

344

The Furling of the Flags

numbered blue legions that fairly crushed us beneath their
weight. The vividness of the memory burns my brain
as by fire, — the ghastly faces of the dead, the unuttered
agony of the wounded, the patient suffering of the living.
Day by day, night by night, we grew less in numbers, and
our thin lines contracted; divisions shrank into regiments,
companies to platoons. Men knew that the inevitable
was upon them, yet smiled into one another's face and
went forth to die. It was pitiable; it was magnificent.
Hungry we fought, unsheltered we slept; our dead were
lying with the enemy, while we who yet lived for the duty
of another day fronted the bayonets with hearts of courage
and sadly prophetic souls. Everywhere to front and rear,
to left and right, stretched that same blue wall tipped
with cruel steel; in constant hail of iron the shells fell
upon us, darkening the day-sky, and turning night into
a hell of flame. There was no retreat, no loophole of
escape; we could but stay, suffer, and perish. Like men
afflicted with some incurable malady, we who were of
that stricken remnant sternly, grimly looked into the
eyes of death and waited for the end.

I saw it all; I held a part in it all. Upon that April
day which witnessed the turning of the last sad page
in this tragedy, I stood without the McLean house, ankle
deep in the trampled mud of the yard, surrounded by a
group of Federal officers. Within was my commander,
the old gray hero of Virginia, together with the great
silent soldier of the North.

Few about me spoke as we waited in restless agony.
No one addressed me, and I think there must have been
a look in my face which held them dumb. We knew
well what hung upon the balance then; that within those
humble walls was being consummated one of the great

events of history. To the men in blue it meant home, and victory, and peace; to those in gray, suffering, and struggle, and defeat.

I know not how long I waited, standing beside my horse, with head half bowed upon his neck, seeing the figures about me as in a dream. At last the door was flung open, and those within came forth. *He* was in advance of them all. In that pale, stern, kindly face, and within the depths of those sorrowful gray eyes, I read instantly the truth — *the Army of Northern Virginia was no more.* Yet with what calm dignity did this defeated chieftain pass down that blue lane, his head erect, his eyes undimmed — as dauntless in that awful hour of surrender as when he rode before his cheering legions of fighting men. Only as he came to where I stood, and caught the look of suffering upon my face, did he once falter, and then I noted no more than the slight twitching of his lips beneath the short gray beard.

"Captain Wayne," he said, with all his old-time courtesy, " I shall have to trouble you to ride to General Hills's division and request him to cease all firing at once."

I turned reluctantly away from him, knowing full well in my heart I was bearing my last order, and rode at a hard trot down the road between long lines of waiting Federal infantry. I scarcely so much as saw them, for my head was bent low over the saddle pommel, and my eyes were blurred with tears.

. . . .

The sun lay hot and golden over the dusty roads and fenceless fields. The air was vocal with blare of trumpets and roll of drums, while everywhere the eye rested upon blue lines and long columns of marching troops. I formed one of a little gray squad moving slowly south-

The Furling of the Flags

ward — a mere fragment of the fighting men of the Confederacy, making their way homeward as best they might. As the roads forked I left them, for here our paths diverged, and it chanced I was the only one whose hope lay westward.

Silently, thoughtfully I trudged on for an hour through the thick red dust. My horse, sorely wounded in our last skirmish, limped painfully behind me, his bridle-rein flung carelessly over my arm. Out yonder, where the sun pointed the way with streams of fire, I was to take up life anew. Life! What was there left to me in that word? A deserted, despoiled farm alone awaited my coming; hardly a remembered face, scarcely a future hope. The glitter of a passing troop of cavalry drew my mind for an instant to Edith Brennan, but I crushed the thought. Even were she free, what had I now to place at her proud feet, — I, a penniless, defeated, homeless man? No, that was all over, even as the cause for which I had fought; love and ambition must lie buried in the same grave. The clothes I wore, that tattered suit of faded gray, soiled by months of hard service in the open, was all I possessed in the wide world, save the starved and wounded animal limping dejectedly at my heels. The mere conception of it, the picture of kneeling thus attired at her feet, brought with it a grim smile, which a deep heartache instantly chased away. Besides, she was not free, and no dream of love might inspire me to toil and hope. With clinched teeth I drove her memory from me, back into that dim past where lurked all that had been worthy in my life. Sternly I resolved that her face should henceforth abide with those others — the shadowy comrades of many a battlefield.

In this spirit I plodded on, my step heavy, my head

347

bowed, wearied alike in heart and body. My temples throbbed with the heat of the sun, my eyes were dulled, my throat caked by the swirling dust. At a cross-roads a Federal picket halted me, and I aroused sufficiently to hand him the paper which entitled me to safe passage through the lines. He was a man well along in years, with thoughtful eyes and kindly face, and I spoke to him out of my sheer loneliness.

"No doubt you are rejoicing that the long struggle is so nearly ended?" I said as he handed me back the paper and motioned me to pass on. "Have you a family in the North?"

"A wife and five children up in Michigan, sir," he answered civilly. "I guess they are counting the days now. And you, sir?"

"Oh, I have some acres of worn-out land over yonder, and but little else."

"Well, you're a sight better off than some, I s'pect. It's been pretty tough on all of you, but if you fellows only work like you fought you'll have things a humming before long."

There was homely comfort in his philosophy which for the moment cheered me. Perhaps he was right; the energy and bravery of the South, crippled as it now was, might yet conquer our present misfortune, and prove it a blessing in disguise. I had gone a hundred yards or more, this thought still in my mind, when I became aware that he was calling after me.

"Hey, there, you gray-back!" he shouted, "hold on a bit!"

As I came to a pause and glanced back, wondering if there could be anything wrong with my parole, he swung his cap and pointed.

The Furling of the Flags

" That officer coming yonder wants to speak with you."

Across the open field at my right, hidden until then by a slight rise of ground, a mounted cavalryman was riding rapidly toward me, the wind blowing back his cape so as to make conspicuous its bright yellow lining. For the moment his lowered head prevented recognition, but as he cleared the ditch and came up smiling, I saw it was Caton.

" By Jove, Wayne, but this is lucky!" he exclaimed, springing to the ground beside me. " I 've actually been praying for a week past that I might meet you. Holmes, of your service, told me you had pulled through, but everything is in such confusion that to hunt for you would have been the proverbial quest after a needle in a haystack. You have been paroled then? "

" Yes, I 'm completely out of it at last," I answered, feeling to the full the deep sympathy expressed by his face. " It was a bitter pill, but one which had to be taken."

" I know it, old fellow," and his hand-grasp on mine tightened warmly. " Of course I 'm glad, there 's no use denying that, glad we won; glad the old Union has been preserved as our fathers gave it to us; glad slavery on this continent has passed away for ever, and so will you be before you die. Yet I am sincerely sorry for those who have given their all and lost. God knows you fought a good fight, fought as Americans only can, even though it was in a bad cause. That is the pity of it; such heroism, such sacrifice, and all wasted. If you have been beaten there is no disgrace in it, for no other nation in this world could ever have accomplished it. But this was a case of Greek meeting Greek, and we had the money, the resources, and the men. But, Wayne, I tell you, I do

349

not believe there is to-day a spark of bitterness in the heart of a fighting Federal soldier. We fought you to a finish because it's in our blood; we whipped you because we were compelled to in order to preserve the Union, but we'd share our last cent, or last crust, with any gray-back now. I know I feel as if every paroled Confederate were a brother in need."

"I know, Caton," I said, — and the words came hard, — "your fighting men respect us, even as we do them. It has been a sheer game of which could stand the most punishment, and the weaker had to go down. I know all that, but, nevertheless, it is a terrible ending to so much of hope, suffering, and sacrifice."

"Yes," he admitted soberly, "you have given your all. But those who survive have a wonderful work before them. They must lay anew the foundations; they are to be the rebuilders of States. You were going home?"

I smiled bitterly at this designation of my journey's end.

"Yes, if you can so name a few weed-grown fields and a vacant negro cabin. I certainly shall have to lay the foundation anew most literally."

"Will you not let me aid you?" he questioned eagerly. "I possess some means, and surely our friendship is sufficiently established to warrant me in making the offer. You will not refuse?"

"I must," I answered firmly. "Yet I do not value the offer the less. Sometime I may even remind you of it, but now I prefer to dig, as the others must. I shall be the stronger for it, and shall thus sooner forget the total wreck."

For a few moments we walked on together in silence, each leading his horse. I could not but note the contrast

The Furling of the Flags

between us in dress and bearing. Victory and defeat, each had stamped its own.

"Wayne," he asked at length, glancing furtively at me, as if to mark the effect of his words, "did you know that Mrs. Brennan was again with us?"

The name thus spoken set my heart to instant throbbing, but I sought to answer carelessly. Whatever he may have surmised, it was plainly my duty to hide our secret still.

"I was not even aware she had been away."

"Oh, yes; she returned North immediately after your last parting, and came back only last week. So many wives and relatives of the officers have come down of late, knowing the war to be practically at an end, that our camp has become like a huge picnic pavilion. It is quite the fashionable fad just now to visit the front. Mrs. Brennan accompanied the wife of one of the division commanders from her State — Connecticut, you know."

There was much I longed to ask regarding her, but I would not venture to fan his suspicions. In hope that I might turn his thought I asked, "And you; are you yet married?"

He laughed good-humoredly. "No, that happy day will not occur until after we are mustered out. Miss Minor is far too loyal a Virginian ever to become my wife while I continue to wear this uniform. By the way, Mrs. Brennan was asking Celia only yesterday if she had heard anything of you since the surrender."

"She is at Appomattox, then?"

"No, at the headquarters of the Sixth Corps, only a few miles north from here."

"And the Major?"

351

My Lady of the North

Caton glanced at me, a peculiar look in his face, but answered simply:

"Naturally I have had small intimacy with him after what occurred at Mountain View, but he is still retained upon General Sheridan's staff. At Mrs. Brennan's request we breakfasted together yesterday morning, but I believe he is at the other end of the lines to-day."

We sat down upon a bank, our conversation drifting back to their uneventful ride northward, and later to our experiences during those last weeks of war. I have often reflected since on the vivid contrast we must have made while resting there, each holding the rein of his horse, our animals as widely differing in appearance as ourselves. Both were typical of the two services in those last days. Caton was attired in natty uniform, fleckless and well groomed, his linen immaculate, his buttons gleaming, the rich yellow stripes of his arm of the service making marked contrast with the blue he wore and the green he sat upon. I, on the other hand, was haggard from hard, sleepless service and insufficient food, my shapeless old slouch hat and dull gray jacket torn and disfigured, the marks of rank barely discernible.

But his manly, hopeful spirit reawakened my courage, and for the time I forgot disaster while listening to his story of love and his plans for the future. His one thought was of Celia and the Northern home so soon now to be made ready for her coming. The sun sank lower into the western sky, causing Caton to draw down his fatigue cap until its glazed visor almost completely hid his eyes. With buoyant enthusiasm he talked on, each word drawing me closer to him in bonds of friendship. But the time of parting came, and after we had promised to correspond with each other, I stood and watched while he rode rapidly back down the road we had traversed together. At the summit of the hill he turned and waved his cap, then disappeared, leaving me alone, with Edith's face more clearly than ever a torture to my memory of defeat, — her face, fair, smiling, alluring, yet the face of another man's wife.

CHAPTER XXXIX

I WALKED the next mile thoughtfully, pondering over those vague hopes and plans with which Caton's optimism had inspired me. Then the inevitable reaction came. The one thing upon which he built so happily had been denied me, — the woman I loved was the wife of another. I might not even dream of her in my loneliness and poverty; the remembrance of her could be no incentive to labor and self-denial. The Lieutenant's chance words, kindly as they were spoken, only opened wider the yawning social chasm between us. The greatest mercy would be for us never again to meet.

I bent my head to keep the westering sun from my eyes, and breathing the thick red dust, I trudged steadily forward. Suddenly there sounded behind me the thud of hoofs, while I heard a merry peal of laughter, accompanied by gay exchange of words. I drew aside, leading my horse into a small thicket beside the road to permit the cavalcade to pass. It was a group of perhaps a dozen, — three or four Federal officers, the remainder ladies, whose bright dresses and smiling faces made a most winsome sight. They glanced curiously aside at me as they galloped past. But none paused, and I merely glanced at them with vague interest, my thoughts elsewhere. Suddenly a horse seemed to draw back from out the centre of the fast disappearing party.

354

My Lady of the North

"Ah, but really, you know, we cannot spare you," a man's voice protested.

"But you must. No, Colonel, this chances to be a case where I prefer being alone," was the quiet reply. "Do not wait, please; I will either rejoin you shortly or ride directly to the camp."

I had led my limping horse out into the road once more to resume my journey, paying scarcely the slightest attention to what was taking place, for my head was again throbbing to the hot pulse of the sun. The party of strangers rode slowly away into the enveloping dust cloud, and I had forgotten them, when a low, sweet voice spoke close beside me: "Captain Wayne, I know you cannot have forgotten me."

She was leaning down from the saddle, and as I glanced eagerly up into her dear eyes they were swimming with tears.

"Forgotten! Never for one moment," I exclaimed; "yet I failed to perceive your presence until you spoke."

"You appeared deeply buried in thought as we rode by, but I could not leave you without a word when I knew you must feel so bad. I have thought of you so often, and am more glad than I can tell to know you have survived the terrible fighting of these last few weeks. But you look so worn and haggard."

"I am wearied — yes," I admitted. "But that will pass away. My meeting again with you will be a memory of good cheer; and I found no little encouragement from a conversation just held with Lieutenant Caton."

She looked at me frankly, her eyes cleared of the mist. "Were you indeed thinking hopefully just now? You appeared so grave I feared it was despair."

My Lady of the North

"It was a mixture of both, Mrs. Brennan. My own known condition furnishes sufficient despair, while Caton's excessive happiness yields a goodly measure of joy, which I have not yet entirely lost. Nothing glorifies life, even in its darkest hour, as the success of love."

She glanced at my face shyly. "Undoubtedly the Lieutenant is in the seventh heaven at present," she admitted slowly. "His Celia has led him a merry chase these many months, before she made full surrender; but that merely makes final victory the sweeter."

"She retains the disposition of a child."

"But the heart of a woman is back of all her playfulness. You are upon your way home?"

"I have just been paroled, Mrs. Brennan. After four years of war I am at last free, and have turned my face toward all that is left of my childhood's home, — a few weed-grown acres. I scarcely know whether I am luckier than the men who died."

I saw the tears glistening again in her earnest eyes. "Oh, but you are, Captain Wayne," she exclaimed quickly. "You have youth and love to inspire you — for your mother yet lives. Truly it makes my heart throb to think of the upbuilding which awaits you men of the South. It is through such as you — soldiers trained by stern duty — that these desolated States are destined to rise above the ashes of war into a greatness never before equalled. I feel that now, in this supreme hour of sacrifice, the men and women of the South are to exhibit before the world a courage greater than that of the battlefield. It is to be the marvel of the nation, and the thought and pride of it should make you strong."

"It may indeed be so; I can but believe it, as the prophecy comes from your lips. I might even find cour-

356

age to do my part in this redemption were you ever at hand to inspire."

She laughed gently. "I am not a Virginian, Captain Wayne, but a most loyal daughter of the North; yet if I so inspire you by my mere words, surely it is not so far to my home but you might journey there to listen to my further words of wisdom."

"I have not forgotten the permission already granted me, and it is a temptation not easily cast aside. You return North soon?"

"Within a week."

I hardly know what prompted me to voice my next question, — Fate, perhaps, weary of being so long mocked, — for I felt small interest in her probable answer.

"Do you expect your husband's release from duty by that time?"

She gave a quick start of surprise, drawing in her breath as though suddenly choked. Then the rich color overspread her face. "My husband?" she ejaculated in voice barely audible, "my husband? Surely you cannot mean Major Brennan?"

"But I certainly do," I said, wondering what might be wrong. "Whom else could I mean?"

"And you thought that?" she asked incredulously. "Why, how could you?"

"How should I have thought otherwise?" I exclaimed, my eyes eagerly searching her downcast face. "Why, Caton told me it was so the night I was before Sheridan; he confirmed it again in conversation less than an hour ago. Colgate, my Lieutenant, who met you in a Baltimore hospital, referred to him the same way. If I have been deceived through all these months, surely everything and everybody conspired to that end, — you bore the same

357

name; you told me plainly you were married; you wore a wedding-ring; you resided while at camp in his quarters; you called each other Frank and Edith. From first to last not one word has been spoken by any one to cause me to doubt that you were his wife."

As I spoke these words hastily, vehemently, the flood of color receded from her face, leaving it pale as marble. Her lips parted, but failed in speech.

"Believe me, Mrs. Brennan, the mistake was a most innocent one. You are not angry?"

"Angry? Oh, no! but it all seems so strange, and it hurts me a little. Surely I have done nothing to forward this unhappy deceit?"

For a moment she bowed her head upon her hands as though she would hide her face from me, conceal the depth of her emotion. Then she looked up once more, smiling through her tears.

"I recall starting to explain all this to you once," she said, striving vainly to appear at ease. "It was when we were interrupted by the sudden coming upon us of Mr. and Mrs. Bungay. Yet I supposed you knew, that you would have learned the facts from others. The last time we were together I told you I did not wholly understand you. It is no wonder, when you thought that of me. But I understand now, and know you must have despised me."

"No! no!" I protested warmly, forgetting all I lacked and recalling only my deep love for her. "It was never that. Not one word or act between us has ever lowered you an iota in my esteem. You have always been my lady of the North, and from the first night of our meeting — out yonder, amid the black mountains — I have respected and honored you as one worthy of all sacrifice, all love."

My Lady of the North

Her eyes were drooping now, and hidden from me behind their long dark lashes.

"I am going to tell you my story, Captain Wayne," she said quietly. "It is not a pleasant task under these circumstances, yet one I owe you as well as myself. This may prove our last meeting, and we must not part under the shadow of a mistake, however innocently it may have originated. I am the only child of Edwin Adams, a manufacturer, of Stonington, Connecticut. My father was also for several terms a member of Congress from that State. As the death of my mother occurred when I was but five years old, all my father's love was lavished upon me, and I grew up surrounded by every advantage which abundant means and high social position could supply. During all those earlier years my playmate and most intimate companion was Charles Brennan, a younger brother of the Major, and the son of Judge David Brennan of the State Supreme Court."

She had been speaking slowly, her eyes turned aside, as though recalling carefully each fact before utterance. Now her glance met mine, and a deeper color sprang into her clear cheeks.

"As we grew older his friendship for me ripened into love, a feeling which I found it impossible to return. I liked him greatly, valued him most highly, continued his constant companion, yet experienced no desire for closer relationship. My position was rendered the more difficult as it had long been the dream of the heads of both houses that our two families, with their contingent estates, should be thus united, and constant urging tried my decision severely. Nor would Charles Brennan give up hope. When he was twenty and I barely seventeen a most serious accident occurred, — a runaway, — in which Charles

359

heroically preserved my life, but himself received injuries, from which death in a short time was inevitable. In those last lingering days of suffering, but one hope, one ambition, seemed to possess his mind, — the desire to make me his wife, and leave me the fortune which was his through the will of his mother. I cannot explain to you, Captain Wayne, the struggle I passed through, seeking to do what was right and best; but finally, moved by my sympathy, eager to soothe his final hours of suffering, and urged by my father, I consented to gratify his wish, and we were united in marriage while he was on his death-bed. Two days later he passed away."

She paused, her voice faltering, her eyes moist with unshed tears. Scarce knowing it, my hand sought hers, where it rested against the saddle pommel.

"His brother," she resumed slowly, "now Major Brennan, but at that time a prosperous banker in Hartford, a man nearly double the age of Charles, was named as administrator of the estate, to retain its management until I should attain the age of twenty-one. Less than a year later my father also died. The final settlement of his estate was likewise entrusted to Frank Brennan, and he was made my guardian. Quite naturally I became a resident of the Brennan household, upon the same standing as a daughter, being legally a ward of my husband's brother. Major Brennan's age, and his thoughtful kindness to me, won my respect, and I gradually came to look upon him almost as an elder brother, turning to him in every time of trouble for encouragement and help. It was the necessity of our business relation which first compelled me to come South and join Major Brennan in camp: as he was unable to obtain leave of absence, I was obliged to make the trip. Not until that time, Captain Wayne, — indeed, not until after our experience at Mountain View, — did I fully realize that Major Brennan looked upon me otherwise than as a guardian upon his ward. The awakening pained me greatly, especially as I was obliged to disappoint him deeply; yet I seek to retain his friendship, for my memory of his long kindness must ever abide. I am sure you will understand, and not consider me unwomanly in thus making you a confidant."

"I can never be sufficiently grateful that you have thus trusted me," I said with an earnestness that caused her to lower her questioning eyes. "It has been a strange misunderstanding between us, Mrs. Brennan, but your words have brought a new hope to one disheartened Confederate soldier."

She did not answer, and with a rush there came before me the barrier of poverty existing between us. I glanced from my ragged, faded clothing to her immaculate attire, and my heart failed.

"I must be content with hope," I said at last; "yet I am rich compared with thousands of others; infinitely rich in comparison with what I dreamed myself an hour ago." I held out my hand. "There will come a day when I shall answer your invitation to the North."

"You are on your way home?"

"Yes; to take a fresh hold upon life, trusting that sometime in the early future I may feel worthy to come to you."

"Worthy?" she echoed the word, a touch of scorn in her voice, her eyes dark with feeling. "Worthy? Captain Wayne, I sometimes think you the most unselfish man I ever knew. Must the sacrifices, then, always be made by you? Can you not conceive it possible that I also might like to yield up something? Is it possible you deem me a woman to whom money is a god?"

"No," I said, my heart bounding to the scarce hidden meaning of her impetuous words, "nor have the sacrifices always been mine: you were once my prisoner."

She bent down, her very soul in her eyes, and rested one white hand upon my shoulder. For an instant we read each other's heart in silence, then shyly she said, "I am still your prisoner."

THE END

www.ingramcontent.com/pod-product-compliance
Lightning Source LLC
Chambersburg PA
CBHW032230010726
47494CB00002B/424